T0035856

OLD
FLAME

OLD FLAME

MOLLY PRENTISS

SCOUT PRESS

NEW YORK LONDON TORONTO SYDNEY NEW DELHI

Scout Press
An Imprint of Simon & Schuster, LLC
1230 Avenue of the Americas
New York, NY 10020

This book is a work of fiction. Any references to historical events, real people, or real places are used fictitiously. Other names, characters, places, and events are products of the author's imagination, and any resemblance to actual events or places or persons, living or dead, is entirely coincidental.

Copyright © 2023 by Molly Prentiss

Rich, Adrienne; "Paula Becker to Clara Westoff" from *Collected Poems 1950–2021* (WW Norton, 2016). Reprinted with permission of WW Norton.

All rights reserved, including the right to reproduce this book or portions thereof in any form whatsoever. For information, address Scout Press Subsidiary Rights Department, 1230 Avenue of the Americas, New York, NY 10020.

First Scout Press trade paperback edition April 2024

SCOUT PRESS and colophon are registered trademarks of Simon & Schuster, LLC

Simon & Schuster: Celebrating 100 Years of Publishing in 2024

For information about special discounts for bulk purchases, please contact Simon & Schuster Special Sales at 1-866-506-1949 or business@simonandschuster.com.

The Simon & Schuster Speakers Bureau can bring authors to your live event. For more information or to book an event, contact the Simon & Schuster Speakers Bureau at 1-866-248-3049 or visit our website at www.simonspeakers.com.

Interior design by Erika R. Genova

Manufactured in the United States of America

10 9 8 7 6 5 4 3 2 1

Library of Congress Cataloging-in-Publication Data is available.

ISBN 978-1-5011-2158-6
ISBN 978-1-5011-2159-3 (pbk)
ISBN 978-1-5011-2160-9 (ebook)

For my mother and my daughter

OLD
FLAME

PART ONE

BIRTH

This story, like all human stories, begins with a birth. My head flew out of a vagina, and there began my consciousness. A gloved hand severed the umbilical cord, and there began my aloneness. The blood kept coming out of the vagina long after I exited. Too much blood. My entrance into the world had created a chasm big enough to swallow a mother. I screamed and screamed. I reached out for a breast, but there wasn't one. The gloved hands held and washed me. They gave me milk from a bottle, which I refused, then gulped. I do not remember any of this with my mind, but I remember it with my body. I remember the harsh lights of my new life, the dark space from which I came, the taste of plastic, the goo of my mother wiped away. I remember the feeling of it. My wholeness stolen. My half self, searching. I would search long after. I am searching still.

PART TWO

BUSINESS

MONEY SIGNS

When I was younger than I am now, twenty-seven to be exact, I found myself walking into a tall office building on Thirty-Fourth Street in Manhattan. It felt like I was being pulled in by a magnet. The magnet was capitalism, but I couldn't see that then. All I could see was an opportunity to survive and purchase potions for my face. I was only in my twenties, but I was already worried about my face, what might become of it as the years passed over it, where the lines would be drawn. I was worried about many things: the homeless guy on my block freezing to death, all the whales dying, how to pay my rent. But also who I should be in this life, how I would get there, what the point of me was. I was, as certain people tended to describe themselves in the days before they began to describe themselves as "anxious," what they might call "a worrier." Other people might have just called me a woman.

The building on Thirty-Fourth Street was the corporate office of an iconic New York department store, where I had gotten a job as a copywriter. This was my first "real" job, the kind that made "real" money that would nestle me comfortably into the "real" world. Before this, I had been a bartender, a salesgirl, a nanny, a waitress, and a tutor to a pair of rich children on the Upper East Side—invisible, energy-sucking jobs that, despite their toll on the body, weird hours, and depressing aspects, were not considered legitimate by the ruling class of New Yorkers or the IRS. I had always worked very hard, but I had always been poor, putting what money I did make into the endless, ever-expanding pit of my student loan debt or into the greedy hands of whichever Brooklyn landlord I was renting from. I always felt nervous, as if I were balancing on a very thin beam that could be yanked out from under me at any moment. I was never, as far as I could understand it, fully in control of any given situation.

On my twenty-seventh birthday a DJ named Darius had given me a baggie of coke as my gift, which I inhaled in the bathroom of the dive bar where I worked at the time with a fellow bartender named Zoe. After she snorted her line through a rolled-up twenty, she told me excitedly that I was too fucking smart to be so poor and declared that I should go into advertising. Advertising, Zoe explained, was the only industry in this godforsaken city where a creative person could make any cash. Her cousin had a job as a copywriter, she explained, and got paid to write fun puns about clothes. "You could definitely do it," Zoe said. "You're always lurking in coffee shops with that notebook of yours. There have got to be some fun puns in there." At first, I wasn't so sure. Like so many young people living in New York City, I wanted to be a "real" writer, not a writer of taglines about sweaters. I rubbed some of the coke onto my gums. When I caught my reflection in the bathroom mirror, I didn't recognize myself—I had money signs in my eyes.

COSTUMES

The department store was at once cheesy and glamorous, with carpeted shoe salons and long escalators, faux-mahogany wall displays stuffed with silk ties. The whole place smelled of many perfumes mixed together, and the beige light made it feel like it could be any time of day. There was a strict dress code: anyone who worked at the store itself or at the corporate office was only allowed to wear black and white. When the employees emerged from the subway in groups, the sidewalks were our chess board and we were the kings, queens, and pawns. We moved up and over, sometimes diagonally. We took elevators in packs of six or eight. We migrated silently between the marble lobby and the ninth floor, using magnetic cards to unlock the doors and turnstiles. When the door to the office opened, it made a very loud clicking sound.

There was Essie. Tiny, hunched, wonderful. Essie was the receptionist, but she was more than that. She was like a mascot for this place, a relic of an old New York full of fur stoles and jazzy types. Every morning I asked her how she was and she said she was wonderful, but she said it in a way that was sarcastic enough to maybe mean she was the opposite of wonderful. Then she always lifted her paper coffee cup and said: "That friend of yours is an angel from heaven."

Essie was talking about Megan, my best work friend, who brought Essie a small black coffee from the coffee cart in Herald Square every morning because she knew that Essie secretly wanted two coffees but would only ever allow herself to purchase the first one. This was the sort of woman Essie was: the kind who denied herself small pleasures in exchange for feeling some other kind of goodness, the kind that came with saving her daily dollar. I respected this and could relate to it; I was the kind of person who refused to take a taxi when the subway existed. I wondered if Essie had always been this way or if there had been a time when she was more generous with herself, when she went to smoky parties at friends' apartments, drank many glasses of wine, left with a man on her arm, looked back at her friends coyly, watching them watch her exit, watching them watch her exist.

The halls were a maze. The lights were bright. The cubicles were chest-high. The overachievers and the mothers of small children were already at their desks, typing away or leaning back, guzzling iced coffees from tall plastic cups, savoring this warm weather ritual even as it edged into Pumpkin Spice season. The coffees were so big back then, a foot tall if you included the straw. The ice made a comforting sound as it sloshed against the plastic, then became smaller and smaller as the morning wore on, squeezing its condensation through the plastic and pooling on the desk. Even the ice wanted out of its cage, shape-shifting in an attempt at escape. By 10 a.m., everyone had arrived.

Emails began to fly across the room. When you caught one and pinned it down, solved its problem, another one flew at you. They stacked up like Tetris blocks, each fitting into the previous one somehow, but only if you were fast enough. If too many went unread for too long, a low-level anxiety began to build. This was capitalism at work: the deep sensation that you were going to start falling behind. Poverty was waiting for you, and then death. An office like this one—its organized plots, its waxy smell and coffin chairs—brought you very close to death; you could feel it lurking. But then it contradicted itself, promising with its padded cubicle walls and cozy chat rooms and plush health insurance that it would hold your very mortality at bay. This promise made you want to stay. It made you feel needy and needed. Two years passed, and then three, and now it was October again. I was still here, and it was time for our team meeting.

Our team meeting was in Linda's office. Linda was the manager of the writing team, a middle-aged single mom from Jersey City who'd been working here since 1994 and still wore business suits from that time period. I loved Linda. She was kind and had a good sense of humor and I found much comfort in her, the way she had seemed to stay the same for so long, how she maintained a buoyant positivity even though her job was mundane and her life as a working single mother was probably pretty hard. But her meetings were pointless, and even she knew it. We'd have to read off our status reports and stare blankly ahead while the rest of the team read their status reports. Then we'd all laugh about something and eat mini candy bars. Hahahahaha Snickers. Hahahaha Milky Way. My team gathered like little chicks in the small room. Linda huddled us under her motherly wings, unwrapped our Twix bars for us, popped them in our mouths. My status was that I was done writing the product copy for the catalog but I had not finished the headlines. Reed's status was that he was done with his headlines but not his product copy. Fiona's status was that she was not done with either, but she had done some research about how other brands were writing about highlighting serums and she wanted to share it with us. She read a poetic verse about morning dew from her phone's screen.

"We need to be talking about dew more," she said.

"I can't argue with that," Linda said, unfolding the wrapper of a peanut butter cup and sliding it into her mouth.

It was Halloween, hence the candy. Linda was wearing a witch's hat. I had painted a mustache on my upper lip and worn a beret. Reed had shaved a five-point star in the back of his hair; he was going as Marcel Duchamp performing *Tonsure*. Fiona had worn bright red. When I asked her what she was, she said, "I'm a person who doesn't work here," and shoved a purple lollipop in her mouth. Then she got out her essential oils kit and asked who needed a pick-me-up. We all did. Linda chose the one in the blue bottle, meant to activate the fifth chakra, which was a throat opener for good communication. Reed always chose the sensual sacral chakra, because he despised sex but wanted to be seen as sexual by others. Fiona chose the one that opened her third eye. I did a blend of survival/grounding (first chakra) and sensual sacral (couldn't hurt). Then we left Linda's office and went back to our own cubicles.

My cubicle! It was all mine. My pics, my pens, my desktop, my mouse. *Click click!* I was the captain of my own ship in here, surrounded by my own shit. Reply all, reply all, oops, didn't mean to reply all. Cold coffee, but I felt cozy. Bad lighting, but it was familiar by now. My reflection in my computer, the universe at my disposal. Clicked to the news and scanned a headline about a French town that had banned clown costumes. Remembered I needed some socks, so clicked to instantly purchase some. Clicked a link Zoe sent me to a video of a group of senior citizens dancing; one of the old men throws his walking canes aside in order to bust a better move. An ad on the side reminded me that I could look better than I did currently if I bought something, anything, whatever it was that was being sold.

I knew I should start working. Reluctantly, I clicked over to a Word document and wrote a headline about fall's new capes: GIVE THESE A WHIRL.

Then I wrote a headline about statement socks: SOCKS TO BE YOU. Then a poem appeared in my inbox; at some point I had signed up to receive a poem a day. Usually I didn't read the poems because I was too busy, but the poem today was called "You Can't Have It All," which intrigued me because I was just starting, in this very moment, to feel like maybe I did have it all. My coffee had begun to work and I was getting things done. I had a boyfriend I'd managed to keep for over a year—a photographer named Wes—and a shitty but workable basement apartment in Williamsburg that, because of my real-job salary, I did not have to share. I finally had health insurance; I was finally making a tiny dent in my student loans; I could finally afford to buy avocados. Why couldn't I have it all?

Barbara Ras was the poet. And although the poem's title suggested depravity or lack, its verbose list of life's succulent stuff—a fig tree, a soulful black dog, the "skin at the center between a man's legs, so solid, so doll-like"—made me feel flushed with so much pleasure I began to see all the world as abundant and forgiving. Ras seemed to be whispering in my ear, singing, almost, as if I were a small child and she were lullabying me to sleep. She spoke of foreign languages and towels and makeup, "buses that kneel," Indian food with "yellow sauce like sunrise." As always happened when I read writing that moved me, I allowed myself to fully succumb to it, taking the poem in through my eyes but reading it with my entire body, until, by the last line—Jesus Christ, her *last line*—I was crying at my desk.

"There is the voice you can still summon at will, like your mother's," Ras finished, "it will always whisper, you can't have it all / but there is this."

I wasn't sure if I was crying because of the mention of the mother's voice—even the word *mother* could undo me if the timing was right—or the phrase "buses that kneel," which made me hear the wheeze of this bus, see its lumbering, gentlemanly gesture, and think of old San Francisco in the wind. I was plunged into a past life on the opposite coast, one that I told myself often I didn't miss but that I occasionally longed for with a bodily desperation that manifested as dizziness or even nausea. I had grown up in Daly City with my adoptive mother, Ann, in a clean and quiet suburban house from which San Francisco taunted me like an inaccessible playground. I moved to the city as soon as I could, when I was eighteen and started college, and for a while I considered it mine. San Francisco had been so charming then, in the same wonderful way that Essie at the front desk was charming, which had everything to do with regional specifics. In San Francisco's case this was the smell of old wood and eucalyptus, Victorian homes perched wonkily on hillsides, food trucks selling corn covered in cotija and watermelon juice, teenagers, high on home-grown weed, traipsing through the Mission in purposefully thread-bare clothes. Since then San Francisco had been digitized and regenerated, an aging face that had gotten some kind of laser treatment. And I had changed, too. Now I spent my days awash in fluorescent light, emailing the minutes away, and the concept of California felt like a distant dream.

The Barbara Ras poem had me suddenly worried. Was I being the woman I had meant to be? The woman I had imagined becoming as a girl? Was this what having it all felt like? And if so, why could the phrase "clouds and letters" from a poem in an email make me question everything, make me crave some alternate version of myself, a self who was more like Barbara Ras, a woman whom I suddenly missed, imagining in detail her bright scarves and her geranium smell, her redwood writing desk, her deep woman's wisdom, even though I had never met Barbara Ras, she was not mine to miss or love, she had her own family, her own daughter, who I found out via Wikipedia was born the same year that I was. I wondered if she and her daughter shared the lives of their minds with each other. I wondered if they drank coffee together in a breakfast nook regularly.

An alert popped up on my screen, eclipsing Barbara Ras's Wikipedia page. Hans, the creative director, had called a last-minute meeting about the holiday campaign. I quickly sent my document of holiday ideas to the communal printer, gathered up my notebook and my iced coffee, picked up my printed pages around the corner, and headed to Megan's cubicle to swoop her up on my way.

WORK FRIENDS

Megan, who was less concerned with punctuality than I was, was busy
in her cubicle, putting the finishing touches on a spread in the Women's
Book. The Women's Book was just a catalog featuring the new styles for
fall or spring, but for the creative department, who labored furiously on
it for months in advance, it was a kind of biannual fashion bible, the cul-
mination of our collective creativity and effort. She was adding a flirty
border to the "Bold Colors" story; this particular spread featured a bony
brunette wearing a bright red crop top and a structured miniskirt of the
same hue. The woman floated strangely in the middle of the page, reaching out toward my headline: WITH FLYING COLORS. Seeing my words in the
context of the catalog made me actually cringe. This was the problem
with writing: your silly ideas printed on real paper, which made them both
more permanent and more disposable than if they'd just gone fallow in
your mind. Someone would actually read the dumb headline I'd written
in the pages of a free catalog. Someone else would throw it in a gutter.

"Looking good," I said to Megan, plopping down in the chair she reserved for cubicle visitors. Like me, Megan was also sporting a painted-on
mustache and black beret.

"Is it, though?" she said.

"As good as it can," I said. "Can't make the clothes less hideous."

"True," she said. "But I didn't get a fucking master's degree to make
borders all day."

I didn't say so, but to me making the border looked easy and fun. I was
jealous of graphic designers because their job appeared to embody an ideal
of mine, which was to be simultaneously artistic and useful. Graphic designers
could fulfill their innate desires to create beauty—and develop mood boards,
and obsess over serifs, and tape color swatches onto their computer screens—
all while slotting nicely into the corporate system. This felt very different from
my own job, in which I wrote using words I would never employ in my own
writing, words like *luxe* and *glow* and *trend*. I always felt like I was lying.

"Smells good in here," I said.

Without looking away from her screen, she lifted an unlit candle she'd stashed behind her computer monitor. "Gardenia," she said.

"Chic," I said.

It *was* chic. Everything Megan had tacked to her cubicle walls was in good taste: an image of the shadow of a monstera plant; a Chanel ad from the seventies, an illustration of a deli coffee cup that said *We are very happy to serve you* on it. There was a framed picture of a Northern California beach, which I'd instantly known was a Northern California beach when I'd first seen it because I was from Northern California, too, and I knew the way the seagulls there behaved.

"No wonder I like you," Megan had said when I'd told her I recognized those seagulls, back in 2011, when we'd first met. "I seem to always find the Californian in the room."

"You mean you seem to find the other perverse bitch who decided to leave the most beautiful place on earth for this shithole," I'd said.

"Yes," Megan had said. "That."

Megan and I had become fast and reliable work friends in those first weeks of making fashion ads together. Work friends were specific: you only went so far with each other, never pressing past a certain outer skin, and there was comfort in this. By this point we'd known each other for three years, but she still felt one step removed from my heart and soul, which I liked. We were bonded by the DNA of our communal effort, the blood of our email chains. We made mistakes and cried in each other's cubicles. But we weren't beholden to each other like real friends were—at least not yet. Our vague similarities—we were both Californians; we both rode the L train to and from poorly renovated apartments in Williamsburg; we both resented the company dress code and tried to defy it with excessive accessorizing—were enough to keep our nine-to-five friendship afloat and ever buoyant.

"Eww, I just realized something," I said, standing to leave for the meeting.

"Hmm," Megan said, not taking her eyes off her screen.

"It's lunchtime. They're going to serve us one of those meeting salads."

"There is nothing worse than a meeting salad," Megan said. "It's like the second the lettuce enters this building it becomes iceberg."

I knew exactly what Megan meant. Even if it was spring greens they were serving, it always tasted crisp and flavorless, utterly devoid of nutrients.

"Hurry up," I said. "It's twelve fifty-seven."

"You and your minutes," she said.

We walked through the bright halls with our arms touching. The new Associate Creative Director for the Women's Department—his name was Todd; he wore suits over T-shirts and had a small hoop earring; we had yet to uncover whether he was gay or straight—joined us on Megan's side.

"Hey, girls," he said, shocking us both into silence. We suddenly knew he was definitely straight. "You headed to this meeting, too?"

MEETING TEXTS

Me: *What's New Guy's deal?*

Megan: *Like in what way?*

Me: *Seems like a hotshot.*

Megan: *No one says "hotshot"*

Me: *I just said it which means people say it.*

Me: *Earring etc.*

Megan: *Reed told me he's making triple what he makes*

Megan: *Guess he found his onboarding packet in the recycling*

Me: *Jesus. But isn't he like younger than us?*

Megan: *I just remembered that Reed makes more than us*

Me: *Because he has a peen.*

Megan: *I'm kind of intrigued, to be honest*

Me: *By Reed's peen?*

Megan: *NO! By New Guy*

Me: *Are you serious? He's your boss, dude. Plus he's BLOND.*

Megan: *What does that even mean?*

Me: *One should never trust a male blond.*

Megan: *Where do you even come up with this stuff? It's like you're copywriting life*

Me: ™

HOLIDAY IDEAS

Hans wanted us to throw spaghetti at the walls. He wanted us to riff. He wanted us to free-associate, to brainstorm, to generate. To use our collective creativity to imagine the very best holiday campaign that had ever existed.

I loved this shit. I was never happier than when I was in a room with many people, all of us aiming our energies at the same thing. It didn't matter that it was for the sake of selling fancy things to rich people. It didn't matter that we worked for an outdated department store that all but refused to enter the new age of digital marketing, that our hard work would end up in old-school paper catalogs with an average readership age of seventy-six. All that mattered was that I was surrounded, encased in collective thought, my brain synapses ping-ponging inside my head as if life were just one big game and I was playing fast and loose.

We considered wrapping taxicabs in large red bows. We dreamed of skyscrapers draped in Christmas lights. We riffed on possibilities for our always-iconic store windows. I wrote festive or funny phrases down in my notebook, calling them out occasionally to spark the team's thinking. *Holiday of lights. Love, unwrapped. Sleigh me. Fleece Navidad.* People loved my ideas and gave me air high fives across the table. I was good at this: selling the feeling of a particular kind of delight. Customers loved to be delighted while they considered which store, out of all the world's stores, they should shop at, and which items, out of all the world's items, they would purchase and own. The more delight and desire a woman felt while looking at a pair of boots, the more likely she was to spend her money on them. I was good at this job because I was a dreamer and an exaggerator. I could not simply live with things as they were. I had to make them shinier, more dramatic, bigger, and more beautiful. I knew what desire felt like—I had been burning with some version of it for as long as I could remember—and I could make other people feel it, too.

A knock on the conference room door meant the meeting salad had arrived. Two young women wearing unflattering black pants and short-sleeve button-ups wheeled a cart into the room and pulled the plastic wrap from five or six oval trays. Hard, lifeless tomatoes gleamed under the conference room lights. A carafe of dressing was the only promise of flavor. The group stopped talking about Christmas and lined up to serve themselves on thick black plastic plates. Those of us who knew what was up got a Diet Dr Pepper, too. No one said thank you to the young girls who'd wheeled the salad in. They were invisible and then just gone.

Megan was uncharacteristically quiet as we ate, just when everyone else was getting friendly, asking about weekend plans. Come to think of it, she'd been quiet during the whole meeting. Where she would normally be the one to come up with the best idea and share it easily, she'd kept her hands in her lap, hadn't written anything in her notebook. She'd re-applied her lip gloss twice. She looked more elegant than usual somehow, in her painter's beret and a blouse with a Peter Pan collar, as if her simple costume had transformed her. Her silence, too, felt unfamiliar, and vaguely worrisome. I kept glancing over at her, as if that might prompt her to contribute, but she avoided my gaze. Despite her silence or perhaps because of it, she looked beautiful.

I had never really thought much about Megan's particular brand of beauty. I had noted an attractive health about her; there was the sense that she was very much in her own body, that she took care of it and felt it fully. I knew she attended exercise classes with names that promised holistic overhaul—Pure Barre, SoulCycle, Physique57—and that she had a noticeably nice complexion thanks to the many potions and lotions she purchased with her discount at the department store and used on her face at night and in the morning; she had what she called a "skin regimen," and it seemed to work. Her eyes were hazel and her hair was hazel, if hazel meant what I thought it did, which was any in-between color that was impossible to pin down. Was her hair blond? Was it red? Was it actually just brown? It was old-fashioned somehow, her look. Edwardian, maybe.

I tried one more time to look at her, but she kept her eyes on her salad as she ate. I saw Todd look at her, too, or at least I thought I did. It could have been that I was making up the look, just like I made up the woman I was writing the holiday campaign for, who was shopping for a Christmas present for her sister, who was dying of cancer. She wanted to find her something soft, maybe a cashmere scarf, so that she would feel comfortable and cozy as she passed slowly into another realm. This woman couldn't know that her sister would be offended by such a gift, that it would make her feel old and sad and sick, and that she would hide it in the back of her closet and try to forget her sister had purchased it for her. It made the sick woman feel distressed, even violated, to be so misunderstood. What she wanted was something shiny, even gaudy, outrageously beautiful. She did not want to sink softly into death but to sparkle her way there.

EXCHANGE

Later that day, around four, I got an email from Megan. When I opened it, I found a line drawing of a salad that she had scanned in and Photoshopped to peak crispness. It was a perfectly disgusting depiction of the salad that was now in my stomach. I laughed out loud when I saw it.

I wrote Megan an email back. It was a short story about the salad girls, the ones who had wheeled in the silver cart. I wrote about them ironing their shirts in the dark dawn, then meeting at the subway stop to ride to work together. They always had a cigarette before going in. They were friends because they had to be, because they peddled salads around midtown together, and without each other's company they wouldn't be able to stand the job. But one day, one of the girls didn't show up at the subway stop. The other girl felt confused, almost devastated. She waited for a long time, tried texting and calling, never got an answer. She finally went to work, and when she got there she asked the boss about the other girl. "Maya got here early for once," the boss said. "She's already on her route." The girl who had been left behind felt awful all day. When she finally saw her friend as they were punching out at headquarters, she asked her where she'd been that morning. "My therapist says I'm codependent," she said. "But I think I'm going to fire her." The girls grinned at each other. They knew things were going to be fine. They smoked a cigarette in Herald Square, looking up at the patch of sky between the tall buildings, and then went to the sale section at the Gap. Each of them bought a pair of shorts for $6.99, which they promised themselves they'd wear all summer long.

As soon as I sent the email off, I felt a thrill. I wondered if Megan would take pleasure in what I'd written, and maybe even want to read more. Would Megan send me another drawing? A sense of possibility announced itself inside of me; I suddenly felt warm. If only this could be my job, I thought, imagining things and sharing them with my friends.

A chat appeared in the bottom right corner of my screen.

Megan: *Let's make a book*
Me: *THE OTHER WOMEN'S BOOK*
Megan: *YES*
Megan: *Sit tight for your next assignment.*

WORK DRINKS

That night after work, still wearing our Halloween costumes, a bunch of us went to drinks. You could do things like that in those days, go out drinking for the sheer thrill of it, with no worry about getting home to anyone or anything, no fear of the future headache or the future in general. We went to a cocktail bar called Skye, where a huge circular bar bloomed out into an atrium-like space. Real birds flew around above us; it was unclear whether they'd found their way in from the street or had been brought in to accentuate the confusion about whether we were indoors or out. The seats were made of the kind of puffy leather you could lose yourself in. We lost ourselves in the leather and in bittersweet drinks made with mescal and Aperol. Megan looked over at Todd, who was talking to Faith, the Associate Creative Director of the Beauty Department. Faith was beautiful, with dark hair and light eyes and wrap dresses, but everyone knew that she was extremely religious, which rendered her unthreatening as far as female competition went. Megan touched her gold necklace delicately with her long fingers, pretending to talk to me while she watched Todd.

I allowed myself to look at him, too. His light eyes were vicious and magnetic. He was unattractive—floppy blond bangs, ruddy skin, a nose too small for the rest of his face—but also intensely handsome, thanks to some invisible force I could only identify as self-satisfaction or accumulated power. Beyond his blondness, the scarf he kept draped around his neck while inside was also a red flag—men who wore accessories for the sake of accessorizing were always trouble. But when he looked in my direction my breath caught, my face heated up, and my pelvis began to tingle. I decided I would have an affair with him in my mind, just to see what Megan's intrigue was all about. I'd been with Wes for long enough by now that even an imagined affair felt scandalous and out of reach, which made me both turned on and fearful—I didn't know if I could go through with it. So I hopped into Megan's body, which wasn't hard since we were both wearing berets and mustaches, and walked up to Todd, right in between him and Faith.

"Excuse me," I said to the version of Todd inhabiting my fantasy, who, like the real Todd, had fake blood coming out of his ears. "Can I steal you for a second?"

Fantasy Todd gave me a surprised half smile. "Sure," he said. He seemed to be pleased with my forwardness, so I kept going with it. I asked Fantasy Todd if he would like to buy me a drink, and he said he'd love

to. I liked the feeling of men buying me drinks, not because I didn't want
to spend money but because I didn't want to deal with the effort of the
transaction. To be handed something bittersweet without having to do
anything to get it was almost perversely satisfying. Then I led him to one
of the leather couches in the darker part of the room and we sat down
with our thighs touching. One of the little birds joined us on the arm of
the couch—Fantasy Todd held out a finger and it climbed on.

"You're the writer, right?" Fantasy Todd said. As he said it, the little
bird flew off his finger and away.

As soon as Fantasy Todd said the word *writer*, acknowledging that I
had failed to inhabit Megan's body and was still in my own, and that he
knew who I was, and that he understood that I was not just a *copywriter* but
an *actual* writer (or at least an aspiring one), I reached my neck out long
like a giraffe and I French-kissed him. Fantasy Todd's tongue was thick
and moist, not like Wes's tongue, which was pleasingly absent most of the
time. I hated this new tongue. But I didn't pull away. If I was going to
fantasize, I might as well get some mileage out of it; Fantasy Todd and I
had to have sex. But where?

Lucky for us, Skye was attached to a hotel called Rume, so Fantasy
Todd and I could just check in (he paid) and head upstairs. We were
in room 508. The room was fine, with gray sheets and a big TV, but
we didn't notice either way. We were too busy kissing like teenagers and
falling on the bed together. Fantasy Todd's dick was hard under his dress
pants. I was incredibly drunk and the dick spoke to me. I grabbed it so
it would shut up. I didn't like talk during sex, but there he went, saying
something about my pussy. I hated that word and I hated that Fantasy
Todd was saying it, but I moaned anyway. I loved the way Fantasy Todd
wanted me. It felt incredible to be wanted like this: as if he couldn't live
without my body. Sometimes I thought that even I could live without my
own body, but not Fantasy Todd. He would perish if he didn't put his
hands all over my breasts, and then his fingers in my mouth, and then his
head between my legs. He would actually die.

"He's wearing a ring," Megan said, which put an abrupt and panic-inducing end to my fantasy. I looked over at him, and he was looking right back at us. His eyes were mouths. I thought for a moment that he was acknowledging what had happened between us in room 508, but in fact he was looking at Megan.

"For the better," I said. "Considering he's blond."

Megan elbowed me in the ribs.

"Wanna go pee with me?" she said.

"Do I ever," I said. I knew she just wanted to walk past Real Todd, maybe see if he kept his eyes on her as she moved. He did. At a certain point I had to look away. His gaze was so dazzling, and I was so afraid.

WES

I'd once been dazzled—though in an altogether different way—by Wes, my own boyfriend, who showed up across the picnic blanket from me at one of Zoe's get-togethers in McCarren Park, armed with a camera around his neck and a small side grin. Though when I think about it, the dazzling was similar in one key way: both Wes and Todd were mysterious; I did not know them yet; and so I could ascribe to them many qualities and narratives that might or might not be true. (Because of this room for speculation and interpretation, the space between meeting someone and knowing them, for me, is intensely charged, erotic almost by definition, because it is within that space that the person in question might fit perfectly into my life, fill all my emotional craters, be exactly what I've been looking for all along.) But this was the difference: Todd dazzled headfirst, coming toward you with a powerful confidence, whereas Wes dazzled by staying to the side, making room for whatever was beautiful to show itself, giving it a frame. Though he himself was beautiful, too. That was also true.

If I were to write the story of me and Wes, I would begin with a particular feeling that, as far as I know, does not exist anymore. It was the

feeling of Brooklyn, specifically of Williamsburg and even more specifically of McCarren Park, on a weekend day in June or July of the years
between 2008 and 2015. The feeling was one of swollen possibility, as if
the condensation in the air was not the gathering humidity but the collective mist of youthful perspective: we were all going to become something, but we didn't quite know what or when, and until then we were
content to sit in small or large groups on small or large blankets on the
patchy grass drinking wine in the daytime and talking about art, books,
changes in the neighborhood, free concerts we'd been to recently, the
particular burdens of our various day jobs, the possibilities of our side
hustles, where we'd move when the law changed and our rent control
lifted, etc. This is all to say that when I met Wes in the summer of 2013,
when I was twenty-nine, the idea of the future felt open and charged
and promising, and the concept of real adulthood still felt far off, and
neither Wes nor I had been significantly beaten down or rejected by the
world yet.

Zoe and the friends in attendance were blowing off steam after their
brunch shift—they all worked at the same restaurant, a beloved bistro
on the edge of Greenpoint that made you feel like you were in Paris.
In my yellow gingham sundress I'd bought at the Goodwill for nine
dollars, I stood out against their waiters' black. But they weren't just
waiters, of course. They were painters and writers and makers of hand-
sewn clothes, each spending their shift money on mimosas made in red
plastic cups, pale skin peeking out of the cuffs of skinny jeans, fresh
tattoos mingling with regrettable ones on calves and forearms, paperbacks sticking slyly from their worn totes. I'd met all of them before at
the restaurant on one drunken night or another, except for one. The
one was Wes.

The one had that Nikon around his neck.

The one wore dirty shoes and lurked at the edge of the picnic blanket
like a shadow.

The one said suddenly, after I'd explained to a girl named Rachel that I worked in advertising: "But I'll bet you're also working on a novel."

"Excuse me?"

"I just mean," he said, "you don't *just* work in advertising, right?"

Green, lazy-lidded eyes that felt both distant and enveloping; if you dove into them, I imagined, the water would be Bahamas warm.

"I write stories sometimes, yeah," I said. "But just for fun. I've never like published anything."

The one nodded knowingly. "I knew it."

"Knew what?"

"That you were probably a writer. The way you're clocking everything, storing it away somewhere. Like you're going to use it later."

I did a half smile. So did he. His green eyes were set off by his dark hair, which he parted on the side and slicked back in a way that had somehow narrowly avoided looking sleazy. He had dark pockets below his eyes that made him seem appealingly worn out, a friendly nose, worry lines between his eyebrows. He was not skinny, but there was something feminine about his body; his collarbone reached elegantly from his throat out to his shoulder, like a ballerina's arm. He was handsome but not conventionally so, and this made me hopeful. Conventionally handsome men always understood that they were handsome; they had known since they were small, which made them choosy and out of reach, too aware of their power. The way I saw it then was that Wes had not capitalized on his handsomeness, at least not yet.

"What do you do?" I said, to distract from the fact that I was clearly checking him out.

"I take pictures," he said, with unexpected seriousness. The seriousness scared and excited me. When he said the word *pictures*, it was like he was suddenly wearing armor, like he had created a wall around himself.

"I tried to be a writer," one of the waitresses said, interrupting us too late for the interjection to make sense, her tattoos flinching as she tipped a bottle of rosé toward my cup. "Went to grad school and everything. Then I couldn't hack it. The constant rejection just ate away at me."

I nodded at her with sympathy, but I wasn't fully listening. I was watching the boy in the armor, the one, whose name I had yet to learn.

"You're a great writer," the boy in the armor said to the girl who had wanted to be a writer. "She's a great writer," he said to me. "I'm Wes, by the way."

I smiled, relieved. He was once again open, extending himself to me. The ends of his words whistled through his teeth.

"And you're Emily," he said.

I don't have to explain what it feels like to have a man with tropical oceans for eyes say your name out loud, how it almost shocks you to re-member that you exist and can be referred to. Everyone who has lived knows what it feels like to be surprised by the fact of themselves in the presence of certain others: the quick match-strike of self-recognition, and suddenly you're alive and burning.

The group laughed. Someone who wasn't Wes and therefore didn't matter was telling a story about a customer at the barbershop where he worked who had specifically asked for a mullet. Wes turned and snapped a picture of the barber, who was gesticulating. I chimed in with something witty that I can't remember now and could barely hear myself saying in the moment, caught up as I was in Wes's presence. I felt myself performing, asking for his attention with my intellect, and I could feel him responding: his gaze was the kind of approval I lived for, his lashes batting up against my banter. And then, from the corner of my eye, I saw him lift his camera again, and *click*, he took a picture of me.

Click, and suddenly I was two people at once: the woman and the woman being watched. And in that moment in my personal history, in those long, youthful days before I knew how to see myself, when a nine-dollar dress from Goodwill was all I needed to play the part of a girl who felt like a million bucks, the woman being watched was exactly who I wanted to be. *Click*, I was smitten.

But just as I was starting to imagine how the night would play out, how we'd all go drinking at one of the nearby bars and I'd eventually find a way to lean my body against his, how he'd tell me I was adorable and I'd look down at my shoes and then up at his eyes in a way that hinted at coquettish but could be written off as casual, Wes announced that he was leaving.

"I think I'm gonna head home and get some work done," he said to the group. Wait, what? Whatever match had been struck was swiftly blown out; I simultaneously felt deflated and more intrigued. I hated that he was going, but I liked his self-seriousness; I liked seeing myself reflected in his armor; I felt inspired by him and wanted to be like him. If he was going to get some work done, I wanted to get some done, too. So when Zoe and her friends went to Enid's for margaritas, I pulled a Wes, explaining to the group with my refusal to get drunk in the daytime that I had a dream for myself, that I would realize it no matter the cost, that my self-actualization was worth a thousand margaritas, a million days in the park, a hundred of Zoe's skeptical raised eyebrows.

Warning, Zoe texted me when we were only a block away from each other. *Your dude Wes is married to his work.*

I've always had a thing for married men, I typed, turning her warning into a joke. I knew she was trying to keep me from getting too interested, trying to protect me from falling for someone unreachable. But the impossibility of Wes only made me more intrigued. The impossible: that was where my gaze always landed. Imagine how good it would feel, I thought, if I were the exception. If the impossible suddenly became possible for me.

PHOTOSHOOT

The week after Halloween, Megan was out of office; she was helping art direct the shoe and handbag photo shoot. Without her, the office seemed quiet and too serious, and I felt relieved when I got an email from her: a drawing she'd done on set of a very large bag slung over the very slender arm of a very beautiful model. Immediately, I put all my real work aside and began to draft my response.

I wrote about what I imagined was happening at the photo shoot: a dance choreographed by money, thin bodies being prodded by many hands. Safety pin, body tape, thong line. Catered breakfast; spinach wraps, ham slabs, granola. No one eats. A leather jacket. A flared jean. A fur collar. Can someone touch Clara up? Clara is blank-faced and silk-bodied, with octopus arms. Eyes as big as coffee saucers. Black coffee only. No sugar ever. The occasional stale birthday cupcake, devoured and then purged. Nicolo hates when she does it, says it's disgusting, that she's too thin already. But by now its ingrained; she was fourteen when she became aware of her beauty, which was when she started to worry about losing it. To lose her beauty would be the ultimate disaster—how would she and Nicolo pay their rent? Not as if Nicolo did anything, besides get stoned with Gunner and watch porn. She'd found it on his computer a thousand times; too baked to clear his history. Some big sultry girl getting it from behind, always with breasts like watermelons. Clara knew he wanted more than she could give him, literally, but she couldn't help that, either. The clothes looked better this way, dangling off her thin shoulders as if she were a hanger. She loved seeing the pictures after they were retouched, when all her flaws had been wiped away. Sometimes she even reached out to touch the screen, pretending her fingers were Nicolo's, and a desire arose within her, warm and terrifying, a desire for more of herself rather than less, and her mouth all over her own neck.

When the photo shoot was over, the photographer, a shorter-than-average but handsome man in a zip-up leather jacket, popped a bottle of champagne. It oozed all over the floor, which had just been swept by an invisible cleaning lady. He grinned, passed the bottle around, lit a cigarette inside. Winked at Clara, who turned her head away in shame. It is my job to be this way, she wanted to say, but didn't. This was the curse of modern womanhood as she understood it. She'd gotten used to being beautiful for everyone else, no matter how ugly they were to her.

THE ITALIAN ANGLE

A few days later, the actual photo of the same bag Megan had drawn came back from retouching. I opened the zip file. The model's face had been cut out; you saw only her elbows and waist, which appeared even thinner in contrast to the bag that loomed large in the foreground. Bits of light flecked off the pebbled leather. Hardware gleamed like ice. Megan's drawing had been so much more beautiful than the actual image.

But I had to do my job, which was writing about this bag—a whip-stitched, textured leather satchel that sold for upward of a thousand dollars—in a way that made people want to buy it. Using my thesaurus, I looked up alternatives to *supple*. As always, there were many options—different combinations of letters that would provoke different combinations of thoughts and feelings in a customer. *Graceful. Malleable. Resilient. Bending.* None of these felt appropriate for the tough-softness I was trying to describe. Perhaps there was no word for it. All I could think of was Barbara Ras's poem—"the skin at the center between a man's legs, so solid, so doll-like"—but of course that would not do here.

I could tell the story of the bag from a craftsmanship angle or from a fashion angle and both would improve the purse's chances of being sold. The purse was handmade with the most careful stitching, and could be worn with the season's 1960s-inspired trench coats. By owning this bag, I could promise my customer, she would feel worldly and worth it, plugged into her own womanhood, desirable, and more complete than she did currently. She would be taken more seriously at work, where making money seemed to hinge on already having it. She would fit in at social gatherings, where other women toted similar bags, eyeing each other knowingly, adding up each other's outfits in their minds.

Deep down, the woman who bought the purse wanted only to be reassured that she was doing the right thing, nothing more. She was like a mother who, when letting her child out of the house in the evening, wanted to be promised that the child would not ingest alcohol or drugs. A firm acknowledgment that she was being seen and heard, despite the nagging feeling that she wasn't. As if a leather satchel—let alone a child's word—meant anything when held up against her gargantuan fears of losing everything she loved most, of destruction, of withering to the point of obsolescence. The woman needed something to hold on to: something specific that told her that this bag—this neat little extension of self— could save her from the aloneness she'd feared her whole life, the kind she'd come to expect if she didn't play all her cards right, purchase all the right signifiers, surround herself with worth so as to appear, at least to herself, worthy.

The bag was made in Italy. The Italian angle was good, yes. When something was made in Italy it was thought to be not only elegant but authentic, as if by purchasing it you could access a part of the Old World, a world where people cared about quality in a way that they didn't in the New World. Women loved Italy. That boot-shaped peninsula had a certain sensual pull—I knew this because I'd felt it once myself; when I was nineteen, I'd seen a study-abroad pamphlet that included a picture of a piazza filled with beautiful people eating cheese while sitting on the ground and taken it upon myself to make my way to that piazza as soon as possible. No matter that Ann had warned me of the impracticality of this choice; I wanted to go to Italy precisely *because* it seemed impractical, which at the time I equated with soulful. I reasoned that Ann had no say about what or where I studied, since she wasn't paying for my education; she firmly believed in bootstraps, and despite a partial scholarship, I'd had to take out tens of thousands of dollars in student loans to make it happen. I spent that student loan money on intensive language courses—I was a quick study, as if the language had already lived inside me somewhere—and then to buy my plane ticket to Bologna and a suitcase, and I went. Italy could do that to a person. It could upend you.

But the customer did not want to be upended. The customer was at point A and happiness was at point B, and my job, as the writer, was to offer them the path of least resistance to get there, to point B, by way of purchasing something. And so instead of diving into the Italy I knew— all shaded porticos and sad stories and secrets that remained secret to this day—I conjured a romantic scene: a piazza at sunset, red glow on the bag's gold-tone hardware, a self-possessed woman on the loose.

INVITATION

In one of those magical moments in life that transcends probability and logic, I received an email invitation—just as I was thinking about Italy— to a wedding in Verona. The invitation sprang out of a digital envelope, releasing 2-D flowers onto my screen. It was written in Italian, sent by the mother of the fiancé of my friend Grace, whom I'd met while studying abroad and had stayed in touch with via email. She was marrying her Italian sweetheart in April; the wedding was going to take place at a villa outside Verona. When I googled it, I found out that this villa had once been the residence of Dante—as in *Dante* Dante. Was it even possible to decline such an invite? In my mind, I was already back there, smelling the old dust and the powder-rose of Renata's perfume.

Renata was the woman I'd lived with in Bologna during my year abroad, who also became my professor. I'd found her by way of an advertisement posted on via Zamboni, the portico-covered street that acted like Bologna's Craigslist, where homeless students roamed, tearing off phone numbers and calling them from public telephones.

Dimmi, she'd said over the phone when I called. *Tell me.*

I immediately wanted to tell her—everything. Renata had one of those voices that made you want to spill yourself. I wanted to tell her that I was homesick, even though I wasn't sure exactly what I was home-sick for—my childhood with Ann, whose prim austerity had made me feel stifled and self-conscious? My rambunctious years in San Francisco, where I had slept with too many people so that I might feel loved, only to wake up every morning after feeling infinitely more alone? Neither of these visions of home was very comforting, and yet . . . neither was Bologna.

I wanted to tell Renata that Bologna wasn't what I'd imagined it would be. I'd been here for a month already, staying at a youth hostel while I worked through a final intensive language course; when I wasn't in class, I walked around all day to avoid the dark, stinking pit of my shared room. The city was shaped like an asterisk, centered around piazza Maggiore, the avenues shooting out from it in all directions. Every street was covered with redbrick porticos, making it feel dark and a bit eerie, shutting out the sky. Instead of the soulful, colorful European vibe I'd had in mind when I'd signed up to study here, Bologna was full of a particular kind of lonely beauty, the kind that rusted your soul. You'd find it at the markets with their cheap earrings and sassy hats; in the statues and the tomatoes; in the red arches; in the saxophone player on via Ugo Bassi; and at the tiny gym where I went to sweat and cry. I was too young to have learned to embody my loneliness, or to use it as a productive force, and so I grabbed one-euro bottles of red wine by the neck, tipped them down my throat, and thought about boys back in San Francisco who were probably not thinking about me. There were skinny street dogs and persistent hashish sellers. There was always an untalented bongo player drumming out an imported beat somewhere at the north end of the piazza. *Mario! Mario!* I heard someone call. It seemed everyone was named Mario in Bologna except for me.

Oh, to be Mario! I thought, my mouth bleeding wine. Oh, to be Mario, with his mother calling him in at night, reminding him that his food was ready and that he'd better eat before he perished! Oh, to be Mario at the discoteca, rubbing his Italian dick up against the foreign exchange students! Oh, to be Mario, his leather loafers reflecting the red of the porticos, his eyes glittering with the knowingness that he belonged here, to a mamma who would never stop loving him, even when he buried her in the earth. Always, he would be hers. Always, this man would be her boy.

Who is this Mario? I wanted to ask Renata. Instead I told her I'd seen her flyer; I was interested in the job and the room.

"Aha!" Renata said, her voice suddenly as happy as a bird's. "How amazing that you found us. I am always surprised when the flyers work. How old-fashioned this place is, right?"

She spoke in rapid Italian, implying that she trusted my fluency, and she immediately got down to logistics, implying that she was offering me the job and that I would accept it. I appreciated both of these things— it made me feel competent and trustworthy. "You'll pick up my girls— Benedetta is nine, Greta is eleven—from school and ballet practice," she said. "I want them to practice English, so you'll speak with them. And I'll pay you four hundred euros a month, plus the room, of course. Can you come on Sunday?"

"Sunday is great," I said. I felt a buoy of hope tugging my heart upward. Maybe, like all the city's Marios, I would have a place to go home to every night, someone to call me in when it was time.

On Sunday, church bells bonged as I clicked over the cobblestones in a pair of uncomfortable boots I'd bought in a fit of determination to look and feel Italian. When I got to via de' Poeti—that was Renata's street's name, the street of the poets—I paused to look up at a pair of arched windows high above the street. Geraniums dangling from charming clay pots, one of the frames slung open, like in the movies I'd seen about Italy. Then: two little heads, popping out over the orange flowers.

"Ciao!" said one head.

"Ciao!" said the other.

I waved up at them. The girls both had deep olive skin and wild, curly hair, and huge grins that spread out across their wide faces. The gate buzzed open. Before I could find my way to the stone staircase that led to the second floor, the girls were already downstairs. They quickly arranged themselves in front of an open doorway on the ground level, making a bridge with their hands in front of the entrance.

"What's the password?" one of them—the younger one—said brightly, in Italian.

I played along. "Hmmm," I said. "Poeti?"

"Noooo!" they both cried, laughing.

"Bologna?"

"Nooooo!"

"Amore?"

"Noooooo!"

Renata appeared behind them, out of a dim, low-ceilinged room with stone walls. She was holding a perfectly folded stack of white cloth that seemed incongruent with her general look, which was fiercely elegant. It was impossible that this woman did laundry, I remember thinking. She looked nothing like the girls; her nose was long and handsomely hooked at the end; her eyes were a striking green, where the girls' were a deep brown. Her hair was jet black but not sharp; it undulated in waves around her pointed face. Her belted jeans made her waist look tiny; a white blouse ballooned around her torso. Her face was pretty, her smile was warm but slightly sad, and her eyes reminded me of a wood stove with a glass window: reflective and cool on the surface, while revealing an internal flame. I felt the buoy again, despite knowing the danger of hope. I already wanted something from this woman, I realized. I either wanted to be her, or to be *hers*.

"Girls," Renata said, "let's walk Emily upstairs, shall we?"

"But she didn't get the password!" the younger girl complained.

Renata leaned over to whisper something to me; I was so focused on the intimacy of the gesture, the moist warmth of her breath in my ear, that I couldn't catch it.

"Sorry?" I said.

She leaned back in. "*Americana*," she said with a little laugh.

"Americana," I said to the girls, who were grinning.

They burst into laughter and hugged me around the legs, which made my throat close up with tenderness for them—so quickly, just like that, I cared for them.

I don't remember everything we talked about that Sunday, or how the afternoon faded into evening as quickly as it did. What I remember instead is the foreign magic that was that house, which felt like some kind of secret castle, tucked behind the street. The walls were made of ancient plaster that was painted in beautiful, unexpected hues: the living room was the color of salmon flesh, and the kitchen, which was massive and full of hanging copper pots, was a delicate rosemary green. The back wall of the place was made of stone, like the walls of that cellar-like room downstairs, though this stone was whitewashed, making it feel both earthy and elegant at once. Half-burned candles rose out of brass candlesticks like deformed sculptures. The couches, of which there were many, were draped in wide-striped fabric, giving the living room a playful and inviting feel. And then there was the art. On every wall there was a painting or a photograph, or many paintings and many photographs, and sculptures sat confidently on almost every available surface. An orange parking cone stuck out of one of the walls in the hallway. A brass woman holding a ball in the air stood giant and proud on a mantel. But the piece that struck me the most was perhaps the subtlest: a small photograph of a woman in a white dress, standing in a living room with a vacuum cleaner, her son playing with a toy on the floor next to her. Something in that woman's face, with her slight smile and vacant eyes . . .

"That's Liliana Barchiesi," Renata said, having noticed the attention I was paying the photograph. "From her series *Casalinghe.* Housewives. Here, I made espresso. Let's sit and chat and drink it."

Just as we sat down on Renata's striped couch, which sank under our weight, a woman with a mane of wild red hair blustered through the back door, off the kitchen.

"Ciao, Evelina!" Renata called.

"Just getting a cracker!" the woman called back in an unexpectedly high voice, one that carried like a laugh through the house.

"Please, take many!" Renata called.

As soon as she appeared, Evelina was gone, out the door she came through, but her presence—the idea of her, and her sweet, sticky smell— lingered. I couldn't help but smile. *This*, I thought, was what I had imagined Italy to be like. Cracking plaster walls and neighbors borrowing carbohydrates. The laughs of little girls, who had disappeared momentarily, echoing from the hallway, running toward us with their arms full of treasures, dumping them on the floor of the living room for me to see. A velvet dress! A doll with button eyes! A special key! A necklace made of tiny freshwater pearls! A chapter book! Paintings they'd made for their mother! A lip gloss on a chain! All the incredible treasures of girlhood: they wanted to share them with me. The older one, Greta, held up a photograph of them as babies.

"If you're wondering why we don't look like Mamma," Greta said, suddenly serious, "it's because we're adopted."

An edict: my own story reflected back on me. It was the moment when I should tell them that I, too, was adopted, but I did not. Maybe I wanted to begin my story anew with them, reinvent myself. Or maybe I just didn't want them to sense my desperation so soon, to see me seeking something in them. Despite whichever of these things was true, this new information doubled my desire to be let into this family.

"And if you're wondering where our papa is," Greta said, "he doesn't live here anymore."

"Yes, Greta's right," Renata said, stiffening. "Massimo was my husband, but he left a few months ago. It's just us now. You may see him around—he teaches at the university where you'll be studying, and he'll pick up the girls every other weekend."

Oh, to be Massimo! I thought, projecting my own assumptions onto the story. To be Massimo every other weekend, getting to be the fun dad who dipped in to buy the girls gelato! To be Massimo at the university, where students shuddered with admiration as he approached the lecture podium! To be Massimo in bed with another woman—there was always another woman—free and unburdened, pumping hard with pleasure! To insert oneself into the story, rather than opening one's legs to let it in . . .

"Would you like to see your bedroom?" Renata said. "If you want it to be yours, that is."

I did. I did want it to be mine. Just like I wanted everything in this house to be mine, including the palpable love I could feel, leaping from one little girl to the other, to their mother, occasionally bouncing toward me, close enough to feel its warmth. I followed Renata down a hallway toward the room that would be mine, far enough away from the rest of the rooms that it felt like its own miniature apartment. Angels painted on the ceiling and books surrounding the bed on three sides. A window overlooking the central courtyard, where birds were busy landing on overgrown branches. I moved in that September, as the city's residents returned from a long August on the coast. It was just getting slightly cold. Hahahahaha the angels said as they watched me try to fall asleep that first night. Hahahahaha the two young girls said as they rifled through my suitcase, stealing my thong underwear to ring around their necks. Renata in the mornings with her hair pulled up in a claw clip. To be her or be hers, I thought, imagining first the claw clip in my own hair, and then my hand as the clip, and then both of us holding each other's hair in our hands, unable to let go lest the locks fall down the other woman's back: that slight discomfort on the neck.

REJECTION

The feeling of that year—the longing and the hope, the plaster walls filled
with too much history, the special buzz of Italian words moving around
in my mouth—descended upon me as I sat in my cubicle in Manhattan,
contemplating returning there. It made me feel both giddy and daunted.
A decade later, I was a new and improved version of myself, not so easily
crushed by my own emotions. I would be different if I went back now, I
told myself. More curious and less sad. I would wander with conviction
instead of melancholy, and I'd take notes in my notebook. I decided I
would go to the wedding in Verona, and then I would go to Bologna,
where I would revisit my loneliness as if it were a landmark, only this time
I would not be alone—I would bring Wes.

I texted Wes: *Italy in April?*

While I waited for his reply, I googled "what to wear to a wedding
in Italy." Numerous dresses appeared on my screen, each a bright ray of
two-dimensional possibility in its little white box. I imagined wearing the
yellow one with the ruffled cap sleeve while dancing with Wes under a
thousand twinkle lights. I saw us taking our seats in the church pews—me
in the long floral wrap dress with the subtle tie at the waist. Which kind of
woman did I want to be at this wedding, and in general? The effortlessly
elegant woman who casually spent her entire paycheck on her outfit because investment pieces were always worth it? The woman whose statement earrings would surely date her ensemble down the road but who, in
the moment, was radiant with relevance? The mysterious woman in long
sleeves? The dress became a vessel for all the feelings I was having about
the possibility of returning, and I began to search obsessively, my eyes
glazing over as the screen looped on an endless scroll.

Finally, my phone buzzed. *What's in Italy? I have New Orleans.*

The dresses on my screen suddenly all looked the same; Renata's
image blurred in my mind. Of course, New Orleans. Wes had been going every spring for over a decade, documenting the same family, whose

house had been washed away by Hurricane Katrina. He had thousands of photographs of them—a big family with a matriarchal grandmother at the helm—waist-deep in water, then in a homeless shelter, then in their new tract homes, holding objects they'd saved from the wreckage—meticulously filed on his hundreds of hard drives. I thought back to when he'd gone on the same trip last spring, how I'd pined for him while he was gone but ultimately loved the idea of it, proud that my boyfriend was doing such important work. Now, as I realized New Orleans was coming up again, and that it would keep him from accompanying me to Italy, I felt a tinge of resentment for it: the place that called Wes away from me, that sat at the very top of his list of priorities. Maybe he could reschedule? Maybe if I explained what Italy meant to me he might reconsider?

My friend Grace is getting married, I texted back. *At DANTE'S VILLA.*

You have to go! Wes wrote. It was amazing how quickly the idea of the future could expand and contract, how easily a vision could be crushed. I didn't want to go to Italy alone; the idea strangely frightened me. I closed the digital invitation without responding to it, and the flowers fluttered back into the envelope. But I couldn't shake the image of the two girls I had once cared for, at their ballet class I took them to on Wednesdays, their slender youthful bodies pulling taut into straight or rounded lines. I realized just how badly I wanted to see them. And I wanted to see their mother, who, very briefly, like a bird landing or a cloud passing, had felt like my own.

SOS

I would have wallowed in this feeling of rejection longer, but I got an email from Megan, which immediately brightened my mood. Getting an email from Megan felt how getting emails used to feel, back when the internet was new and people poured their hearts into it, when friends and lovers used email like it was simply an electronic version of actual letter writing, filling each other's inboxes with meaning. These days, emails were just another form of to-do list, packed with unpunctuated directives and crazy links. But not Megan's. Megan's emails were like little walnuts that you could crack open to discover whole tiny worlds. Her drawings were both art in themselves and invitations, for me to dive into them and root around for the story. Our exchange had become the thing I went to work for; her name in my inbox felt as exciting as a new lover's.

Megan's email included a drawing of a lamp. The lamp was familiar, but I couldn't place it in my mind at first. It was square and modern, with a tweedy shade. And then it dawned on me: it was Todd's, the one in his office that he'd brought from home. "Who brings a lamp from home?" I'd chided Megan the week before. "Do you have to judge *everything* everybody does?" she'd said, a comment that had stung and that I'd stashed away, likely saving it to make myself feel worse during one of my self-critical shame spirals.

Fuck, I thought now, because I knew exactly what the lamp meant. It meant that something had happened with Megan and Todd, or that she wanted something to. My hunch was confirmed when I got a text from her a minute later.

SOS, she'd written. *Can you get a drink after work?*

CONFESSION

At 6:00 p.m. on the dot, Megan and I elevatored to ground level and then escalatored into the bellows of the subway. We took the R to Union Square and transferred to the L. Megan had made it explicit that she needed a drink before she told me whatever she was going to tell me, so we were mostly quiet on the subway. A woman who looked homeless shuffled the length of the train car, holding out a shoe. The woman's gray hair was matted into three distinct paddles, like a trifecta of beaver tails. Megan reached into her purse for a dollar, which encouraged me to do

the same. I felt reflexively bad for this woman collecting the public's pity
in a Reebok, and wished I could offer something more than a tiny bit of
money. But when Megan and I reached our dollars toward her, attempting to slide them into the shoe, she waved us away and gave us a dirty
look. When the subway's robotic voice announced we were arriving at
the Bedford stop, and we stood to get off the train, I peered into the shoe,
where a tiny mouse, no bigger than the end of a teaspoon, crouched in
a nest of ripped newspaper. The mouse made me feel both stupid and
happy; the woman had not been begging at all, but caring for something
small and vulnerable, perhaps loving it. It's so easy to get the story wrong,
I thought as the subway dinged open. We were back in Brooklyn.

Megan and I were funneled out with the Williamsburg crush onto
Driggs. After an unnecessary consultation—we both knew where we'd
end up—we walked to one of our favorite bars, a goth dive on Grand
Street that had somehow resisted aesthetic overhaul. As all the other bars
commenced to subway-tile their backsplashes and invest in low-wattage
lighting, trying in vain to catch up with the ever-evolving global aesthetic,
desperate to resemble everything else so as not to fall out of general favor, this bar stayed comfortingly the same—an old lover who remains
frozen in place and time in your mind, immune to age and change.
A few of us had held on to the place with a kind of desperation, crouch-
ing in the dark with our cheap beers, trying to ignore the Dunkin Donuts
that had descended on North Seventh, the deliberately camouflaged
J.Crew on Wythe, pretending that the neighborhood hadn't turned into
a giant shopping mall overnight. I liked the booth in the front window
best, because it felt both private and public at the same time; the passersby on the street could not hear your conversation, but they could
watch it without the sound on, and it satisfied me to feel like a character
in a show.

Happily, this favorite booth was open, and so we claimed it with our
purses while we ordered tequila sodas. After one sip, before we were even
all the way seated in the booth, Megan dove in.

"Okay, so you know how we went on that team field trip," she said. "When the art team went to the MoMA last week?"

I nodded. I was wildly jealous that the designers got to do things like this, going on set to photo shoots or spending workdays at museums to jog their inspiration, while I was stuck writing product copy for seventeen styles of the same bra.

"So we all walk up there, and it's that fun vibe of like being free from work with your coworkers, everyone's joking around and being kind of playful, and Todd walks next to me, doesn't say much, but I can tell he's like listening to me banter with Mara and kind of getting a kick out of it."

"Does Mara even know how to banter?"

"Not the point of the story," Megan said scoldingly.

"Sorry, keep going."

"So we get into the museum and everyone goes their own way. I knew there was this Klimt painting that they were showing and it was the last week it was up, so I went straight to that floor. I don't even really like Klimt all that much, but this particular painting moves me for some reason. Especially in person. It's of Adele Bloch-Bauer, but not the one everyone's obsessed with, with all the gold. It's done in purples and greens and blues, she's in the center of the composition, wearing these robes or a big scarf or something, with this really particular expression on her face. It's like she's very worn down, almost exhausted by life, and she's surrendering a little bit in this moment. Either that or she's just learned some crazy bit of news and she can't breathe for a second."

I nodded, urging Megan to go on, desperate for her to get to the point. She fidgeted with her cocktail napkin before she continued.

"So I'm in front of it for a while," she said. "And then at one point I feel that there's someone standing right behind me, like really close. I know it's him even before I turn around, I just *know*, you know?"

"Todd?" I said.

"Yes, Todd," she said. "And he knows I know it's him, right? And it's this fucking *crazy* erotic experience, knowing he's there, feeling his breath on my neck, looking at this painting of this huge woman. We stood there for like fifteen minutes."

"Whoa," I said. I could feel the exact tension that Megan was describing, the proximity and the knowing. It was erotic even now, in the telling, as if it were happening to me.

"So we have this museum moment," she says. "And then we all go our separate ways to go home, and I'm getting on the Q train, right? And I see him get in the car next to me. He doesn't look at me, but I know he knows I know he's there, and he knows I'm there, so close and so far away, and we ride the train like that, a car away, feeling each other. And when we switched to the L, it was the same: him in the next car, me feeling him through the walls."

"Jesus," I said. "Kind of creepy, no?"

"It was but also wasn't," she said. "It felt like nothing I've ever felt before—like there was so much feeling that it was in the *air*. Like it was this tangible thing."

"Whoa," I said again, unable to craft a coherent reaction.

"And *then*," she said, "right before we get off the train, I get a text from this number I don't know."

"How the hell did he get your number?"

"I have no idea. Maybe Reed? Anyway, he goes: *Did you feel that too?*"

My heart was racing.

"Oh my god," I breathed.

"I *know*," she said.

"So what'd you say back?" I said.

"Nothing," she said. "I never responded. I went home to my depressing full-size bed and he went home to his wife."

Megan and I had done some internet sleuthing and found out that Todd's wife was a fair and voluptuous redhead named Gabrielle, who evidently made expensive jewelry by hand. The jewelry was extremely dainty, almost invisible, with sparkle-size diamonds and strips of gold as thin as strands of hair. Gabrielle's skin had a similar quality to the jewels: it sparkled and you could see through it to her blue veins and rosy flesh; if Megan's look was Edwardian, Gabrielle's beauty went even farther back, to the pale, pressed prettiness of the Victorians. Needless to say, Megan and I had developed a mutual fascination with her.

"Wouldn't it be lovely," Megan said, "to be married to someone whose presence resembled a bit of moon glow on the surface of a lake?"

"But then sometimes you probably just want to dive in," I said, which was supposed to make Megan laugh but didn't.

"So how are you feeling about it now?" I said.

"Fucking crazy!" she said. "I mean, what am I supposed to do, you know? I didn't even really like him all that much . . . I mean, I'd had a crush on him, obviously—I was intrigued. But it wasn't *real*, you know? It was a work crush, something to take my mind off my stupid job, some fantasy that would never be anything more than that. It had felt small and safe, contained. But now I'm like . . . I don't know. It's so strange, I almost feel like I'm hypnotized or something. Like I've been told to be infatuated with this person, and so I am."

"I don't know, Meg," I said. "I feel like you've gotta get out now, before anything happens."

Megan let her eyes wander up to the ceiling of the bar, where hundreds of bottle caps had been nailed into ugly designs. She sighed.

"But what if . . ." Megan said, dropping her gaze to look at me with terrified lamb eyes. "What if it's real?"

"Well, it is *real*," I said, trying to make her feel validated. "You do feel something. But it's just lust. It's not . . . substantial. It can't be. You don't even know each other."

"I know," she said. "No, you're right, I totally know."

Megan's cocktail was almost gone, so I took the liberty of ordering her another one from the heavily tattooed woman behind the bar, whose judgmental gaze made me feel at home because I knew it so well; I used to give the same look to other women when I tended bar. But though I knew this, though I had been this woman, I still let it slice into me: the cut of another woman's eyes on you as she sized you up, certainly deciding that you came up short. Why did we do this to each other? Were we each so protective of our own tiny sliver of self that we had to defend it with a steely distrust? Or were we all just a little bit pissed off, tired of pouring people's shots, the soles of our feet aching from too many hours in our clogs?

"I think she poisoned my drink," I reported to Megan when I returned. "But yours should be fine."

Megan smiled half-heartedly and said nothing. I could see that she was only partly there, her mind reeling with images of Todd. We drank quietly for a while in the booth, taking in the gravity of the situation. I began to feel as guilty and parched as if I were the one lusting over someone I'd never have. It felt crazy good at the same time as feeling crazy bad. The way Todd's eyes could swallow you whole.

"You're lucky you found Wes before the window closed," Megan said.

"Oh, come on," I said. "What *window*? You're thirty-one. Nothing's *closing*."

"Oh, it's closing all right," she said. "I'm going to wake up one morning and look around and realize everyone has found their place, their person, their *thing*. And I'll just be standing there, alone, dressed like a corporate penguin, lusting after my married boss."

I reached out and put my hand on top of Megan's. I knew that what Megan was getting into would probably hurt her in the end, and that it probably hurt her now, but I was also moved by it. That feeling of falling for someone, the burn of that wanting, and then letting it take hold of you—I understood it, even coveted it. We were asked to follow so many rules, to be so many things. To follow our conscience but follow our heart, even when they conflicted with each other. To be desirable while disregarding our own desire. Sometimes, just sometimes, we wanted to not have to choose how to be. We wanted to be told to feel a certain way, to be hypnotized into feeling held.

NOSTALGIA

When I left Megan that night, I took my time walking back to Wes's place. I was charged up in a weird way, agitated. Even though it was November and cold out, I felt warm and ready, though I did not know what for. I felt like doing something bad, so I bummed a cigarette from one of the Wall-Street-cum-Williamsburg dress shirt dudes and smoked it on a stoop on the south side of Metropolitan. It tasted like 2012, like freedom, like Wes, who was waiting for me to climb into his bed with him so that we could fit ourselves into the shapes we'd constructed over our nights together: two S's pressed up tight at the curves.

I put the cigarette out with my boot after a few puffs; I didn't actually like the feeling of smoking itself, it was the *choosing* to smoke that I liked, the tiny act of rebellion that felt like freedom, or at least a gesture toward it. I turned right onto Wythe and then left onto North Fourth. Wes's was the last old loft building on the block: it sat like a stubborn, original artifact in the middle of the tall and gleaming condominiums that had shot up around it. I let myself in through the back alley entrance. The smell was the same as it had always been—plywood and pot—and instantly took me back to that first time I'd come here, my second encounter with Wes. It was a few weeks after meeting him at the park, and I'd run into him on one of my long walks around my neighborhood. He had a cigarette dangling from his mouth and was carrying two fistfuls of tinfoil: egg and cheese sandwiches, still steaming. "Wanna eat some breakfast?" he'd said, so casually I couldn't tell how to take it. Was he asking me on a breakfast date, or did he think of me in a way that was so unromantic that he thought we might bro down over an egg and cheese? Either way, I wanted in.

"Two sandwiches, huh?" I said in a jabby, flirtatious way that showed I could be casual, too.

He grinned, tossed the cigarette down and put it out with his sneaker. The confidence with which he carried out this simple action made me wonder if he did know he was handsome after all.

"One's for my roommate, Kasper," Wes said. "He's very bad at feeding himself."

"Sounds like a winner," I said.

"But it could be yours," he said. "If you want it to be."

"And let Kasper starve?" I said. "I couldn't possibly."

Seamlessly, suddenly, without knowing exactly how I'd arrived there, I was at the door to his loft building.

"It used to be a pantyhose factory," Wes had said as he led me inside, shoving the brick that was holding the door open with his foot. As we stepped into the cluttered hallway, I tried to imagine the gauzy peach piles of sheer pantyhose fabric, the whir of those old sewing machines, the gossip of the workers. Now it was full of busted IKEA furniture and free clothes boxes and crates of empty mason jars, the little evidences of lives lived and phases outgrown, someone's brief dabbling with making kimchi or short-lived affair with bucket hats. Bikes leaned on every available wall, against the scribblings of drunk street artists who'd made their contributions during parties that flowed from one unit to another, from one night to the next, from year to year, until all the parties ran together like the art on the walls did: messy remembrances of decades come and gone.

The smell of Wes's unit was the more specific olfactory blend of so many Brooklyn boys: stale cigarettes and dirty laundry, whatever food was in the trash, and vinegar; I'd later learn this was his photo developer, which he used to print photos in the cement box of his makeshift shower. The place had been built out by crafty previous tenants: there was a lofted space over one half of the big room, and then a smaller structure nestled into the opposite corner of the ceiling, built to resemble a Japanese pagoda. Between these upstairs rooms was a working drawbridge. The big arch windows looked out onto Kent Avenue, where the season's fashions (that first summer it was tank tops with really big arm holes) were being paraded by hipsters on their way to the food truck lot down the block. A chandelier made of bottles hung from a naked rafter.

"Wow," I'd said that morning. "You're really living the dream."

Wes laughed, perhaps thinking I had been making a joke about the makeshift space, but I was being serious. Wes lived the life that people in Williamsburg were supposed to be living, the life this neighborhood was known for. I had been to parties at lofts like this but had never known someone who actually lived in one; they were slowly getting torn down, being converted into condos by developers who were actively capitalizing on the neighborhood's gritty cool factor. But Wes's building was the real deal, and so, I conjectured, was Wes. Everyone else I knew had given up on their creative dreams, tabling them while they pursued more realistic careers at advertising agencies and tech start-ups and direct-to-consumer mattress brands. But not him. A hundred photos of his were stuck on the wall above his desk with blue artist tape, forming a beautiful, messy collage. The loft completed the picture of Wes as a person who prized authenticity over practicality, which was highly attractive. I loved the thin-paned windows that made the light dance across the floor like water. I loved the blue tape. I loved the high ceilings and huge beams—Wes's own industrial sky.

I gravitated toward Wes's desk, where I touched the edge of a picture of a small child standing in a flooded street, holding a hamster in his hands. Both the child and the hamster looked wet and worried.

"Those don't really pay the bills," Wes said. "So I do this stuff on occasion."

He shook the mouse of his computer to reveal a screen filled with shining Bacardi bottles.

"I try not to do too much ad work, though," he said. "Lest I become corrupted."

I burned. I was corrupted; the photo on his screen had the exact overly retouched sheen of the ads I worked on every day. A pang in my belly: I wished I had chosen to be more like him.

I couldn't help myself; I picked up a stack of black-and-white photos from the desk and began to sift through them. I audibly gasped when I saw the one of me that he'd taken at the park: there I was in my thrift-store dress, laughing at god knows what, with *something on my face.* I looked closer. It was a small triangle on my right cheek.

"What *is* that?" I said.

Wes laughed. "I think it was a piece of a chip."

My whole body flushed with the warm prickle of embarrassment. Was *that* why Wes had taken a picture of me? Not because he thought I was beautiful or interesting-looking or worthy of capturing on film, but because I had a chip on my face? More important—*why* did I have a chip on my face? I didn't even remember having eaten chips.

"It was this perfect triangle," Wes said, perhaps trying to justify what he'd done: capitalized on my messiness for a good picture. "Right there." He placed his warm finger on my cheek, which burned as he touched it. I realized that Wes must be the kind of man who never had anything on his face—he was somehow immune to crumbs and boogers, even rogue eyelashes. His own messes were somehow sensual: dirt rubs on his canvas sneakers that he wore without socks, the worn fly of his jeans. The fact that he'd honed in on my accidental and very unsensual mess felt doubly embarrassing. Out of the two of us, I saw, I was the crumby one.

Then he said: "You became an abstract painting for a second."

I melted again. I'd settle for being crumby if I could also be a painting.

"Kasper!" Wes called up to one of the lofted rooms. "Breakfast!"

I heard rustling, groaning, and then feet padding down the shoddily constructed wooden plank stairs from the mezzanine, where I assumed the bedrooms were. It was the middle of the day, but this Kasper person had clearly just woken up. Wes tossed the egg and cheese into the air and Kasper caught it. Of course Wes was a sandwich thrower. He probably opened beer bottles with his keys, took stairs two at a time, slid down banisters. Despite his smallish stature and elegant collarbone, he seemed manly to me in this particular way: that understanding of physical objects in space, and of himself in relationship to those objects.

"You're a good friend," Kasper said in a funny, too-sincere way as he unwrapped his now-congealed egg and cheese. Kasper looked and sounded European, Swedish, maybe. He was tall, with broad shoulders and a ruddy, uncomfortable-looking face, like he didn't know how to fill the bigness of himself.

"This is Emily," Wes said to Kasper. "I picked her up on the street."

"Good morning, Emily," Kasper said. "Welcome to our palace."

I smiled. "Thank you," I said. "It's beautiful."

"Too quiet, though," Kasper said, crossing the room toward a shoddily constructed DJ booth I hadn't noticed until now. "We need tunes." He shuffled through a stack of records and slid one onto the player. The music that emerged was not the Euro techno I'd expected. It was slow, just piano at first, and sad.

"Kasper is an amazing musician," Wes said. I noted how easy it was for Wes to give compliments, remembering how he'd praised the writing of Zoe's friend at the park. It took a certain kind of confidence to be so free with flattery, and also a touching kind of devotion.

"Is this you?" I asked Kasper.

Kasper smiled. "I wish. I'm just playing DJ right now. This is a Danish guy, pretty famous, he's also called Kasper." Kasper let out a little laugh, as if this coincidence of names was one of life's fun little jokes.

We all listened to the sad song contemplatively. I tried to think deep thoughts but instead I thought about how close Wes's body was to mine, just a few feet away. I snuck a glance at his collarbone, which was visible just below the thin neck of his T-shirt; I imagined myself reaching out to touch it. I felt both preoccupied by desire and deeply present in a way I hadn't in some time. I felt all the things happening in my body: the tingle in one of my knees, the air moving in and out of my nose, my feet on the loft's plank floor. The dust in the air sparkled. The beautiful light from the tall windows found my face. I willed Wes to lift his camera again, to capture this moment on film, to capture me as I was now, existing in the delirious, hopeful space before anything had happened, where everything is built of pure imagination, the entire future a fantasy. But he did not.

"Want to see my plants?" Wes said instead.

"And he has *plants, too*?" I said.

Wes grinned and led me up the plank stairs and across the lowered drawbridge to his pagoda. Inside, a white square of bed and a hundred houseplants, immaculately tended to, lined up under the window: a large open square, looking out onto the living room, that had been sawed out of the drywall of the lofted room. I thought of him touching the leaves gently. I imagined him touching me like he might touch the plants: tips of fingers on my stems and leaves, tending to me. *Who is this person I am sitting across from?* I remember thinking. *Could he love me? Will we be together? Will we be together always?*

When he did touch me it was not delicately: Wes grabbed the back of my head with both hands and tugged it eagerly toward his, and suddenly we were kissing very passionately. It happened so quickly I almost didn't register that it was happening at all, so when we pulled away from each other, I must have appeared shocked.

"Sorry," Wes said. "I couldn't help myself."

"I liked it," I said, smiling, though I wasn't actually sure I had. It had been jarring—I hadn't gotten to experience the most pleasurable part of a first kiss, which is the part where you know it's going to happen but it hasn't yet. I realized I had told him I liked it because I felt tender toward him and wanted to protect him; I didn't want him to feel self-conscious. But then I wondered if he did anyway; he now had a concerned look on his face that made me think he might regret the kiss entirely.

"Are you okay?" I asked.

"Yeah," Wes said. "It's just. I want to tell you something before anything else happens."

"Okay," I said. I felt nervous suddenly, thinking Wes might tell me he had some kind of disease, or that he was moving out of the country soon, or that he already had a girlfriend.

"I try not to kiss people unless I really like them," he said. "And I know I've only met you twice, but I'm pretty sure I like you. I could tell after the park—I couldn't stop thinking about you afterward."

"Same," I said, lowering my gaze and then lifting it again: a practiced flirtation.

"But it worries me," Wes went on. "Because every time I've been with someone, I've fucked it up. I need my space, and my time, my work, you know? I'm particular about it—I've sort of had to be."

"Why's that?"

"I moved here when I was eighteen," he said. "When I decided to study photography, my parents basically told me they weren't going to have anything to do with supporting me—I was totally on my own. They're conservative and practical, they've never left Iowa, they have a fucking American flag on their front lawn. They didn't get who I was, why I wanted to do what I wanted to do. They don't believe in art, and my politics scare the shit out of them, and my photos, if they've ever even bothered to look at my website, would most definitely push my mother over the edge. Anyway, I've had to make my own life from scratch; I moved into this place when the neighborhood was still scary as hell and I was just a teenager, and I feel protective over it—my space and my time, the only things I really have that are my own. Not the best for my relationships, though. I always end up getting resentful when my time or space is cut into, and pulling away. It's happened a few times now. It's not the girl's fault, of course. But it seems that she always wants more than I can give, and I always end up feeling bad."

"I don't want to make you feel bad," I said, kissing the collarbone I'd admired at the park. "Just good."

Wes lay back on the bed, looked up at the ceiling. I lay down next to him.

"It's a weird thing to feel like you don't have anyone," he said. "You get used to doing it all alone, and then you kind of exist that way by default."

"I know exactly what you mean," I said, which was both true and not true. I knew what it felt like to be alone in the world, yes, but my response to that aloneness was to surround myself—with friends, lovers, anyone who would fill up the emptiness. I already knew Wes and I were deeply different in this way: my defense mechanism was togetherness, his was separation. *Will he hurt me? Will I hurt him? Will there be explosions? Will we survive them?*

He shifted onto his shoulder and turned to look at me. Then he took his index finger and ran it over my nose, down to my lips, over them and onto my chin, then down my neck to my clavicle and then my stomach. At my belly button he stopped, circling idly for a moment, looking at me with those tropical eyes of his.

"You know what's lucky?" I said.

"What's lucky?" he said.

"The preposterous thing I'm trying to do might just require as much time and space as the preposterous thing you're trying to do."

Wes smiled. "You mean writing?"

"Yes," I said, not knowing where my confidence was coming from. "Unfortunately for the social animal that lives inside me, I've chosen to take up a vocation that requires long spans of insane-making aloneness."

"Go on," Wes said, climbing on top of me now, letting his mouth fall onto all the places where his finger had just been.

"I disappear for whole days or nights," I said. "No one can find me. They text me frantically, telling me to meet them for happy hour or brunch, but it's as if I can't hear them, so deep am I in the pit of language I've been busy digging."

Wes laughed. I was joking, and we both knew it, but I was also deliberately pleasing him, which only I knew, by painting a picture of the
woman I knew I could be, if only I tried harder. My writing habits, at
that time, weren't really habits at all—I wrote in fits and starts, on subway
platforms and late at night when I couldn't sleep. But I could see that he
liked the idea of this writer-loner I was describing, and I liked it, too. In
fact, it seemed to turn both of us on. The sex we had then—in Wes's little
pagoda full of plants, in the middle of the day—felt like more than sex:
it felt like a promise, or a pact. From then on, we would be together so
that we could be alone. So that we could withstand it, the brutal solitude
required to make something actually good. It felt like an incredible relief,
that promise. It was a promise to myself as much as it was to him: I would
become a real writer, and Wes would hold me to it. He pushed himself
deeper into me, and it felt good, and our pleasure intensified simultaneously, mine enhancing his and his enhancing mine, in the infectious way
of laughter, and sometimes fear.

—

This midday sex led to more sex, and the sex got better as my affection
for Wes deepened and intensified. I found out that he was self-taught and
well-read, that he could keep up with me in social situations, that he showered daily, sometimes twice, and that he woke up very early and made
coffee, so that when I woke up it was ready. I liked all these things about
him, and I told him so. In return, he told me what he liked about me: that
I went down tunnels in my mind, that I asked millions of stupid questions,
that I knew many poems by heart, and that I looked good naked. He took
pictures of me naked. He also took pictures of me clothed. He taped the
not-nude photos above his desk, adding to his ever-evolving collage of the
things he found beautiful. When I passed his desk, I saw myself in many
forms: laughing while eating noodles, reposed on his couch, concentrated
with a book, wistful by the water. If I were to see those pictures now, I

know I would feel nostalgic. Not because I was happier then, but because Wes had captured, with those photos, something essential about the way I was back then: in all of the photos I looked slightly different; I was still malleable, changeable, and open to that change; I hadn't solidified yet, and there was freedom there; I could be anyone I wanted to be, in any moment. I don't know where those photos are now; Wes took them down at one point, though I can't remember when, or what he replaced them with.

—

Now I climbed up Wes's precarious stairs to the mezzanine, let down and crossed the drawbridge, and slid into bed with him. The world of Wes was familiar to me now, in all its particulars. The romantic hassle of this drawbridge, the absurd-to-the-point-of-hilarious volume of Kasper's snoring, the freezing air that shot through the floorboards in the winter. I still loved it here, and I even felt a certain amount of ownership over the space now—early on, Wes had surprised me with a small desk he'd found on the street that he'd hauled inside and set up under the big window: my very own writing desk. In the little drawer of the desk he'd tucked a worn-out copy of *The Elements of Style*, and atop it he'd placed one of his house-plants, a succulent he'd smuggled back from a trip to California. The way I'd imagined things had not been far off: Wes's ambition served to make me more ambitious, and often we'd spend the whole weekend at the loft together, me with my notebook at the little desk, Wes editing photos on his computer across the room. Breaks for shared cigarettes; long dinners with Kasper at the end of the day; sex in his strange concrete shower; beers on the roof before bed. When Monday morning rolled around and I had to go back to work, I felt a deep pit of loneliness as I left the loft and set off for midtown, knowing I probably wouldn't be back until Thursday or Friday; Wes liked to have a few uninterrupted shooting days at the begin-ning of the week. I'd gotten used to this rhythm, and despite—or perhaps because of—the days of distance that punctuated our togetherness, I was always rendered mute and loopy by his smell: fresh clothes tinged with musky body odor, warm breath laced with tobacco. I felt that familiar dizzy desirousness now, as I climbed into bed with him and kissed the back of his neck.

"Hey, goober," he said sleepily.

"Hey, special friend," I said.

"How's Megs?" he said. He raised his naked arm out from under the sheet to stretch.

"Oh, you know," I said. "Same. We went to Iona. Had our drinks poisoned, the usual."

I generally told Wes all my stories, spilling out a week's worth of silly office gossip and New York City shenanigans when we met up on Thursday or Friday. So why did I feel hesitant to recount Megan's Todd story, wanting to keep it close to my chest, as if I were protecting it?

Because it's not even a story yet, I said to myself, setting in motion one of those interior conversations that could continue all night if I let it. Nothing even happened.

And yet it's got you all hot and bothered, another part of me replied.

I'm just worried about her, I defended.

Or are you jealous of her? I countered.

Why on earth would I be jealous of her?

Because she's in the throes of erotic imagination. A state of pure desire. Because she's experiencing that once-or-twice-in-a-lifetime feeling of being carried completely away. Be honest with yourself: You miss it. The feeling of not knowing whether something will happen. That time when the question is more important than the answer.

As if to prove myself wrong, I slung my leg over Wes's waist to straddle him. He smiled in a way that could have been reluctant or amused, I couldn't tell—mostly he looked sleepy. I ignored the smile and shimmied his boxers down, first with my hands and then the rest of the way with my foot. And then—I couldn't help this, it occurred like some kind of hypnotic mind trick—I imagined I was Megan pulling down Todd's boxers with *her* foot. My foot was Megan's foot; Wes's dick was Todd's dick. The thought electrified me. I liked being someone else, anyone else, free from my own psychic loops and too-familiar body. As I lowered my body onto Wes's, I imagined Todd's startling gaze below me, and the horror and novelty of it gave me an orgasmic shiver. I cried out with pleasure in a way I usually didn't. Wes put his hand over my mouth; Kasper was home! And that's when the spell of it broke, and I was forced back into my own body, forced to remember that I could not, no matter how hard I tried, be anyone other than myself. I zipped my mouth shut, stayed silent while I came.

MARATHON

The next morning was one of those November days that feels like glass: bright and fragile, empty and waiting to be filled, clear enough to cut through any strange feelings from the night before. Wes said he wanted to post up by the park; the New York City Marathon was happening today, and he wanted to take pictures of the runners. The sidewalks were packed, the endorphins of the athletes had bubbled over and infected the crowds on the sidelines. The communal elation made me feel buoyant, as I always did when I felt like a part of something bigger than myself. A man with prosthetic legs bounced by like a gazelle. A woman who must have been in her nineties shuffled by, waving at everyone as if she knew them. It felt like she did know them, like we all knew each other. We were all bodies careening through space and time, some fast and some slow, some old and some young, some jiggling along happily and some bounding forward like running machines—but none of the differences or intentions seemed to matter: as long as you had joined the race you'd done it. You'd lived.

I texted Megan: *Running is beautiful and so is life! Come meet us!*

She agreed; I told her we were on the corner of North Twelfth. But then Wes started walking south, wanting to catch the runners from a different angle.

"But we're meeting Megan," I said, following him reluctantly.

"You're meeting Megan," Wes said with a tinge of annoyance in his voice. "I'm working."

"It's Saturday," I said. "I thought this was just for fun."

"There are too many good faces out here today," Wes said, as if I had insulted him. "I can't miss them. I'm going toward the bridge." He kissed me in a way that felt like a goodbye; I stopped and he kept walking.

A strange sensation overcame me then, watching Wes's body disappear into the crowd. For a second, I had the feeling that nobody could see me, that I had become completely invisible. I don't mean this in a metaphorical sense, but in a very real one: I felt as if I didn't exist. The world around me carried on, cheering and pulsing with vigorous health, as I retreated into nothingness. It only lasted a moment. When I snapped out of it, a very clear thought occurred to me: that whatever I had just felt—some kind of cosmic neutrality—was the exact opposite of what Megan had felt on the train, with Todd. Megan, enlivened by the gaze and wonder of someone else, even through the metal walls of train cars, had felt her own existence throbbing in her ears, felt the blood rushing to every part of her body, recognized the fullness of herself, perhaps even admired her own reflection in the train window. Did we need others to remind us we were there? To make us whole? And if so, had I chosen the right other? Wes was always looking—his job was to look, to see—and so why did it feel, in this moment, like he couldn't see me?

A few minutes later, Megan got there. But she wasn't really *there*. She had been sucked into her phone, which she held like a mirror close to her face, so that it made her cheeks glow. She was texting with Todd, I knew. I thought about telling her to stop, warning her against what could become of this, but I couldn't. Her face looked so happy, and beautiful, too, glowing, as if by being admired it had been transformed: a different girl altogether.

ENERGY

Megan and Todd's sexual energy began to leak out into the office. Everyone felt it. Computers ran hot, overheated. Meetings ran long, allowing for extra furtive glances. I masturbated in the bathroom, came silently and hard. Megan wore tight jackets and smelled different; she'd finally invested in the perfume she'd wanted forever, 40 percent off with our store discount. Peonies and sea glass, whatever that smelled like. Her Edwarian skin shone like the inside of a shell, flushed pink at the mention of Todd's name. Essie in a tizzy at the front desk when somebody's key didn't work. Linda leaving little star-shaped Christmas chocolates on our desks.

In the ping-pong that was our creative project, it was my serve; I still hadn't responded to one of Megan's drawings, the one of the lamp. I searched my inbox for it, stared at the drawing for a long while, then typed: TODD'S LAMP HE BROUGHT FROM HOME. I began writing a detailed description of what I imagined Todd's apartment to be like, down to the automatic window shades that sheltered the expensive furniture from the sun during the day, the glass swizzle sticks on his bar cart. I then began to write about Megan entering Todd's apartment for the first time. I saw her touching his expensive leather couch, pressing her fingers to his window glass. I saw him making her a gin and tonic, handing it to her, putting his hand on the small of her back. I spent two paragraphs on their first kiss—I felt incredibly turned on as I described their tongues—but only two quick sentences on what happened next. *They finally had sex, licking each other's ears and nipples. There was one moment of transcendence before the condom broke.*

Whoa. I deleted the sentence from the screen; it felt hot and dangerous. Plus, I knew HR could see everything I saved on my computer, and I didn't want anyone to find this. The story had gone somewhere unplanned—I would never be able to send it to Megan as part of our project—but I couldn't stop writing it. I opened my notebook and rewrote the sentence by hand. Then I kept writing. It flew out of me in one long natural pull, like a scarf from a magician's hat. Megan was easy to write

about because I knew her, and also because she fascinated me in a particular way: she was like me, but she was not me; I could carry out my own
obsessive thinking, but through her, as a kind of cypher. I followed her,
but I also led her. I imagined what she might do or think, but also what I
might do or think, but because it was her and not me doing it or thinking
it, I was off the hook in a crucial way. Suddenly Megan was squatting
over a toilet in a midtown Au Bon Pain, peeing on the magic wand of a
pregnancy test. Suddenly the test was positive. She opened the bathroom
door a crack. "Get in here," she whispered. Or I imagined she whispered.

I had taken Megan's story to unfathomable territories, charging it toward some crazy end, while in reality it lingered in the hot space of a beginning. While the pregnant Megan in my story debated an abortion, the
real Megan fucked Todd with her eyes across a conference table, never
having touched him.

Where's my story? Megan chatted me from across the office at some
point that afternoon.

Sorry, I'm swamped, I lied.

With what? she wrote. *I thought you finished all the copy for the Women's Book.*

I'll send you something by EOD, I said. But I didn't. I spent the rest of
the day working on this secret story about Megan, unable to stop myself
from sliding into her predicament, sliding into her skin, losing myself in
her longing.

THE BREAK

Weeks passed; the world seemed to be turning faster than usual; the office
spun around us; Megan, Todd, and I were encased in our own bubble of
creativity and lust. Megan sent me new drawings; I sent her new writings;
The Other Women's Book had over thirty entries in it by now. Nothing
had happened between Megan and Todd, but her desire had deepened
and grown with each passing day, and it showed up in her drawings as

they became more intimate, more direct, more brutal: her foot after a day of wearing heels, the erotically chapped lips of one of the models in the Resort catalog, Todd's ear with his earring. My stories followed suit. When Megan drew the empty tampon machine in the office bathroom, I wrote a piece about Greta, the girl I took care of in Italy, getting her first period. I had picked her up from ballet practice and she was crying, beside herself with terror and disbelief, as if she had just been robbed. In a way, she had been. Her childhood had been extinguished, just like that. Far too early, I'd wanted to tell God, though I didn't believe in God, of course. But I needed to blame someone for Greta's period, and that someone had to be a man. I'd cursed him, and all the other hims, too, as I showed Greta how to nestle a pad into her underwear, though I myself hated pads, the way they bunched up, and how after you'd bled on them you had to deal with the gruesome painting of what was inside you, admiring it for a moment and then, horrified, throwing it into the trash.

Megan and I were recording our surroundings but also our personal histories and our inner lives, and I was genuinely proud of what we were making. I was writing more than I ever had on my own, too, continuing the story I'd started about Megan and Todd in my notebook. It was as if each feeling and impulse fed the others: desire begetting energy, energy begetting creativity. I wanted things to stay that way forever, charged with possibility and eros, but I knew in my heart that they wouldn't. I understood that something would break, and it did. Megan and Todd finally kissed in real life, on the subway of all places, just before everyone left town for Christmas. And then, dutifully, as if it was their job to follow through with what they'd started, they finally had sex, at Megan's apartment, in the daylight, in the new year. They both called in sick to work on the same day, and I knew exactly where they were. I went to the office bathroom and cried for her, imagining the ache of her pleasure mixed with self-disgust. Later, in our booth at the bar, I asked her how it was. "He had these dark hairs on his chest," she said, a new sadness in her eyes. "I hadn't expected them because he's so blond. They kind of made me want to puke."

SUBWAY TEARS

In late January, a storm descended on the city. Snow began to fall and wouldn't stop, and wind rattled the office building. Megan seemed rattled, too.

"What's up?" I asked as I passed her cubicle, seeing that she was leaning on her forearms on the desk.

"Not feeling great," she said.

"You should go home," I said.

"No one ever goes home," she said. "I can't be the person who goes home."

I knew what she meant; there was an unwritten rule at this place that you came in no matter what, even if it was just to spread your germs around the office. The individual body mattered not at all when held up against the corporate body. We all needed to be here all the time.

But just then our phones dinged simultaneously; a company-wide email appeared in both of our inboxes. There had been a weather warning—we'd officially crossed into blizzard territory—and transportation might become difficult as the day went on; we should all head home as quickly as we could.

"Thank you, tiny baby Jesus," Megan said. We filled our leather tote bags with all the heavy, mostly unnecessary shit we carted around every day—gym clothes, multiple lip glosses, extra shoes, cheap umbrellas we'd bought from street vendors that morning, when the snow had been wet and sleety—and walked out into the storm together.

"Oh shit," Megan said, after we'd charged for a block with our heads down and made it to the subway platform.

"What?" I said.

I looked where she was looking: there was Todd, on the other end of the platform, shaking the snow out of his hair.

"I just don't want to see him right now," she said.

Todd looked over at us and waved, but did not approach. When the train came, we got in different cars. Megan seemed relieved but still distressed. I felt like I could see what was playing out in her mind: the memory of the first time they'd ridden in adjacent subway cars, how different—how much worse—it felt now.

"What's the deal?" I said. "What's happening with you guys?"

Megan shrugged. Her rosy skin was wet from melted snow, and I wanted to wipe it off with my finger but didn't. This new version of her, the Megan who had actually really fucked up, confused me greatly. I had only ever seen her do the right, good thing: tipping way too much at Chipotle, taking calls with her grandma's nursing home in the office lobby, bringing Essie coffee. She refused to let Essie pay her back; it was only a dollar, after all. And she never cared if the Chipotle employee saw that it was *her* who slipped the twenty-dollar bill in the jar that said *Tips are HOT*. She just did nice things because she was actually nice, because it made her feel good, because she *was* good. But it seemed that her goodness had broken down when it came to Todd, that the pull of his weird, magnetic power was too strong. It had gone too far, and she knew it, and she couldn't take it back.

"I think it was a mistake," she said.

"Yes, it probably was," I said, as kindly as I could. "But it can be over now. Please just tell me it's going to be over?"

"I don't know" was all she said. "I don't know what to do."

I hugged her around the shoulders. She leaned into me and began to cry. The people across from us on the train did not stare or acknowledge her crying, and I loved them for it. I love you, woman with the many plastic bags. I love you, dad carrying your kid's light-up scooter. I love you, girl with the gold necklace that spells out your name, confidently telling the world who you are. You get it. You've been here; we all have. In a moment of regret so deep that it can't wait for you to get home before it comes out through your eyes.

RIDING THE FERRY WITH TODD

The next day, the L train was down because of the storm, so I had to take the ferry across the river to get to work in Manhattan. I texted Megan to see if she wanted to meet me at the dock, but she said she still wasn't feeling well and was going to stay home. To my surprise, Todd was on the boat, sitting on the lower level with an empty seat beside him, wearing a cap that made him look like someone who peddled caps.

"Morning, friend," Todd said when he saw me, as if the world were normal and we actually were friends.

"Good morning," I said. "Didn't expect to see you on here."

"I'm on here every day. It's actually the easiest way to get to midtown from Dumbo."

"Dumbo, huh?"

"Williamsburg, huh?"

"Touché," I said.

"Have a seat," he said, and so I did.

This was awkward; I felt like a spy. I knew everything about what had happened between Megan and Todd, and he had no idea I knew. Or maybe he figured I did and thought that somehow bonded us? Either way, Todd had a certain power over situations, and by the time we'd sat down on the lower deck of the boat he had me feeling as normal as he seemed to feel, even a bit giddy from the coffee and the thrill of being moved across the top of water.

"You know, you and Megan talk the same," Todd said.

"We do?" I said.

"Yeah," he said. "Like I'm not sure I could tell you apart if we were on the phone."

Though I felt embarrassed by this fact, I knew it was true. I knew that when I was around Megan, the cadence of my voice changed to be slightly more like hers, and that hers probably changed to be slightly more like mine. I even noticed us doing little things that the other did sometimes, for no real reason, just to see how it felt. Tugging our hair up into piles on top of our heads, only to let it down again a few moments later. Rapping our pens on our notebooks during meetings. Sighing to ourselves, picking at our teeth with our salad forks, laughing from our bellies over something no one else would think was funny. I knew we were more than work friends now. Without even knowing it, through art and through secrets, we had crossed over.

"So did you always know you wanted to be a copywriter?" Todd said with a kind smirk.

"Oh yes," I said. "I've known since I was five or six that someday I'd work for a department store in midtown, spinning yarns about sweaters."

Todd gave me a courtesy laugh. "So what did you think you would be?"

I knew then why Megan had fallen for him in the first place. It was *this*, this kind of attention paid, these kinds of questions, questions nobody asked these days, as everyone hustled to keep up with everyone else, their eyes on their own prize. *What did you think you'd be? What do you really want? Who are you, actually, under all the pretenses you put up each day to prove that you're deserving of being alive?* It felt like the first time in a very long while that someone had asked me what I wanted, or what I had originally wanted, before I'd let reality rake itself over me. I felt special in Todd's eyes right then, just as I had once felt special through Wes's camera lens, and it made me want to reveal things about myself that I never revealed to anyone.

"I was always making up stories," I said. "Inventing things—stories that weren't necessarily true, or at least fully true. My adoptive mom would kind of ridicule me for it, tell me I was exaggerating or lying; and I internalized it as this deep flaw, like I was *bad* or something, or wrong, or too dark, maybe. Then, when I was eighteen, I finally found out my birth mother's real name—my adoptive mom gave it to me on a little blue sheet of paper, told me I was an adult now and it was my right to know who my biological mother was. So I google her, right? Moni Lastra. And the first thing I find—the only thing, really—is a story, which she'd apparently written, in a small literary magazine in San Francisco called *The Haight*. The story was called *The Girl and the Whale*; I read it in a matter of minutes, as if I had been hungry for it my whole life. It was set in a small beach town in southern Italy, and was from the perspective of a teenage girl who finds a dead whale on the beach. That was the whole plot. A girl finds the whale and doesn't tell anyone about it, keeps it to herself for a whole evening and night, until it's discovered by the town in the morning. Anyway, I find the story and something clicks. I see myself in the story somehow: not in the character, necessarily, but in the writing. I had a revelation like: Oh, maybe that's the reason I am the way I am. Maybe telling stories isn't such a terrible thing . . . maybe it's in my blood, maybe it's what I was made for. Telling stories that aren't true but are maybe truer than true. Like how an imaginary whale can be more real in the mind than an actual whale."

I stopped abruptly, surprised I had said so much. Had I shared this story about my birth mother with anyone before? Had I even shared it with Megan, or with Wes? I was pretty sure I hadn't. So why was I sharing it with *Todd*?

"So you're adopted," Todd said. I nodded, disappointed he'd taken the conversation in this direction; I'd wanted to keep talking about writing.

"I used to dream about being adopted," Todd continued. "I had this image of what an adoptive mother looked like. Blond shoulder-length hair. A warm bosom."

I laughed unexpectedly. "You'd be surprised," I said. "Ann was . . . well . . . the opposite of a warm bosom. She was deeply religious, like pray-before-eating vibe. I think she adopted me out of genuine desire to do good; she always wanted to do the right, good thing, and I think she'd convinced herself that adopting was this way to save herself or something. She went to crazy lengths to make it happen—a lot of agencies didn't want to send a baby to a single-parent household, so she had to pull strings at the church— but I never really understood what the deeper desire was for her, like why she wanted me in the first place, since it seemed like all I did was bring unwanted chaos to her life. She had this really rigid way of being, and she wanted me to be that way, too. Same outfit in different colors every day. Same job at the bank for twenty years. Everything in its certain place. Nothing messy. And when I was messy—not just like I spilled something, but if I was complicated, or if I cried and my face got blotchy, she would sort of tweak out, as if she couldn't compute or handle what was going on. It made me feel like there was something deeply wrong with me, even though I know that wasn't her intention. Oh, and her hair was down to her butt— she had a thing about not cutting it—so there goes your vision of the bob."

Todd laughed sadly, looked out at the choppy river through the rain-streaked window. Once again I knew I had overshared, but it was like I couldn't stop telling him things, it was all just flowing out.

"One Christmas," he said, "when I was five or six, my mom got really sick with what she said was the flu, though I know now that she was withdrawing. Then my little sister got the chicken pox. I remember thinking: I am the man. I have to take care of everything. But of course I didn't really know how. I stood on a chair and made soup from a can, and I knocked over the pot."

Todd held out his arm to show me his wrist, which had a splotchy burn mark on it. For whatever reason, it made me think of the black hairs on his chest that Megan had been so offended by. All of a person's imperfections, the gross deformities that made up a body and a life. The bad things we've done. The mistakes we've made. The burn marks. I suddenly felt a love for him, as if he were all of humankind trapped in one scrawny body.

"Wow," I said, not knowing what else to say. I took Todd's forearm in my hands and lightly touched the burn with my fingertips. I'm not sure why, but this felt like a completely normal thing to do in the moment, or maybe the only thing to do. Todd looked up at me. There was something hot happening between us, some intimacy that wasn't necessarily sexual but was as intense as if it were. I was sure he felt it, too. It was an invitation of some kind, to join him in his darkness. I felt that he had seen a similar darkness in me, and he was inviting me to exist within it, with him. The idea of someone who found this part of me compelling, even attractive, made me feel at once repelled—was Todd the actual devil?— and incredibly turned on. I imagined him leaning toward me and taking my earlobe in his teeth.

"What else did you find?" he said, his gaze holding. "When you searched for your birth mother."

"There wasn't anything else," I said, still holding his arm in my hand. "Aside from the obituary, which was so short and banal—it just said that she was second-generation Italian American, unmarried, and that she died from complications during childbirth, leaving behind an unnamed new-born daughter. It was the most depressing thing I had ever seen. It said nothing about who she was. It only positioned her in relationship to other people, made it seem as if she hadn't mattered at all. Like how could a life be reduced to that? A few lines that could have been about anybody."

I didn't try to articulate the thought that was just occurring to me now, which was that maybe a woman's life could never be captured in words, or with a story. Maybe she was always going to overflow, refuse to arc properly, rebel against the very page she was written on, or just shrivel up before anyone could pin her down . . .

"Why didn't you get in touch with the editor?" Todd said.

"The editor?"

"Of *The Haight.* See if she'd ever read anything else by your mom. Or if she knew her."

"I hadn't thought of that," I said, feeling stupid. The idea of it exploded like a bomb in my mind just as the ferry jolted into the dock, yanking Todd's arm from my hands, and the conversation was cut short. I understood as we deboarded that we'd never pick it up again, that this was the first and only time I'd be the center of Todd's attention, the first and only time I'd tell this story the way I'd just told it: so raw and real, unplanned and fresh, like a confession. I felt briefly saddened that the moment was over, until we got into the cab that would deliver us to the office and Todd was very rude to the driver. He told him haughtily not to

take the street he was taking, there was too much traffic, and then scoffed
as he looked at his watch. There was a photo shoot scheduled for this
morning. He was in charge, and this incompetent cabbie was going to
make him late.

EMPTY INBOX

When Megan came back to work, after taking an entire week off
with what she'd described as a "gross flu," things felt different. She
no longer bubbled over with sex; she stopped wearing her sea glass
perfume; there was a general chill about her. She told me she was
fine, but I knew something was off. At the department-wide meeting that week, Todd gave a presentation on the fall trends: school-
girl plaid, cropped jackets, grunge bridal, granny panties. *Granny
panties*?! I texted Megan, but she didn't look at her phone. She scribbled
in her notebook, refusing to look up. I tried to see what she was writing or
drawing on the page, but she covered it up with her long hand. She didn't
send me any drawings that week, and I felt their absence like a presence
in my inbox.

CEO

A few weeks later, in February, the CEO of the department store announced that he was stepping down. He gathered us all on the first floor
of the store, in the perfume section, to say a few words and pass the baton.
The current CEO's speech had a lot of gravitas and was inspiring in the
way that corporate speeches can be, where they briefly make you want to
be a better person. I suddenly wanted to live with integrity, pull myself up
by my bootstraps, make mistakes and then be graceful about fixing them,
evolve as a human, etc. The feeling was fleeting. When the CEO finished,

he handed over a symbolic paperweight to another man in a suit, and I forgot that integrity existed. The new guy took the spotlight. He had red hair and patchy sideburns.

"They say that you should do what you love," he began. "And when I look out at this group, I see that you've all done just that. You've followed your dreams and ended up here, with us, ready to care for your customers and for each other each day with spirit and gusto."

I looked around. People were smiling. It was the same rhetoric our generation had been fed from the start—that our jobs should not only make us money but say something about us, fulfill some innate desire in our deepest soul—and we loved to be told we were executing on that expectation, that we were turning our own dreams into realities, even if we were just selling people granny panties.

The new CEO moved on to the subject of corporate loyalty. "We're all in this together," he said. "When the sea rises, so do all the ships."

Was he talking about global warming? Or butchering that idiom about the rising tide lifting all boats?

"This is more than just a company," he continued. "It is a family."

Suddenly, sharp pangs of anger began bubbling up from somewhere deep inside me. I started to think about how crazy this was, that hundreds of us were standing here inhaling air that had been spritzed with a thousand perfumes, listening to some guy in a suit tell us we were his family. What we were doing here had nothing to do with family and everything to do with money, and to confuse the two was so problematic it made my head spin. If this was a family, I wanted to say, where was the mother? Why were there only fathers, standing above us in suits, telling us what to do? Why did they give their sons bigger allowances than their daughters? Why, when we were sick, did we feel bad about staying home?

"Our woman wants to feel taken care of," the CEO was saying now. "And that's what we can give her that none of these online retailers and direct-to-consumer start-ups can. We can make our woman feel special.

We can give her real attention. Personal attention. Real-time fashion advice. In-house tailoring. Real, valuable loyalty perks. Because at the end of the day, she deserves it."

I felt my face pucker up when he added, "And we deserve a share of her wallet."

The employees let out an obligatory communal chuckle. Hahahahaha we were going to snatch money from every New York City woman's purse! Hahahahaha we deserved it! I looked over at Megan, who rolled her eyes, no doubt thinking the same thing I was. I'd always hated this phrase, *share of wallet*, which reduced people's livelihoods and lives to a pie chart, of which every company and brand wanted a piece. But I hated it even more now, attached to the CEO's vision of "our woman." As if the department store owned the women who slid so gracefully through their automatic doors, who had done all they could in their lives to become their own individual selves, who had agonized over how they wanted to smell and appear, who had cried while looking in the mirror, who had gained unwanted weight when they had babies, lost too much weight when their fathers and mothers died, who made love with their husbands when they didn't want to, fucked their bosses when they knew they shouldn't, made pacts with themselves that they would be better, that they would try harder to be better, which only added to their deep exhaustion, their understanding that no matter what they did, no matter how hard they tried, they could not escape the traps that had been set for them: an escalator offering to take them away, into the impossibly aspirational Designer section. The whole operation suddenly seemed unrelenting, oblivious, even cruel.

I wanted to walk out, but I was not the kind of person who walked out. I wanted to say something, but I was not the kind of person who said something. What kind of person was I? What was I doing here? The perfume was going to my head. This wasn't my life; it couldn't be. But also—if the place where I spent fifty hours a week wasn't my life, then what was? Suddenly I felt claustrophobic, like I needed to get out. When

I got home that night, I decided, I would search for places to stay in Italy. I'd go alone if I had to.

TRAVEL PLANS

It was the first option for Bologna Airbnbs in my price range: the room with the angels that I had once occupied. My heart stopped when I saw that room—those familiar books, that window that looked down onto that poetic courtyard—then quickened when I clicked in and saw the host: Renata, of course, her triangular face surrounded by the glossy tentacles of her black hair, her glowing eyes. The coincidence was too uncanny. I hadn't been in touch with Renata since I'd lived with her a decade ago; neither of us had made the effort to keep up via email. But that didn't stop me from feeling deep recognition: Renata, even an image of her, felt like a part of me, and also like a hole where a part had been ripped out. I stared at her for a while before committing. But then my finger clicked without my permission: BOOK NOW. Very quickly, before I could even think about changing my mind, a response: *EMILY! It's Greta. I do Airbnb for my mom.* ☺ *I cannot believe it's you! That you're coming to stay with us! I promise not to steal your underwear, but I can't vouch for Bene. BACI BACI BACI! See you soooooooon.*

BOWLING BALLS

Once I'd bought my plane ticket, I felt like I was already gone. I did my work quickly and thoughtlessly, then embezzled even more time than usual to tinker with the thing I was writing about Megan—it was getting quite long. I felt good in there, in Megan's world, doing things that women did, facing problems head-on. Problems were never really problems when they belonged to your character and not to you.

Megan's current fictional problem was that she was pregnant, and she had to decide what to do. Or rather, I, the writer, had to decide for her. This part did feel hard, but only because of the discrepancy between what Megan would do in reality—get an abortion faster than someone could say Todd's one-syllable name—and what I needed her to do for my story, to make it keep going. I found myself drawn toward the unrealistic narrative, the one where Megan kept the baby that Todd had impregnated her with; I wanted to discover what would happen if I played it out. What did this otherworldly transition feel like, bringing a human into existence? How would I, as Megan, move through it? I wrote about her first ultrasound, how her face was illuminated by the glow of the screen as she watched the spermy shape of her child wiggle and pulse. I wrote about her morning sickness and her aching back, things I thought I knew how to describe but didn't really. I wrote about pregnancy as if it were a series of scenes, when actually—as I would find out later—it was one long blur of body violence and hormonal euphoria: indescribable if you haven't known it. I made it all go too fast. Before my lunch break I'd already almost finished the pregnancy montage and gotten to the scene where I took her shopping for maternity clothes.

Megan needed leggings. Tunics. Bigger and more comfortable shoes. So I took her to the department store we worked for. We rarely actually went to the store, which was funny since we talked about it, wrote about it, and sold the image of it every day. We entered through the revolving doors and were immediately accosted by our own slogans, designs, color choices, and displays. I spotted a tagline I'd written over near the sweaters section: *Cashmere is for always.* We were selling ourselves to ourselves; we had set the trap, and now we were taking our own bait. Megan and I touched many sparkly and soft items. We didn't even like the stuff in this store, it wasn't our taste, but we began to feel the desire to possess all the variations of beauty that were on offer to us: signature scents and dark sunglasses, bronzing powder, pearls. We were not pearl people, Megan and I, and yet even the gaudiest jewels seemed appealing in that moment. We could be any kind of women, we imagined, if we invested properly, and if we listened to our own lies. When you repeated something enough times—that cashmere was a necessity, that one should always try to look younger than one was—did it begin to take hold inside you? Did you believe it? I knew what Megan and I were doing was just a newer version of what women had done for decades, internalizing the stories they read in magazines and saw in television ads, then repeating them to each other until they solidified into something real, but it suddenly seemed like a kind of violence, and I was shocked to see so plainly that I was a part of enacting it. My enticing words were like clubs, hitting women over the head just when they thought they could see straight.

We took many escalators up to the maternity section, which was very small and very sad. There were a few muumuus and some soft jumpsuits, all of which were hideous. There were jeans whose front pockets were tiny and fake, to allow for a large piece of stretchy elastic to bloom up from the fly. I felt angry on Megan's behalf, that her options were so limited and bad.

"I'm surprised the brand isn't called Patriarchy," Megan said, holding up a pair of faux-snakeskin leggings. "The options are pregnant nun or pregnant whore."

"Let's get you some bras," I said, leading her away from the elastics.

"I'd like to see you *try* to find a bra that will fit these," Megan said, cupping her breasts.

"They're great," I said.

"They're *bowling balls*," she said.

I laughed with her.

Megan paused for a moment and looked at me with uncharacteristic sentimentality. "Will you be there?" she said.

"Be where?"

"At my birth," she said.

"Me? Are you serious?"

"You're the only person I'd feel super comfortable yelling at," she said. "Like if I need to really scream."

I laughed. "Of course," I said. "I'd absolutely love to be yelled at while watching a head come out of your vagina."

"Good," she said, removing a very large bra from a rack of very large bras and holding it up to her chest. "Do you think my balls will fit in here?"

I had made myself laugh, but I knew the scene wasn't very good. I simply wasn't a strong enough writer yet to portray a feeling exactly how I imagined it. I didn't yet know how to make sure the reader knew what I knew, which was that Megan was hard and soft at the same time, as if she were wearing a crab shell. Inside there was a bunch of sensitive mush, all her complicated feelings and desires, her messy parts, her girl memories, her private lust, her shame. This scene only showed her from the outside: fondling garments, washed with unflattering light. I wanted to go in. I wanted to go somewhere crazy and deep. I wanted to write a birth scene, though I had never given birth or seen a birth in real life. It seemed like the precipice of existence, the core, the central moment. I felt attracted to the blood, the question of whether the woman would make it through. I liked to imagine what it might feel like, to push a being out of you, shitting out a life. Mostly, though, I liked the idea of being asked to be at Megan's birth, even if it was a fictitious one. I liked the idea that someone could trust me this much. Trust me with their whole life.

DOWNSIZING

As part of what the new CEO called a "downsizing," which happened in March, the receptionist, Essie, was the first to go. I watched as she hung up her telephone for the final time, then gathered her down coat and her very small purse and shuffled out the door. She did not look back at her desk, or at me. She was the kind of woman who only moved forward, who diligently trained her eyes on the nearest part of the future. I imagined her leaving the office and walking the whole way from Herald Square back to her apartment on Sixty-Fourth Street. Sometimes she took the bus, but today she had all the time in the world, and so she strolled as slowly as she wanted to. She stopped to treat herself to a cappuccino, which she couldn't finish. The acids hurt her stomach, which made a few embarrassing sounds, forcing her to get up and leave the café. It was still late morning. How cruel, I thought on Essie's behalf, to fire someone in the morning. A glass of sherry was still hours away. What would she do until then?

I had to stop thinking about it; I knew that compassion's close cousin was pity, and I did not think Essie would want me to pity her. Plus, the thought of her not being at the front desk every day actually hurt my heart. My heart hurt easily in those days. It was part of my codependency, which was part of why I stayed in that job so long. I liked to feel the hearts of many other people beating inside my own. I liked the comfort of being moved around like a pawn, decisionless and safe. Which is probably why I survived the downsizing, because I was so easily moved.

Many other people got fired. Some salespeople whom I'd never noticed, and a couple of junior-level something-somethings. There were two people besides Essie who mattered, at least to me. There was Gus, whose job was to circulate materials from one person's desk to another's in large, heavy plastic sleeves. Gus was huge and old and kind and often irritated—I adored him. He sometimes stopped at my desk to drop off old issues of *Poets & Writers*, which he confessed he stole from the lobby in his apartment building; whoever had subscribed had long since moved out. Gus's circulation job had become obsolete long ago, replaced by less cumbersome computer programs, and yet they had not fired Gus because, like Essie, he had worked here for more than half his life; he had spent more time with the company than anyone else there; it simply wouldn't be fair to dispose of him. And yet the new CEO had. When Gus was asked to clear out his desk, he sat in his chair for a long time, unable to comprehend what had just happened. When one's life was one's job, what did one do when one was let go? I imagined him releasing his large hands, letting the plastic sleeve full of materials fall to the carpeted floor.

The other person who got fired was the least expected, and for me, mattered the most. I didn't fully understand what was happening at first, even when I got an invitation to a last-minute creative team meeting that seemed ominous in its lack of description. I still didn't understand it when I got into the conference room, that terribly lit den of whiteboards, and saw that Megan was not in attendance.

Where u at, I texted her.

They fired me, she responded.

My entire body sparked with rage, as if it had happened to me. The three dots of her typing blinked at the bottom of my phone.

Or should I say he fired me, she typed. I knew, of course, that she meant Todd.

IMPULSE DECISION

I left work early and met Megan at Bemelmans. We couldn't afford to go there, but fuck it; Megan had just gotten laid off, and I knew she loved the paintings on the walls—whimsical hand-painted scenes by the children's book illustrator the bar was named after—and so I told her I'd buy her a thirty-dollar drink. *Or six?* she'd typed back. *If it comes to that,* I'd written. I found her with her chin on the bar, already thirty dollars in the hole.

"What the *fuck*," I said, trying to find the coat hook under the bar, for my purse.

"I should have fucking *known*," she said, shaking her head. "Of *course* I should have known."

"He's a snake doggy," I said. There was no hook; I let my purse drop to the floor.

"A full-blown snake doggy," she said. "Do you know what he said to me?"

I waved to the bartender. "What?"

"He said that he was sorry he was the one to have to let me know. I was like, Oh, really? Because I'm sorry I let you stick your dick inside me."

I couldn't help but laugh.

"I feel like it's some kind of retaliation," she said. "For being distant with him lately, for not letting things continue. I knew it was going to backfire, of course it would. But I just couldn't do it anymore. It was eating me alive, Em. The guilt, and his smell, the way he talked to me at the office. When he asked me to turn in those catalog images last week? I wanted to be like, '*Fuck you*, you don't get to tell me what to do.' But of course he does. That's the whole thing of this, isn't it? He never stopped telling me what to do. He told me to be in love with him and then I just was."

"You were in love with him?" I said. "Like actually?"

"Of course," she said. "Why the fuck else would I have let this happen?"

"I'm so sorry," I said. I touched her arm in a gentle way that reminded me of the way I had touched Todd's arm on the ferry; I had a brief moment of panic that I had somehow betrayed her by being so friendly, even intimate, with him that day. Megan's arm had light downy hair on it that seemed childlike and tender, utterly innocent. Her plight was pathetic and poetic all at once; I felt deeply for her.

"What do you love about him?" I said, surprising myself with the question.

Megan thought for a minute. "I love that he looks me right in the eye," she said. "He doesn't look away from me. It's like he doesn't care about the bad parts of me, or the ugly parts. It almost feels as if he likes those parts the best. He like kisses my cellulite, you know? I don't know how to explain it, but it just felt . . . it felt like he wanted *me*, you know? The real me. And I was myself in this way that I wasn't with anyone else."

I didn't say what I was thinking, which was that Megan had been acting like the exact opposite of herself lately—wearing too much perfume, clamming up in meetings, shedding weight and claiming she just wasn't hungry—because I knew the exact feeling she was describing, and I knew how good it felt.

"But those aren't things about *him*," I said instead. "That's just how he made you see yourself."

"Isn't that what love is?" she said, with a new earnestness. "Two people making each other feel better about themselves?"

"Maybe," I said. I was starting to feel sad. Megan was twirling her olive stick around in her drink, her mind far away from where we were sitting. I noticed that she was wearing a silky white blouse that I'd never seen before.

"Is this new?" I asked, pinching some of the silk between my fingers.

"Wanted to use my discount one last time," she said. "It's Chanel."

"Damn," I said. I thought about how Megan and I, according to the lifestyle marketing biographies the sales team had invented, were "Style Eccentrics," meaning that they could not predict our shopping habits. One day we would buy a coat at the Goodwill and the next day a Chanel blouse. We were unfavorable as consumers, impossible to pin down, and I liked that about us.

"Maybe I should sue him," she said suddenly, shocking me. I laughed uncomfortably.

"You just said you loved him," I said.

Megan's face became hard, which made it more beautiful than it was when it was soft.

"Maybe I'm serious, though," she said, her eyes narrowing. "I mean, don't you think I have a case? He's married. He came on to me on a work field trip. He gets pissed that I want to break things off, but also refuses to leave his wife. Then he *fires* me."

"I don't know, Meg," I said. "I feel like that could get so messy."

"It already *is* messy," she said.

"But then you'd be known as the girl who slept with her boss," I said. "And it might mess up your chances of being hired again."

"You're right, I know."

"Not that he doesn't deserve it."

"No, you're right."

The jazz music playing in the background calmed down a little bit; it had been getting steadily more erratic since we'd arrived. I looked at my sad friend with her hazel hair and her expensive shirt, her pretty skin. I imagined us being old together at this same bar, when we could actually afford it, meeting here on Friday nights. It was a nice, simple thought that made me feel very hopeful.

"Do you want to come to Italy with me?" I asked. It was impulsive, but I trusted impulse—probably more than I should have. Impulse, to me, felt honest: the thing you would do if you didn't think through all the reasons you shouldn't.

"Italy?" Megan said. "You mean to the Dante's villa wedding?"

I was drunk off half the martini; I felt electric with this new idea.

"Yes," I said. "Come on. Italian wine. Italian men. It'll be perfect. You can get out of here for a while."

"I don't know," Megan said—the thing anyone always said when they were asked to do something outside of their own box.

"Well, I don't know, either!" I said. For some reason this made her laugh, which made me laugh. We laughed just long enough to have broken something between us, one of the many barriers that humans erect to defend their organs or feelings. It occurred to me that I loved Megan. I'd felt this way about only a few people in my life—my childhood best friend, Casey, whose sister was born with a severe disability that required their mother to devote nearly all of her time and energy to caring for her, and who was both fearlessly independent and fiercely kind as a result; a high school friend named Ricardo, whose wicked sense of humor made me feel understood; and my college roommate Lila, who insisted I read all the same books she did so she'd have someone to talk about them with—I read more in those years than in the rest of my life combined. I now knew that I could confidently add Megan to my tiny list of beloved humans, those who would leap to my defense if I was in trouble, and whom I, in turn, wanted to protect. Yes, I thought. I wanted to protect Megan, and to go through life with her in it.

"To Italy," Megan said suddenly, lifting her glass for a toast.

"To you," I said. "They don't know what they're losing."

Megan smiled sadly, took a sip.

"Oh, sure he does," she said.

CONCEPTION

When I told Wes about the layoffs that night at the loft, he was livid.

"You've gotta get out of there, Em," he said. "You can never trust a corporation. That shit should be illegal, firing people who have been there for thirty years."

"I can't just leave," I said. "I have my loans. And my rent. Unless you want me to move in with you, of course."

I nudged Wes playfully to make clear this was a joke, not me actually asking to move in with him. But he did not respond in kind.

"The loft is my studio, Em," he said. "You know I can't lose that. And then there's Kasper."

"Whoa, chill," I said. "I was kidding. But god forbid I would joke about sharing something as precious as your *loft*."

In my sarcasm there was anger, and he could feel it; we both could. I hadn't even realized I was angry until now, but it seemed I had been for some time; reserves of resentment came bubbling up. I began to make a list in my head of all the times I'd felt dismissed or rejected lately—that morning at the marathon; the previous Friday night, when I'd wanted to go on a walk together but Wes had, once again, had too much work to do.

"This is what you get with me," Wes said. "I've been clear about it from the beginning."

"Yes, you've been explicit," I said. Suddenly my hands felt hot. "And it's been fine, it's been great, sure. You work, I work, we work all the time. We work *all weekend, every weekend.* We've stopped doing anything else to-

gether, anything that might be inspiring, or god forbid *fun*. But what are
we working *toward*?"

"We're working toward this," Wes said, gesturing around the big
room. "Toward making the things we want to make. Living the life we
want to live."

"But *this* has nothing to do with me," I said. "This is all yours."

"You stay here all the time, Em. You have your writing space. What
more do you want?"

"I want to feel like we're not just making our own things, but that
we're making something together. That I am a bigger part of your life
than just a desk in the corner."

"Here we go," Wes said. "I told you this would happen. From the very
beginning I told you. Out of nowhere comes this whole backlog of resentment I didn't even know was there in the first place. I genuinely thought
we were on the same page, Em."

He had a point, I knew. Where *was* this coming from? Did I actually
want to move in with Wes? If so, I hadn't articulated the desire to him
before, or even to myself in a real way. But it felt clear to me now, as if a
curtain had been pulled back: the way things were was not how I wanted
them. I wanted more. Simultaneously, I felt ashamed of this wanting, like
it was bad, or preposterous, or unbecoming, or all those things. Why did
it feel so embarrassing to want?

"I'm just . . . I'm starting to feel like the way we've set things up . . .
isn't working for me anymore. Like all this work is just a wall around you,
keeping me from getting any closer."

"That's not what it is at all," Wes said. "It's literally about logistics. I
need space to work. I need time. My work takes time."

"Well, maybe it's good I'm leaving for a while," I said, feeling the pang
of anger again. "Lots of time without me getting in the way."

"Maybe it is good," he said, not unkindly. He batted his eyelashes
over his green eyes. "And for you, too. Maybe Italy will inspire you."

I shook my head at him, bewildered and insulted. Why did he assume that I was uninspired? I felt like he should know that I was in a productive phase, that I had been churning out pages in my notebook, but he was writing my efforts off, as if what I'd been doing was unimportant, even silly.

"I know you think I'm just some corporate drone," I said. "That I'm a fraud, that I'm not even really a writer."

"No," Wes said calmly. "That's you. *You* don't think of yourself as a writer. I'm the one standing here encouraging you; I have been since day one. But you've gotta do something with your writing if you really want to be a writer, Emily. Get it out of your notebook. Put something in the world."

I frowned at him. "Not everyone's as lucky as you," I said. "Some people have to work real jobs. Do dumb, shitty stuff that has nothing to do with their dream. But somehow you just get to be exempt from that."

"I've *chosen* to be exempt from that," Wes said. "I make sacrifices in order to be exempt from that. That's why I have to have my studio at my apartment. That's why I have a roommate."

"But why wouldn't I be your roommate?" I said, realizing as soon as I said it that it sounded whiny, pathetic.

Wes seemed flustered. "If you want to talk about that in a real way, fine, we can talk about that. I just thought things were good how they were. It seemed like a good balance."

"I want to sacrifice things like you do," I said. "I do. I want to not want more than I have, to not need anyone. It's why you're so good at what you do. You give everything to your work. But I can't, and I realize that I don't think I'll ever be able to, and maybe that means I don't have what it takes to be a real writer. Maybe I should just stop trying. Maybe it won't ever work."

I felt the chaos of tears behind my eyes. Wes pulled me close, seeing that I was about to break.

"You have an incredible mind," he said. "All I want to do is read the book you write someday."

I allowed myself to press my face into Wes's bare chest and cry. It felt good to cry, cathartic, though I knew it wasn't really warranted. How had we even gotten here? Why had that anger bubbled up, out of nowhere? I didn't need to move in with Wes to be happy. The way things were now—it was enough. His arms around me were enough. His smell enveloping me. His collarbone jutting from the frayed edge of his T-shirt; I kissed it, then kissed his neck, then let him kiss my mouth. I felt exhausted from crying, wrung out, the way I remembered getting as a child when I could not be consoled. Ann had never been good at consoling, but here was someone who was. I let Wes's body console me. A body taking mine over, consuming it. Pleasure as eraser. The loft's wood floor on my back; the worry of splinters creeping in to remind me that I was in the body that was feeling these things, flexing in these ways. I felt a familiar desperation coming over me: the need and desire to merge completely with another human, to have them inside me and me inside them, to complete each other in some essential way that could only be achieved by real, physical osmosis. Sex was as close as I'd ever gotten to this, and I knew it didn't achieve the total results I was after; I wanted more than was possible, I wanted to escape myself as I entered the realm of another, giving myself away entirely. I love you, I thought but did not say, as I pulled Wes close just when he was about to pull away. Instead, as I let him come inside me, I whispered that it was okay, it was okay, there was nothing to worry about, it was all going to be okay.

PURE BARRE

The weekend before we left for Italy, I met Megan at an exercise class she'd gotten a free pass for. I was annoyed that we were substituting burning calories for consuming them; we'd made a habit of going on boozy brunch dates at Roebling Tea Room on Sundays, and now I was supposed to spend my weekend morning sweating and in pain. I rolled my eyes when I arrived; Megan told me that my ass would thank me.

During the class, a toned twenty-three-year-old shamed us into moving various parts of our bodies very quickly in tiny motions that resembled a baby bird trying to take flight. She told us we had to "work it harder" if we wanted to get that "Pure Barre seat." I didn't know what that was or if I wanted it, but I flexed my abs and ass and pumped, praying that these muscles I hadn't known existed could keep up with what the teacher called "pelvic micromovements" and "gluteal lifts." Despite utterly depleting my energy reserves, I did not break a sweat, which Megan told me afterward was the whole point. Getting toned without messing up your blow-dry.

"But I don't have a blow-dry," I said.

"But you could," she said. "And if you did, you'd be grateful you hadn't ruined it."

I tried not to make fun of what we'd just undergone, knowing that Megan was in a fragile state. All her job interviews had gone terribly so far—one agency she'd applied for told her that her portfolio lacked nuance; another had asked why she'd left her old job and she'd broken down crying. She'd also started going on Tinder dates, as many as she could fit into every free evening, which were going just about as well as the interviews. I told her I'd treat her to a smoothie, which she convinced me to order on Seamless so that we didn't have to wait in line. I obliged, and by the time we arrived at the juice bar down the street our massive green drinks were waiting for us like healthy prizes. Click a button for calories, and they appear for you. Pump your pelvis fast enough, and you'll transform your body into a lean, long line. Swipe right, swipe right, swipe into oblivion. Faster, faster. Smaller, smaller. Shrinking down and down and down, until you're a sliver of yourself, or maybe all the way gone.

"You're judging me," Megan said as we walked toward the river.

"Never," I said with a smirk.

"Go ahead," she said. "Call me basic. I know you want to. It's right there on the tip of your tongue."

"You're the opposite of basic," I told her. "Which is why I find it fascinating that you subscribe to this whole corporate wellness racket. I'm not judging, I'm just amused."

"Well, I'm glad I can entertain you," she said. "Honestly, it doesn't really feel like a choice. I feel like I have to do these things if I want to . . . keep up."

"Keep up with what, though?"

"With the other women! With life! I feel like if I don't keep doing these things women are supposed to do, I'm going to be left behind. I'll be like a disgrace to women everywhere. The one who stopped trying. Who let herself go. Who . . . I don't know, failed."

"You're a long way away from letting yourself go, Megs."

"It doesn't feel that way," Megan said. "I feel old. Like my youth has been stripped out of me. Just . . . ripped out."

Megan's eyes were technically watching a small dog piss on a planter box, but they were actually far away. It seemed like she was on a plane all her own in that moment, referencing something I knew nothing about. I wondered what wounds Megan hid from me, what scars of her past still lived beneath her smooth surface. I felt sad that I might never know.

Did we want to save the planet? A heroic young person asked us from behind her clipboard. We made motions with our hands that meant that we were so sorry but right now, in this very moment, we really didn't have time for saving the planet. We passed a pair of women in workout clothes, and then another woman with a stroller, also in workout clothes. Each woman was a mirror for the next, a different version of the same thing, part of an algorithm of bodies and outfits moving through the same spring day. A freshly shaven man yelled into a cell phone about needing better content. *We can't bullshit content,* he was saying. *It's got to be authentic. It's got to feel real. Can you do that for me? Can you make this shit feel real by Friday?*

Maybe this was what Megan meant, this terrifying sameness, this new world order, stripping us of the things we once treasured. I thought of Todd saying *What did you think you would be?* Did we think we would be here, drinking fourteen-dollar smoothies, watching all the humans morph into each other and into their surroundings, as if it were all just one gi- ant Photoshopped image? Everything around us felt like both a promise and a threat. Capitalism disguising itself as wellness, as intelligence, as community, as grace. The smoothie was disgusting, creamy and thick from the avocado Megan had forced us to add to it. The shop windows showed us things we should want but couldn't afford. Everything had been designed especially for us, to lure us in like some kind of trap. I felt the jaws of the neighborhood open up to swallow us.

"Italy is going to feel good," I said.

"Yeah," she said. Though the way she said it felt sad and hopeless, and I wondered if she still even wanted to go. If I had known what Italy would do to us, I would have stopped her in the street right then. Looked her in the eyes and said, "Let's not go. Let's stay right here. You and me in the sunshine on Bedford Avenue. Best friends, frozen in the chaos of our time."

PART THREE

PLEASURE

DEPARTURE

"Oh no you don't," Megan said when I tried to take the aisle seat. "I get crazy claustrophobic if I'm not on the aisle."

"I get pee-phobia," I said. "I spend the entire flight worrying about when I'll have to pee, then agonizing about asking the person in the aisle seat to move so I can get by."

"But the person in the aisle seat will be me," Megan said.

"It doesn't matter," I said. "The pee-phobia knows no difference. It mortifies me to inconvenience someone. Even if that someone is my friend."

The guy in the row across from us laughed at us and offered to trade his aisle seat for the window seat in our row. We were both massively relieved.

"You're a saint," Megan said to the guy, who winked at her in a gross way.

We settled in. Plugged our headphones into the seats. Pulled our books from our tote bags and tucked them into the seat backs in front of us. Megan's book was called *I Love Dick*.

"The title resonated with me," she said with a smirk. And then, with a sigh: "I'm so, so glad to be getting out of here."

"Me too," I said.

"It's a crazy thought," she said. "That I'm not leaving anything at all behind. Literally nothing."

The previous week, the lease on her apartment had expired and she'd decide not to renew it; she'd find a new place when she got back. I'd helped her get all her things to a storage unit in Ridgewood. The place had felt like a morgue, full of stuff people had once loved but had probably forgotten by now. Going there had made Megan very sad, I could tell, as if after putting the objects she owned out of view, she couldn't understand who she was.

"You're free," I said, unsure if I believed that was a good thing.

"Freedom is overrated," she said, reading my mind. "Responsibility to others, or to things, is what makes you matter, what grounds your life in reality."

"Maybe reality is overrated," I said. This part I believed.

"You would say that," she said.

The plane took off; we blasted into the ether; we each felt the existential hope and fear of being suspended in the air between worlds. Vacant-eyed European flight attendants handed us wine without our even ordering it. We toasted across the aisle.

"I know it's sick," Megan said after two miniature bottles of bad chardonnay. "And I know that technically it was me who called things off between us. But I miss him. Or maybe I just miss feeling special."

"I get that," I said. "It's hard to feel special anymore. Especially when everyone in New York is special."

"Exactly," she said. "It's like you're just one in a million women who went to art school and then ended up designing ads. One in a million women who listen to the same songs while they get ready to go on dates that won't pan out, where they'll leave halfway through and get in a cab and start swiping on their phone again, trying to find love on the internet. I always think about how many people have swiped no to me. Who looked at my face and thought, 'Nah, no good.'"

"Well, I can tell you for a fact that those dudes are idiots," I said. "Just like Todd is."

Megan leaned her head back against the head rest. "He once told me he couldn't live without me," she said. "Which of course is like the most cliché thing in the world. But it felt real at the time. It made me feel so powerful. Like I was this force."

"You are a force."

"But then of course it wasn't true," she said. "He could very easily live without me. He's living without me right now."

"He's miserable, I guarantee it."

"I don't want him to be miserable," she said. "That's not what I want."

"I know," I said.

I reached my hand across the aisle toward her, and she reached her hand out to meet mine. Her fingers were dry and warm.

"Maybe I'll start painting again," she said. "While we're here."

"That's so good," I said.

"They're supposed to have beautiful paper in Verona," she said. "I read about it online."

I nodded, smiled, tucked my empty wine bottle in the seat pocket next to my book.

"What are you worrying about?" Megan said.

"What do you mean?" I said.

"You're doing the thing with your eyebrows," she said, "which means you're worrying about something."

"I'm kind of nervous to see her," I said.

"Who?" Megan said. "Renata?"

"Yeah."

"What's the deal with this woman?" Megan said. "You're so specifically affected by her, but I don't really get what happened."

"It's all kind of complicated," I said. "There are so many prongs to the story."

"We still have four more hours on this flight," Megan said, lifting her hand to ask the flight attendant for more wine. "Give me all the prongs."

THE MANY-PRONGED STORY OF RENATA

"Okay, so remember how I told you Renata was a professor? She taught art history at the University of Bologna, where I was studying. I was an

English major, but when I found out she taught a feminist art history course I immediately enrolled. I'd been living with this woman for a few weeks, right, drinking wine with her on the couch every night after the kids went to bed, getting to know her and kind of falling under her spell. And so I showed up for her first lecture—it's in this giant auditorium made of dark wood, with these massive chandeliers. All of the lectures were held in places like this, rooms that looked like palaces, that seemed to be meant for high-profile court hearings or high-society balls or something. And then Renata walked in—she was wearing this great black blazer and ruffly white blouse—and even though I'd been living with her, even though I'd seen her eat breakfast in her robe and giggle with her children, she completely took my breath away when she walked on the stage. Her presence was literally electric. The students around me perked up as they watched her open her chic leather bag and take out her lecture notes. And then she flicked on her projector and the room hushed. A photograph beamed onto the wall behind her, of an older woman sitting in a chair.

"'This is my mother,' she said. Her voice was loud, crisp, authoritative. She went on to tell us that Giuseppina Bachetti, her mother, who was born in Prato in 1934, had a photographic memory. She could memorize large swaths of text; she could conjure details from years past in her mind; she could learn other languages by reading foreign dictionaries. But because the first seven years of her life were spent under Mussolini, who was of course deeply anti-intellectual, she learned from a very young age to suppress her rare gift, and she grew into a frustrated person, constantly confused and angry with the world. Renata told us that Giuseppina married her father out of a sense of duty when she was twenty-three, had a child for much the same reason two years later, and now lived in a tiny apartment above a Chinese restaurant in the town where she'd spent all her life. Then she said: 'She calls me every evening to remind me I am as worthless as she's been made to feel.'

"The class let out a hesitant laugh; Renata switched the slide. The next image was of a piece of paper with hundreds of numbers printed on it, in pristine handwriting that went all the way to the edge of the page.

"'This,' Renata explained, 'is a page from my mother's notebook that she keeps in her kitchen. It is a record of every number she has heard, seen, or come in contact with on a given day. The bills she's paid, the price of the clams at the fish market, the temperature of every region of Italy from the weather channel. Also every numerical thing about me, her daughter: my height, my weight, how many euros she spent on my shoes, how many ravioli I ate for dinner. She stores these numbers up in her mind, and then releases them onto the page in the evening. She does this every day.'

"The class breathed and shuffled. It was as if everyone was thinking the same thing: *Seems pretty crazy.*

"'Seems pretty crazy, right?' Renata said. 'Until . . .'

"She switched the slide again to reveal the same page of numbers, framed and mounted on a white wall. It did not look out of place as a work of art; in fact, it was quite beautiful.

"'At what point does compulsion become art?' Renata said. She cupped her hands and shook them in that Italian way. 'At what point does the personal become worthy of a frame? At what point does a woman's daily life—her grocery shopping, her child's shoe size— become a topic of critical discourse? And at what point does art become an agent of change? These are the questions we'll work through in this course.'

"I was totally captivated. At one point I caught Renata's eye. She did a little wink, a flick of her face that was our secret. I felt more enlightened than the other students in the class because I knew her better than they did. I lived in her house, bathed in her shower, used her towels. Tonight we'd sit on her white couch with our glasses of red wine, discuss the lecture: my own personal office hours.

"The class was epic. Every lecture changed form and blew my mind in some new way. This was masculinity under Fascism; this was first- and second-wave feminism; this was 1978, when Italy erupted with the feminist conversation; this was Carla Lonzi and the Rivolta Femminile, this was when she spit on Hegel; this was Ketty La Rocca and her words pasted over images; this was Tomaso Binga, pretending to be a man. Each class seemed more vibrant and impassioned than the next, and after each one I felt somehow closer to Renata, as if by learning from her in this formal context I was cementing my bond with her: if I could meet her intellectually, I thought, perhaps she would respect me enough to love me.

"I can't explain why, Megs, but I wanted this woman to love me. I *needed* her to. And for a while I thought she might, that we were getting close in some important way—she gave me extra reading for the class, left little xeroxed poems in the envelope with my monthly payments, kissed me on the forehead when she left for the day, got a wistful look in her eyes when she said *Cara Emily*. She even let me borrow this locket of hers—I complimented her on it one day and she took it off her neck and put it on mine. 'It was my mother's,' she said. 'I'll give it to Greta one day, when she's old enough not to lose it. You can wear it until she's ready for it.' The tiny picture inside the locket was of Renata as a child, maybe five or six, already with so much bright fire in her eyes. Wearing her around my neck made me feel brighter myself, as if some part of her were pulsing through the gold, against my clavicle. There was something special between us, and both of us knew it—you know how when you meet certain people, you just feel connected to them? It was like that."

"Like when I met you at the water cooler," Megan said, smiling. "And I knew right away, as I watched you fill up that reusable BPA-free water bottle, that we were destined to be together forever."

I grinned. "Exactly," I said.

"So when did it get complicated?" Megan asked.

"One day in November," I continued, "when we were walking home from class together, she confided in me, telling me that her ex-husband's new girlfriend, Vittoria, was pregnant. She explained to me that she'd run into her at the market; they were both reaching for the same decorative squash. She saw the stomach first, dipping into the squash bin like the woman's own personal pumpkin, and then looked up to the face. Renata's blood had turned into flames, ripping through her veins.

"'When are you due?' she found herself asking, surprised at how calm her own voice was.

"'End of January,' Vittoria said serenely, rubbing her stomach. 'But I have a feeling she'll want to stay in there as long as she can.' *A girl.*

"We arrived at the apartment and Renata let us in with her big key. Her hands were shaky. As soon as we got inside she opened a bottle of wine, poured us each a glass. Massimo was picking the girls up after ballet to take them for gelato, so we were alone. Part of me felt satisfied by our closeness in that moment, proud that she'd chosen me to confide in. Another part of me felt unmoored, the way a child might feel when they first see their mother afraid, suddenly realizing she isn't the unflappable woman they'd always believed she was: without warning, in her tenderness and fear, the mother becomes mortal.

"'It's the timeline,' Renata said, tossing back a bit of wine. 'The baby is due in January. Massimo left us in the spring, in May. He got her pregnant before he left. How was I so *stupid*?'

"'You're not stupid,' I tried. 'He's just a giant asshole.'

"'But I should have *known*,' she said, leaning forward and shaking her head. 'I think I did, deep down. That he had been embarrassed, or maybe ashamed, by his inability to get me pregnant. Indignant, almost. That he wanted to prove to the world, or maybe just to himself, that it hadn't been his fault. That he was, indeed, as virile as he'd always believed he was.'

"She poured more wine, began to pace. I had never seen her like that: her hair wild, her eyes glowing with fury. It was if a switch had flipped inside her, morphing her into a different woman entirely. No longer the calm art professor, but now the unhinged ex-wife. I felt almost blindsided by the change in my perception of her: how quickly my feelings for her moved away from awe, then into fear, and then, in an imperceptible shift, toward pity. But I knew from being a woman myself that there was always a risk of this: you could be stripped of your power in an instant, simply by getting hurt.

"'You know what hurts the most?' she said. 'More than Massimo keeping this all a secret? Is that the girls didn't tell me. That they chose to protect him over me. After everything I've given up for them. My whole life, really. My career? Gone. My whole sense of self? Gone. And what did Massimo give up? Exactly nothing. And to think he was the one who wanted to adopt in the first place. It hadn't even occurred to me. I didn't want to.'

"A deep sadness rose within me then, Megs. Sadness mixed with shame. Though part of me knew it wasn't what she meant, the easy way she said it—that she hadn't wanted to adopt them—felt like a confirmation of this thing I had suspected for so long, that adoptive mothers could not possibly love their children like biological mothers could. And to expect that child to carry the burden of hurting her own mother, when I knew for a fact that all those girls were doing was trying with all their might to be loved entirely by her? I felt like crying suddenly, but I contained myself, not wanting to turn the story toward myself.

"Then, something truly crazy happened. Out of the corner of my eye, I saw a blur of white. When I looked up from my glass of wine, I realized it was Greta, Renata's older daughter, standing in the doorway in her ballet leotard, like a child ghost. I looked over at Renata, but her back was turned; she was getting more wine. And when I looked back to the door, Greta was gone. But I knew—I *knew*—she had overheard her mother speaking about how disappointed she was, how much she'd been forced to give up, how she hadn't even thought to want them in the first place.

"And when I looked over at that empty doorway where she'd been standing, Megs, I felt the world shift beneath me, and I felt myself inhabit Greta's body, which was actually my own body at her age. I was at church, waiting for Ann while she went to confession. I'd brought a book with me—I never went anywhere without a book as a kid—I was reading the Laura Ingalls Wilder series. The family in the book was packing up their wagon and the mother was sweetly waking up the children when I heard a little cry from the confession booth. I moved closer to it, quietly and slowly. It had been Ann's cry, I could tell, because her voice was shaky, as if she was still crying a little bit.

"'I try so hard every day,' Ann was telling the priest. 'I wear myself to the bone. But she only acts out. She yells at me, Father. She seems to hate me. Honestly, I don't know if I have the strength anymore.'

"'The strength for what, dear?' the priest said kindly.

"'To be her mother,' Ann said. 'God forgive me—I just don't want to be her mother right now.'

"I pretended I didn't hear her, and I opened my Laura Ingalls Wilder book. In the firelight and candlelight, Ma was washing her daughters, then combing their hair and dressing them. Over their red flannel underwear she put wool petticoats and wool dresses and long wool stockings. She put their coats on them, and their rabbit-skin hoods, and their red yarn mittens."

"Oh my gosh," Megan said, her eyes reddening at the corners, her Edwardian hand pressed against her heart. "I'm so sorry, Em. That's heartbreaking."

"I had this weird feeling around Renata after that," I said. "I'd had this vision of her—this picture of a woman who had figured out how to be both: a mother and a mind, the ideal woman. But then it kind of broke down; I kept thinking about Greta in the doorway, remembering myself outside the confession booth, feeling the pain of being that young girl. I pulled away; I missed some of Renata's classes, I began eating dinner out with the other American students, rather than at home with her. I left the locket on so as not to hurt Renata's feelings, but I felt distinctly that it had lost its power. I did my job with the girls, picking them up from ballet and doing their English homework with them. I became especially close with Greta. She started coming to me instead of her mother—when she was bullied at school, or when she got her period. I could sense that things with her mother had shifted for her as they once had for me, and it broke my fucking heart. I wanted to be there for her, but I could only do so much.

"Weeks passed in this weird limbo, and then it was time for our final exams for Renata's class. I'd missed so much by now, and I knew I wasn't going to do well. And the way they do their exams there—they're *oral* exams. You're meant to give kind of essayistic responses, but out loud. In front of everyone in the class, in this giant cathedral-style classroom. I've never been so terrified in my life."

"That's my actual nightmare," Megan said.

"Same," I said. "Especially when the professor is the woman I live with, who I've got this complicated vibe with now. So there's Renata, sitting above her sea of scholars on a gilded throne. One by one, her students approach her, like lawyers approaching a judge to deliver a closing statement or receive a final verdict. No notes, no paper, no way to sidestep or avoid the questions asked of you. I parked myself at the very back of the room, hoping I might never get called on. But of course I got called up almost immediately. Sweat formed like little spikes in my armpits. I moved through the room toward Renata's throne, sat down in front of her in a seat that was lower than hers. She blinked but didn't smile. She had inhabited her role as *la professoressa*, and she didn't break it for me.

"'Tell me about the 1970s,' she said. 'What was so powerful about that decade for Italian feminism?'

"I regurgitated what I'd written in my notebook, which I'd memorized. I talked about the feminist groups that began coalescing in Turin, the Wages for Housework campaign, about Mirella Bentovoglio curating all-women shows. These were all things I'd learned in her early lectures, the ones I'd actually attended.

"'Provide a concrete example of female marginalization,' Renata said, saving me from the bumble of my previous answer, 'that you've witnessed in your own life.'

"Here, I was totally caught off guard. I had not expected my own life to be of service here, but then I thought about all the ways Renata had brought her own life into the classroom and I realized I should have prepared for this. Renata nodded once in a way that meant: *This is a test*, and so I started to talk. I heard myself beginning to talk about my birth mother.

"'My mother wanted to be a writer,' I said. 'Or at least I think she did. I read a story she wrote in a literary magazine. But when I searched for more stories, there weren't any. I have a feeling that if she were a man she would have published more. She would have had the world at her back. She would have had the confidence, or maybe just the time.'

"'And did you ask her about this?' Renata said.

I realized that Renata thought I was talking about Ann, who she knew as my mother.

"'I couldn't ask her,' I said. 'She died when I was born. Ann adopted me two weeks later.'

"Renata tilted her head, clearly confused. I felt confused, too. Why hadn't I told Renata sooner that I was adopted? It didn't make any sense.

"'She died because I was born,' I said, as if to clarify something, though I don't know what.

"Renata put her hand on mine, squinting. Once again our boundaries blurred: Were we student and teacher? Friends? Did I matter to her? Did she matter to me?

"'You didn't tell me,' Renata said, her face turned slightly to appear perplexed.

"I shrugged, unsure of what to say. Renata squinted at me again, as if she was trying to figure me out.

"'You seem to want closeness,' Renata said. 'And yet you don't have a lot of trust in people.'

"I looked up at her. She was dead on, and it terrified me. I had never once had someone articulate my way of being so acutely; it stung like getting a shot, brief and hot, and then over."

"That's not how I think of you," Megan interjected, which made my whole body warm. "If that means anything."

"It does," I said, smiling. "I think with Renata I was that way, though, because I wanted something specific from her; I wanted her to be a mother to me, and I knew she couldn't be that, but I wanted it anyway, and, well, it made for a kind of impossible dynamic."

"But what about Ann? Why didn't you want that from Ann?"

I thought about this for a moment. "When I was little I did. So badly. I tried so hard to please her. No whining, straight A's, perfectly clean room, because it seemed like that's what it would require to be loved by her, for her to accept me, or love me. But at some point I realized that Ann responded better to me from a distance. When I was eight, I did a little experiment, where I called her by her first name instead of calling her 'mom.' It was so weird, Megs—she instantly seemed to relax when I said it. It was like it took the pressure off the relationship or something, and it instantly warmed her to me. So I never called her 'mom' again. I just had to come to terms with it, that this was how it would be. Always a little bit removed, you know?"

Megan nodded sympathetically; I could tell she didn't know what to say.

"But back to the exam," I said. "We got back on track; she asked me a question about a specific artist, whose name I had forgotten and whose work completely eluded me. I got that pit of nervousness in my stomach, and I knew I wouldn't be able to pull off an answer. I started talking, but I knew I was totally blowing it, just bullshitting, trying to find my way out of various holes I dug myself into. I was aware that I was doing terribly, and yet I could make myself do better. I felt lost, stupid, out of control.

"'Listen,' Renata said when I stopped talking. 'Do you want to come to Christmas with us? At my mother's?' I wondered if any of the students in the lecture hall were hearing this, though no one seemed to be paying any attention.

"I wanted more than anything to say yes, Megs. I wanted so badly to be a part of Renata's family, a real part of her life, to have her cut roasted chicken off the bone for me, serve me a taste with her fingers, pour me more wine. I wanted her to give me stupid Italian advice about the importance of blow-drying one's hair. I wanted to be in her class forever, learn about every artist she'd ever discovered, listen to her lectures on repeat. I wanted to be hers; I wanted her to be mine; I wanted us to be an us. And yet I knew that I couldn't want these things, that I shouldn't, that they weren't possible. We were practically strangers, two women whose ties were as flimsy as the scrap of paper I found her phone number on. So I told her I wished I could come to Christmas, but I had plans to go to Naples with a friend."

"But you didn't," Megan said. "Have plans."

"Nope," I said. "I ended up going alone. I slept with some cheesy Australian in a gross hostel by the harbor. He kept telling me this was supposed to be fun, that I should be laughing."

"While you were having sex?"

"Yeah," I said. "Which of course just made me cry."

"Naturally."

"And then . . . things got weirder after that."

"With the Australian?"

"With Renata."

"Wow, this *is* a lot of prongs."

"I warned you!"

"Go on."

"So I got back to Bologna after Christmas and everything felt totally different. Renata was acting super weird. She seemed almost nervous or something; I'd never seen her that way. At first I thought it was because of me—that I had wounded her in some way by not coming to Prato with them. But then the girls crawled into bed with me one night and told me some shit that made me think something had happened in Prato, though I couldn't understand what."

"What'd they tell you?"

"Something about a police station," I said. "And Renata having to see a specialist. Which made me feel really scared; I started thinking she'd tried to commit suicide or something, or been assaulted, maybe—I came up with a hundred stories about what had happened in my mind. I knew I couldn't get the real story from an eleven- and a nine-year-old, and I knew I wasn't brave enough to ask Renata about it outright—to this day I have no idea what happened that Christmas. I've always wondered. Sometimes I still have dreams about it."

"Whoa," Megan said. "That's so intense."

"Totally intense," I said. "I felt like I was caught in this story I didn't even understand, but that I was picking up all the feeling from it—like I was living in a movie. And *then*, she asked me if I'd meet her for coffee one morning, and I knew something was off because we'd never had coffee out before, we'd always just made it at home. I thought she was going to tell me she didn't need me to watch the girls anymore, that she wanted me to move out."

"And did she?"

"She told me I failed the exam," I said.

"Oh, fuck," Megan said.

"Yeah," I said. "She said she was sorry, and that if I wanted her to she would give me a passing grade, but that the truth was that I had not answered the questions sufficiently, that technically I had failed, and she wanted me to know so I could decide for myself what to do. And it felt like . . . I know this sounds dumb, but it felt like she was just saying I failed, in general. At living with her, at being in her family, at existing. I took it really hard."

"Of course you did!" Megan said.

"Being the Goody Two-shoes that I am, I said that I'd take the test again in the spring. She said that was the right thing to do and that she was proud of me; she knew I was interested in the material and that I would do well if I applied myself. She also said that the test would be with another professor, that she wouldn't be available."

"And you hear: I won't be available for *you*."

"Exactly. I remember leaving the café and walking away from her and thinking: I've got to get out of here. I have to leave. It was way too much, just too much. I literally walked straight to via Zamboni, which is where everyone advertises rooms and apartments, and found a flyer for a house full of American exchange students. I told Renata I was moving out the next week."

"And you never saw her after that?" Megan said again.

"I saw her once," I said. "At IKEA. When I was buying furniture with my new roommates. She and the girls were in the home office section. I imagined that she was setting up an office for herself in the room I'd been living in, which made me happy for her and also terribly sad. I wanted to run over to her, to hug her and the girls, but I didn't. I just let them walk away. Sometimes I feel like my whole life has been a series of things I could have done but didn't."

"And the necklace? Did you give it back?"

"She told me to keep it," I said. "To give it to Greta when I thought she was ready for it."

"So she thought she'd see you again," Megan said.

"I guess so," I said.

"And now you're going to," Megan said.

"I guess so," I said.

"What do you think it's going to be like?" Megan asked.

"I have no idea," I said. "Which is why I'm so fucking happy you're here with me."

ROME

Megan and I had purposely arranged for a two-day layover in Rome because why not. Rome was Rome. You couldn't not go to Rome. For two days we trip-trapped down long sets of stone stairs. We ate mountains of gelato. We indulged our tourist side. We were not sad. The sky over Rome was always gray. The buildings in Rome were always yellow-gray-stone-gold. Productivity had never mattered here, and still didn't. It was about enjoyment and so we enjoyed. It was about food and so we ate. It was about life being life and so we lived. Slipping around Rome felt like tap-dancing through history. Nobody gave a shit what we did.

We were too old for hostels, so we splurged on a room at a place near the Trevi Fountain. The room was heavy-draped and dim, with one queen bed. I hadn't imagined sharing a bed with Megan; I could have sworn I had booked a double room. She didn't seem fazed, plopped down, sighed. I liked the way she looked on the bed, and wanted to write about it. I wanted to describe how her plopping and her sighing had felt like acting, like the thing that the character of her would have done in a movie, and how she had done it so easily, as if it was second nature to enact the gestures and motions that the audience of the world expected of her. She was drunk off the negronis we'd had at dinner, which didn't stop me from opening a bottle of prosecco we'd picked up on the way home.

"I'm going to get some of that good paper when we get to Verona," she said, putting her hands behind her neck and staring up at the ceiling, which had a chandelier blurting out of it. I didn't remind her that she'd told me this already, on the plane. Instead I let her linger in the creative fantasy that I indulged in all the time: the feeling that someday you would make something, when there was time and you were in the mood and everything was in its place. Someday you would create something really beautiful, so beautiful that it filled all the holes in your heart and mended or at least depicted all the cracks in your psyche and transcended your smallness and smoothed out all the bumpy surfaces of your existence.

"That sounds good," I said, handing her a water glass full of prosecco.

Megan propped herself on her elbow, took a sip.

"What should I do with myself, Em?"

"What do you mean?"

"I mean with my life. I can't figure out what I even want anymore. It was like Todd was the first thing in so long that I actually *wanted*, you know, like actually *felt* something about. It's like everything else in my life was so easy and shiny, and then this thing, even though I knew it was wrong and bad, was something I actually *wanted*. And then when that ended, when that wanting stopped . . . there was nothing left to fill it. Now I just feel . . . empty. Nothing I do *means* anything, nothing feels like it matters. I just fly to Italy and get drunk, and no one cares."

"I care," I said. This, I knew, was a nice thing to say, but it didn't do anything to help Megan. No matter what I told her, she wouldn't believe me. I understood this. We had been conditioned to believe men, not other women. It was men who could make us feel beautiful, smart, sexy, or worthy by telling us we were. Even if we didn't like them, even if we *hated* them, even if we didn't trust them: we still believed them.

"Did I ever tell you about his dick?" she said.

I shook my head. Megan created a small space between her thumb and pointer finger, held up her hand.

"No way," I said. And then we both started laughing so hard that prosecco came out of our noses. Megan fell asleep with her clothes on, and I stayed up reading the book she'd brought, which, like so many orders of past dinner companions, looked more interesting than my own.

READING *I LOVE DICK* IN ROME

Though I had spent most nights of my life staying up late to read, as I am a notoriously bad sleeper and because succumbing to the dream of other people's stories makes me feel calmer than succumbing to my own unpredictable thoughts or dreams, that night was different in that I didn't go to sleep at all. The book was too good, too weird, too full of buzz and eros, and so I just kept going, rubbing my eyes when they got blurry, urging myself to go on even as I knew I would pay for it with exhaustion the next day. The book was made up of letters, cataloging a husband and wife's mutual obsession with a man named Dick. By midnight I had become as invested in the triangulated desire as if I were a part of the triangle myself.

Toward the end of the book, I came across a sentence that stopped me in my tracks. "Why does everybody think that women are debasing themselves when we expose the conditions of our own debasement?" Chris Kraus, the author, wrote. "Why do women always have to come off clean?" She goes on to describe a concept she'd dubbed the "female monster": a woman who overtly prized and revealed her own experience, used it as her singular mode of expression, blasting open the personal in a way that ended up coming off as grotesque. Kraus as narrator, incredibly, declares that she *wants* to be this way, that she *aims* to be a female monster, that it will be her goal in both the project of the book and in her life to embody this woman the world finds so disturbing.

I immediately thought of a drawing I'd seen in Megan's sketchbook, which she'd left open on the plane when she nodded off for a nap. It was unlike most of her drawings in that it was a self-portrait; I had only ever seen her draw objects or settings, maybe a few faces in the distance, never her own. But in this drawing Megan's face was front and center, caught within the rectangular frame of an iPhone screen, along with part of her naked body; Megan's boob was visible in the lower corner of the screen. She wore an expression that was somehow both innocent and erotic, as if it was up to the viewer to decide whether or not she knew exactly what she was doing. At the top of the screen it said *FaceTime* . . . as if the phone were in the process of initiating a video call. I knew, of course, that it was a portrait of her calling Todd. The drawing had made me catch my breath; I felt scared, somehow, upon seeing it, though at the time I could not pinpoint why.

Currently, Megan was asleep next to me on the bed, with her mouth slightly open. The space between her lips was so innocent, it reminded me of a child. I began to wonder if Megan, in that drawing, hadn't been doing something akin to Kraus—displaying her own dubious desires, her infatuation with her own story of infatuation, her personal monsters, revealing these things not to debase herself but to reveal the conditions in which she existed, the trap of her own femaleness. Could Megan's affair with Todd, her active part in pursuing her own desires, have been considered a feminist act? Or did it only become such when she turned it into art? Did looking at her through this lens make it all more valid, or more twisted?

I grabbed my notebook from the nightstand. *IS MEGAN A FEMALE MONSTER?* I wrote in my notebook in big, blocky letters. *WAS HER WRONGDOING POLITICAL? DO WE SYMPATHIZE WITH HER BECAUSE OF THIS, EVEN AS WE DISAPPROVE OF HER ACTIONS? DO WE LIKE HER? DOES IT MATTER IF WE LIKE HER?*

I closed the notebook and looked back over at her sleeping face. I had the urge to stroke her cheek lightly, because I liked my own cheek to be stroked and I thought maybe she would, too, but I did not do it. It was strange, I thought, that intimate gestures like this were only permitted within romantic relationships. I would have stroked the cheek of a man I just slept with for the first time, whom I would never see again, but I did not stroke my friend's. Instead, I turned my back to her and read the rest of *I Love Dick* in one long, horny stretch. The sun was already coming up when I finished, and Megan's breath was emerging hot and putrid from the slit in her mouth. I stroked the side of my own face as I finally closed my eyes.

RENATA COUNTRY

Early-morning sun through the slit in the drapes; the sounds of the shopkeepers hollering at each other downstairs as they opened for the morning. Megan still asleep. Me: crackling with the adrenaline of my sleepless night, of the electric book I'd just read, of being back here. I realized that I could feel her, all the way from here. It was as if she were radiating toward me, buzzing through the Italian telephone wires. Ciao, Renata, I felt myself think. I thought I heard her say something back, but I couldn't be sure. I could never be sure with her.

VERONA

Verona was humbling. All this old stone. All this marbled paper. All these pristine Italian women, their hair in elegant banana clips.

"They love a trench coat here, don't they," Megan said.

"Who doesn't?" I said.

We were at an outdoor café, eating pizza. It was blustery, and the sky was spitting. We were supposed to go to an opera in an outdoor amphitheater, but it had gotten rained out. We were semihappy about it. This was what it was to be young: we were allowed to be excited about missing the opera. The wedding wasn't for two more days; tomorrow was the rehearsal dinner, but we weren't invited to that part—another thing we were semihappy about. We joked about not even attending the wedding at all; it seemed boring; we didn't know if we believed in marriage; even as we doggedly pursued monogamous love we were still at the point in our lives when having options felt more important than feeling safe.

Megan had bought a drawing pad at one of the paper shops and was making a small sketch of a pigeon that was feasting on our crumbs, using the restaurant's ballpoint pen. I was envious that she could make something out in the open like this, without feeling the sting of self-consciousness. I wanted to be writing like she was drawing, but I couldn't bring myself to open my notebook in front of her, or in front of anyone. Though I'd shared so much of what I'd written with her over email, the act of writing itself was private for me, something I had to do alone. I needed to feel free to be bad at it, maybe. Or maybe I was just embarrassed to be seen trying, putting in time and effort for something that might never pan out.

I drank my wine and watched the sky for a while: puffy gray clouds and specks of rain landing on the umbrella above us. I felt bloated and lethargic. It was the middle of the afternoon; there was no opera to go to, it was too rainy to see the sights. What were we doing here? I remembered this exact feeling from when I'd lived in Italy years before: the sensation that time was infinite and there was nothing to fill it with. Megan's presence made it impossible to do anything I wanted to do, like reading or writing or simply thinking, and suddenly I was angry that I'd asked her to come here with me. I imagined how nice it might be to be alone in Verona, cruising through the streets with a large umbrella, coming upon a shop filled with rare books, where there would be some kind of warm drink mulling in a copper pot and an old gray cat in the window. I'd sit in there and read and write all afternoon. But no. I had to eat pizza and drink wine endlessly, until I exploded.

"Want to chill on your own for a bit?" Megan said, shutting her notebook. It was as if she had read my mind. "I want to go back to the hotel and take a bath."

As she stood to leave, I felt panicked suddenly, even though I had just wanted her gone.

"See you in a little?" she said, leaving too many euros on the table for the meal.

"'K," I said.

A bit of late-afternoon sun forced its way between the clouds, making me feel more depressed than if it had stayed all the way gray.

IMPOSSIBLE WOMAN

With Megan gone, I told myself, I could finally get some writing done. I pulled my jacket over my head and walked down the block to another café, where I sat down at a metal table and ordered an espresso that came with a small cookie. Across the street, a shop that sold crystals and wind chimes was just opening, and an old, hunched Italian woman was pulling a rack of the chimes out onto the street. As the cart bumped and jostled over the cobblestones, the wind chimes clanked and sounded off, their many tones mingling to create a sound that reminded me of lonely California gardens, cheery pansies, butterfly wings. It was a beautiful moment—the chimes singing through the skinny Italian street, the cobblestones wet and shining from the rain, the old woman touching the long silver tubes with her leathery hand—and I wanted to write it down.

When I reached into my tote for my notebook, I discovered a rogue envelope, floating around next to my grubby ChapSticks and receipts. I opened it. It was one of Megan's drawings, of a hand resting on a book, whose title could be seen between the fingers: *I Love Dick*. Megan's hand: so particular it couldn't be anyone else's. The drawing captured a certain nuance: there was a sadness to it; you could tell the hand in the foreground wasn't quite steady, that the heart that pumped blood to it had recently been broken. Like I did with all the drawings Megan gave me, I considered this one a prompt. I forgot about the wind chimes and returned to what had become my favorite subject: my friend Megan.

I tried to write something that captured the same nuance of Megan's hand as portrayed in her drawing, but after writing a single sentence my pen ran out of ink. I shook the pen. It told me to stop. Stop shaking or stop writing? The latter. Fuck. The pen had found me out. It saw what I was trying to do and it set out to stop me. It was bad, my writing, it always had been, and there was no reason to keep doing it. The empty pen told me I would never get Megan right, that it was impossible. *She* was impossible: there were too many versions of her, too many intricacies, too many stories I'd never know, all swimming around inside her singular body. A better writer might be able to render her particular contradictions—angelic and devilish, smooth and spiky, self-assured and caught up in the opinions of others—but not me. I was an amateur; what I had to say wasn't even worth the ink.

I closed the notebook, sighed loudly, left money under my tiny espresso cup, and walked back toward the hotel. I spotted a shop with art supplies in the window, and bought Megan a tube of blue paint. It was a beautiful blue, and it was expensive. I thought about something I'd read once: that there had been no concept of the color blue before there were words to describe it. I tucked the tube into my bag to give to her later, and the little weight of it made me feel better somehow. I knew in my heart of hearts that words did matter, I just had to get better at using them. I wasn't good enough now, but maybe, with practice and time, I could be.

I felt very hungry all of a sudden, even after our pizza and my cookie. Specifically, I wanted a long and skinny sandwich like the kind I'd gotten so often in Bologna. The kind where the bread cut the roof of your mouth.

LONG DISTANCE

Back at the hotel, I called Wes from the lobby, using a calling card because I hadn't set my cell phone up for international calls before I left. It was still morning in New Orleans, and I assumed he was working, but surprisingly he picked up. I could hear beeping and banging behind him—the sounds of a distant city, a different world. I'd been gone only a few days but it felt like a lifetime had passed; the distance between us was palpable as we spoke.

"So how is it?" Wes asked. "I can't believe you're there. I'm jealous."

"Beautiful," I said. "Verona is pretty magical. I wish all the streets in the world were made of cobblestones."

"Sounds gorgeous," he said.

Magical? Gorgeous? Our conversation felt stilted, like we were both trying too hard. I felt a sinking feeling, a feeling I'd known for my whole life. The other person pulls; I claw for them, trying desperately to keep

them close, get more of them, get all of them. The clawing hurts or an-
noys them, which only makes me want to claw more. *Don't claw,* I told
myself. *Stay calm and don't claw.*

"How's the shooting today?" I asked. I realized before he answered
that his response wouldn't satisfy me, that whether his day went well or
poorly I would still want more—some kernel that let me know: he was
slightly miserable because he missed me.

"It's been really good," Wes said. "I wish it could be longer. I feel so
much pressure to get it all in these few days, you know? But the family is
good. The older daughter just had a baby. Super cute."

"Aww," I said. "So sweet."

"I'd say thirty percent sweet and seventy percent insane." Wes
laughed. "But yeah, it's cool to see. I mean, I've known her since she was
thirteen, and now she's a mom."

"I'm imagining that's how it's going to feel to see Bene and Greta," I
said. "Like whole lives have passed, but somehow they'll still feel familiar."

"Oh crap," Wes said. "I'm late. I met these other journalists from the
city who are all at this Future of Media conference that happens to be
going on while I'm down here—they're going out to this Creole place for
brunch."

"Sounds fun," I said. *Brunch?* Wes hated brunch.

"Kind of intimidating, actually," Wes said. "It's this guy I've been
tracking forever, Matt Davis from the *Times.* And then this woman Sarah
Hughes, who writes for *The Atlantic,* sometimes *Harper's.*"

"Wow," I said, though in reality I was not impressed but annoyed.
Why was Wes going to brunch? And why was he giving me these people's
biographies? It felt weird, on top of all the other ways this phone call felt
weird, or perhaps just distant. We are so far away, I wanted to say. Instead
I sent a kiss sound through the receiver, said goodbye in a way I knew
sounded clingy, and hung up, returning to the hotel room, where Megan
was waiting for me with a bowl of olives and a bottle of wine: our ideal
dinner.

TAN

Megan had brought a bottle of fancy self-tanner with her; she'd gotten it at the department store. Before bed that night, we rubbed it in circles up the backs of each other's legs, on the knobs of each other's shoulders. We did this silently, solemnly, as if what we were doing—painting each other with an orange-brown gel to create the illusion of having been irresponsibly exposed to sunlight—was perfectly normal, even required. In the morning, I would find streaks of the stuff in the crevices of my elbows, on the bridge of my foot, which I knew looked worse than the original skin, untouched and pale. But it was the application itself that made us briefly happy: the feeling of productivity that came from trying to be and look better. I liked the sensation of Megan's long hands rubbing swiftly down my arms, like she was brushing off the ugliness, making way for the beauty.

DRESSES

"What does one wear to Dante's villa?" Megan said as we strutted down via Mazzini the next morning, hooked together at the elbow.

"I'm imagining yards of kind of dirty linen," I said. "Just like, draped."

"Or maybe velvet," Megan said.

"Yes, velvet," I said. "And some kind of headpiece, either golden or made of leaves."

"Do you think any of these places will have that?" Megan said.

"Hard to say," I said. "But it's worth a shot."

We ducked into one of the many fine-looking boutiques on what Google had informed us was the best shopping street in town. It was so unlike going into a shop in the States that I actually wondered if it was closed. No one accosted us or asked us if we needed any help. No one sprayed perfume in our faces. Pristine garments lined the walls like reeds on the bank of a river. The smell—something fresh mixed with an underlying earthiness—reminded me distinctly of Renata, and I once again felt my nerves prickle as I thought of seeing her in just a few days.

Megan floated around the store touching things, running her hands over cashmere sweaters and through racks of silky dresses. Wordlessly, a tall and thin saleswoman wearing a dress that was also a blazer delivered three dress options for Megan: a gray maxi with a high neck, a short black cocktail dress, and a silky long blue thing that looked like it was made of water. For whatever reason, the saleslady did not offer me any options, which made me wonder what it was about me that made people think I didn't want to be helped. Did my current clothing make me look like someone who didn't spend money on clothing? Did I carry myself in a way that suggested I was Megan's sidekick, only along for the ride? I tried to forget about being glossed over so blatantly and acted excited while Megan modeled the first dress option, but I felt miffed and bruised, and so when Megan was in the dressing room with the blue dress I left the store and went back out into the street.

It was warmer today, and the sun felt good on my face. I closed my eyes. Why did I feel like crying? Who cared if a saleslady overlooked me? But it wasn't that, I knew. It was an old ache, something so deep I couldn't even fully identify it. It was Wes cutting our conversation short, as if he hadn't heard that I was just about to say something that was important to me. It was crying so loud in my bedroom as a child and Ann not hearing me, or simply deciding not to respond to my distress. It was going unheard, being forgotten, so many times and for so long.

Megan emerged with a large bag. She put her hand on my shoulder.

"You good?" she said.

"Yeah," I said. "I just needed air."

She took my hand in her hand, the one that wasn't holding the bag.

"I got the blue one," she said.

"It looks like water," I said.

"Exactly," she said. "And now to find something for you."

"Remember that it can't touch my body," I said. "And that it should act like a personal parachute should I decide to jump out of any planes or windows."

Megan laughed. "You have an amazing body," she said. "I don't know why you always want to wear these sacks."

"That's just the thing," I said. "I don't want anyone to know I have any body at all. I want to appear bodyless. Just a floating head."

"What about that one?" Megan said, pointing into the window of a shop with an awning that just said the word MAGAZINE. I moved closer to see what she was referring to, which was a bright red silk dress, floating on a clear hanger, that was shaped like a Roman column.

"Could be just shapeless enough," I said. So we went into Magazine.

This shop felt less intimidating than the one where Megan had gotten her dress, which I was both thankful for and annoyed about; of course I would get my dress from the less chic of the shops. I approached the saleslady and asked her in my best Italian if I could try on one of the red dresses hanging in the window, in a small.

She wagged her finger and made a *tsk* sound that I remembered from living with Renata. She was scolding me.

"No smalls left?" I asked.

"There is only one of those dresses."

"That's the last one?"

"That's the only one," she said. "It's one of a kind. They all are."

She moved her thin arm around the store, gesturing toward so much uniqueness.

"I see," I said. "Is it possible to try it on?"

"Of course not," she said. "It's in the display."

"So you're not going to sell it?" I said. This was *classic* Italian. To sell the unsellable. To prioritize the window display over the customer. To make it impossible to do a simple thing like purchase a dress.

"What's she saying?" Megan asked me.

"She's saying that it's the display dress," I said.

"So it's not for sale?" Megan said.

"It technically is, but I can't have it."

Megan scoffed. "That's insane."

She went over to the window and tugged lightly at the dress. It slipped easily from the hanger and gathered in her hands; it looked like a giant crumpled rose petal. She handed it to me, eyeing the saleslady.

I grinned at her. I had no need or desire to try the dress on; it was shapeless and would obviously fit. I set it on the counter and smugly watched as the saleslady rang me up. It was too expensive, but I didn't care. I felt like Megan had saved me, that she had known exactly how to scoop me up when I needed her to. I squeezed her ribs as we walked out of the store and into the bright daylight. We like her, I thought. It matters that we like her.

THE RIVER

Back out in the street, swinging our bags full of expensive fabric, Megan and I walked happily toward the river, and she updated me on the follow-ups from the Tinder dates she'd gone on the previous week.

"It's bleak out there," she said. "That one musician dude completely dropped off, probably just wanted sex. And then that French guy ended up having a girlfriend and lying about them being in an open relationship. And then that Brian guy just kept being busy, but you know, the kind of busy that isn't actually busy."

"Busy Brian," I said.

"It's almost getting existential," Megan said. "There's this feeling of: If I don't find the right guy right now, like right right now, I won't ever find him. Or it won't matter if I do, because I'll be beyond procreation by then. And what is a woman without babies? Is she even real?"

I laughed.

"And then let's say I find a suitable guy, right? Like a guy who is busy enough but not too busy, who doesn't have any habits disgusting enough to turn me off completely, who doesn't already have a wife. In order to not have a 'geriatric pregnancy' or whatever they call it, I'd have to force him to get me pregnant like the first week we're together. What guy wants to sign up for that? They can feel it, the desperation. They know when you're worried your eggs are going bad."

"Your eggs are not going *bad*," I said, laughing. "We're not that old, come on."

"I'm older than you!"

"By like eight months!" I cried.

"And *then*," Megan continued, dismissing me, "say you convince him it's time, or that time is important in the equation at all, even though he feels no pressure whatsoever from his own biological clock; then you have to start *trying*. Which honestly seems like a recipe for disaster. How would you ever get pregnant when you were *trying* to get pregnant? It's like when you're trying not to eat sugar and all you can think about is Swedish Fish."

"And did you know," I said, "that on your *main* ovulation day, like the *only* day of the month you can actually get pregnant, you only have like a twenty-three-percent chance? I mean, why didn't they tell us that in high school?"

"Instead they told us that a drop of 'pre-come' was going to knock us up immediately," Megan said, laughing.

"Exactly," I said. "I made my high school boyfriend wear like three condoms on top of each other."

"*And* you were on birth control."

"Yep," I said. By the time we got to the river, we were warm with laughter.

Verona was one of those cities where the water was everywhere. You had the sense that if you walked long enough in any direction, you would run into the river. Bridges leaped across it at regular intervals, which was comforting: you always had a way to get somewhere else if you didn't want to be where you were. Megan and I made our way to one of these bridges and began to cross it. In the middle, we stopped to look down at the water. It did not rush, like an American river might. The mass of it moved calmly and all at once, without bump or eddy, as if it were a sheet of glass atop a freight train.

"Did you get my little drawing?" Megan asked. "Of your hand?"

I thought about Megan's drawing. What did she mean, my hand? I reached into my tote bag and pulled the drawing out of my notebook, reexamined it. Oh my god. I had assumed the hand was Megan's—I had been so sure of it—but I now saw that it wasn't, couldn't have been; it was a *left hand*, the hand Megan used to draw with.

Suddenly, I was unable to speak. It was in that moment, on that bridge, that I realized I had gotten the story all wrong, seen it from the wrong angle, confused everything. It wasn't Megan's hand; it was mine. It wasn't Megan's story I had been writing, but my own. It was not Megan who was pregnant, but me.

PART FOUR

PAIN

WEDDING

At a tiny decrepit church atop a spindly hill, my friend Grace got married. I watched her lithe, nervous form float down the aisle and I wept. It was a Catholic ceremony, which meant that Grace and her Italian groom had to kneel and rise at intervals throughout the priest's heavy Italian sermon. As Grace's slender body lifted and sank, her huge white dress thinned and puffed. It was as if the dress were breathing. Megan seemed moved by the ceremony, but despite the fact that I was crying, I was distracted. My hand, though I did not will it to, found my stomach through my red dress. The dough of my own flesh felt warm just below the fabric. I wondered how hard I would have to press to kill whatever was living inside me. But I did not press. Instead, I petted my own stomach as if it were a small head. I did this very subtly, with tiny motions, so as not to appear conspicuous.

Afterward, at Dante's villa, we were served a thousand-course meal. Each course came with its own wine pairing. I took the opportunity to get wasted before I knew for sure that I shouldn't. Surrounded by beautiful Italian people and grapevines and literary ghosts, we brined ourselves in beauty and abundance. The dinner already felt like a memory, like something Megan and I would look back on with intense fondness: the way you looked back on anything that was the last or only one of its kind. We knew it would be the only time we would feed each other mozzarella di bufala with our fingers. The only time we would be served prosciutto straight from the bone. The only time we would dance to European techno in a room that had once held Dante's inferno. Megan looked radiant in the

DJ's flashing green lights, her long dress swishing around her while she moved. The way the Italians danced was the divine kind of comedy. We opened our mouths wide to laugh.

The sister of the groom, Simona, came out of nowhere, shoved me and Megan into a corner. She was fiercely beautiful, with cat eyes and arched eyebrows, a body as long and slim as a worm's. "Do Americans like to have fun?" Simona wondered. "Is it like in *O.C.*?" She explained to us, in stilted English, that she loved that show, *The O.C.* It transported her to another time and another world, she said. A world where feeling bad was supposed to feel good. "When Marissa gets in trouble or has anorexia," Simona said, "I am glued to the television. I know it's retro, but I love Marissa's clothes." She dug a key into a small bag of coke, held the key up to Megan's nose. Megan sniffed at it. She held the key up to my nose but I put a hand up, declining.

"What is it?" Megan said, her tone both skeptical and concerned. "What's wrong?"

Megan knew I didn't decline things that could alter my mental or physical state, that I was a *yes* person. To say no when you are known as a yes person is an affront to anyone who thinks they know you. By saying no, I was revealing to Megan that I was not the person she thought I was. Instead, I was an entirely different kind of careless. She dragged me to Dante's bathroom, where I drunkenly told her what I suspected and feared: that I was pretty sure I was pregnant with Wes's baby.

WES'S BABY

Would be heavy-lashed and disciplined. Would have one set of estranged grandparents and one very practical and distant grandmother. Would be raised in a tiny basement apartment without laundry or else a giant, decrepit loft. Would learn photography early. Would need to go to public school. Would not have married parents. Would grow up in a world that was getting hotter by the day. Would have to learn how to make money to survive. Would witness beauty and experience unfathomable pain. Would get stressed out, fuck up, break down, go to pieces. Would trip and skin a knee, break a bone, question everything, form opinions, age, and one day, die.

PREGNANCY TEST

"I thought you had an IUD," Megan said, in a way that managed to be not accusatory. We'd just gotten a pregnancy test at the Italian pharmacy and were looking for a bathroom for me to take it in.

"I *did*," I said. "Until like two months ago, when it expired. I hadn't gotten a new one yet because our company health insurance was transferred to a new provider, and I hadn't gotten the new insurance card in the mail. I didn't want to deal with the hassle of being reimbursed once I got the card."

"They never reimburse you," Megan said.

"Exactly," I said.

We found a public bathroom near the train station, where we'd been dropped by a party bus after spending the night at the villa. I went in alone and noted how dismal this all was: the orange tile of the floor, the scuzzy mirror, the pregnancy test like a ticking time bomb in my purse. I pulled it out. The brand of the pregnancy test was called Screen Italia. It made me laugh because it reminded me of all the ways in which Italy was absurd. They watched dubbed television and called buses "pullmans." I fucking hated this place, I was just remembering that now. I squatted over Screen Italia and peed.

"You okay in there?" Megan said through the door. "Want me to come in?"

I unlocked the door and she squeezed through. I put my head in my hands.

"I can't be pregnant," I said. "It's the worst possible timing."

"Not the *worst* worst," she said. "You're squarely out of your twenties. You have a job. You have Wes."

"Just say you get it," I said.

"I do get it," she said sadly. "You know I get it."

The test was positive, so I cried. Megan held me while my pants were still down. I gripped her back the way people grip other people's backs in movies. It moved me that she was here with me, squatting so close to my naked vagina.

"Here's what we do," Megan said. "We go get cacio e pepe at that place near the piazza, we abstain from alcohol just in case, we discuss practicalities but prioritize feelings, and we decide. You can call Wes and tell him or you can not. It's up to you."

"You mean just *not* tell him that I have his baby inside me?"

"Sure."

"That seems nuts."

"It seems nuts that he blasted off inside you and never thought twice about it."

"To be fair, it was kind of my fault."

"All I'm saying is that this is one hundred percent your shit. You don't have to tell anyone, including Wes, until you're ready, or until you know what you want."

I thought about what she was saying. I thought about Wes, about how far away he'd seemed on the phone, and how far away he could seem when we were in the same room. I had no idea what he would think about this new information, how he would react. I had no idea if telling him would increase the distance between us or shorten it, pull us together like a magnet. I also had no idea how *I* felt about it, other than that I knew it would stop my writing life before it had ever started.

"I want to write a book," I said to Megan.

"I know you do" was what Megan said, petting my head like a mother might. She tucked the pregnancy test into the small wastebasket, the kind with a plastic hood that swings open and sometimes all the way around.

MY MOTHER'S PREGNANCY TEST

Two blue lines: one for my beginning, and the other for her end.

TIME

Megan and I were due to go back to New York in just three days, and I felt paralyzed by all of it, both my immediate future and my larger one. In the morning we were supposed to go to Bologna, which was full of ghosts and memories, and I didn't know if I had the energy to see Renata in my current state. But New York seemed even more hostile. New York was not a baby-friendly place, even for babies who might not ever be born. New York zoomed and honked, spit money, stayed up late. It didn't seem like the right place to make a decision about the small, vulnerable thing that had burrowed inside my uterus.

Because I needed time, I became obsessed with how quickly or slowly it was passing. "What time is it?" I said to Megan, though I had just asked the same question a few minutes earlier. Kindly, she humored me. "Five thirteen," she said. "Five sixteen. Five seventeen." I was drinking a glass of red wine even though pregnant people weren't supposed to drink. I defended myself for no reason: "They say it's fine to have one glass."

"Five twenty-two," she said, pouring me a finger more.

It had occurred to me on more than one occasion on this trip that Megan was a very wonderful friend. The points at which this realization struck me were the points where I felt Megan was reading my mind, like when she took that dress down from the hanger in the window, or like now, when I could tell she sympathized with my predicament, even empathized with it, taking it on as if it were her own. This was my favorite kind of love, the kind that felt like two people had enmeshed into one body or brain, when you felt like someone was deep in the shit alongside you.

"You're becoming my favorite friend," I said. "I just thought you should be aware."

Megan smiled sadly. "I have to tell you something," she said. "I had an abortion. In January, when I was gone from work that week. I'm sorry I didn't tell you, but I just needed to do it alone. It was Todd's, which was just, ugh, it was awful. To tell you the truth, though, the abortion part wasn't so bad. You're probably going to go that route, I'm assuming?"

"Yeah, probably," I said impulsively. I was used to going along with Megan, liking what she liked, choosing what she chose. It felt easier that way, more fluid, to be the same.

"Megs, I'm sorry," I said.

"No no," she said. "It wasn't a thing. I'm totally okay, promise. And you will be, too."

I hugged her very hard, so hard that my own eyes bulged from their sockets.

MIRRORS

The news of Megan's aborted pregnancy called forth the sensation of looking into a mirror when there's a mirror behind you as well, creating an incalculable layering of reflections. There was the Megan in my story, who had gotten pregnant and decided to keep the baby. There was the real-life Megan, who had gotten pregnant and decided not to keep it. There was the Megan who hadn't gotten pregnant in the first place, or who I hadn't known to be pregnant in the first place— the version of reality I had believed the whole time. And then there was me, who was pregnant now, facing the same decision she had not so long ago. We all looked at each other. We moved in tandem, like dancers who'd memorized a routine, in sync until we weren't. And that's when the strangeness occurred: the moment when one of us split off, reached an arm up as the others were bending down, making a decision to divert from the choreography without informing the others, separating herself, becoming suddenly different, suddenly rogue, suddenly frightening, suddenly all alone as she freed herself, doing whatever she wanted with her body.

HEART SINK

Back in the lobby, where I had gone to sit at the bar and eat olives while Megan showered and changed, I texted Wes. *Miss you. Wanna talk later?* He didn't respond immediately; he was probably out in the field. I imagined Wes with his camera bag, glued to the present moment, hunting for the shot, intensely focused on capturing whatever was in front of him. I wanted to be working! I wanted to have a project like New Orleans, one I could return to with conviction and certainty every year. I felt envious of Wes in that moment—alone and happy to be alone, working and happy to be working, having taught himself so thoroughly that what he had inside himself was all he needed.

I opened Google on my phone, aware I was using precious and expensive data, and typed: *Should I have a baby?* There was a quiz, which I clicked on. I felt about quizzes like I did about horoscopes: they were only accurate if you wanted them to be.

1. When you think about starting a family, how do you feel?

     a) Neutral. I don't really think about it.

     b) Extremely anxious.

     c) Excited but nervous, too.

     d) Deeply happy.

Already, I felt confused. Why was there not an option for *All of the above?*

2. Are you willing to compromise some of your own autonomy and personal agenda for the sake of your child?

    a) No, I like my life as it is.

    b) Yes, I'm ready.

    c) Possibly. It depends.

Jesus, who had written this thing? I clicked on A, then paused and clicked on C. Then I felt someone watching me, and I looked up. The hotel's receptionist, a beautiful olive-skinned woman with thick eyebrows and a name tag that read RHEA, was looking right at me. Though I knew she couldn't see what was on my screen, I felt embarrassed and clicked out of the quiz. My phone buzzed with a text from Wes.

Hey goobs! Going out with that same crew again tonight. Can we chat tomorrow? There was the heart sink again.

Me: *Glad you hit it off! Yes tomorrow's good.*

Me: *Wish I was there.*

Wes: *Wish I was THERE.*

Me: *Touché.*

Wes: *Heading out now. Kiss on the neck.*

Me: *Kiss on the eyelids.*

I made my way upstairs, feeling unmoored and aggravated. Why hadn't I just told him? Forced him to call me, explained everything right away? I knew it was silly, but there was part of me that felt like I shouldn't have to, like Wes should telepathically know he'd gotten me pregnant and write me a message corresponding to that truth. I had the absurd thought that if Wes could get pregnant and did, I would know about it, even from all the way across an ocean. I felt betrayed by his not knowing, even when I was the one not telling him.

The hotel's ornate Italianness suddenly felt oppressive. I craved a minimalism I knew I wouldn't find here. I wanted to pare everything down. My thoughts, the drapes, the thing living inside me. I wanted to give the world an enema. Flush everything away. I took the stairs up to our room and unlocked the door with the old-fashioned key. It did not feel charming. I wanted a plastic key card that made a tiny light turn green. At least I had Megan, I thought. Megan would know how to make me feel better.

But when I opened the door she was sitting on the bed, her long legs crossed, her cheeks flushed with either embarrassment or anger, perhaps even horror. Then I saw her lap. She was holding my notebook in her hands, and it was open to the exact wrong page.

"Shit," I said.

For a moment that felt like a universe, she did not say anything.

THE FIGHT

"What is this?" she finally said, holding up my notebook.

IS MEGAN A FEMALE MONSTER? I could see from across the room, in my stupid, blocky handwriting.

Fuck. I felt caught, like the time I'd cheated on a math test in seventh grade and suddenly felt the teacher's shadow over me, knowing punishment was coming. But I also knew I didn't totally deserve to be punished; this was my private notebook, where I should be able to write freely, knowing no one would ever see it.

"It's my notebook," I said. "That you, apparently, have just read?"

"Why are you writing about me?" Megan said.

"It's not *actually* you," I said. "It's fiction. It's just a story."

"'Is Megan a female monster?'" she read from the page. "Was her wrongdoing political?" She paused, looked up at me. "My *wrongdoing*? What the fuck, Em?"

"It was something from that book," I tried, knowing my explanation would fall flat. "The Chris Kraus book. Those are her ideas."

"Hmm," Megan said. "Looks like your handwriting, though."

"It's just a story, Megs. Notes for a story."

"I'm just trying to understand why you would write this stuff down, though," Megan said. "What is this, even? Are you writing a novel? About *me and Todd*?"

"It's not a novel, it's nothing," I said. But when she said it out loud I knew it was true; I *had* been trying to write a novel, I simply hadn't admitted it to myself yet. "No one was ever going to see it."

"But I saw it."

"Well, what do you want me to do about that?"

"I don't get you," Megan said. "One minute I think you're the only person who understands me, the only person I can tell all of this shit to, and the next minute I realize you've been fucking *judging* me this whole time."

"I wasn't judging you. I was just, I don't know . . . trying to figure it out. Trying to figure out why everything happened with Todd, what that was. I was . . . interested in it."

"And? What conclusions did you come to? I'd love to know."

"I think he had power and you were drawn into it, and then you couldn't see straight from inside his hold on you, or your infatuation, or whatever it was. I was trying to imagine what it would be like to be in that position."

Megan let out a weird laugh.

"What?" I said.

"You *are* in that position, Emily."

"What are you even talking about?"

"You're talking about being unable to see the reality from inside a relationship? Look at your own! You're pregnant, with a dude who you don't even live with, who hasn't *asked* you to live with him because he's too protective over the precious lifestyle he's created for himself to let you fully in. Talk about power dynamics."

I felt the pit in my stomach swell. I thought of the fight I'd had with Wes, the one that had led to the sex that had gotten me pregnant, how privately wounded I'd been when he'd so quickly rejected the idea of living together. I hadn't even told Megan about it—the rejection had felt too embarrassing—but it was as if she'd seen through me, found the painful spot and pushed on it.

"You have literally no idea what you're talking about," I said now, with defensive spirit. "He has a roommate. He's not going to just kick him out."

"Oh, Kasper? The Danish musician with a trust fund? Kasper would be just *fine* without Wes, Emily. And so would you, if I'm being honest."

"Wow," I said, incredulous. "And how long have you been sitting on this? The fact that you hate my boyfriend?"

"I don't hate your boyfriend. I just think you're never going to get what you need from him. And this is a moment when you're going to need things. Like actual support."

"Wes supports me. He's one of the only people who pushes me to keep writing."

"Of course he does! He's trying to get you to fit into his annoying artist fantasy—the loft, the writer girlfriend, whatever. He doesn't even acknowledge who you actually are, which is a girl who still works for the company that fired her best friend."

"Wait a second. You expected me to quit?"

"You could have at least *considered* it. I mean, how could you not? You watch them fire all the old people who have lived their entire lives at that place, and your best friend, and you act like nothing fucking happened. It's like you're in this delusional world where your choices don't matter. But they do."

"How is being able to finally pay back my loans delusional? I'm swimming in debt, Megan. This is the first time I've ever had my own money."

"Get a job somewhere else. Literally anywhere else. You're a college-educated white girl. It's not that hard."

"You're actually pulling the privilege card right now? You're the one who sends a money request and your dad just wires cash into your account; you don't even have to *talk* to him. You've never had to worry about not having enough. Not ever."

"I'm not talking about *money*, Emily. I'm talking about decisions, about the choices you make. You talk every fucking day about the 'capitalist bullshit' we have to put up with, you write these stories about all the problematic ways we're engaging with the system, about how horrible these powerful men are, but have you ever done anything besides complain about it? No. You somehow remove yourself from the decisions that would actually mean something, as if you had no choice. But you do. You're part of the fucking problem."

"This is insane. You're giving *me* advice about taking the moral high road? The girl who, let's see, fucked her married boss, broke things off with him, and was then somehow *surprised* when she got laid off?"

Megan's face morphed into an ugly grimace. "Just fucking say it," she said. "Just say it to my face, instead of thinking it, or saying it in some secret code, or writing it in your fucking novel."

"I don't know what you're talking about."

"I am a monster," Megan seethed, tears rising in her eyes. "That's what you think, isn't it? A monster who deserves everything she got. Go on, say it. Tell me I'm a monster."

I felt tears gathering in my eyes, too. I could feel myself in the trap of my own anger, unable to get out. I was in too deep; all I could do was fight back.

"You're a monster," I said, very plainly, as if I had no feelings at all, as if I were made of stone.

"And you're sick," she said, her face fierce now. "Sick and selfish. I really hope you decide to get an abortion, because you'd make a terrible mother."

Our eyes met then, and there were knives in our gazes. We had never spoken this way to each other, not ever. We had always been the kind of friends who agreed with each other; agreeability was one of the pillars of our connection. But we had broken everything, the whole veneer of our friendship, and I felt one of the sharp shards of feeling slice into my abdomen. I choked on a sob as I left, slamming the door behind me.

I sat in the hallway for a while, fuming, replaying what we'd said to each other. Megan's accusations stabbed me harder as they repeated on a loop in my mind. I knew many of them were true. Maybe I was sick. Maybe I was selfish. I probably would make a horrible mother. But the fact that she had *said* these things—I almost couldn't stand the pain of it. Did she really believe them? Or had she said them in anger? Either way was bad, and I fumed as the loop in my mind gathered speed and power. Finally, I went down to the lobby to book myself another room. The woman I'd seen earlier, Rhea, typed loudly on the keyboard of an old boxy computer and smiled kindly at me, as if she knew something must be wrong. She placed the room key in my hand very gently, letting her fingers rest on my palm for an extra second.

"Can I do anything else for you?" Rhea asked.

I shook my head. "No, thank you," I said. "I'm good."

But I wasn't good. I knew that when I woke up the next morning, Megan would be gone. That she wouldn't be mine anymore.

BOLOGNA

The train to Bologna was full due to an Italian holiday I'd never heard of, so I had to sit on the floor in between two cars. The train rumbled madly beneath me, liberating some of the tension in my body, shaking it into a melted kind of exhaustion. Two Italian businessmen stood above me, talking about numbers. Their masculinity made me feel calmer; I had a brief fantasy that when we got off the train, they would offer to drive me wherever I wanted to go in their little sports car that was conveniently parked at the station. The fantasy soothed me and gave way to sleep. When I woke up, the businessmen were gone, and we were there, at Bologna Centrale. The first and last place I had set foot in this city, so many years ago. I hurried to gather my things. I was exhausted in a way I didn't remember ever having been, as if sleep were a drug that I needed more of. I tumbled out of the train and into the station, which was just as depressing as it had always been, with all that beige stone, the espresso vending machines, the lackadaisical bustle. At least, I told myself, Bologna didn't have to be mine. It was only on loan to me. I was only here for two nights.

Via Marconi had not changed. The same trash blew around in the gutters. The same yellowish clouds hung overhead. There was the store where we got calling cards for our Italian cell phones. There was the guy with a pushcart full of old, jangling keys. There was the poignant pigeon. There was the building my American friend Sam had lived in with his roommate Marco, who had killed himself that October. He had jumped off the roof of the building. Sam had been out of town that weekend, visiting a friend who was studying in Amsterdam. When he came back, Marco's girlfriend was weeping in the kitchen. She had been sitting there for two days. She couldn't move. I had never been able to walk down this street afterward without thinking of that woman's elbows, how they must have hurt from digging into the Formica table for so long, holding her own face while she wept.

Finally, I stepped off via Marconi into the center of everything: piazza Maggiore. Jesus Christ, there was the Fontana del Nettuno! I remembered this dude. A vast gray-green hunk looming over the front end of the piazza, casually dragging his trident and surveying his kingdom below. I hadn't remembered Neptune being this hot. He had a full beard and wild waves of hair, and a chiseled body. He wore the grimace of a man with responsibilities. One of his feet rested on a large conch shell. His penis was made purposefully small, I remember overhearing from a passing tour guide, so as not to be lewd, but what was lacking was made up for when you looked at him from the side, at which point his outstretched thumb mimicked a good-sized erection. Below him, surrounding his raised pedestal, four women squatted above a fountain, squeezing water from their round breasts. The water flew upward in eight glorious arches, then tinkled into the fountain below, filling it. I had never once thought about

OLD FLAME 137

this statue when I lived here; I had taken it for granted, written it off as a historical bore. But now it spoke to me as very real and very powerful, the depiction of the serious if poorly endowed man, concerned with the wider world, while the women below him were consumed with the task of expelling liquid from their own bodies to quench the thirst of the community, their babies, everyone else but themselves.

Neptune made me want to have an abortion immediately. I could not become one of these kneeling women, milk projecting out of my tits. Shit everywhere. No time for myself, for my writing, for my own dreams. Neptune made me want to claw my own insides out. I felt my face flush and tears rise into my eyes. I leaned over the fountain and put my hand under a stream of water. I cupped my hand and lifted it to my mouth. I hadn't realized I was thirsty, but I drank for a long time.

PART FIVE

GLORY

REUNION

I rang Renata's buzzer. The sound—a deep, churning jangle—was so familiar it flicked a switch on inside me. *You're here.*

"You're here!" Bene's wide face appeared above me, leaning out over the geraniums. She grinned. "A little late, no?"

"I'm sorry," I called. "The train."

"The trains are the worst!" she called.

"Let me in!" I felt like I still knew her, that she was still very familiar, though she had been only nine when I'd seen her last, and now she was a teenager, her round face covered in innocent pimples. I wonder if she tried desperately to treat them, as I once had, with too-strong drugstore chemicals—salicylic acid, benzoyl peroxide—only to find that those rinses and washes left her face chapped and raw, sensitive to sunlight, vulnerable feeling, worse off than before.

The gate clicked open and I let myself into the magical world of their stone courtyard. The morning glories crawling up the stone wall turned their heads and stared at me. I smelled jasmine and cooking garlic. I felt nervous suddenly, and wished I hadn't come. It seemed like so much effort, this reunion, and for what? I was just a girl who'd lived here once a long time ago, for a matter of months. In the scheme of their lives, I was so small, almost nothing.

But as soon as I got up the stairs I felt two sets of arms—Bene's, Greta's—wrapped around me so tightly I could barely breathe, and I remembered the feeling of the girls so vividly: the fresh smell of their hair and skin, the way they laughed for no reason. I thought of the chapter

books I'd read them before bed, their ballet leotards with the bit of extra fabric in the crotch. I thought of the way they'd smelled then—like
blossoms and skin—and how now there were new smells layered on top
of their original smells: soaps and deodorants and spritzes of youthful
perfume. I felt myself grinning. I'd missed them.

"We missed you!" Bene said jubilantly.

"You look older for sure," Greta said.

I swatted her on the arm. "*You* look older," I said. "Last time I saw
you, you had pigtails."

The girls parted for Renata. Before I had a chance to feel the nerves
I had expected, she swept in and hugged me tightly, then pulled her face
back to look at me. I imagined that she was noting the new lines that had
appeared around my eyes, the part of my neck that had already begun to
sag, the wrinkles in my button-up shirt. She was, as ever, perfectly coiffed,
in a burgundy silk shirt tucked tightly into high-waisted jeans with a black
belt. I felt instantly resentful about the possibility of being judged, but the
resentment felt so familiar it was almost comforting. I didn't remember
the last time I had been looked at so closely.

"Emily," she said, and it made me feel warm to hear her say my
name. She took my jacket from me and hung it somewhere.

"I'm sorry I'm late," I said.

"Tell Greta," she said. "She's the one with her timers dinging every
five minutes."

A timer dinged, as if on cue. We all laughed. Greta hustled back into
the kitchen to peek into the oven, nudge something casserole-like with a
fork, and close it up again.

"Needs five more minutes," she announced.

I surveyed their familiar kitchen: handmade Italian tiles for the back-
splash, with little chickens painted on them in blue. Those beautiful copper pots. How strange it was, to be back around the things I had once
lived with. It seemed like a miracle that those shiny, rosy pots were still
hanging there above the stove, the little espresso maker still parked on

the back burner like a faithful butler. I flicked my eyes over at the living room wall: there was *la casalinga*, frozen in her own living room with her vacuum.

"Both the girls work at the osteria now," Renata explained. "Bene's a server. And Greta works in the kitchen, as one of the cooks."

"Wow," I said. "How'd you get that job?"

Greta laughed. "Because I was a terrible waitress," she said. "I was always tasting the food and asking the chefs how they made it, telling them to add more salt. Then one day the manager says, 'We're putting you in the kitchen.'"

"Ha!" I said.

Bene poured us all wine from a bottle without a label, passed around the glasses. I wondered for five seconds whether or not I should drink it, then did. It was delicious. I had forgotten about this part of living at Renata's: she always had the very best wine.

"You're still a vegetarian, right?" Greta asked, opening the oven again.

I froze. I didn't have the heart to tell them that no, I was not a vegetarian anymore, that my vegetarianism had been short-lived and half-assed, a righteous environmentalist phase I outgrew when I left the Bay Area after college. I didn't want to out myself as a woman who lacked conviction, who changed her mind with every whim or season, so I nodded vaguely, then dipped my finger into a sauce on the counter. "That's fucking delicious," I said, which it was. Greta grinned and her obvious pride made me feel happy.

Suddenly my stomach lurched with nausea, and I had to abruptly excuse myself and rush to the bathroom. Of course, I thought. Of course I would get sick in the very moment I wanted to appear pulled together, when I wanted more than anything to be the best version of myself— for this family to be reminded of my gracefulness, which might, if I was lucky, come off as goodness. In the bathroom, I crouched over the bidet and dry heaved. Nothing came. I heaved again and coughed up a wad of bile and phlegm, but it only made me feel worse. I stood up and splashed my face with water from the sink, breathed deeply a few times. Luckily, I could feel the queasiness easing up, releasing its clutches. I towel dried my hands and went back out into the living room.

At the very same moment, the apartment door blew open and Evelina, Renata's neighbor, swooped in like a confused crane. Her long red hair floated behind her. Her glasses were crooked.

"Emily!" she cried, flying toward me. "Look at you! You were so much fatter when you lived here!"

I laughed. The Italians had no trouble being frank about things like this: how fat you'd been, how old you looked. But I loved this about them: it seemed real in a way that Americans were incapable of being. I hugged Evelina. "Ciao, Evelina."

"Madonna, you'll never guess the pains I've gone through today! My meat guy—Rena, you know my meat guy—has stopped carrying the right mortadella. So he tries to cut me some from this nasty log filled with eggs, and I tell him, hold on now, where's the one with the olives that you know I like? And he tells me he stopped getting the one with the olives because he had a fight with the guy who made it. And I say, you let a fight get in the way of your business? You let a fight get between you and your most loyal customer? I had been his most loyal customer—that is until today, when I had to go to the guy at the stall across from his, to get the mortadella I needed. I felt like a traitor! But I had no choice! He's the one who stopped carrying the right mortadella!"

I smiled at Evelina. I was happy she was here; she made things feel looser, released some of the pressure. Greta announced that dinner was almost ready and we could head down to the courtyard; we were going to eat outside tonight, she'd bring things down. I watched her in the kitchen, stirring pots with Renata's wooden spoons. She looked graceful and in her element, adding a dash of salt here, a sprig of parsley there. I had known this about her when she was younger, but it became clear to me now: Greta had a specific confidence that made you trust her to take care of things. She'd always had her ballet bag perfectly packed when it was time for practice; she'd made her own school lunches; she'd tucked her younger sister in every night. She did things with precision and care, naturally, without being asked. You could see sureness and capability in her every movement, and this was something that I admired, and also envied.

Then we were in the garden, which was newly bursting with April's expected bounty: daffodils in every nook and cranny, night-blooming jasmine in full night bloom. It smelled of rain and flowers and cigarettes—a neighbor was smoking on her balcony, closing her eyes while she exhaled. Everything was very romantic back here—lush and almost sexy. Greta's food was heaped in abundant piles on platters that snaked down the center of the table. Bene passed out cloth napkins; Renata lit tall candles; Evelina gave dramatic thanks to the heavens above for producing such abundance.

"God breaks our balls sometimes," she hollered, "but he sure has fed us well tonight."

"Greta has fed us well," Renata said, and I saw pride shine in her eyes as she touched her daughter's hair.

Home, I thought, because I couldn't help myself.

CHOREOGRAPHY OF A FEAST

An adopted daughter serves a meatless ragù to an adopted daughter. A professor passes a cloth napkin to her former student. Estranged friends catch up on the last ten years over braised fennel. A mushroom frittata soaks in a decade's worth of banal gossip. An American explains her marital status between bites of charred broccolini. A newly tenured professor urges her precocious daughter to elaborate on her plans for the future.

"Greta, tell Emily about New York."

"Mom," Greta protested. "I haven't even gotten in yet."

"She's applied to study abroad at NYU for next fall," Renata said.

"That's amazing!" I said, genuinely excited. "I'll meet you in Union Square! I'll show you all my favorite places near the campus—The Strand for books and then shopping at this consignment store off St. Marks and then the oldest bar in the city for black-and-tan beers."

Renata raised her eyebrows in a jokingly disapproving way. Greta laughed and said it sounded fun.

"What do you *do* in New York?" Evelina said. "For your job?"

An aspiring writer chews through a tough but tasty mushroom.

"I work in advertising," I said, feeling depressed after saying it out loud. "I write advertisements."

"You'd make a good writer," Renata said. "You notice things. I remember you always had that notebook when you lived here."

"Yes, I try to write other things, too. Little stories about people and things I see. Nothing real."

"Did you write about us?" Evelina chimed. "You were here for all the drama, after all."

I saw Renata give Evelina a look, though I couldn't place the expression.

"Oh, what?" Evelina said to Renata. "Don't tell me you never told Emily about your run-in with the Prato authorities!"

Renata shook her head, tried to smile—but I could tell she wanted Evelina to stop talking. So, apparently, did the girls, who stood up in tandem and began to clear our plates.

"I'm supposed to meet Chiara at the cinema," Greta said.

"Fede's picking me up in ten," Bene said, balancing a stack of plates on her forearm.

Two teenage girls kiss their ex-nanny's cheeks, leaving swipes of iridescent grease.

"Have you ever noticed that teenagers are always leaving?" Renata said to her daughters' backs.

"We love you!" Bene shouted back at her, which made her smile.

"They're good girls," Evelina said. "You did good, Rena."

Renata sighed. "Oh, don't fluff me, Eve. We all know it's impossible to be a good mother."

"Well, you're as good as it gets," Evelina said, bending over to kiss Renata on the forehead.

A lipstick mark lingers. An eccentric neighbor begs off; she's tired, ready to cuddle with her Chihuahua.

It was just us now, me and Renata. The night air felt thicker suddenly, as if it were closing in around us, the smell of jasmine becoming syrupy. Renata sipped her wine with her signature elegance, the candlelight bouncing off one side of her face, leaving the other in shadow. I reached for an almost-empty wine bottle, began to pour.

"You probably shouldn't be drinking so much," Renata said.

I stopped pouring, shocked.

"What?"

"You're pregnant," Renata said, very simply, as if it were an obvious fact. "Aren't you?"

"How did you know?"

"I spent many years of my life clocking pregnant women," Renata said. "Back when I was trying to get pregnant myself. There's a certain look a woman has. In her eyes. In her face. Plus, I heard you retching in the bathroom earlier." She winked at me. Reflexively, I reached up to touch my cheeks. They were hot and soft, oily from the warm dinner.

"How are you feeling?" Renata said. I couldn't tell if she meant physically or emotionally or both. No one had asked me this yet—no one *knew* about this yet, except for Megan—and it broke me open. A complete gushing occurred. A waterfall of wounds pushing through the retaining wall of my exterior self. The river in Verona. The Screen Italia test. The notebook and my terrible story. The fight with my favorite friend. The boyfriend back home, whom I still had not told.

Renata didn't say anything, didn't push on any of the subjects I brought up, but simply let me spill the contents of myself, as if I were a bowl, tipping. Her response—or lack of response—felt like a friend's; if she had been my mother, I knew, or my sister, if I had one, she wouldn't have been able to handle my pain, she would have tried to fix it, to patch me up so that I wouldn't leak out, so that she would not have to witness the unraveling of a life so deeply intertwined with hers. This, oddly, disappointed me. Why couldn't she worry for me, join in on my frenzy, like a mother would? Why was she being a friend to me, as sturdy as a column for me to lean against and as open as a vessel for me to pour myself into?

"Let's go inside," Renata finally said, leaning over to blow out the last of the candles. I wiped my wet face with the back of my hand. "I'll tell you about what happened in Prato."

I didn't know if Renata was simply offering up this story as a distraction from my own, but I didn't care. I had wanted to know this story for so long, and here I was, face to face with its protagonist, who I could already feel myself rooting for.

WHAT HAPPENED IN PRATO

"When we were in Prato that Christmas," Renata began, settling into the couch with her wine, "I ran into an old lover. Sandro Levi, that's this man's name. We were together before I moved to Bologna, when I was in my early twenties. Sandro was an artist, a painter and a sculptor. He was older than me by five or six years, so he was already living the life he knew he wanted to live, whereas I was still trying to discover who I was and what I would become. His self-possession was intoxicating. He had a studio in Prato's Chinatown, in a big warehouse with factory windows. I loved that studio almost more than I loved Sandro, though I loved Sandro quite a lot. He was the first man I ever really gave myself to all the way. He taught me about art, how to see it and how to talk about it. I thought he was everything, and that our love was forever."

I leaned forward, closer to Renata. I felt like I was in her class again, watching her orate, hanging on her every word, completely rapt.

"But as we well know by now," she continued, "no love is forever and no man is forever, right?"

I smiled as if I agreed, but felt daunted by what sounded like a premonition. I didn't want to think about the possibility that my love for Wes could burn out, not right now.

Renata raised an eyebrow and smiled slyly. "Anyway, when I was twenty-four, the year I decided to move to Bologna to continue my studies, I found out I was pregnant with Sandro's baby. I knew immediately that I did not want to keep it. During my years with Sandro, I had come into my own as a feminist and a thinker. I believed women should be able to pursue careers before they had children. I had just gotten into the art history program at the University of Bologna, and I didn't want to ruin my shot at earning my degree, or interrupt my studies with the responsibilities of new motherhood. I conferred with Sandro and he agreed. I had the abortion at a clinic in Prato. It was relatively quick and only painful for a little while. I moved to Bologna that fall, and Sandro and I split up. The distance was too much for us, and it felt natural to give each other the time and space to study and be with other people. Though I thought about Sandro often, I didn't feel regretful about our breakup, and I rarely thought about the abortion. I always thought Sandro and I would return to each other someday, but we never did. He married another artist in Prato, and I married Massimo, who was a mutual friend of ours."

Renata's wineglass was empty; I took the liberty of pouring her some more. Renata nodded in thanks but didn't touch the glass. I couldn't help but place her story up against my own, like a piece of tracing paper. The artist's loft, the unwanted pregnancy—the similarities to my own life were almost uncanny. I had felt this way before, when I lived here, and I felt it again now: that Renata's fate and mine were somehow intertwined, or that her fate was indicative of my own. This feeling was both unsettling and comforting: if my story was simply a reproduction of another that had come before it, perhaps the choices I made didn't matter as much as I thought they did. Perhaps the predicaments we found ourselves in were simply reiterations of previous ones, in which case all our pain was communal, historical, both lesser and greater than we'd imagined it to be.

"After I graduated," Renata went on, "I tried to get a job as a professor, but could not. There wasn't much room for women in academia back then, or even now. I worked at a film archive for a long time, cataloging and labeling the reels. All of the filmmakers were men. I tried to get the archive to invest in women-made films, but it was like trying to move a brick building with my weight, and plus, there weren't that many films made by women in the first place. I remember feeling very angry during that period, trying to claw through the thick walls of Italian sexism, never getting anywhere, and coming to a sort of resigned conclusion that I would just give in. I would become a mother, and do the things women were expected to do—caring for small people, cooking, making their husbands happy. It seemed like the only way, and I no longer wanted to fight it. And even though Massimo had fallen in love with me for my independent spirit, he ended up liking this subdued version of me very much. He had wanted kids for a long time, and finally I was coming around. We began to try to get pregnant."

Renata went on to tell me that this trying had gone on for years, with no success. She spent the first half of her thirties being prodded and judged by doctors and specialists. They'd tracked her cycle and gone to special clinics, paid for by the university, where Massimo taught. She'd injected hormones into her own abdomen, kept logs of her diet, taken a series of pills, which always got stuck in her throat. Her mother, whom she called weekly despite how terrible she felt after these calls, told her that it was Renata's own fault for having waited so long. Women were so selfish these days, her mother said. Trying to live out their dreams while their uteruses dried up.

But Renata knew that the problem was not with her. She had gotten pregnant before, with Sandro, and she had a feeling, somewhere deep, that she'd be able to again, that she was still quite fertile. The problem was with Massimo, she knew, or with her compatibility with Massimo, and yet she never dreamed of telling him this. She knew what this knowledge would do to Massimo's gargantuan ego—it would destroy him. The few times he'd been unable to get an erection resulted in his sulking for days on end, and then becoming angry with her, as if his penis's failure was her fault. Plus, she'd never told Massimo about Sandro, let alone having been pregnant with Sandro's baby, and this did not seem like a good moment to bring that information to light. Confident that it was his wife's body that was failing them and not his, Massimo suggested they adopt. "A little girl," he said. "A little brown or Black girl."

Renata rolled her eyes at this. "He actually said that. A little brown or Black girl. Which I knew had something to do with my mother, who Massimo perceived as racist, which admittedly she kind of was. She'd been raised inside a nationalist fervor; Mussolini lived in her ears. My parents hated the Sicilians, they hated the Slovenians, then the Armenians, then the Africans. They were even wary of people from as far south as Naples, where the girls were born, to a mother who was too poor to care for them and put each in foster care just after giving birth, stipulating that she wanted them to be adopted together. And the second Massimo saw them he was in love, and so was I, and so there were two. Massimo couldn't stand the way my mother looked at the girls when we first took them to meet her, with a barely veiled disgust. He said that we shouldn't allow her to see them, if she was going to act so openly hostile. But I couldn't do it, I couldn't keep them from their grandmother. And, of course, my mother came around."

"Yes, she loves them now, doesn't she?"

"Oh yes. Madly. The truth is, it was mostly my father coming through in the beginning. It took her a long time after he died to get rid of his voice in her head; he was her other dictator. When he died a few winters after we brought the girls home, my mother changed. Almost like she was starting over. She's great with them now. She even offered to watch the girls while I went out at night over Christmas, which I hadn't done in eons. I went to this art opening that the city had organized, in the cathedrals. And that's when I saw Sandro, standing there in the middle of the first church I entered, looking up."

"How did he look?" I asked, liking the gossipy feeling of this part of the story.

Renata shook her hand as if she'd touched something hot. I laughed.

"Oh, Sandro is beautiful," she said. "Slender and tall, with some northern blood. But mostly it is his freedom that makes him so attractive. He has always been free, Sandro. Not in the same way Massimo is. Massimo is very, like you Americans say, 'keep up with the Joneses.' Sandro—he has released himself from society in this way that has always astounded me. He does what he wants and when, but somehow it never feels selfish, it only feels authentic. He truly does not care what anyone around him thinks."

"You've always seemed that way to me," I said.

Renata laughed. "Oh, far from it. I burn with shame. I live for the approval of my mother, even when I disagree with most of her opinions. And I've allowed men to shape my entire life."

I stayed quiet, in awe of her blunt self-awareness.

"I watched Sandro for a while, looking at him looking. Eventually, I lifted my gaze to the ceiling, too. I couldn't even see the painting up there, my vision was so clouded with Sandro's image. I saw Sandro swimming on the ceiling with the gods and cherubs. When I looked over at him again, he was looking at me."

"Did you talk to him?"

"Oh yes. And much more."

I yelped with the delight of Renata's promiscuity. I love her, I thought. Now more than ever.

"So what happened?"

"I went back to his studio with him—the same studio he'd had when we were young. Everything was exactly the same; it was almost like I was having déjà vu. The cigarettes, the coffee cans full of paintbrushes, the little husks of his paint tubes. The big, cold windows. It was like we were twenty again, neither of us with responsibilities, just two young people in love. He told me all the things men tell women to get them to sleep with them. That I looked beautiful, that I hadn't changed a bit, that my ass was still perfect. He grabbed it and pulled me to him. We kissed like I haven't kissed anyone in years, with the passion of teenagers. We slept together on the cot he's always kept in his studio for this exact purpose. I went nuts for it. I hadn't had sex in so long, not since I'd found out Massimo was cheating on me."

"How did you find out?" I asked, instantly regretting it because I knew it interrupted the flow of her story.

"Oh, the usual way," she said. "I saw them together. At a café near the university. Nuzzling."

"Men are shit."

"Well, of course," Renata said. "But it's never really about the men in the end."

She gave a little smirk, then looked into the near distance, seeming to come to some new conclusion.

"This strange thing happened when I was lying with Sandro on that shitty cot after we'd made love," she said. "I began to think about that baby, the one we hadn't had. I had honestly never thought about it before, or had any regrets whatsoever about getting the abortion, and still, it wasn't regret I felt. It was curiosity, or . . . imagination. I began to imagine my life if I had stayed in Tuscany with Sandro, raising our baby in his big, cold art studio. I began to live the life from front to back, like a montage in a movie, only it felt more real. The pregnancy and the birth, the nursing, the resentment I felt for Sandro when he painted while I took care of the baby, the books I read late into the night simply to feel like I was myself for some fraction of the day. It was so vivid, this life I hadn't lived. I could actually feel these things: the pain of the birth, the exhaustion, the resentment. I was truly having an out-of-body experience, while Sandro was apparently having a totally perpendicular thought process, imagining the possibility of a future together. He tells me suddenly that he's moving to Bologna that spring; he's been offered a professorship at the university. That Massimo had pulled some strings to get him the job."

"Wow," I said, not knowing fully what this meant. Renata's sharp eyes grew sharper, narrowing into little angry slits.

"I'd been up for a full professorship for eleven years," she said. "No strings had ever been pulled for me. I felt a burning inside me, some latent fury that had been there for decades. It was heating up. I suddenly saw the unfairness of the whole thing, clear as day. I saw myself as a little girl, smarter than any boy in my class, but being passed over for the literary prize, as if the teacher hadn't read my paper at all. A boy named Bruno got the prize. Bruno was every boy and I was every girl. Bruno was Massimo, who suckled on his mamma's teat until he was four, who was secretly bad at spelling, who had me read over all his papers, but who got to present himself in the world as the smarter of us, the one with the professorship, the one with all the accolades, all the female students drooling over him during office hours. Where was I this whole time? I was at home with the babies, warming up their milk, trying to steal time for myself when they were asleep. But I swear to god they knew when I opened a book, Emily. As soon as I opened a book their little eyes would pop open, as if they could sense that I was trying to use my brain for something other than marking their shits on a chart.

"Why did Massimo's mind matter more than mine? Why did Sandro get his freedom to be an artist, without having to answer to anything or anyone else, slipping into a professorship without ever even trying? Why had my father gotten away without washing his own underwear for thirty years? I saw so clearly everything I had given up in my life, despite trying so hard to live by my own standards. I realized that I hadn't just given things up for these men, but for myself, as I tried to become them, to want what they wanted, to embody the masculinity that kept them invulnerable. I thought that if I could be stronger, if I could emulate their strength, their confidence, I could be invited in. But I never was. I was left there with the milk. I had no idea who I was anymore. I don't know if I had ever known."

I had tears in my eyes then. It crushed me, to hear Renata talk like this, to lay out the anger so plainly. If Renata couldn't withstand the weight of being a woman, no one could.

"I left Sandro's place in a huff," Renata continued, "and went back to my mother's. I had expected the girls to be asleep, but they weren't; they were wide awake, running around the living room as if my mother had given them each a bag of candy. I asked what was going on, and my mother's face looked pale. I could tell she knew something she didn't want to tell me. I yelled at her to tell me what was going on. And she said very flatly that the baby had come. Massimo's baby. A baby girl, so excited to come into the world she'd arrived a month early. My mother had gotten a call from Massimo's mother, who still insisted on keeping up with her despite our separation; they had become quite close when Massimo and I were together, as both of their husbands had died around the same time."

Renata paused and took a breath, taming one of the waves in her hair by tucking it behind the shore of her ear. I watched her face change, as if she were watching a particularly affecting scene in a movie. Her brows leaned toward each other; her glassy eyes grew clearer. She looked beautiful and fierce.

"Something happened then," she said. "I heard about Massimo's baby, and this put me over the edge. The dam broke. I became furious. I mean, *furious*. Down to my bones, deep inside my stomach. This rage occurred inside me, it was like a bomb going off. Strangely, I was not envious whatsoever about the fact of the baby itself, or that Massimo had succeeded in procreating naturally with someone who wasn't me—I had my children, whom I loved; that was enough for me. And sure, I was a little peeved, in some petty way, that he'd gotten to prove his stupid point, that his precious sperm had finally done their job. But mostly—and this shocked me—I was angry for Vittoria, on behalf of her. I imagined her changing the baby's diapers while Massimo slept in, waking in the night to check if the baby was breathing, staying up late to fret about how she would teach her child to be kind. I thought about her crying when she couldn't get the baby to stop crying. I thought about her thinking through all the minor logistics, the timing and temperature of the bottles, the naps, the fevers, the doctor's visits. And I found that I no longer had any resentment or hatred toward her. In fact, I found the image of Vittoria beautiful, tender, heartbreaking. I knew her; I had been her; I *was* her. She was me. She was looking out the window of her apartment, longing to go outside. But she was stuck. Massimo wouldn't be home until after seven. The baby would be in bed by then, and Massimo would have a calm evening to himself, reading and drinking his amaro in that big leather chair of his. I imagined myself as Vittoria, staring at him. Anger swelling from somewhere deep, eyes like daggers. I wanted to do it for her. I wanted to physically harm Massimo for Vittoria.

"My mother tried to get me to sit down, offering me broth and tea. But I couldn't be bothered with sitting or drinking. I felt almost possessed, as if something had taken hold of me. Without saying anything to my mother or my children, I turned around and left again. It was raining by then, I didn't bring an umbrella, I flew across town in the pouring rain, running back to Sandro's studio. I banged on the door and he let me in. I looked at him viciously, and I felt that I wanted to kill him, as if he were Massimo, or maybe all men. I didn't, of course, but I wanted to. Instead I began yelling, screaming, rushing around in a furious flurry. Then I found a pair of scissors on his table. And I suddenly had this vision that I could ruin him, that I could slash through all his beautiful paintings with these scissors, and that by destroying his art I could destroy some aspect of men in general, that I could wreck their inherent, beautiful confidence."

"And did you?"

"I would have," she said. "I really had gotten to that place where I would have. But Sandro grabbed my wrist and held it, and we stood there like that, locked in a battle of strength, which of course Sandro won."

I was stunned by this image, and my hands flew to my mouth.

"I'm not proud of this, by the way," Renata said. "Sandro didn't do anything wrong, aside from being the man who was nearest to me in my fit of rage. The way he handled me in that moment . . . he had this calm face, his eyebrows cocked, almost like he felt bad for me. In the moment, I became mortified very suddenly; I dropped the scissors and fell to my knees, crying and screaming that I was sorry, that I didn't know what was wrong with me, that I was going mad, forgive me, Sandro, for going mad. He helped me up, hugging me, but then I heard sirens outside. I still don't know whether Sandro had somehow found a way to call the carabinieri when he saw me grab the scissors or if they had been passing by and heard the commotion of my wailing, or maybe saw us fighting through the huge loft windows. Either way, they were suddenly there, taking me outside by the arms. Sandro looked at me like he was sorry as he put me into the back of their car."

"But you didn't do anything. Why would they take you away?"

"I guess they thought I was dangerous. Wielding a weapon. Unhinged, et cetera. In the end, they let me go, under the condition that I get psychiatric help. My mother and the girls had to come pick me up. It was the middle of the night. I thought my mother was going to go berserk, but she didn't, not at all. I remember her coming toward me in the police station and reaching out to me. I collapsed into her arms and wept, and she let me. I didn't remember any other time when she'd hugged me like this. It was as if, in my anger, she finally understood me. Like she was telling me with her body that she had been here, exactly where I was, at some point in her life."

"My god, Renata, I'm so sorry. I never knew you went through this!"

"How could you have? It was a hell of my own making. I didn't want to drag anyone else into it. And I don't want to dwell more on it now. Emily, we must talk about you. Tell me: What are you going to do?"

The question caught me off guard; Renata's story had transported me far enough from my own reality to forget I was pregnant. Now that reality landed back in my hands like a hot stone—I wanted to throw it.

"I have no idea," I said.

"Your boyfriend, this . . . Wes," she said. "Is he a good man?"

"Yes, of course. He's brilliant, and hardworking, and kind. But he's distant. In that way some men can be, you know? Where you wonder if he can really see you, which makes you question whether you're actually there."

I felt a deep anxiety after I said this out loud; I'd never articulated this about Wes before, even to myself.

"Does he want children?"

"We've never talked about it directly—like if *we* want to have children together. I've heard him tell people he wants them, someday, in theory. But I can't really imagine it. I think it would really freak him out. The idea that he'd be responsible for someone else. That he'd have to give up his freedom in some way. He's worked very hard to get where he is, and I think he'd resent having to give any of it up."

"And you? Do you want children?"

At this I felt the tears returning, pushing at the backs of my eyes and then squeezing out of the corners.

"I'm scared," I said, so softly it was almost a whisper.

Renata's hand found my knee. "Of course you are," she said.

"My birth mom," I said, wiping my face with the back of my hand. "She—"

"That's not going to happen to you," Renata said, cutting me off. "You're not going to die. And you're not going to stop writing, either, if that's what you're worried about."

I looked up at her; it was another one of those times when I felt like she could read my mind.

"You'd probably write *better*," Renata said. "Because you'd actually know something. You'd actually have felt something in your life."

"But what about the story you just told?" I said. "About giving up teaching to be with the girls? Didn't you feel like you'd lost yourself? Didn't you feel like *la casalinga*?"

Renata's eyes were glassy, like marbles, and they were filled with her signature elixir of compassion and fire.

"Look," she said. "Being a mother is the most complicated thing I have done in this life. It's as if, overnight, you have lost the self you once knew. She's gone, missing in action. And sometimes—sometimes that is unbearable. And yes, sometimes you are the housewife, you are standing there with the laundry and cursing to yourself, you are ready to scream, you think: How can I exist in this domestic scene when I have all these thoughts, all these things I want to be doing, all these things I want to say! But it was only after I adopted the girls that I began to actually see what life was. Before them, I thought life was about making a splash. I used to like to make a splash—entering a party in a fabulous dress, or saying something that would make the man across from me spit out his olive pit. I thought that to be myself I had to be in a state of constant transformation, that I had to be constantly at odds with what came before me—upturning my family history, the whole history of Italy, with every move I made, every word I said. I thought feminism was about me, you see. My own power."

Renata paused, placed a finger on her closed mouth. I thought she was going to continue, but she settled into the couch in a way that made me think she was done speaking, that she had come to the end of her thought.

"But isn't it, a little bit? About your own power? Isn't that the point?"

Renata smiled sadly.

"Being a feminist is about love," she said. "It's about finding power in love, finding a politics of love. Once I had the girls—well, I finally knew what that meant. A mother's is the deepest love that exists. There's nothing else that comes close. And it completely changed my scholarship. Almost as if I had gone back to school, gotten a new degree."

I studied her from across the couch. I thought about how, when I'd lived here, I'd thought about her in black-and-white terms. She was either loving or not, mine or not, perfect or not. Now I was seeing the messy, colorful painting of her. How so many contrasting strokes could be layered on top of each other inside someone. Of course, I thought. Of course.

She pressed herself up with her hands, as if she were preparing to get up. We had rowed across the lake of our conversation, and now, I knew, we were coming to its shore. I felt sad just thinking about my time with her ending; I almost wanted to reach out and clutch her wrist, tell her not to go to bed, not yet. But Renata stood up, put the cork in the wine.

"The child—my child with Sandro—would have been just your age now," Renata said, her gaze flickering, as if she were both here and transported, closer than ever, but also farther. Then she kissed my forehead and disappeared into her bedroom.

THE ANGELS

The angels on Renata's library ceiling did not laugh at me this time. Perhaps they could sense that I was in too fragile a state to handle being laughed at. I looked up at them looking down at me, tried to shut my eyes, couldn't. I realized that one of the angels was Renata, one of them was Megan, and one of them was me. We were all holding on to each other's wings and frowning. We couldn't let go, or else we'd risk floating in separate directions. But if we kept hanging on, none of us would be able to flap our wings to stay flying. Both options seemed less than ideal.

I desperately wanted to talk to Megan. I wanted to tell her about the dinner I'd just had, how Greta had cooked vegetarian even though I was no longer a vegetarian, and I hadn't had the heart to say anything about it. How the girls went out after dinner now, how adult they were, how it pained me to see these once-innocent creatures morphed into people with responsibilities, with boyfriends, with breasts. I wanted to tell her about Renata's story, about the abortion, the sexy artist, the paintings that had nearly been slashed but that remained intact. How it had felt to sit on the couch with her again, how familiar and real.

I ended up telling these things to Megan the Angel. She was a good listener. She asked thoughtful follow-ups that made me feel understood.

Megan the Angel asked: "Did the story make you want to keep the baby at all?"

I pulled the blanket up to my chin and nodded. I felt cold, and deeply afraid suddenly, wanting to take back the nod. It wasn't the point of Renata's story, I knew. The story hadn't been meant as some kind of threat, that if I aborted my child it would come back later, to haunt me, and I would end up rageful, wielding a pair of scissors. But I couldn't get it out of my mind— she'd offered proof that there would be a future in which this decision would mean something to me, even if I didn't understand it now. I also couldn't shake what she'd said about trying to embody the very masculinity that had kept her down; it felt familiar and true—all the times I'd quelled emotions and gut feelings for the sake of appearing capable or logical or strong. And I thought about what Megan had said during our fight, about the way I made decisions, how I always ran away from the hard ones, waiting for someone else to make them for me. Did I really want only to be free and prolific, like I imagined I did? Or had I been conditioned to prioritize ambition, individualism, myself over any other self? Why did writing a book seem so much more important, legitimate, interesting than creating a human life? And what was this elusive "book," anyway? It didn't exist. In the end, my brain was probably much less interesting than my body. With my body, I was growing a *person*. Why was I working so hard, spinning my wheels, to separate myself from everyone else, when in fact what I had always longed for was togetherness? Wasn't it what I had been searching for my whole life? A home in someone?

"What if I just tried to reframe it?" I said to Megan the Angel. "To consider it more of a blessing than a problem?"

"Please don't use the word 'blessing,'" Megan the Angel said, which made me laugh.

"I didn't mean *blessing* blessing," I said. "I just meant . . . I don't know what I meant. I guess I'm just . . . I guess I'm just wondering if it could be beautiful."

"It would be hella hard," Megan the Angel said.

"I know," I said. "I know it would be."

"I'd be there," Megan the Angel said. "If you would want me to be, that is."

"Of course I would want that," I said.

Swaddled in the comfort of the angels, these women who were caring for me and watching me close my eyes, I sank into a heavy sleep—only to be woken up a few hours later by a rare and distinct and dreamy urge to write.

SYNCHRONIZED BIRTH

In an impossible conflation of time and space, Megan and Renata went into labor with their aborted babies simultaneously. They were admitted into the same hospital on the same day. I could not understand what year it was, or what time of day. I could not discern whether this hospital was in Prato or New York. Did it matter? No! Megan and Renata were in labor! I had to get to the hospital as fast as I could.

This is how Megan went through labor: like a fucking American phoenix. Hair wild and hazel eyes wide with rage, rocking back and forth on all fours, gown splayed open for everyone to see her ass. Megan's backside was usually small and compact but now it loomed, the farting sun that the room orbited around. Everything smelled like body. Metallic blood and stale breath, vagina gunk. She was radiant, moaning, sexual, needy. She wanted water, ice, soda, soup. She wanted the world to spin and bend for her. She wanted Todd to squeeze her hand while she contracted. She wanted Todd to bash his head against the wall while she contracted. She wanted me to get her the fucking nurse. She wanted the fucking epidural. She wanted Todd to give her the fucking epidural. She wanted to cry, she

wanted to cry but she couldn't, she was past crying, she was past screaming even, she was crowning, she was pushing, she was reaching between
her legs and finding *a human head there*, she was wailing with joy, with pain,
with ecstasy, with orgasm, she was coming, the baby was coming, it felt
so fucking good, it felt amazing, and here he was, the hand, the foot, the
penis, the cry, here he was on her chest, her own fluids pooling in his eyes,
here he was, this small thing she'd made, here he was, and no one else
mattered now, and I understood that somehow, I watched her forget me
entirely as she honed in on her child, and so I did her a favor and I left.

I went to Renata's labor room, which was just down the hall.

This is how Renata went through labor: like a plant that opened with
the sun. All night she had been closed, quiet but for some low moaning,
but with the day's light came her readiness, her unfurling, her electric and
determined energy, and she dilated consistently for four hours, centimeter
by centimeter, until, around noon, she was fully open, the sun from the
window beating down onto her vagina, out of which a human foot was
emerging like a stamen, and the doctors, white-faced suddenly, became
frenzied, as if they had never seen such a plant, as if this were an entirely
new species, how could they not have noticed it before, they wondered,
that this plant's stamen was foot-shaped rather than head-shaped? They
turned into a small militia of plant scientists, gathering around the foot.
Should they cut her open now? Too risky. Should they try for the breech
birth? But what about the shoulders; what if the shoulders didn't fit? Renata moaned. The doctors held their breath. Then all at once the baby
fell out of her: a little girl. The doctors breathed out. Renata yelled. But
then there was a problem with the baby, and even though she couldn't see
the baby, Renata knew there was a problem, because she couldn't hear
her crying, and they always cried, they cried right away, but hers was
silent.

A puddle of fluids on the bedsheet. An unnecessary plastic crib, being
wheeled away. Renata lying on her back, all the life sucked from between
her legs. A fury. A gash. A pair of scissors.

I didn't know how to comfort Renata. I stood by her bed and waited
for her to need me. But she, too, seemed oblivious to my presence, ab-
sorbed in her own private hell of loss. Her placenta had slid out and left
a large dark stain on her gown. I began to scrub at the stain with a cloth
I found in a bucket of soapy water. I rubbed more and more aggressively,
as if cleaning the mess could help at all. I dipped the cloth back into the
water and splashed it onto the hospital gown. I kept scrubbing, scrubbing.
It wasn't fair. The stain wouldn't lift. No matter how hard you tried, you
couldn't clean up other people's messes. You couldn't erase their pain.
Renata's baby— or was it my baby?—was dead. I heard Megan's baby—
or was it my baby?—crying from his room down the hall. He screamed
as if the world was ending. Maybe it was, or maybe it had just begun, or
maybe those were the same thing.

LONELY BEAUTY

When I woke up, my body ached as if I had been run over. My brain
felt cracked open, confused. The angels smiled down on me lovingly. I
touched my stomach, as if to check if anything was there. Nothing was, of
course, aside from the regular paunch under my belly button. My throat
was very dry, as if I had been breathing stale hospital air. My notebook
was splayed open beside me. When I flipped through, I saw that Renata
had met Megan in my pages, that the stories I'd been dwelling on for so
long had finally converged in the bloody mess of a birth scene.

Renata was already gone when I went out into the living room; she
was teaching her feminist film course this morning. I had the day to myself, before we all met again for a final meal that evening. In the kitchen,
Renata's smell lingered. I made myself an espresso, drank it while looking
out at the street. Then I went into Renata's room and touched the things
on her dresser: old-fashioned bone hairbrush, gold earrings shaped like
flowers, silver-framed photos of her and the girls at the beach in Naples,

in the town where the girls were born, the town of my mother's whale, the town I had run away to one winter with the silly thought that I might find something intrinsic to my mother or myself, only to find myself in bed with some terribly boyish man, cackling on his twin hostel cot. I thought about leaving the locket, which I'd packed in my toiletry bag, on the dresser, but decided not to—I'd promised Renata I'd give it to Greta at the right moment, and this wasn't it, I somehow knew. When I caught my reflection in the mirror, I had the strange sensation that some of Renata's features had blended with mine, that in an off-kilter way, around the eye sockets, maybe, I looked like her. I made a face at myself, baring my teeth. Who was I kidding? I didn't look like anybody.

I dressed myself and headed outside, Renata's gate clicking closed behind me. Via de' Poeti was familiar and clean and cool, dark with the shade from the red buildings. The seamstress who worked out of her house across the street was batting a rug outside. She waved at me like I'd never left, and I waved back, knowing that tomorrow I would leave yet again. There was a lump in my throat. As I entered the market, the bustle of people and food swelling around me, I had a viciously clear thought: I did not want to go back. I wanted to stay here, with Renata and Greta and Bene and the seamstress across the street. I had never known this to be true before, but it felt clear as day now. Bologna, however lonely it had been, was the place I'd felt most like a part of a family, even if it had only been for a few months. Would I ever feel that way again? Would Wes ever be able to make me feel that way?

I dug for my phone in my bag, texted Wes. *Two more dayyyyyyyys*, I typed.

Until I smooch your faaacccceeeeee, Wes typed back.

It should have made me feel better but didn't. He didn't know the whole story. Would he still want to smooch my face if he knew I was pregnant? *Seventy percent insane*, I heard him saying in my mind, about someone else's child.

I walked over to piazza Santo Stefano. There was the man who sold chestnuts. There was the bongo guy. There was the woman in the Prada loafers, the same loafers I had written about for the department store just a few weeks earlier, which now seemed like a lifetime ago. *Pebbled calf leather with gold-tone hardware.* It felt impossible that I had written that, and that I would continue to write things like it when I returned. The heavy stone of reality lodged in my throat, sank down into my chest and then farther into my belly; going back to that office sounded like the most depressing thing I could imagine.

What if Megan had been right? What if by failing to make any decisions at all, I had, by default, made all the wrong ones? What if the security I'd thought I'd been working toward—my cushy job, my relationship with Wes—was just an illusion? What if Wes only loved a version of me that wasn't the real one? What if he and I had simply been seeing what we wanted to see in each other this whole time, caught in the narratives of the fantasies we'd each prized?

I thought about a night the previous winter when Megan had joined me to attend a group photography show Wes had been a part of, at a tire shop turned gallery in Bushwick. The photograph Wes had submitted was one of his New Orleans pictures, of a woman wading through waist-deep water, carrying her small baby above the surface, her arms clearly straining from the weight. Megan and I had stood in a corner, commenting on people's outfits—that winter it was cropped pants with geriatric tennis shoes—and keeping to ourselves, watching Wes bask in his artist glory. He shined in these situations, his long lashes batting with admiration as he talked to people whose work he loved, praising them openly, as Wes was apt to do. I remember adoring him in that moment, feeling proud of him, until Megan said something that threw me off.

"Does he ever introduce you to these people?" she asked.

It felt like a slap in the face. I hadn't known that I'd wanted to be introduced until right then, when she said it.

"I think it's an industry thing," I said. "Where they just geek out over apertures or whatever. I'd rather talk shit in the corner with you."

I had tried to brush off the feeling I'd had after that, that Wes wasn't proud enough of me to introduce me to his photography friends, but it returned to me now. I felt the doubt again, stirring in my stomach. What if I didn't know Wes the way I thought I did? Could any of us ever know each other all the way? Was a complete love possible? A love that took every person's truth into account?

I needed to stop. To turn around before I went too far down this anxious path. I decided to distract myself by spending the day soaking in all the lonely beauty Bologna had to offer. I went to the Salaborsa, the library off piazza Maggiore, and looked at the Etruscan ruins that had been preserved beneath the glass floor. I liked walking on top of this very old world, which reminded me that I was no more than an extra in the never-ending movie of history, that I barely mattered. I walked to La Piella and looked through the tiny hole in the wall that revealed an old waterway, allowed myself to feel depressed about the brown color of the water. I went to the record stores I remembered loving on via del Pratello, where the smell of hash mixed with tobacco hung heavily and the music was uncomfortably loud. I cried in one of the red phone booths, for no reason and all the reasons. When my sobs turned to sniffles I comforted myself with a pleasant thought: I had one more night under the angels, and dinner with Renata and the girls was just an hour away.

DUE INSIEME

On my way to the train station the next morning, I felt ravenous, which seemed impossible considering the large quantities of pasta I'd eaten the night before with Renata and the girls; we'd gone to a quiet trattoria on their street and had an uneventful, cozy dinner that had left me feeling deeply satisfied on all levels. I still didn't want to leave, but I also knew I needed to, and the angels, when I looked up at them from under Renata's quilts after dinner, had reminded me that maybe, possibly, things would all turn out okay. As I trudged down strada Maggiore with my suitcase, I spotted Pizzaria Due Torri, a place the abroad kids used to go to late at night, and decided I couldn't resist: I ordered two slices with anchovies. The young woman who was serving the pizza smiled and said, "Due insieme?"

"What?" I said. I knew what it meant—*two together?*—but it caught me off guard, and I had thought for some reason she was asking if I was eating for two, or ordering for two people. I rolled the words around in my mind, and then in my mouth. *Due insieme. Two, together.*

"*Sì,*" I said. "*Insieme.*"

The woman's bright smile flashed again, and I had the feeling that she knew something about my pregnancy, though I reasoned that she couldn't possibly. She looked to be about my age, and from the grayish circles under her pretty eyes I assumed she must have a small child at home, a person she loved so much it wore her out. I wondered who was looking after her baby now, as she served pizza at the *due insieme* place. I imagined her mother, *la nonna*, feeding the baby spoonfuls of yogurt. It took a village, they said. But I didn't have one. I only had Wes. Wes and I probably wouldn't have this baby, but if we did we would be all alone with it. Maybe the angels were wrong. Maybe things wouldn't be okay.

The woman stacked one of the two on top of the other, anchovy sides in, like a pizza sandwich. I thanked her and paid, then ate the pizza standing up, dripping grease onto the sidewalk. I watched a few pigeons peck at my grease stains. It was amazing to eat. The sun shifted slightly in the sky, so that it suddenly shone out from behind the famous *due torri*, the two towers at the end of the main avenue, one of which was tall and skinny, one of which was shorter and leaning. I felt pity and affection for the leaning tower, which I knew was a symbol of failure—the towers had been built in a power feud between two families in the 1100s, and it had clearly been the loser—and though I knew I needed to get to the train station soon, which was in the opposite direction, I walked toward it. For a second, it was as if someone else were with me, walking alongside me, looking at the same glowing, leaning silhouette. I felt a warmth in my right hand, as if someone were holding it. But who? It was just me. The sun shifted behind the shaft of the losing tower; a bit of oil dripped from my fingers and stained the old stone beneath me. I was alone and also full, expanding. I needed to get home. I turned away from the towers and into the piazza, took one more drink from Neptune's maidens' breasts, and then I left.

HOLLOW

Inexplicably, Megan was not on the plane. It seemed like too grand a gesture, I thought, to have missed or changed her flight because of our argument. It made me feel like things were worse than I'd even thought they were. I'd held on to an unarticulated hope that we'd figure things out on the way home, that we'd convince another kind man to switch seats with one of us again, then drink enough tiny wines to become gushy and forgiving, eventually reaching out across the aisle to touch each other's hands. But her absence now was total: an empty seat, an empty feeling in my body. Though empty wasn't the right word, not exactly. I thought of the word *hollow*. As I waited for the plane to take off, I typed it into my Italian translation app. *Vuoto*: void, vacant, bare, vacuous. *Sordo*: deaf, dull, impervious, voiceless. That was it, I thought. All of those things, hollow in all of those ways.

PROS AND CONS

The city was still cold when I got back, which made me feel as if no time had passed, when psychologically speaking it had been a lifetime since I had taken the L train to Lorimer Street and made the ten-block trek to my little basement apartment. The streets were both familiar and foreign, the same way the Bologna streets had felt when I first arrived, as if I had lived here years and years ago and was just coming back for a visit. There was the gourmet grocery store that had once been a crappy coffee shop. There was the bougie coffee shop that had once been a Puerto Rican grocery store. There was the houseplant and candle store that had once been a comic book and incense store. Everything in Brooklyn just kept giving birth to other things, a vicious and endless cycle of renovation that spit people and businesses out in its wake. The idea made me feel exhausted.

Wes was waiting for me outside my apartment when I got home, armed with a fistful of bodega daffodils. His ignorant cheerfulness made me want to cry.

"I have to tell you something," I said, taking the flowers, pressing them to my chest.

"Tell me," he said. He kissed my forehead.

"I'm pregnant," I said. I could feel my eyes bulging with the pressure of tears.

Wes's face fell.

"Fuck," I heard him say, and an electric sadness coursed through my chest. "Are you kidding? From the one time we weren't careful?"

I nodded. A tear broke loose and fell down my cheek and I didn't wipe it away.

"I'm sorry," he said, wiping the tear for me. "I just wasn't expecting this. I'm just . . . in shock. Here, let's go inside."

I clumsily dragged my suitcase down the stoop steps and through the basement hallway. I sat at the little breakfast table; Wes grabbed himself a beer.

"I wanted to tell you when we talked," I said. "But it seemed weird over the phone."

"Yeah," Wes said. He had gone into his own head in the way that he could; I could tell he was trying to make sense of it all, comprehend it like he could comprehend a photograph, always knowing exactly what he'd have to do to edit the image to his liking.

"I'm assuming you don't want to have it," I said.

Wes's eyes shot up and met mine; I read his look as hopeful. "Is that what you want?"

"I honestly don't know what I want. Part of me thinks having a baby is creative suicide, the worst possible decision, totally insane. The other part . . . I don't even know where the other part is coming from, but it's the opposite feeling."

Wes nodded, clearly agitated. "I think we need to think. We need to really think it through. Maybe we should make a list. Pros and cons."

"Pros and cons? This isn't an off-site retreat."

"What's an off-site retreat?"

"You know, where they take all the company bigwigs and make them do icebreakers."

"And teach them team-building techniques that are actually just ways to manipulate their employees."

"Exactly."

We smiled at each other. I felt a little bit better already, making jokes with Wes. Maybe this didn't have to be such a big deal; maybe we could navigate it together, and no matter which way it went we would manage. He took a piece of paper out of my printer and wrote PROS and CONS at the top.

"Okay, pros," he said.

"Continuing the human race," I said. He wrote it down.

"Cuteness?" I said. He wrote it down.

"Would probably be a cool kid," he said.

"Loving something more than yourself," I said.

Wes solemnly wrote down what I'd said. Under it he also wrote: *Tiny feet*. This made me smile; I imagined the molecules inside me that would somehow, magically and naturally, form into miniature toes.

"Okay, cons," he said. This was easier. He wrote without asking me: *Careers, sanity, sleep, money, social life.*

I laughed when he finished, because the list was kind of funny and it made me feel lighter about things. But I also knew this wasn't the way to make this decision. I wanted him to think about this with as much intensity as I had. I'd flown over oceans, conferred with the angels, drank from Neptune's maidens' breasts, all while listening to my biological clock, ticking forcefully and incessantly between my ears. Wes had just learned about this right now.

"Why don't we think about it for a few days," I said, "and then talk about it again. See how we're both feeling."

Wes nodded. He seemed nervous suddenly, as if more time would give things more weight, and he didn't want more weight. As if he'd actually thought this could be as simple as a pros and cons list.

"Okay," he said. "Yeah, that's a good idea."

I nodded, too; we were both sitting there nodding. But inside I was screaming. I felt angry, suddenly, that I was the one with the child inside me. Either decision, in the end, would impact me more than him. I would "lose" or "keep" the baby. My body would change or not change. Both of our worlds would shift, but it would be mine that would explode. A head would emerge from between my legs. Or else it wouldn't.

TERMINATION

I couldn't sleep at all that night, the pros and cons list vibrating in my mind, Wes curled up against me like a long-lashed puppy. In the morning, I was exhausted from the jet lag and sleeplessness, overcome with the stress of this decision, and in the throes of an impossible bout of morning sickness. After puking twice in the toilet and once in the shower, I called the head of HR at my office, a robot lady named Angela, to tell her I needed to take the day off.

"The thing is," Angela said in a distant, nasally way, "you've already gone over your allotted number of vacation days, and I see here that you've also maxed out on sick days, which I'm assuming you also used as vacation days? I could put you on probation for this, but I won't because I'm decent. You'll need to report into the office today."

"So if I don't come in today . . . what happens?" I said.

"You'd be terminated," Angela said. I imagined the bit of lipstick that had dragged outside of her lip line.

"Terminated," I repeated. The word lodged in my throat. It was the same word doctors used for abortions. If I was terminated from my job, I knew, I would not have the resources to have the child that I had thus far failed to terminate but might or might not terminate soon. I felt as if I were walking through a battleground, with people throwing the word *terminate* at me, hoping to obliterate me with it.

With much resentment, I dressed myself as neatly as I could, trying to make up for the bags under my eyes. I chose a prim collared top with a black skirt and silver loafers. I was seething on the subway, barely managing my nausea, watching the people around me supplement—or perhaps supplant—their consciousnesses with content from their various devices. No one looked at each other. No one reached their hand out and put it on someone else's hand, told them it was going to be okay. We were each alone with our own pros and cons, zooming toward our cubicles, where we would labor for the next eight hours, shoving our personal baggage waaaay down, swallowing it when it rose in our throats like more vomit, so we could email, email, email until seven in the evening, at which point the sun would have lowered behind the tall buildings and our spirits would be sufficiently crushed and we would step back on the human conveyor belt of the subway that would deliver us to our next inhumane obligations: thirty minutes of cardio at the gym; drinks with someone we'd been flaking on for months; feeding ourselves in ways that prioritized convenience over nourishment, speed over satisfaction, so that we could fall asleep watching the streaming service of our choice and do it all over again the next day.

I walked up the crowded subway stairs. Just as I emerged onto the sidewalk, I dropped my iced coffee by accident. A man in a suit stopped to help me pick it up, shoveling the ice back into the cup as if it could be saved. It was the Chief Marketing Officer, one of the slick-haired guys at the top whom I'd lumped in with all the other slick-haired guys at the top. Though I knew who he was, I was positive he wouldn't recognize me.

"Oh dear," the Chief Marketing Officer said, cradling the dirty ice.

"Oh, you don't have to do that," I said.

He stood, handed me the cup. Then he held up a finger in a way that meant: *Wait here for one second.* He left me there on the sidewalk while he ran into a bodega on the corner. He emerged moments later with a new iced coffee, which he presented to me with a boyish grin.

"Wow," I said. "Thank you so much."

"It's nothing," he said. "Truly."

"It's something," I said. Because it was. The Chief Marketing Officer had reminded me that we were all just people, picking up each other's gross ice, trying to be good to each other. Together, we walked into the vacuum of the office building, accepting its freezing yet oddly comforting embrace. Before he dipped into his corner office, he turned and smiled. "I might get this wrong, but . . . Emily?" I grinned and told him yes.

THE YELL

My work family zoomed toward me. Reed practically had to shield me from Faith, who went in for a religious embrace. Hans tossed me an air kiss when I saw him in the hall. Fiona dabbed my wrists with Calm blend essential oil, which she thought I'd probably need after seeing all the emails that had amassed in my inbox.

I tucked into my cubicle and got down to business. It felt as if I had walked into a life-warping machine and then been spit back out into my previous reality. So much had changed and nothing had. Megan was gone; I had a secret tiny human inside me; they had switched out my office chair and this one was worse. And yet under the sterile lights of corporate America everything was just the same as it had always been. I had thousands of emails, and I began to sort through them one by one. I took calm sips of coffee from my tall cup, until I wondered if I should be drinking coffee, just in case. I googled it and it said it was okay to have a certain small number of ounces that I couldn't compute. I kept sipping, scrolling, responding. A bland spell was cast on me, and the feeling of safe productivity settled my nerves. For the first time in days, I felt okay about things. My nausea subsided. I wrote a headline for the Kids catalog. *Here comes the sun.* I wrote ten product descriptions. Easy. I could do this.

Then a poem appeared in my inbox. It was called "Paula Becker to Clara Westhoff," by Adrienne Rich. It was a long poem, and at first I didn't feel like I should read all of it because I had too much work to do. But as soon as my eyes drifted past the first few lines and landed on this one—"The moon rolls in the air. I didn't want this child."—I knew I would stay with it, embezzle whatever time it took to read it in full.

The poem took the form of a letter or confession from Paula Modersohn-Becker, who I found out through a Google search was a German painter, to her friend Clara Westhoff, a sculptor and the wife of Rainer Maria Rilke. Paula is pregnant. She is unhappy. She knows the child will be her responsibility and not her husband's. She is searching for inspiration everywhere but cannot find it. She recalls the inspired days she and Clara spent in the studio together, and meeting in Paris years later, when they were both married. And then the narrator, Paula, confesses that she had dreamed of dying as she gave birth to the child.

I shuddered, dreaming of my mother giving birth to me.

Was this what I was afraid of? Becoming my mother as she became nothing?

The poem moved on with more hopefulness, landing back with the relationship between Paula and Clara. Paula can, through the cracks in her desperation, see a future full of work and love, a future with Clara in

it, Clara who can "hear all I say and cannot say." If Clara can hear her—
if *someone can just hear her*—she will be okay.

In one of those disorienting perspective shifts I'd experienced only a
few times, the characters in the poem became the characters of my life.
Paula was my birth mother, her existence erased by her own child. Paula
was also me: full of herself kicking her own insides, fully aware of the
pit of her future and yet emboldened by it, staring it down, knowing she
will plunge, with part fury and part relief. Full of love for Clara, who was
Megan, of course, who even now, after so long without real contact, could
hear me saying all I could not say. I clicked the X in the corner of the
poem and it disappeared from my screen. I had tears in my eyes. I knew
right then that I was going to keep the baby.

Holy shit, I was going to keep the baby.

There it was, clear as day.

I was going to keep this baby.

Can you hear me, Megan? I am going to keep this baby.

I stood up from my desk and rushed through the halls to the elevator.
I needed to get outside. I swung through the revolving door and onto the
sidewalk, where spring had announced herself flamboyantly. Corporate
tulips stood at attention in every office planter box. Everyone in Herald
Square was either sneezing or recovering from a sneeze. The world was
one big damp hallelujah, and I felt like part of it suddenly, as if I had
grown roots that connected me directly to the earth. I began to walk away
from the office building, through the hell of Herald Square and down to
Twenty-Sixth Street, where I turned right and made my way into Chel-
sea. I did not feel happy, but I felt strong. My decision stayed with me, firm
and close. The cherry trees were on fire with blossoms, and some of them
rained down onto my hair.

I kept walking—too far of a walk for a workday, I knew—until I
found myself at the park on the edge of Manhattan, where it scrapes up
against the Hudson River. I stood at the railing and stared out at New
Jersey. I closed my eyes. I didn't want to look at New Jersey's tall buildings.

I only wanted fresh air, pink blossoms, earth under my feet. I had a primal urge for the natural; I wanted nothing man-made or false. I wanted to yell really loud for some reason, but I didn't want to attract attention, so instead I clutched my hands and yelled out at half volume, sending a noncommittal *ahhhhhhhhhhhhh!* soaring out over the river.

My phone buzzed in my pocket just as my yell ended. It was a calendar alert for the weekly department-wide meeting. A pulse of fear ran through me; I couldn't be late. I speed-walked back the way I'd come, now tense with haste. Finally I was back, sweaty and flustered, stuffing myself into an elevator packed with men in suits, no doubt returning from one of their long lunches. I used my magnetic key card to unlock the gates to my financial existence. In our largest conference room, under the blasting rectangles of light, Todd welcomed me back from my trip.

"You look different," he said, not unkindly, as we settled in around the conference table.

"I haven't changed anything," I said.

"No, there's something," Todd said. "You look . . . brighter or something."

I averted my eyes, looked down at my hands.

"I meant it as a compliment," Todd said.

Now my hands were shaking for some reason, and tears were forming in my eyes. I felt a strange desire for Todd to hug me, for him to take me into his arms right there in the conference room and tell me I was going to be okay. I wanted him to see me, like he'd seen me that one day on the ferry, to ask me what I wanted—what I had once wanted and what I wanted now. The fact that he would not hug me, that he would never think to, was perhaps what made me want him to. I coveted his freedom from the tethers and burdens of others. It made me see myself as the emotionally porous person I was, letting everyone else's story mingle with mine and contaminate it. But Todd was pure in this way; by his calculations he had no binding obligations to anyone, not even his own wife, and this made me feel strangely safe with him, as if I were a sieve and he was a bowl I could set myself in, covering all the holes. But instead he clapped his hands once, which resulted in the quieting of the noisy room. And just like that I was irrelevant. We had to discuss which woman should be the face of our next campaign: the one with the well-placed freckles, or the one with the different-colored eyes? Different was the new perfect, Todd reminded the room. We were looking for a woman who looked only like herself.

THE DECISION

I texted Wes to ask him if he'd meet me at the Thai place after work. The Thai place was our place; we'd gone there most Friday nights since we'd been together. We always sat at the same table in the back corner if it was cold out, and on the roof, right under the Williamsburg Bridge, if it was warm. Wes always paid, despite the fact that his money situation was erratic and he made, on average, much less than I did. This made me feel taken care of in an old-fashioned way and nervous in a new-fashioned way: I was always vaguely worried about Wes's money, if he would have enough of it in any given month; if and when his credit card would be declined. Still, I was more protective of his ego than his bank account, and so I always let him buy me my eleven-dollar noodles.

Probably warm enough for the roof, Wes texted back.

I got there before he did and went straight upstairs. No one else was on the roof yet. Below me, I watched a crew of construction workers dig the street up with their shovels and jackhammers. In the yard of the bar below, a guy was talking loudly about how IPAs were "chick beers." *WOMEN LOVE HOPS*, he said, which made me smile. It was something Megan and I would have repeated for weeks if we'd overheard it together. Above me, the J train screeched toward the Williamsburg Bridge, gearing up for its loud, slow ride across the water. Wes got there just as the construction crew took their cigarette break, arriving in a cloud of their smoke.

"Hi, you," Wes said, kissing my forehead.

"Hi, you," I said.

Below us at the bar, a group of drunk people sang happy birthday to David.

"I had a birthday at that bar once," Wes said. "I think it was twenty-four."

"I can't even imagine," I said, "what it feels like to be twenty-four."

"All ambition and Maker's Mark," he said.

"For me it was performed malaise and crop tops," I said.

We were stalling. Bringing up the past so that we could live in it a while longer without thinking about the future. But we both knew what I'd called him here to talk about. I decided to get it over with.

"Okay, so I know we said we'd wait until Saturday to decide," I said. "But then I read this poem and it made me realize all these things, and . . . I know it makes no sense and it's probably crazy, but I think I want to have this baby. And I want you to know that if you don't want to be a part of it, that's fine, I can do it by myself."

Wes saw that I was about to cry, and he pulled me close to him before I could start. He was good at this. He was good at pulling close at the right moment, and this, to my mind, counted for a lot. He rubbed my back with his hand and kissed my head. It was a long while before he said anything, and in the silence I traveled deep into the woods of future regret. What if I did have to do this by myself, but I couldn't? I thought about that quiz I'd started in Italy: *Are you willing to compromise some of your own autonomy and personal agenda for the sake of your child?* What if I failed at motherhood like I had failed at becoming a writer, or if motherhood was what kept me from becoming a writer in the future? What if I wasn't cut out for it in the first place, and was as selfish as Megan had said I was?

"You can't do this by yourself," Wes finally said, into my hair.

"Thanks for the vote of confidence," I said. "But I'm serious. You're allowed to not want this. I would totally understand if you didn't. I'm giving you an out."

Wes took a big breath, releasing me. A gust of wind blew a flap of his hair over his eyes. I honestly had no idea what he was going to say. But just as he began to speak, a train screamed toward us, the sound eclipsing Wes's words as he said them.

I can't hear you, I mouthed.

"I don't want an out," he said, too loudly now that the train had moved farther into Brooklyn, carrying its sound with it. "If this is what you want, we'll do it. I'll do it."

I smiled. I wondered if I could trust this. If I could trust Wes to mean what he was saying, or if I should take more heed of what Megan had said. Was there room in Wes's life for this? Would he make room?

"Are you sure?" I said.

"Not at all," Wes said. But his eyes looked sincere and solid, and so I let myself feel happy for a second. Maybe we could do this. Maybe this would be good.

A gorgeous waiter with a tall hairstyle appeared on the roof, emerging from below as if by magic. He asked if we'd like anything to drink. Wes ordered a beer; I ordered a seltzer. It felt strange and right not to get a drink, a firm commitment to my decision—*our* decision now—by way of self-denial.

"Oh and I think we already know what we want," Wes said to the waiter, who jotted down our usual order: drunken noodles for Wes, pad see ew for me.

"Wow," Wes said when the waiter left. "So I guess we're doing this." He lifted his face to the sky, as if he thought the heavens might send something down to save him from his choice.

"I guess so," I said.

Then Wes looked at me with a specific kind of admiration that I'd never seen before, kind of squinty.

"Only you could read a *poem* and convince yourself to have a kid," he said.

I smiled. *He sees me*, I thought, with enormous relief. The noodles arrived shortly after that: warm and familiar, exactly like they'd always been.

GODDESS

The public loved my pregnancy. As my belly grew, I morphed into a goddess. Strangers touched my midsection, cooing over it. Passersby regarded me as if I had strength, beauty, and pathos. People nodded approvingly as I waddled. I parted seas of subway passengers with my girth and glow. Grandmothers stopped me on the street to tell me how their daughters were pregnant with their second, or their third. I was ushered to the front of lines, given extra helpings and all kinds of advice. Questions flew at me from out of the blue. Was it a boy or a girl? Did it kick or was it calm? Did it have wings or hooves? Hahahaha. One woman, on a crowded subway, yelled across the train car to ask: "ARE YOU GOING TO HAVE A VAGINAL BIRTH?" I nodded slightly, hoping to express without having to verbally reply that a vaginal birth was indeed what I was hoping for. Though to me, at that point, hope seemed irrelevant. To desire or wish for anything at this stage felt absurd, which made me feel absurd, considering that pre-pregnancy, I'd had nothing but desires. Desire to make something beautiful. Desire to be beautiful. Desire to love and be loved, to read and be read, to announce myself to the world and have the world fold me kindly in, as if it had been waiting.

But the public gave zero shits about my desires, it turned out; they just loved the fact that I was going to become a mom. Moms were so pure! Moms were so nice! Moms made snacks! Moms had milk in their bulging tits! Moms held down the fort! Moms listened! Once I became one, the public conjectured, I would rapidly embody all these things, as if by pushing a separate self out of my vagina I might lose my original self in the process. And who cared if that self was gone? The public did not. That self was nothing compared to the creation of new life! Wasn't this the entire *purpose* of a woman, after all? To birth, and to mother? Wasn't this why women were *invented*? Without this capability, what even *were* their capabilities? What were they worth? Who would they be? This was *it*, the public said. This was the pinnacle of womanhood, on display for the world to see. They rubbed my belly as if it were a Magic 8 Ball, asking wholesome, prying questions. To all of them I delivered the same answer: CANNOT PREDICT NOW.

BIRTH CLASS

Birth class was not optional. Not in this day and age. Not in Brooklyn. It felt as mandatory as recycling, to go to a weekend-long course during which you would learn the evils of the hospital system and the powers of your own female body. I had convinced myself, or had been convinced, that if I did not sign up for birth class I would end up being the kind of mother who didn't keep track of the sign-ups for picture day and whose kid ended up pictureless as a result, the kind of mom who gave her kids Cheetos because she lacked the conviction to say no. I felt that if I did not attend birth class, I might come across as a lazy and unprincipled pregnant person, the kind of woman who cared little about natural birth, who just wanted the fucking drugs.

Even though I *was* this person, the person who wanted the drugs, I bull-dozed my way down Manhattan Avenue, stomach first, to arrive at what felt like an urban ashram to attend the weekend-long seminar. I walked through a palace of healing crystals and an artisanally tie-dyed curtain into a room that was as dark as a womb, filled with women and their husbands. Wes had wanted to come, but he'd gotten an assignment to photograph a protest in the city at the last minute, so I was here alone. I moved my lonely body through the space, searching for where I might sit, until a large inflatable yoga ball rolled toward me. I sat down on it. I bounced.

We went around the room and introduced ourselves. The teacher explained that she herself was a doula, that she'd been present for over two hundred births, and that she had five children of her own. Then she got right down to business. She pushed a doll out of a fake pelvis. She reached a hand through a ten-centimeter-wide hole in a piece of wood. She turned on a video that had been shot in 1968 of a woman giving birth in a wooden bathtub in an open-air house in California. She explained that hospitals loved money, and that doctors hated waiting, and that once we were in the system we'd be there for good. Don't let them give you an IV unless it's medically necessary, she warned. Once you have an IV? You're tethered. And she wanted us to move! She wanted us to squat! She wanted us on all fours, if it was more comfortable! She wanted us to walk! To bounce, like we were bouncing now! She wanted us to relax our pelvic floors. I imagined my pelvic floor was the opposite of a glass ceiling. A kind of mushy, quicksand-style floor that, if relaxed properly, would allow my child to pass through it easily, and then slurp back just as quickly, retracting itself. She warned that none of this would be possible if we didn't have someone to advocate for us during the birthing process.

"Who here has a doula?" she asked the group. The women around me raised their hands; their male partners did not. This told me that it had been the women in each of these couples who had researched and sought out their doulas, met with them and signed them on. The men had not done these things, and therefore did not feel comfortable claiming with a raised hand that they had a doula. They did not have anything. They were just wiggling sperms who'd been forced to spend their weekend attempting to visualize the unimaginable and inevitable widening of their partner's nether regions.

"And you?" the doula said, training her gaze on me. I didn't know what to say. I had not thought about a doula, let alone arranged for one. I shrugged. "I guess I should look into it," I said. "But I just kind of feel like I'd want someone I know there."

The doula morphed in my mind; suddenly she became a doula of empathy. Instead of pulling new bodies into the world, she dove *into* existing bodies, inhabiting their physical being and their psyche, and presently she dove into mine.

"What about Megan?" this imaginary empathy doula inquired.

I swallowed. "What about Megan?" I said.

"I think Megan would make an excellent birth partner," she said. "You feel comfortable with her, and she's pragmatic yet loving. She can make you laugh. These are ideal qualities for a birth partner, even if they aren't trained."

"I'll think about it," I said, but the truth was I already had. I'd already acknowledged that the only person I wanted by my side while my child made its way into the world, aside from Wes, was Megan. How I'd already imagined her cheering me on from the sidelines, *Push, biatch! Push!* And how I imagined all the snacks she'd buy for the hospital room: her favorite granola bars and coconut water and, because she was a badass who was not a slave to natural ingredients, a huge bag of Doritos. But I knew it was just one of my fantasies. Megan and I hadn't talked at all since Italy—almost six months ago now.

The woman bouncing next to me burped and excused herself. She was very beautiful, with dark straight hair, and the burp seemed incongruous with the rest of her presentation. She wore a luxurious sweater that I wanted to nuzzle my face into. I thought about how Megan would talk shit about the sweater. She was good with brands, and she'd be able to tell that this particular sweater had cost this woman $420 because it was hand knit in Spain using eco-friendly wool. She would talk about how ridiculous it was, these signifiers we used to show our status and our wealth, and how this birth class was just another one of them. "We spend so much time trying to feel good about our decisions," she'd say. "Listening to all these podcasts and researching naturally dyed fabrics and meditating or whatever, and it's all just another way of saying that we belong to this elite group of educated New Yorkers who can afford to listen and learn the same way. This birth class is like a fancy car. The Mercedes-Benz of vagina monologues."

The doula continued with her scheduled programming; she'd transformed back into a regular doula in my mind. We learned that Pitocin
was our enemy and C-sections were a last resort. We were taught that we
were beautiful goddesses who were part of a long lineage of women who
had all given birth. We were told to pack coconut water in our hospital
bags (yeah, Megan *knew* that) and coconut oil for our lips, and lavender
spray for the room. If we could get away with it, the doula told us, we
should try to plug in Christmas lights in the labor room. Everything was
better with good lighting, she said. The pregnant women around me, for
the first time all day, let out a twinkling of little laughs.

WES ESPECIALLY

During my pregnancy, Wes and I lived in what felt like a womb of our
own. I wasn't drinking, so we didn't go out, which Wes didn't mind as it
gave him more time to work in the evenings. We decided I would move
into the loft before the baby came, and gave Kasper notice that in a couple of months, he'd need to find somewhere else to park his DJ booth.
He was sad to leave but happy for us, and Wes had started calling him
Uncle Kasper. We cooked dinner together and watched movies on Wes's
projector. Wes talked to the baby through my belly and played it songs on
his old thrift store guitar. He accompanied me to my many appointments,
watching in awe as the doctor shed light on my insides, pointing out the
features of the ghostlike blob dwelling in the dark circle of my uterus. It
seemed we'd both firmly gotten on board with this new development, and
the energy between us changed and brightened: this person inside me
was our collective project. We told different versions of the same story
to various friends. We were totally surprised, like freaking, but now we're
happy about it. Unprepared, yeah, but really excited, actually. Right, I
mean nothing can prepare you, that's true. My friend who's a mom said
that being surprised is actually easier. Because you don't have to analyze

everything so much, you know? Not really thinking about marriage, no. Not our thing. We were totally ambivalent about the sex. But then Emily basically knew already; she'd had a sense from the start. And we were so happy when the doctor confirmed it was a girl. Wes especially.

BODY

The lips of my vagina swelled like raisins left in water. I emitted goo. My sweat glands erupted, creating a stench I had never before smelled, something between skunk and persimmon. My feet swelled two whole sizes; I was now wearing nines. My face ballooned. My hormones oozed a honey-like happiness. My lips chapped and cracked. I was a more disgusting and happier version of myself. I was more and less beautiful. More and less alive. My feet disappeared, and after that, a whole chunk of my sadness. On a number of occasions, I found myself stopping in the middle of the sidewalk to touch or lean against a particularly beautiful tree, just because it felt so good to touch another living thing.

Uncharacteristically, I didn't worry about writing. I wrote when I could, and when I wasn't writing, I calmly grew a human. I felt my center of gravity shift, both literally and figuratively. As I leaned back to support my weight, I leaned away from my ambition. As my ankles ballooned, my curiosity withered. The bigger my body became, the smaller my ego got. I didn't even miss her, my old self, because this self felt so much *easier*. More convinced of her place in the world, less worried about everything, more easygoing. More like the woman I'd imagined I should be.

During those months, when the light hit the buildings in a certain way, I felt a new dignity, perhaps the kind women had been experiencing for generations before me, forever. There was a point to my existence. I was useful. It was glorious. Or maybe it was me. Perhaps I was glorious.

PART SIX

PAIN

BIRTH STORY

On New Year's Eve, in the middle of the night, in a room full of lights and hands, a human body was extracted from my human body.

There had been thirty-two hours of labor, ten of which were painful and twenty-two of which were pain-free, after I had rounded my back over my large belly to accept a very thick needle into my spine.

At hour thirty-one, a monitor had beeped differently than it had been beeping previously. A team of experts closed in. I was wheeled with businesslike haste into the bright room, cut open with what I imagined to be a large scalpel. I shook violently the whole time. I burned with fever, lurched with nausea. I yelled out, but I don't know what I said. It all seemed to be taking too long, and I remember being afraid that something was going wrong, that there were unforeseen complications, that I was going to die. Wes, in full scrubs and a face shield, looked entirely unfamiliar to me, and his face was white with what I assumed was a terror that rivaled my own.

When they brought my daughter over and held her out for me to see for the first time, I vomited into a pan shaped like a quarter moon, which was too small to contain the vomit and so overflowed onto the floor of the operating room.

My daughter was then taken away, to an area of the room that felt very far from where I was having my stomach sewn up, to have her stomach pumped and an IV inserted and a respirator clasped over her very small nose. She had been strangled by her umbilical cord. She had swallowed some of her own shit.

I vomited again, and then again, and then again.

I was not an American phoenix. I was not a night-blooming flower. I was none of the women in the stories I had written or dreamed or read about birth. It hadn't felt like a story at all, at least not the way I understood stories. Stories were meant to have protagonists whose desires and motivations drove the story forward. I felt like I had been driven over, and was now lying on the ground helplessly, unable to move or get up. My baby was not in my arms or sucking on my breast. She was in a small incubator on a different floor of the hospital, being treated for the trauma that had occurred during her entrance into the world. I tried to imagine what it felt like to be blindsided by the mortal world. To be *delivered*. To experience that blast of light, that painful first inhale, that impulse to cry out—for care, for comfort, for love, for anything that might ease the pain of existing, and then not getting it. It wasn't hard to imagine. I was feeling all of it, too. I was two floors away from my baby, but we were crying out in the same key.

A MOTHER'S HUG, PART ONE

I fell asleep for the first time in forty hours, and I woke up to a dreamy shock. In the chair where Wes had been, the only chair in the hospital room, was Ann. Sitting primly in her blouse and cardigan, reading one of her paperbacks, her long hair pulled back in its signature braid. The presence of someone so familiar and sturdy made my throat close up with emotion. How was she here? I had told her, of course, that I was pregnant, but I hadn't let her know that I was going into labor.

"Wes called when labor started," Ann said, in her low, stern voice, answering my question without my having to ask. "I flew out as fast as I could."

She offered a half smile. Ann's bland energy brought me right back down to earth from where I had been floating, on a sea of dreams and blood.

"When did you get here?" I asked.

"Last night," she said. "I got to see her first breath."

"What?" I said, confused. "You were in the room? How did I not know?"

"Wes convinced the doctors to let me in," Ann said. "I stayed off to the side. And you were in your own world."

Ann leaned in. I could smell my own stale breath and hoped she didn't smell it, too. Ann was a stickler about dental hygiene, and I could hear her scolding me to brush my teeth in my mind. But she didn't say anything about my breath, or what she'd seen in the operating room, which I imagined was the messiest, most horrific thing she'd ever witnessed.

"That must have been scary," she said. And this—the simple acknowledgment of what I had been through, the acknowledgment of me as a feeling self, it tipped me over the edge. Ann leaned in to hug me, and I began to weep into her cashmere cardigan, which felt soft and homey on my wet face. Ann had never said anything like this to me before, and it felt like she was offering it up for my entire past, as well—that must have been scary to have lost your mother; that must have been scary to have become one.

ANN AT THE BEACH

Once, when I was twelve, Ann and I had gone on a weekend road trip from Daly City to San Luis Obispo. We never went on trips that didn't involve the church, so this was different, and still stands out in my mind as one of the fondest memories of my childhood. We rented a motel room by the beach in Morro Bay that smelled of cigarettes and had a bed that shook if you inserted a quarter, a feature Ann seemed particularly embarrassed about. The first day, Ann sat on her towel, reading one of her mysteries under the shade of a pop-up tent, while I swam in the ocean for hours on end, shrieking from the thrill and thrust of the waves. On the second day, though, I was tired and crabby, sunburned to the point of blistering from the day before, angry I didn't have anyone to play with. Ann noticed me sulking and stood up very suddenly. She pulled off her shirt and her shorts; I hadn't even known she owned a bathing suit, but there she was, in a modest black one-piece, squinting out at the water with her hand over her eyes. I remember that my heart began beating faster when I saw her start to walk away from me, and it quickened even more as her pace turned into a run. Ann ran away from me and into the water, and it was thrilling, and I instinctively ran to the shore after her. I watched her dive like a dolphin under a wave, and when she came up she was grinning, her mouth wide and open and then calling to me: Come in, Emily! It's fantastic! Come in with me! And we swam together for over an hour, Ann and I, and it was the closest I ever felt to her in all our years as mother and daughter, when we were diving under the same waves together, then coming up laughing about nothing other than how the ocean was making us feel: wild, tumbled, buoyant, different from the people we were on land.

NURSE

She morphed as the hours passed. First she was Maria, then she was Lizzy, then she was Anabelle, then she was Tricia. She came in at all hours of the day and night to take my vital signs and to ask if I had farted yet. I looked at her with my battered face and begged her to take some of my pain away. Not just the physical pain in my abdomen but the pain of being a mother. The pain of not being able to hold my child. The pain of not knowing my child yet, of wondering if I would be able to love her. But the nurse couldn't take much of it, or any at all, because she was already full. She was on the sixteenth hour of her shift. She'd just bailed her brother out of jail. She'd seen a baby die that morning. She'd just watched a homeless teenager give birth to a baby boy she couldn't afford to keep. She'd been filling herself up with the pain of others for years, a different kind of empathy than I'd ever be able to know. She had seen ten thousand women become mothers. I was not special, my pain was not special, my baby was not special. I held out my arm and the nurse wrapped a blood pressure cuff around it, pressed a button to fill it up with air. I liked the feeling of the cuff squeezing against my skin. I relished in the pressure of it, the dull pain of the closeness.

BOW

I was put in a wheelchair and rolled down to the second floor, where my baby was being contained in an incubator. I peered in, part of me hesitant to look. Was she beautiful? I couldn't tell. Her face was covered with tubes: two in her nose and a large one covering her mouth. Circular Band-Aids had been placed on each of her cheeks, like the round dots of blush on baby dolls. Her tiny arm was in a stiff, gauzy splint, protecting the IV tubes that were hooked into her forearm. She looked totally foreign to me, like a thing from outer space, attached to so many machines and cords. On her head she wore a knit cap with the name of the hospital on it, adorned with a large knit bow. Under any other circumstance, I would have hated that bow, I knew. I would have thought it absurd that they needed to announce her gender with such a gaudy statement of girliness. But in this moment I latched on to the bow, coveted it; it seemed like the most human thing in the room. Soft and silly, that bow, no real reason for it to exist aside from its obvious gesture toward beauty. Someone, one of the NICU nurses who flitted around her like angels, had thought it was beautiful. And it was, I wanted to tell them. It was. She was.

A MOTHER'S HUG, PART TWO

Two days later, when they took the breathing tubes off my baby's face and the IV out of her tiny arm, Wes and I were finally able to hold her. He went first; I felt frightened, and wanted someone else to do it before I did. I watched his dexterous fingers—used to working with machines, clicking buttons, turning lenses—wrap all the way around her little human body. I watched his own fear morph into awe as he studied her sleeping face. Who was she? I wondered, as I watched him watch her. What would her life be like? What would her heart be like? Her face, as it changed over time?

"Your turn," Wes said, gently lowering her into my arms. She squirmed, then settled into my body, her head nuzzling my breast. I tightened my grip. I clutched her in a way that I had not clutched anything before, with a desperate fury. I felt simultaneously that I was going to lose her and that I was going to hold her this tightly forever. Had there been time for my birth mother to hug me like this, just once, before she was gone? Had our existences overlapped enough for one furious squeeze? If so, I do not recall it, with my mind or my body. I had tried my whole life to find a hug this tight, but I was just finding it now. For the very first time. Just now. Just now. Just now.

PART SEVEN

PLEASURE

NAMES

Our baby had light eyes, like Wes, and dark hair, like both of us. I couldn't stop smiling at her, unless she was crying, in which case I would cry, too. We cried constantly together, and it felt amazing and horrifying, like the falling of a dam. Wes and I couldn't decide on a name, so at first she was just Baby. We didn't have any good family names; Wes's grandmother was named Prudence, which was obviously out of the question. Wes's mom was named Shannon (also a hard no), and even though it probably would have been nice to name our child Moni, my birth mother's name, I felt strange about it; I didn't know if I wanted to name my baby after a ghost. We considered Franny, which we liked because it was old-fashioned, and we considered Madeline, which reminded me of the frisky orphanage outlier in her vine-covered house in Paris, from the story books. Neither stuck. For now, she was Baby.

Over those last two days in the hospital, as we waited for Baby to fully recover from her birth trauma, while Ann read her paperbacks and Wes darted in and out with to-go containers of udon and burgers, I checked my phone with a new diligence, as if it would offer me some kind of answer to the predicament I was in: being a new mother without a clue of how to be one. I was comforted by the scroll of bright images that offered a sense of pleasure and productivity. Instagram notifications pelleted me while Baby whimpered in her sleep in her plastic crib. The app had found out I'd given birth, apparently, because the ads had changed from maternity clothes and nursery decorations to baby clothes and bottle nipples. My phone was identifying my needs as they arose, which felt like some eerie form of ESP. Breast pump, ad for breast pump, hospital shower, ad for body wash, bloody underwear, ad for underwear that soaked up blood. The pictures of these items had a great effect on me. I felt that I needed all of them, desperately, or I would somehow fail as a mother. If I did not warm her wipes up with that wipe warmer, her ass would freeze! If I did not buy her that tiny pair of knit pants, her ass would freeze! If I did not sign up for a sixty-dollar breastfeeding class, I would certainly not know how to do it properly! If they did not offer Prime on the tiny fingernail clippers, they would get to us too late, and my baby might claw out her own eyes! I sent invisible money through the internet. When we got home from the hospital, my hallway would be full of all the shit I had bought, which made me feel somehow calmer, as if the boxes would create a tall wall around me and my baby, safeguarding us from the hazards of the world.

I refreshed my email incessantly, checking in on the status of the orders I'd placed, clicking through to tracking numbers, watching digital versions of real trucks drop things on the stoop of the loft building. Then I saw Renata's name in my inbox, and my heart leaped with a totally different kind of anticipation.

Cara Emily, the email read. *Congratulations on your new baby—Bene said she saw the Instagram announcement. I am glad to know she has arrived so I can think about you and send you good thoughts. I know these early days are very surreal and can be nerve-wracking. Remember that you are a smart, kind woman with a strong heart, and that you can do this. I am always here for you, and so is your room with the angels, whenever you want to come back.*

On another note, Greta will be coming to New York earlier than expected—she ended up choosing to do the intensive summer program at NYU. She'll be in the dorms starting in May, but she's insisted she wants to go early to get to know the city, and will be living in an apartment in the city by herself until then. I wonder if you could meet her for the occasional coffee (or pint of beer, if you must) just to check in. She would love to see a familiar face in the big city, I am sure, and she certainly does adore you. As do I, of course.

Tanti abbraci to you and the piccola,

Renata

An image popped into my mind, one that I hadn't known I'd remembered. I'd been leaving the Salaborsa in piazza Maggiore, and I'd seen them—Renata and eleven-year-old Greta—across the square, walking away from me. I thought I might catch up with them so we could all walk home together, but then, out of nowhere, Renata had stopped walking, picked Greta up by the waist, twirled her around, and then in an uncharacteristic display of affection kissed her hard, right on the mouth. I never knew why she'd done it, but it had moved me greatly. I had lingered outside the library, letting them get farther away from me, knowing my presence would break whatever spell they were under. In that moment, I had wanted so badly to be Greta—young again, utterly loved, getting lifted into the air by her mother, suspended above the mortal world just for a moment. But now, as I relived the moment as a memory, I saw that my position had changed entirely. Now, whether I liked it or not, I was the mother in that scene, the one doing the lifting.

"Let's call her Greta," I said to Wes. He did not say anything, but simply kissed our baby's head in agreement.

WHEN ANN LEFT

I sobbed uncontrollably, which I never would have predicted. Before she went I clung to her, balling her sweater up in my hands. When she pulled away, I looked into her clear blue-gray eyes.

"Thank you for being here," I said.

"I'll always be here," Ann said, putting her hand on my chest, over my heart. It was uncharacteristically sentimental, and it moved me.

"Ann?" I said. "What do you want Greta to call you?"

Ann looked unprepared for this question; her face fell.

"What do you want her to call me?" she asked.

"If it's okay, maybe Grandma? Or does that make you feel old?"

Ann laughed in a surprising way: a bit too loud. Then she looked me in the eyes.

"I'd love to be Grandma," she said.

I nodded. "Then it's settled," I said.

She took a sip of air and smoothed her sweater with her hands. "I'm going to miss my flight unless I leave right now," she said. And then she was gone, and the hospital room was silent except for the beeping of machines, now tethered to no one, built to monitor the breath, the pressure of the blood, the heart.

HOME

The protocol was that I had to be wheeled out of the building in the wheelchair with Greta in my arms. Even though the wheelchair was just a formality, I felt actually paralyzed. The sensation of being unable to walk overcame me. The fresh wound of my scar pulsed as the wheels turned. When we got outside, the winter daylight blinded me. It was a new year. I had a baby. I couldn't see. Everything was too bright and real. Greta wriggled helplessly in my arms.

We took a taxi back to the loft. Greta looked like she was swimming in her infant car seat that Wes had gone to pick up at Babies R Us. I barely noticed the city whirring past us outside; I was too concerned with making sure Greta was still alive in the seat. I felt incredibly nervous about going home, about being left alone with her. In the hospital, the nurses had acted like a hundred mothers, both to me and to Greta, changing our diapers and feeding us, making sure our levels never dropped. Now it was only me and Wes. Suddenly we were responsible for everything. Why had they trusted us with a whole life?

Wes had cleaned the loft as best he could, but as I entered it with Greta in my arms, I realized just how insane of a place it was. I noticed nails I'd never seen before, jutting from the wooden stairs. Electrical sockets magnified and multiplied. There was no bathtub, only the concrete slab of the shower, covered by those moldy pieces of wood. Where would we give Greta a bath?

Wes could see I was panicking, so he put his hand on my back. "It's gonna be fine, Em," he said. "Why don't you lie down for a bit while she's sleeping."

I hadn't even noticed Greta was sleeping; I was too busy clocking all the ways she could die. I handed her gently to Wes, who set her down on an old sheepskin rug on the floor.

"Don't put her *there*," I said. "That thing's disgusting."

"Where do you want me to put her?"

"I don't know, *hold* her maybe?"

"I need to bring all the stuff you bought in from the hall."

I looked at him icily and picked Greta back up myself, my scar wincing as I bent. When I picked her up she woke from her slumber and began to wail. Her face puckered up like a raisin and turned purple. Wes looked at me like he'd told me so.

"Do we have that big ball?" I said. "They say bouncing helps them feel like they're in the womb."

Wes retrieved the yoga ball I'd bought after the birth class from the closet. He had deflated it.

"Can you please blow it up?" I said, annoyed that he didn't do it without my asking him to, that he couldn't read my mind.

Wes found the pump and began the awkward process of pumping on it with his foot. I watched the big bubblegum-pink ball grow and become taut. He plugged up the hole and I sat down on it with Greta in my arms. The bouncing genuinely seemed to soothe her. I bounced and bounced and bounced, until the pain in my abdomen was so great I forced myself to stop and move to the couch.

Wes brought the bags in from the hall and made us eggs. Greta began to cry again. I intuited that she was probably hungry. I tried to undo my nursing bra, but the clasp was hard to unhook. I had to set the baby down and tug at it. The baby cried when I set her down. I tried to speak to her calmly, but she was not rational. She did not want to hear that the milk was coming, she wanted it now. She magnetized herself toward my nipple and latched on. She slurped. It wasn't a good latch. I pulled up the You-Tube video on my laptop and rewatched the instructional latching video. I had to stick my pinky into her mouth to unlatch her, then try to get her to relatch. Her head dangled. She wouldn't relatch. I flipped her over to try the other side. I set her down on the couch and undid my nursing bra on that side. Now both of my breasts were hanging out of the bra like large, tough balloons.

Wes delivered the eggs to the couch and I tried to eat them while balancing Greta in one arm. I was suddenly starving, unable to re-member the last time I'd eaten. A crumble of egg fell on Greta's face. Distressed, I flicked it off her. It landed on the dirty loft floor. She began to wail again. I set the eggs down on the couch and shoved my other boob into Greta's face. She latched but it was a bad latch. I let her keep sucking even though it hurt my nipple. I was giving up. I would rather have my nipples bleed than hear my child cry. When my child cried, I felt a ripple of panic move through my entire body, all the way to my toes.

"Do you feel that?" I asked Wes.

"Feel what?" he said.

"When she cries. Do you feel like, electricity in your veins?"

"I believe that's adrenaline," he said. "Probably a mom instinct."

"So you don't feel it."

He shook his head. He fed me a bite of egg with a fork.

When she was full, I brought her up to my shoulder and hit her lightly on the back. She let out a large burp, and then spit up on my shoulder. I scanned for a burp cloth but couldn't find one in my vicinity, and Wes had gone upstairs to unpack our bags, so I just let the spit-up soak into my sweater.

Greta made a funny face. She was pooping. I felt my own eyes scrunch up. It was as if I could feel the poop coming out of my own butt, that's how intimate it was to watch my baby poop. When she was done, I took her to the changing table, which was actually just the kitchen counter; Wes had put a pad down. I took off the diaper gingerly and marveled at the amount of yellow poop. I told her that she had done a good job.

"She pooped!" I called to Wes.

"Cool!" he shouted from upstairs.

I took her back to the living room, laid out one of the striped flannel blankets they'd given us at the hospital, set her gently on top of it. She looked up at me without any curiosity whatsoever. She had eyes, but they did not focus anywhere. I cooed at her and I showed her a book. She did not care about the book. I kissed her face; I wanted to eat her, she was so beautiful. Then she pooped some more.

I took her back to the kitchen to change her diaper again. This time I briefly considered how disgusting it was that her changing table was in the kitchen, then reminded myself there was no other clear surface on which to change her in the loft; our desks were covered with the stuff of our now seemingly obsolete creative lives: notebooks and scanners and computer monitors and books. I defiantly threw her poopy diaper into the kitchen trash can. This was New York living, I thought. At least we were not spoiling her with too many surfaces, surfaces willy-nilly and for no reason, who needed surfaces? Once again I had the thought that this was an insane place to raise a child, full of inconveniences and hazards; the very things I had once found charming—the hand-built plank stairs, the goddamned drawbridge—I now realized were liabilities. But who were we, without our hazards? Who was Wes, without his drawbridge? A pang of loneliness was stirring in me, loneliness mixed with crazy. I felt a little bit crazy, and though I was articulating it to myself, I knew that I had no control over it. I hoped it would not expand and conquer me, but I also knew that hope was irrelevant here. Hope, like the old flame of desire, had been removed

from the equation of this new life. Here, now, I could only look down, coo
at her, wipe her clean.

THIS NEW LIFE

Panic when Wes went out to get groceries. The epic fear of being the only
one in charge.

The promise of naptime: during this brief window of sleep, I would complete all necessary tasks with time enough to dip back into the unnecessary ones, like writing.

A refusal: *I will not let motherhood take me over.*

Hilarious, how much Greta resembled a burrito when we'd wrapped her
in a swaddle. "Or a turkey wrap," said Wes. "My little avocado turkey
wrap." "Wraps are so nineties," I said. "And also gross." "Don't talk about
my baby like that," Wes said, grinning.

The hopeful sadness of lullabies when you are a person who grew up
without lullabies.

The dread of the alarm, waking me every three hours for a feed.

The new banality of impossible fantasies: sitting alone in a café.

The sincere pride of getting four ounces of milk from a pumping ses-
sion, occasionally worth the degrading feeling of hooking myself up to
the hornlike flanges, the horrific sound of their honking, like a goose
breathing.

How the sky, or perhaps the miraculous question that was the sky, seemed
bigger now.

How we bounced and bounced and bounced and bounced and
bounced.

How we watched the baby as if she were a show we were bingeing: with rapt attention that we couldn't pry away. Just one more episode. And then one more after that.

A refusal: *I will not pry myself away.*

The metaphor that was my scar.

The reality that was her body: jerky arms, creased and mottled skin, tummy like a little balled-up fist.

JOY

On Greta's second-month birthday, which we celebrated on the last day of February, Wes gave her a plant. It was a Chinese money plant, or pilea, with leaves as round and green as tiny lily pads. He'd written the number 2 on a Popsicle stick, stuck it into the dirt. When he touched a leaf to her finger, she grinned. We hadn't known she could grin! I laughed out loud. A warmth overtook me. Why had I never thought of this before, that my child could be specifically happy? I waited for her to do it again, my eyes darting back and forth between her and the plant. I loved them both: young and green and round as they were. I loved them in some new way that I'd never loved things before. Tenderly. Physically. With my whole self. Greta smiled again. Maybe it was happening to both of us at the same time, this very first happiness. Because I don't think I knew what joy was before this. I just don't think I knew.

A VISIT

Fiona, from work, came over to meet the baby. She brought scones and we ate them on a blanket on the floor so Greta could lie on her back like an overturned bug.

"She's fantastic," Fiona said, but she didn't look at her for long. What-ever was happening on her phone was definitely more important and more interesting than my baby. An email from Todd about the spring Women's Book. A sale at Barneys. Her meditation app, telling her to check in with herself. She took a deep breath, then told me she had to get back to the city soon, where she was meeting friends for a bottomless brunch.

"Do you want to hold her before you go?" I asked.

"Not especially," Fiona said. "No offense."

"None taken," I said, though I was definitely offended. Fine, Fiona, go. There's nothing here for you to see, anyway; I have no new stories to tell. Unless you want to hear about the diapers? Before you go, Fiona, do you want to hear about the diapers? No? Well, too fucking bad.

THE DIAPERS

So get this: We have a diaper subscription. Yes, exactly, like a magazine, or like HBO. You wouldn't believe the batshit series of choices I had to go through to decide on these particular diapers: it was one of those tedious exercises in conscious consumerism that makes you feel like you are only made up of your choices and, because your choices are bad, you are bad by default. I had thought about using cloth diapers, which were less wasteful and less expensive, but I imagined washing them in the loft's communal laundry room and decided that would literally and figuratively stink. I read up on composting diapers, which seemed like a good eco-alternative, but there was no composting service in our neigh-borhood, so we'd have to take the diapers with us on the subway to have them composted, which also sounded bad; I imagined the subway car clearing out, as it did when a homeless man soiled himself during his nap on one of the benches. We'd have to get disposable diapers. But which ones? I spent many hours during Greta's naps reading reviews,

blogs, and advertisements for different kinds of diapers, each one claiming to be perfect for my baby's butt and my lifestyle for a different reason. I was forced to choose between best diapers that "gave back" and
best diapers for my budget and best diapers for convenience and best
diapers for the planet.

My budget and the planet squared off. My conscience and convenience waited on the sidelines for their turn in the ring. Somebody—the
Earth or my wallet—was going to get hurt. Either way, I was making
the wrong decision. Either way, I was irresponsible. Either way, I would
regret what I chose, knowing I could have worked harder at seeing all the
angles, weighing them, finalizing the decision that reflected my true val-
ues. Like so many of the choices I'd had to make lately, the choice of the
diapers felt actually impossible.

After a long battle with myself, I settled on the subscription service—it
catered to my convenience, and in the end, it turned out, ease of any kind
trumped everything in this moment. The Earth moaned, bloody and dis-
figured on her side of the ring. My convenience, who hadn't even planned
on joining the fight, stood victorious, raising her arms and pumping her
fists in the air. My wallet had indeed taken a pretty good beating. The
subscription cost seventy-nine dollars a month and came with enough
diapers but never enough wipes. We kept having to get more wipes at the
expensive organic grocery store across the street. Those wipes cost five
dollars a pack. We were spending about a hundred dollars a month on
diapers, or more, depending on how shitty of a week it was.

"That's not nothing," Fiona said.

I shook my head. "Definitely not nothing."

"Though you're probably going out less, so that saves you a lot, right?"

I looked at Fiona. Her gray-green eyes were very innocent and clear,
very not-tired looking. "Yeah," I said. "It all balances out in the end."

Fiona nodded, kissed my cheek, stood up to leave. Before she did, she
added salt to the wound she'd exposed. "Hey, have you talked to Megan
lately? What's she up to now?"

"I haven't, actually," I said, swallowing. "Not sure what she's up to."

. "I miss that girl," Fiona said.

"Me too," I said reflexively. And then, after feeling how good it felt to say it out loud, I said it again. "I miss her, too."

MISSING MEGAN

I missed Megan like I'd once missed old lovers after they'd left me or I'd left them, with the desperation that comes with powerlessness. I knew she was off-limits now, that our stupid fight and minor betrayals—my writing about her, her reading my private writing, us saying cruel things that we couldn't take back—had created some irreversible, angry awkwardness that neither of us knew what to do with or how to transcend. She'd deleted her Instagram, so I couldn't keep track of her as I might have, furiously reloading her profile to see how fine she was without me. She didn't know about the baby. I didn't know whether or not she'd gotten a new job, or where she was living now, or if she'd gotten her stuff out of storage. It was as if she'd snapped her fingers and disappeared.

I missed her worst at night, when I was up with Greta, or when I was unexpectedly reminded of her: passing our dive bar window seat while cruising the neighborhood with the stroller, or hearing a song I knew she loved. But the loss was most poignant when I felt the stirring of an idea inside me, when I wanted to write something down. I'd think, *I have to tell Megan*, and then remember that we weren't doing that anymore: the telling, the writing and drawing, the making. Without her there to catch them, I imagined my words floating through a wide-netted sieve, drifting away into nothingness. I allowed myself to think about a future in which I'd have the "bandwidth," as they called it at work, to write something worth sending her, something that could break through whatever wall had been erected between us. But for now I just compiled them in my head: imaginary stories that filled the bodies of imaginary emails, unwritten and unsent chapters in the book we'd left unfinished.

UNWORKABLE REPLACEMENTS

One early-spring morning, I saw a woman in the mother corner of McCarren Park who looked like Megan. Her face was rounder, but it had the same romantic quality, the blush of her blood showing through in her cheeks and nose. Her eyes and hair were the same in-between color. I walked toward her. I was used to being drawn to other mothers—we coveted each other, attracting each other like magnets. She gets it, I'd think, the second I saw a woman holding a bundle of cloth tightly to her chest, performing crazy acrobatics—squats, lifts, weightless bounces—to get the bundle to stop making noise. We drew each other in, whispered about the particulars, spoke of all the necessary and unnecessary things. *BabyBjörn*, we said, as if it were a secret code. We wondered if other women's children slept through the night. We inquired about dream feeds. We sometimes broke down, crying to someone we'd just met, explaining we were just so tired, so fucking tired, and the woman would reach over with her soft hand, smelling of sour milk, and touch the other woman's shoulder lightly. And somehow this touch from someone who was not her child would be enough to get the other woman through the day.

"How old?" I asked the mother who looked like Megan.

"Four months," she said. She laughed unexpectedly. "I think I'm supposed to be using weeks still, but I have no fucking clue how many weeks it is."

I smiled. It was something Megan would say. I felt a surge of hope that this other mother could be my new Megan, filling the void my friend had left behind. After a few more pleasantries, revealing that this woman, whose name was Maggie, was a playwright (a playwright!), I went out on a limb.

"You remind me of a friend of mine," I said.

"It's funny," Maggie said. "I get that a lot. I think I must have a familiar look. Or maybe I'm a shape-shifter." She raised her eyebrows mysteriously.

I wanted more from this woman, so much more. I wanted to stay with her all day, and then to call her the next morning and meet here again. Maybe we could arrange some kind of routine, where we'd watch each other's babies while the other worked, like Anne Sexton and Maxine Kumin had; I'd just read an article about their writerly friendship, how their careers were made possible by this sharing of childcare. Could Maggie be the answer to all my problems?

"Oh shit," Maggie said suddenly, gathering up her things and shoving them into a large, ugly diaper bag. "We actually have to catch a plane at four. It takes me like two hours to pack this tiny person's tiny suitcase."

"Where are you going?" I said, with no small amount of desperation.

"We're heading home, actually," she said. "We live in Toronto now, where my husband's from. I never wanted to leave New York, but then when we had Archie it was a no-brainer. Free health care, subsidized childcare. A little less exciting than Brooklyn, but I'm kind of over exciting."

"What does exciting mean again?" I said jokingly. My heart was breaking.

"It was good to meet you, though," Maggie said. "If you're ever in Toronto . . ."

I smiled. "I'll look you up," I said, knowing I never would. My world was tiny now. The size of the bundle in my own arms. I watched her walk away under the weight of her child and all his things, the diaper bag slipping from her slim shoulder at one point, throwing off her balance.

SMALL FIRES

Later—how much later? Days? Weeks? Time had become an utter abstraction—I tried to take a shower. Out in the living room, Wes was

doing a bad job at trying to calm Greta down. I could hear her screaming as I shampooed. I hadn't showered in three days before this. I'd been
getting served thousands of Instagram posts about self-care for moms,
images of clean-haired mothers in smoothing yoga clothes, their babies
nowhere to be seen. These women weren't real, I knew, and yet seeing
them made me feel bad. Why couldn't I be a well-kempt woman? Why
was I always such a mess?

Determined to shave, I located an old razor and lathered my legs
with bar soap suds. Greta's crying persisted, and I could feel the anxiety
course through me as I dragged the razor up in long strokes. Because I
was rushed and the razor was probably dull, I cut my shin. Orange blood
leaked out and mingled with the water being swept down the drain.

"Fuck!" I shouted. I gave up. I put the razor down and climbed out
of the shower and twirled my hair up in the towel and smacked a square
of toilet paper on the cut and put on the same disgusting sweats I'd been
wearing for days and retrieved Greta from Wes. She immediately calmed
in my arms. I was magic in this way; my simple presence could soothe
her. I felt both proud of this and angry at Wes for not possessing the same
magic.

"I asked for *ten* minutes," I said.

"And I gave you ten minutes," Wes said. "You need to get more comfortable leaving her with me. She's fine."

"She's *screaming*. How is that fine?"

"It's fine because she's fine. I'm taking care of her. If she doesn't like
that, oh well. She's got to get used to it. Or else it's just gonna be this, you
having to jump back in every ten seconds, taking her away from me."

"You didn't even try," I said. "There are easy ways to calm her. Did
you even try the ball?"

"My whole body is sore from that fucking ball," Wes said.

"Yeah, well my body is still sore from carrying her around for nine
months," I said. "Figure it out. Do what you need to do to keep her happy
for ten fucking minutes."

"All I do is keep her happy, keep you happy. Have I done one thing to make myself happy in the last three months? No. I haven't. All I do is follow your crazy schedules and protocols and rules. It's literally all I do. Give me some credit here."

"You met up for *drinks* with Kasper two nights ago," I said. "You've gone to *four* art openings. Meanwhile I have seen exactly no friends, done exactly no things."

"Then do things! Do whatever you want! I told you, I'll watch her whenever."

"How would you watch her for a whole evening? She doesn't take a bottle yet, remember? You wouldn't be able to put her down. You don't have a boob."

"Exactly! Do you hear yourself? You're asking for something impossible. I can't do what you do, I just can't. It's not physically an option. I'm just not sure what you want from me."

"I don't know, maybe some acknowledgment? Just like, recognition?"

"Look, Em, you've gotta loosen up here a little bit. Trust me with her. Teach her how to use the bottle. Let the fuck go."

By this point I was seething. "You think I want to be like this?" I said. "You think I want to be some anal-retentive person who does nothing else except care for her kid? You think that's what I want? No! It's the reality of the situation. It's what it is right now. I don't have a choice."

"You box me out, Em," Wes said. "You're mad that I don't help enough, but you don't let me. When I try, you say I'm doing it wrong. You don't let her lie on me, get used to me. She only wants you because you keep her to yourself. It's as if I'm completely out of the picture, as if I don't exist."

I felt briefly sad for Wes; I realized I hadn't once looked at the situation from his perspective, and therefore had no concept of how the way I was behaving might make him feel. But I was also angry; he had made me feel like I was stupid, or crazy, for following my instincts. It was so confusing, to feel two ways at the same time.

"I'm gonna go out for some air," Wes said, which we both knew meant he was going to smoke a cigarette. This was a double fuck-you, as he had agreed to quit smoking when we had Greta.

"Yeah, go right ahead," I yelled after him as he walked out. "Go fucking kill yourself with your fucking cigarettes!"

Wes didn't say anything back. I looked out the window to where he usually stood and smoked, watched the single flame of his lighter glow brightly and briefly in the dark. It was the loneliest thing I could think of, that tiny fire that he kept to himself.

MATERNITY LEAVE

It was over, just like that.

DRINKING PROBLEMS

Before I could go back to work, Greta had to learn how to consume her calories from a bottle instead of a human body. We spent a hellish few days trying to get this to happen, ordering countless bottle nipples off Amazon, yelling at each other about what we should try next. She hated us. We hated her. She cried. I cried. Wes lost his patience with both of us.

"You need to get out of here," Wes said. "She can smell you. It's like trying to get someone to eat margarine when there's butter on the table."

"Where am I supposed to go?" I said.

"Go meet someone," Wes said. "Have a drink or something."

I couldn't think of anyone I wanted to get a drink with except Megan. I found my phone in the diaper bag and searched for her name in my texts. What if I just texted her? I scrolled up: the last time we'd texted was before Italy, on our way to meet each other to catch a cab to the airport. It had been early in the morning, still dark.

Megan: *I'm getting coffee what do u want*
Me: *You're an angel from heaven latte pls.*
Megan: *Everything I do I do it 4 u*
Me: *Pulling up in cab! Andiamo biatch!*

We'd been so casual, so carefree, but that wasn't how things were anymore. I couldn't just start up the thread again like nothing had happened. But what *had* happened, even? Every time I went over it in my head our fight seemed like a smaller deal. Why had we made it such a big one with so much silence? And why couldn't I bring myself to break it? I sighed and pressed the button on the side of my phone, darkening its screen.

"Fine," I said. "I'll just go out by myself."

I put on a sweatshirt and went to a bar across the street, where the light was dim and they were playing "Bad Days" by the Flaming Lips. Next, I knew, they'd play something by Sonic Youth, then the Yo La Tengo sweater song. My generation knew this Spotify playlist by heart—a nostalgic soundtrack to the glory days of our younger years, when we had time to be curious about music. I liked it, and Spotify's algorithm had bet on the fact that I'd like it, which should have made me feel weird, or at least predictable, but did not; I relished in the soft solace of being uncannily known.

The bartender, an aging pixie with bell sleeves who looked insanely familiar, asked me what I wanted while she circled the inside of a pint glass with a gross towel. She had the look of a bartender-for-life, someone who refused to give up the freedom service work provided, to pursue the things she actually loved. What did she actually love? How did I know her?

"A glass of dry white wine," I said. I immediately regretted my order, realizing it was that of an old, sad white lady. "Actually, a martini. A gin one." Still an old white lady, but a more fun one.

The pixie said nothing and began to make my drink. She was good at her job. She knew where everything was by sense memory, not having to look as she reached for the spray bottle of vermouth. She slid the olives into the glass with boredom and pride.

Predictably, Spotify segued to Bon Iver. I took a sip of the martini: all ice and brine, thrill and spark. For a full twenty seconds I was her again: the girl I'd once been, sitting at a bar alone, the night spread out in front of her like an empty road, a little pot of desire burning in her, waiting to be stoked. Where would it take her, this night? This life? Who would she talk to? Who would she kiss? What would she write down about it after it happened?

I pulled out my phone again and reopened the text thread with Megan. The sip of martini gave me the confidence to start typing.

Drinking a martini and wishing you were here, I wrote, then deleted.

Megs, I'm sorry, I wrote, then deleted.

Megs, we can't keep not talking to each other forever, I wrote, then deleted.

Megs, why did you have to read my journal and ruin everything, I wrote, then deleted.

Megs, I have a baby now, I wrote, and then immediately felt tears pushing at the back of my eyes. But before I could let any tears fall, before I could send any text to Megan, time snapped back like a rubber band. The martini suddenly tasted like poison in my mouth. What was I doing? I had to go home to my baby! I had to pump! My milk would be full of gin! I wasn't allowed to drink a martini! Greta was probably losing her shit by now, starving and abandoned. I had abandoned her.

Flustered, I asked the pixie for my check and paid in cash. Bon Iver lamented my abrupt departure with a harmonious wail. I tried to apologize to the bartender from the doorway, miming the action of a breast pump with my hands, but I knew it didn't make any sense, that I seemed like a crazy asshole squeezing the empty air in front of her boobs. I jogged back across the street to the loft, and was utterly surprised to see that Wes had successfully put Greta down to bed alone, with the bottle.

"Wow," I said. "Dad of the year."

"You could have stayed out longer," he said. "It was so much easier with you not here."

"Sorry to make things so much harder," I said, annoyed by my own hormonal sarcasm.

I sank into the couch and closed my eyes. Then I saw her: the pixie bartender. She was on a stage, flanked by red velvet curtains. Two silver tassels were fastened miraculously on to her nipples, making helicopter-style circles as she expertly bounced her breasts. That's where I knew her from! I'd seen her doing burlesque a million years ago, at some hole-in-the-wall on the Lower East Side. I wondered if she still performed, and tried to imagine her now, her breasts lower and longer, her thighs dimpled with the soft craters of age. I imagined her telling the crowd in her surprisingly husky voice: "If you want to make a woman happy, you've got to figure out what she really wants. And how do you figure out what she wants? By fucking asking her." The crowd would roar and she'd shimmy; her tassels would spin faster; her skirt would peel off, and there she'd be. A heavenly thing, a woman in her element.

BLACK HOLE

Later that night, when I finally brought myself to plug in to my breast pump, it started speaking to me. *Black hole*, the pump said, out of nowhere. *Black hole, black hole, black hole.* I wondered if it was talking to me specifically, or just to anyone who would listen. I figured it was the former, and that the crazy had finally overtaken me.

"Wes, come here," I said.

He came.

"Listen to this," I said. "Do you hear this?"

"I don't hear anything," he said.

"It's *talking*," I said. "I think it's trying to tell me something."

"I think it's trying to tell you that you need a break from this," he said. "Maybe going back to work will actually feel good. Normalize things a little bit."

I swallowed. I couldn't imagine going back, but I also knew I had no choice. Greta's pediatrician was part of a network of doctors who had collectively decided to accept only the top-of-the-line insurance, the kind you could only get by having a "real" job. I'd looked into it. If we wanted to switch her to a different doctor, one who took the shitty insurance we'd have if we were both freelancing, the closest available doctor was in deep Queens. We didn't have a car, so we'd have to take the subway there, and the ride would be over an hour. What if baby Greta got really sick? An hour on the subway would not do.

My breast pump seemed to know all of this and was becoming increasingly apocalyptic about it. *Iceberg, iceberg, iceberg*, it sang when I set it to the "drop down" setting, in an effort to get my flow going. As the streams of milk spurted sideways, upward, in all directions, I had a very clear thought: *This is how I spend my time now.* Not writing, not reading or thinking or working, but being verbally and physically accosted by a milking machine. I turned it off before I'd gotten enough milk. I knew I'd pay for it later, that I wouldn't have enough reserves, that my supply would dwindle due to lack of demand. But I just couldn't listen to the world as I knew it ending anymore.

Two days later, I pulled black tights up over the bulge of my C-section scar and winced. I grasped at my baby. Wes was staying home with her, which was a temporary situation, until we found daycare or a nanny that we could afford. Until then, it was cheaper to have one of us be with her, and made us feel better, too. I descended underground to the subway, and emerged into a Manhattan I had never seen before. Steep and foreign, too bright, nearly violent with all its harsh lines. For three months I had lived in a cocoon of gauzy swaddles and baby cries, and now I was back in the surreal inferno of the city, sparking as it burned through money and fumes. Its glow was both disorienting and inviting; I felt myself being drawn toward the office like a moth to a flame. Key card, turnstile, elevator, Essie's empty desk. My team sprang up to greet me, begged me for pictures of the baby. "She's perfect," they all said, but I wondered how they knew that. To understand her perfection, I wanted to tell them, you had to *breathe her in through your nose.*

WORK-LIFE BALANCE

That first day back, as I read through my emails and began to check off my to-do list, I felt a strange mix of elation and resentment. This was So. Fucking. Easy. To sit in this chair and send messages through the ether, to engage my brain in ways I was comfortable with: it was a cake walk. If I were home right now, I would be bouncing Greta on the yoga ball or spilling precious quantities of my own breast milk or trying to find a pacifier that had fallen onto the loft's disgusting floor. One of the laborious tasks that was required of mothers and fathers that was somehow not considered labor, that was somehow forgotten right after it was done, erased from the record. When I had been a bartender, people had thanked me with one-dollar bills. Now, I was thanked with shits and burps, moments of coveted silence that, to be fair, felt like a million bucks. How could it be possible that I was paid to write a newsletter called *Your Weekly Chic* but not paid, or even recognized for, keeping a vulnerable human being alive? It seemed utterly insane.

Just as I was starting to feel productive, my breasts began to hurt. I left my desk and went to HR to ask them where the lactation room was, as I had never seen it. I guessed that lactation rooms were one of those invisible spaces, rooms that no one noticed until they desperately needed one, like elevators for people in wheelchairs. The CEO had probably never known where the lactation room was, or if there was one at all—why would he? The HR lady escorted me to an old supply closet. Inside, there were many reams of old paper, sad stacks of Post-its, and a chair with a small desk next to it. A gloomy, round Spectra pump gleamed on the table, beckoning me. I asked the HR lady where I should wash the pump parts and she shrugged.

I got down to business, undressing and plugging in. I flipped the switch and waited for the inevitably dark conversation to begin with the pump. But it turned out that this pump was a workhorse without a personality. It said nothing. This pump was a fucking robot, it didn't have anything interesting to offer, it was the kind of fear-fueled work-aholic that ate lunch in front of the computer. This corporate pump had maxed out its 401(k) and wasn't worried about retirement. In fact, it couldn't wait to retire. Right now it was just going through the motions until it could be done.

I missed my pump at home, which just that morning had wanted to talk about books. On its highest setting, it had begun to repeat a line from a book I'd read in spurts while breastfeeding in the middle of the night. It was a new book by a novelist I liked, about being a mother, and I had underlined many lines in it. *The baby had an orange spoon*, my breast pump said. *The baby had an orange spoon*. At first I thought it was taunting me, re-minding me that I had not written anything down about being a mother, that I had failed to write anything at all in many months. But then I began to hear it as a kind of song. An invitation, an offering. *The spoon is in the literature*, the pump said. *The answer is in the problem*.

Someday I would write again, I told myself. And all of this—the breast pumps and the sleeplessness and the spoons—would make it in there. But for now I lactated in the supply closet, scrolling through In-stagram on my phone. There was nothing there, just pictures of beautiful things that I loved looking at, that somehow made me feel like I was doing everything wrong but that maybe, someday, I could be the kind of person who could do everything right. When the milk stopped flowing, I kept the pump on anyway, and looked at pictures of Greta sleeping. This was

the reason I embezzled time now. To reopen moments that had already
closed.

SEX

Not now, I said to Wes, when he tried.
Never again, I said to myself as I closed my eyes.

PHOTO MONKEY

Just when I thought we'd gotten into the swing of things—a schedule had
emerged from the chaos, offering a helpful, if meager, sense of control—
Wes came home from a weekend photoshoot in a shit mood. The job had
been for the department store I worked for; I'd gotten him a gig shooting
cosmetics so he could bring in a little extra cash. I could tell he was in a
shit mood because he went straight to his desk without even stopping to
kiss me or asking about Greta, who'd gone down to sleep an hour ago. He
put on his headphones and plugged in one of his old hard drives.

From across the room I could see him pulling up pictures from years
earlier, stuff from last year's trip to New Orleans, and from a shoot he'd
done in Laredo, Texas, of immigrant children whose parents had been
deported. I knew exactly what he was doing, because I had done it, too—
going through old notebooks, pulling up documents I'd written eons ago.
He was trying to access some previous version of himself, trying to remember who he was, what he'd once loved more than anything before
he had a child.

I wanted to let him know that I understood, so I went to him and
touched him gently on the back. "We'll get back there," I said. "And you
have New Orleans coming up again."

"New Orleans for *three days*," he said. He was referencing the fact that we'd agreed he'd go on a truncated version of his yearly trip this year, to avoid my missing too many days of work to watch Greta.

"Still," I said. "It's something."

"Just do me a favor," Wes said. "Don't ever get me work again."

I withdrew my hand. "What happened?"

"Nothing *happened*," Wes said. "I just . . . I can't do that shit. I can't be their little photo monkey. I can't play the part they want me to play. It's not worth it."

"We need the money, Wes. If we're ever going to hire anyone to help us we need to start saving."

"It's just not what I signed up for," he said. "It's actually the exact opposite of what I signed up for."

I felt genuinely baffled. "Work rarely is," I said. "Sometimes you just have to do shit you don't want to do. Sometimes it's not about you and your creative vision but about actual obligations to people and things. Like us, me and Greta."

"That's just not how I see it," Wes said, bafflingly. "I think you can make things work without succumbing to all the pressures of society. We don't need all the shit, all this gear . . ." He gestured randomly around the room at various pieces of baby equipment.

"Actually we do need it," I said. "Which maybe you don't understand because you're not the one to research it and find it on Craigslist and go pick it up—I do all that. So you're welcome."

"Thank you for doing all that. I'm not trying to negate all that you do. I'm just saying I don't want to sell my soul to the man on a regular basis, okay?"

"Like I do, you mean? Like how I work full-time so that we can afford to have Greta? I haven't written in literally months. You do one dumb commercial shoot and you have some massive identity crisis. But it doesn't have to mean anything about you, Wes. It doesn't make you less of an artist. We just need to make a little extra right now."

"You know what, forget I said anything," Wes said, closing the file of images on his computer. "It's fine. I'll keep taking pictures of mascara wands for the rest of my life. If it's what I've gotta do to keep our kid in expensive diapers."

"You're being a huge asshole," I said.

Wes shrugged and went to the bathroom; I heard the shower turn on. I went up to bed early and pulled Greta from her crib to join me. We usually didn't allow this, as Wes had made it clear that he wanted to keep our bed *our* bed. But I needed someone next to me, someone who didn't know what freedom was yet, who wouldn't want it if she did.

GREECE

We decided to try to eat at a restaurant. We chose the Thai place because it seemed easy and familiar. I put on a baggy dress that always made me feel confident thanks to the way it eliminated my corporeality and took it up a notch with some hot-pink lipstick.

Weirdly, there was an hour wait; someone was having a bachelorette party on the roof, and there was only indoor seating. We decided to go to a bar next door for a drink first—something we'd done often in our life before Greta. The stroller didn't fit in the entryway of the bar, so we had to leave it outside. We ordered our drinks—a glass of wine for me and a whiskey for Wes—and drank them standing up, passing Greta back and forth when she got heavy or fussy. Inevitably, after we'd gotten about a quarter of the way through our beverages, Greta began to cry in earnest. I took her to the bathroom to see if she needed a diaper change. The bathroom was lit only with candles and had no changing table. I had to lay her on the floor, which was made of poured concrete. She wailed as I undid her onesie and checked her diaper, only to find it empty. Maybe she was hungry. I sat on the toilet and pulled my dress all the way up; she drank a few sips and then began to cry again. This was why people didn't take their children out, I realized. Because it wasn't fun.

"This isn't fun," I reported to Wes when I got back to the bar. He was looking at his phone.

"Holy shit," he said. He was kind of grinning.

"What?"

"*Harper's* wants me to shoot for a story," he said. "Fucking *Harper's!*"

Even though Greta was still crying, I managed to be genuinely elated for Wes for a moment, jumping a bit and then wrapping my free arm around his neck.

"This is incredible!" I said.

Then I saw his shoulders sink a little bit as he scanned the email.

"Holy shit," he said again, this time with defeat in his face. "It's in Greece."

"Greece? What's in Greece?"

"The refugee crisis," he said. "They want photos for a piece about the camps there. I guess it would be with Sarah, that writer I met in New Orleans. I wonder if she pulled some strings for me? I know she's done a few things for them over the years . . . it seems random that they'd reach out to me out of the blue."

"Sarah Hughes?" I said.

"Yeah," Wes said, still scrolling.

From Sarah Hughes's Instagram profile, which I'd done a deep dive into when Wes had first mentioned her over the phone when I was in Italy, I'd pieced together a basic understanding of this woman. She was quite accomplished (she had written many pieces for the *New Yorker* and had won some major journalism prize), had a mutt named Zeus (an animal lover! a mythology buff!), lived on the Lower East Side (independently wealthy?), and was quite pretty (could pull off baby bangs). Raised in Minneapolis, Waldorf school, small ponies and flower crowns, Sarah Lawrence for college, dabbled in screenwriting, got an essay in the *Paris Review* before even graduating, dated famous writers whose cred rubbed off on her. Had a public breakup with a *Vice* editor—she'd written a piece about it for *Guernica*. But heartbreak had only made her more attractive; now she was steelier and sharper than ever. I'd pined for her through my screen, quietly hoping Wes wouldn't keep in touch with her.

But here she was again, pulling strings for him.

"It's an amazing opportunity," I said, bouncing Greta aggressively so that she'd stay quiet.

"I probably can't go, though, right?" he said. "I'd have to cancel New Orleans entirely. And what about you and Greta? Yeah, it seems like too long. It would be for three weeks."

"We'll totally manage," I said, though my throat was closing up as I said it. I was trying my hardest to be what he needed me to be, to give him what I knew he needed me to give him: the freedom he'd lost when I'd made the decision to keep Greta. I kept it light, to keep it from getting heavy. "I'll be like a war wife," I said. "Only less terrified you'll die."

I was casual, convivial, convincing, and I was being this way because I knew I had no choice. I had this feeling, somewhere deep, that Wes needed this, and that I was going to lose him if I didn't let him have it. And so I would.

"Are you sure?" he said.

I nodded. A heaviness climbed onto my back like an animal and stayed there.

CARE

That Monday at work, I spent most of the day trolling the internet trying to figure out childcare for when Wes left for Greece. I'd tried to do this with Wes the previous evening, but it had only made me mad at him.

"Do you think we should look into that place on Grand Street?" I said. "I think they speak Spanish with the kids, which is cool, but there's a waiting list so it wouldn't be a sure thing by next month. Plus it's four hundred dollars more a month than the one on South Fifth."

"Okay, then let's do the one on South Fifth," he said.

"But they only go until three," I said. "So we'd have to find a sitter to get her at three and bring her home before I get off work."

"Okay, then let's find a sitter," he said.

I'd sighed aggressively. "You're not *in* this," I said. "I can feel you halfway checked out."

"I'm sitting here talking it through with you," he said. "How am I not in this?"

"I know it's fucking boring!" I said. "I'm bored, too!"

"I think it doesn't have to be as hard as you think," Wes said. "Let's just pick something and we'll figure out how to make it work."

"Picking something is the work," I said.

I'd stopped talking to him and obsessively reviewed twenty daycare options alone, then come to the firm conclusion after looking at all of them that it would be simpler and more comfortable and basically the same price to get a nanny. So now I was on my work computer trying in vain to figure out how to find one.

Craigslist was all BEST NANNY EVER GOOD REFERENCES BRONX MAN-HATTAN BROOKLYN QUEENS!!!!! I looked on a site called Sitter.com, but felt similarly sketchy about it. I realized I didn't want to find the person who would take care of my child all day on the Internet. I wanted to run into them on the street, or to have a friend of a friend pass them on to me, with glowing reviews—something kismet yet solid, the perfect fit at the perfect time. I found myself paralyzed, unable to make any calls, set up any meetings. I texted one woman from a Craigslist posting, just to say I did something, but when she responded I didn't text back. I was flailing. I texted Wes that I was flailing. *I could tell my mom to come,* he texted back, which I knew was an empty offer. Though Wes and his mom had recon-nected recently over email—her apologizing for his father's rigidness and their lack of support, Wes vaguely forgiving her but privately holding out to see it before he believed it—they hadn't seen each other in years. When they'd found out Greta had been born, we'd only gotten a card: *Congratu-*

lations on the birth of your baby girl. Later, I'd found the card in the recycling. I knew its formality had made Wes feel farther from his parents than if they'd sent nothing.

I was stalling, and I knew that my stalling was not about finding the right person, not really. It was about not being able to leave her. Not being able to physically leave my baby with someone who hadn't helped to make her out of thin air.

Finally, as Wes's departure date closed in, I forced myself to call the number for a nanny listing I found on a neighborhood message board. A Mexican woman who was around my age arrived at the loft the next day, panting from what had clearly been a long walk. She explained she could watch Greta from 9 a.m. to 3 p.m., when she would have to leave to pick up her own children, who were being taken care of by another woman; she had to pick them up in Ridgewood by 4 p.m. Where did that woman send *her* child? I imagined her dropping her baby off at one of the dingy subsidized daycares I'd seen throughout the city, with their faded colorful signs and depressing names—Kid Zone, Play Town, ABC Club. I imagined the simultaneous panic and relief she felt as she passed the baby into the arms of yet another woman, the look the women shared as they made the exchange. Both of them knew what this was, how sad it was. The dim basement room would be full of crying and shit smell for the rest of the day, and no one could do anything about it. The "early childhood educator," as she was called, would not have time to eat a snack or go pee until noon, but even then, even when she gave up her own needs to give her whole self to these babies, she could not console them. She was not their mother, and they knew it. She smelled different, spoke differently, made a different kind of shushing sound. The early childhood educator's patience was incredible, but it wore over time. Dark circles formed under her eyes. The crying seeped under her skin. When she passed the baby back to the mother at the end of the day, she hardly felt relief anymore. "She did good today," she'd say, like she always said. "Two poops, both yellowish-green."

It seemed impossible that this chain of caretaking could exist, so many women giving their offspring away to each other while they each tried to earn a living. I felt sad and also disappointed. I liked Miranda, the Mexican woman who was sitting in the loft kitchen, chugging water. But I needed childcare for the second half of the day, too, from 4 to 7 p.m., which was when I got home from the office. I explained this to her, and her eyes fell to the floor in a disappointment that mirrored my own.

An elderly Russian woman came over next. She pinched Greta's nose and gifted her a tube of Russian diaper cream. She somehow used a baby voice and also screamed when she talked to her. She had a limp and could hardly make it up the stairs to the mezzanine, where Greta slept. At one point, she whisper-screamed at Greta that she had to be good for her or else! Hahaha! I told her I would get back to her soon, knowing that I wouldn't.

"She was fine," Wes said when she left.

"She was *not* fine," I said. "She *yelled* at our baby."

"She was joking," Wes said.

"She could hardly walk," I said, as if that settled it.

Wes was leaving next Monday. By Thursday, we had figured nothing out. I thought about asking Zoe for help, but I couldn't imagine her taking care of an infant, and all my other friends had "real" jobs, meaning they were unavailable during the hours I'd need. I called the daycares I'd originally considered—even the depressing ones—but all of them were full; Greta wouldn't get a spot until next fall.

Greta cried extra hard that evening, during what the baby blogs called her "witching hour." Her wails pierced my eardrums and frazzled my nerves. I strapped her to my body with a complicated carrier contraption and prayed for her to sleep. I pressed my hand against the inside of the big loft window, longing with my entire being to go outside, to leave this screaming child for someone else to deal with. *What did I want before I wanted childcare? What did I once burn for?* I drank a glass of wine and was pouring my second—my anxieties about getting Greta drunk off breast milk were overpowered by the kinds of anxiety that could only be addressed with booze—when it came to me. Greta—the original Greta, from Bologna. She'd written me a few months earlier; I looked back at the email; yes! She was getting to New York this week.

PART EIGHT

BUSINESS

AN ARRANGEMENT

I met Original Greta at a Starbucks on Second Avenue in the city, per her suggestion; it was near her dorm. I had Baby Greta strapped to me in the carrier, and I felt shaken from riding the subway from Brooklyn with her screaming in my ear the whole way. Now, thankfully, she was quiet, almost asleep, but I was already counting down the minutes I had until she woke again, mentally preparing my next steps in my mind. If she woke while we were still in the coffee shop, I'd nurse her there. If she woke afterward, on the subway back to Brooklyn, I'd have to give her the bottle I'd packed, which I needed to put in the front pocket of my back-pack so I could access it easily. Awkwardly, I spun the backpack around to the side of my body and dug around for the bottle. Then I unzipped the pouch and tucked it in there. This all took an incredible amount of effort with Greta in the carrier. I was sweating by the time I entered the Starbucks, where Original Greta was waiting at one of the always-wobbly tables. She wore a denim overall dress over a long-sleeve black shirt, and in front of her was a huge coffee drink topped with whipped cream.

As soon as I saw her, I felt a pit in my stomach—a guilt I would feel over and over as a mother, of having made the wrong call. What was I doing? Greta was a Frappuccino-drinking twenty-two-year-old. Was leaving my infant with her totally insane? But then again, I had been younger than her when I'd looked after her and Bene, so maybe it was fine. But they had been nine, eleven—my Greta was only a few months old. I didn't know what was fine and what wasn't. At least it would be temporary, I told myself. Just three weeks, until Wes got back.

When Greta saw me, she grinned nervously. "I had to get one of these crazy drinks," she said in English, rather sheepishly, holding up her caramel Frappuccino. "Do I look like a celebrity?"

I laughed, and instantly felt better. I remembered how mature Greta was, and how funny. Humor made me feel taken care of somehow, or at least understood.

"You *are* a celebrity," I said. "So much so that I named my baby after you."

Greta's face eased into a warm smile. "My mamma told me. *Ma che bella*," she said as she peered into the carrier at Greta's sleeping face.

I smiled and hugged her. She smelled young and nostalgic: like the inside of a Bath & Body Works. I imagined her going into one before she met me, spritzing herself with all the American scents. I remembered doing a similar thing when I lived in Italy, thinking that maybe smelling like everyone else—baby powder and orange blossoms—would make me fit in there, which it did not.

"You smell good," I said.

"Thank you," she said proudly.

I told her I was desperate for coffee, and went to wait in line. It smelled like poop and Christmas, the smell of Starbucks everywhere. While I waited behind a woman in exercise gear, I read the label on the back of a bag of coffee beans. The beans were from Chiapas, Mexico, and were described as having a crisp and nutty flavor, pleasing acidity, and a round body. I couldn't help thinking these coffee beans sounded sexual. Then it was my turn to order, but I was distracted, thinking about the round bodies of the workers who picked these coffee beans in Chiapas. I had read somewhere that it was the poorest state in Mexico. I had never been to Mexico, but I thought I could imagine it: long hours in the sun, the ever-present feeling of thirst picking the coffee beans that would be overnighted to the mustached baristas up north. The women, I imagined, couldn't afford to leave their children at home, and so brought them out to the fields, carried them like I was carrying

Greta now, while they bent down again and again. I felt guilty for so many reasons I couldn't count them: for drinking a beverage that some other human had had to do such painstaking work for, for taking so long to decide what I wanted, for even thinking I should pawn my baby off on Greta. I ordered a black coffee that I knew I wouldn't drink and returned to the table, freshly frazzled.

"So, I'm going to come right out and ask it," I said, switching to Italian, thinking she'd feel more comfortable.

"Let's do English," she said. "I like to practice."

"Oh yes, totally, of course."

"You need help with Greta."

I laughed anxiously. "How'd you know that?"

"My mom said I should offer anyway."

"I know school starts soon. But I was thinking . . ."

"Of course," Greta said, her voice breaking slightly. "I'd love to. And it's perfect—I have a few weeks until classes start, anyway. I wanted to get here early." She grinned.

"It would start like immediately," I said, praying that this fact didn't change her answer. "I have to go back on Monday."

"It's no problem," Greta said, smiling.

I couldn't help myself; I pulled Original Greta toward me and hugged her, so tightly that I knew I'd probably wake Baby Greta. I didn't care. I felt so relieved I thought I might cry, and I also felt moved. This girl whom I had once helped with her first maxi pad, who had once run around the house whipping my thong underwear above her head like a helicopter—now she was going to help me with my baby. *Someone*, anyone, was going to help me with my baby. I felt the world opening up, right there in that Starbucks. I had the momentary audacity to imagine myself sitting at one of the wobbly tables and writing.

I filled Original Greta in on Baby Greta's temperament and schedule. I told her about the yoga ball trick, the white noise machine, tummy time, naps. She took notes in a small purple notebook and nodded at everything I said, which I realized sounded crazy. The endless lists of protocol, the finicky details. I stopped myself for a second.

"But also, Greta," I said, trying to sound cool, "just be yourself. Use your instincts. Just take care of her like you would if I didn't tell you any of this bullshit."

"I'll take care of her like you took care of me," Greta said.

"So, like you have no idea what you're doing?" I said.

"No way," she said. "You were the best. I wanted to be you when I grew up."

"And look at you now," I said, squeezing her hand. "Grown and brilliant."

She smiled and offered me a sip of her Frappuccino, which I accepted. It was overly sweet and delicious, like Original Greta's smell.

DEPARTURE

Wes got picked up in a black car from in front of our building at four in the morning. It felt eerie and lonely to watch him leave. He told me he would miss us. He had his Ray-Bans propped on top of his head. I had this bad feeling, like maybe I'd never see him again. But I chalked it up to it being 4 a.m., the hour when the mind's anxious volcanoes erupt, when everything seems bleaker than it really is. It was just three weeks, I told myself. I could do three weeks. And I went back to sleep until Greta woke me again an hour later, when my mind was still molten.

UNSENT EMAIL TO MEGAN

Hello from the depths of the hellish mind tunnel that is 4 a.m. Are you awake, wherever you are? Where are you? I'll tell you where I am: on the hideous glider chair we found on the sidewalk on North 9th and installed on the mezzanine, feeding Greta again. You don't even know about Greta, which is so weird. How can you not know I have a daughter? But that's not why I'm writing. I'm writing because I need to write something, and I can't seem to write something without knowing I will send it to someone, and that someone has always been you. So here goes.

A young woman met a young man in Brooklyn and they fell in love in a very Brooklyn way that had a lot to do with developing their individual and combined identities and aesthetics. There was just enough tenderness and need for the relationship to evolve into something real, or at least *realer* than the relationships they'd had before, being that they'd romantically transacted for most of their adult lives in a land of mirrors where it often felt impossible to know oneself or another in a deep way that went beyond the signifiers they each held in front of them like some kind of cultural armor: artists and books they loved, tote bags emblazoned with institutions or causes they theoretically supported, clothing that was very tight or very loose, very punk or ironically prim, always in reference to already-established identities that could now, in this collage of a decade, be donned and discarded like snake skins. These two, the protagonists in this story, were really trying—they both wanted to be good at what they did, and they also wanted to be good in general, and the world worked against them sometimes and for them sometimes, and together they felt better than they did alone.

They had a baby, and the existential and visceral mood of that shift made the woman see things differently from before. Her world got smaller and bigger at once. She became an island of feelings, of new tenderness and new, inexplicable rage. The man did not undergo this transformation in the same way, and continued to pursue the things he had always pursued in earnest, as if the hierarchy that had existed in his small world remained entirely intact. He accepted a job that took him very far away for a number of weeks, and the woman was left to inhabit her island alone, knowing that for these weeks she would not have any ship or dinghy that could return her to the mainland of what she'd come to understand as the real world.

The trip elevated the man in a professional sense, making him even more real to the real world than he already was. But while he was gone, the woman and the very small child had become one thing, a kind of amoebic blob that suckled on itself, surviving on an endless supply of milk and flesh and love. When the man returned, he told the woman about his newfound success, and she just laughed. He asked her what was so funny, but she couldn't explain it. You were gone for so long, she said. You'd never get the joke. The husband felt left out, of course. When his phone rang he answered it eagerly, knowing it might be another assignment, someone who wanted him to be somewhere, who thought he'd be the best man for the job.

Greta started crying, and the story wasn't going anywhere anyway, so I saved the email to drafts, where it would sit indefinitely.

THE MOTHER'S DAY CATALOG

After a few days of Greta watching Greta, which seemed to be going surprisingly well, I got back into the groove at the office, my feet planted firmly in the corporate soil. It helped to be busy, and I was very busy trying to write the Mother's Day catalog. The theme of the catalog was that moms could still be sexy and fun. The model they had chosen was a semifamous writer who was also a mom who was also very beautiful and funny. She had it all, and the point of this catalog was to provoke the desire to have it all alongside her. The mom who was flipping through this catalog would feel both envious and inspired by this beautiful semifamous writer in her sexy pajama shirt or mid-height block heels, and in a fit of self-possession that took the form of a nineties rom-com montage, take it upon herself to circle the item of her envy-desire for her husband or teenage child to find later, this catalog splayed open on the kitchen table, surrounded by chipped coffee mugs and newspapers full of more bad news. Amid the messy realities of her real life, a circled object pointed to the possibility of an alternate existence.

Usually, I was good at writing women's catalogs because I could easily imagine myself as the person who might be reading them, even if I did not particularly like the merchandise on offer. When I wrote about dresses or bras or jeans I could identify the yearning that might arise upon seeing the item of clothing, that particular hopefulness that wearing it might actually change your life. I understood how it felt to desire a fabric, to want to feel the tight crush of new denim, to imagine oneself arriving to a dinner date looking just like the model in the photograph, only more real. I also knew that this desire wasn't necessarily about beauty, but about existence itself. We wanted the clothes not because we thought we would look good in them, necessarily, but because they confirmed we were alive, that we were a body that needed to be clothed, a self that deserved to be expressed through the ways we chose that clothing. A dress that a thousand other women had could make us feel vital and viable, even special. But this specialness, this feeling, was not designed to last. The dress's power decreased every time you wore it. It would inevitably expire with time, not unlike a life.

Usually, I loved this shit. Entering the pleasurable psychology of considering a garment, contemplating the semiotics of fashion, diving into the minds of the many women who might read the catalog I had written. But I was having a terrible time with the Mother's Day catalog. I found myself unable to tap into the part of my brain that understood my customer, partly because I knew that I *should be* that very customer but was not. Before becoming a mother, I was able to find my way out of my own life for long enough to inhabit another, to imagine that I was wealthy enough, for example, to buy the expensive dress that I was selling. But when I looked at the $350 pajama shirt draped so elegantly on the bony body of the semifamous writer-model-mom, I found that it was so far away from anything I could imagine that it actually enraged me. I wanted to point out that the bra the woman was wearing was not a nursing bra; I could tell by the lace peeking out just above the neck of the pajama top. I wanted to place a bet on the fact that this woman had full-time child-

care. I wanted to rip open her pajama top and inspect her stomach for a
C-section scar, which I knew would not be there; most likely, she had
expressed the baby from her vagina quite fluidly, with the kind of grace
and quiet power that a naturally competent woman should contain within
her. This was the kind of mythical woman who didn't get the drugs.

Yes, she was mythical; she was a myth. In my logical brain, I understood that the woman was a construction, that her reality looked much
different than these images suggested. She'd most likely leaked breast milk
onto one of the silk pajama tops on set, destroying it and setting back the
whole shoot schedule. She probably had the bags under her eyes that all
mothers had, that had been erased by a team of skilled retouchers. She
may or may not have gone through a period, a few months after her baby
was born, where she was so depressed that she no longer wanted to wake
up in the morning. But the real her had been preened and flattened and
augmented by creative directors and Photoshop wizards, by stylists and
makeup artists, by fashion directors and "storytellers," with the intention
of making us want to be her. But did I want to be her? Or was I furious
at her? Or was I furious at myself for not being her? Would I have been
more inspired by her story if it exposed her truth? Or was I addicted to
the feeling of impossibility that the catalog version of her gave me, the
sense that I was coming up short but that no matter how hard I worked,
how much of myself I tried to change, I could not be the thing I was supposed to want to be?

I sat with the catalog for too long, just looking at it. It could have been
days; time eluded me now. Finally, Faith, who had taken on the manage-
ment of the Mother's Day catalog as a favor to Todd, called me into her
office, wondering where the copy was. I told her I was still working on
it. "Sweets, the deadline was yesterday," she said. "Let's shoot for EOD
today, yeah? We've got to pass on to prepress."

It was as if Faith were speaking another language, or as if I had forgotten the language we once shared. I wanted to respond to her in my own
mother tongue, vocalizing the speedy chaos that was streaming through my

head. If I'm going to get the catalog copy done today, I wanted to say, I'll need to do it in the next hour because I have to pump at noon, and then I need to make sure I have time to get lunch. I'll get that salmon bowl from Pret to be healthy so that my milk is healthy so that Greta is healthy. Greta needs to be healthy because Greta cannot get sick while Wes is gone. I can't take her to the doctor alone because I'd have to take the subway and I can't take the stroller down the stairs without Wes's help, and I can't force Original Greta to take on more hours. Maybe I'd just take her in the carrier. Although last time I took her in the carrier she didn't seem to like facing inward. I wonder how old they are when you face them outward? Either way it is hard for me to clip the buckle by myself. I'll need to ask the dude across the hall to help me, the guy whose cooking smells like old compost. Shit, I need to figure out dinner stuff for me and Greta. Maybe that chicken thing with the arugula. If I get the arugula at the organic place by the loft it will be expensive. I need to write this fucking catalog or I won't have enough money to get arugula. I need to stop spending so much money. I hope Wes starts making more money, or we'll never be able to afford real daycare for Greta. I need to look up how much that Montessori school costs. I bet it's a fortune. Maybe they'll have financial aid but we probably wouldn't qualify because we make too much money to deserve financial aid but not enough to deserve child care. My boobs hurt. I need to pump soon. Maybe I should pump before I write the catalog copy, but then I'll probably not have time to get lunch. I'm starving, actually. Maybe I'll get a burrito.

Of course I did not say any of this out loud to Faith. Instead I nodded obediently and left her office. I knew that no one who did not have a child could possibly understand the kind of psychological torpor that I was experiencing. I didn't expect them to, and yet I was baffled that they didn't *try*. It perturbed me, for example, that Faith did not think to ask me whether the Mother's Day catalog made me terribly, terribly sad. Whether looking at the photographs of the semifamous mom-writer made me want to close my eyes tightly and never open them again. Or alternatively, in other moments, take an ice cube out of my coffee and set it on my computer keyboard, so that it would melt into the keys and render them unusable for the dire task at hand.

TEXT FROM WES FROM GREECE

How's my beautiful brilliant girl today?

A tiny spark of an old flame, when for a split second I believed he was asking about me.

SKYPE

Greta was on Skype with Renata when I got home from work that evening. She was holding Baby Greta up to the screen, showing her off to her mother. I heard Renata cooing through the computer, singing little ditties to my baby. I joined the Gretas in front of the camera and waved to Renata. The image of her was grainy and there was a delay, but I liked seeing her face in my kitchen, and it made me miss her.

"We miss you," I said. I felt panicked just after saying it, fearful that she wouldn't say it back.

Renata smiled, her eyes flickering with that flash of wildness I'd seen before: all the things I'd never know about her, the things she got to keep for herself. She did not say it back.

"I'm glad you're all taking care of each other," she said instead, which was unsatisfying, but felt true.

PRESENTATION

I was supposed to present the Mother's Day catalog to the entire creative team on a Monday. I hated public speaking and was nervous through the weekend. On Sunday night, Original Greta called me and told me she had to do a meet-and-greet with her econ class, so she couldn't make it over on Monday. I was in a bind. I emailed HR to tell them my predicament. I did not hear back until it was too late, and I had already missed the meeting, having stayed home with my tiny child to feed her milk from my breast and rub my nose against hers for many minutes at a time. I got the email from HR Angela late Monday morning. *You're going to need to figure this out*, it said. *You cannot keep prioritizing your family over your job.*

I stared at the email for a long moment, wondering if I had misread it. Could it possibly be that Angela expected me to care more about my advertising job than my child? That she believed that my capacity to make money for her company was worth more than my capacity to produce nutrients from my body? That I could be either my brain or my body, but not both; I had to *prioritize*? Yes, that's exactly what she expected and what she meant. I needed this job to provide for my child, and she knew it. I knew that Angela had kids of her own; I'd seen pictures of them on her desk. But her empathy, if she had it, had been squashed by the system in which she performed. And so she had learned to be callous; I imagined her shrugging her shoulders as she extended this threat. I began to cry. Greta began to cry. I sucked my own emotions into my body to tend to hers, trying in vain to figure out what was wrong, which ended up being that she was struggling to poop but couldn't.

THE DRAWINGS

The morning of the day Wes was due to come home—he'd arrive very late that night—Todd called me into his office. I figured he was going to yell at me about missing the presentation, or about how bad the Mother's Day catalog had turned out. Instead, it was about taking me out for cocktails. Did I want to go out for cocktails with Todd sometime this week? Maybe Thursday? Would Thursday work?

I felt confused, angry, and slightly intrigued. I looked around at Todd's office, taking special note of the square lamp Megan had once drawn. He had pictures of his wife in modern silver frames.

"Is this . . . a joke?" I said.

"Why would it be a joke?" Todd said. "I thought we were . . . friends? A little bit? No?"

"We used to be a little bit friends before you fired my actual friend," I said, surprising myself. I knew I shouldn't be speaking like this to Todd, who was many rungs above me on the corporate ladder and could probably get me fired. But I was angry. I was angry that I was here at this carpeted office instead of home with my child. I was angry that I was tasked with writing about sexy moms when I was leaking milk out of my breasts. I was angry that Todd had fucked Megan and then fired her. I was angry at myself for not having backed Megan up when she'd wanted to sue him.

"Oh, come on," Todd said. "You know it wasn't my choice to let her go. I don't have that kind of power."

The blood in my veins grew hot and my skin prickled, the way it did when I went from angry to furious.

"Of course you do," I said.

Todd tilted his head in a display of confusion.

"Of course you have power," I said. "You've always had it, just by being born a man you've always had it, living within you from the very start. So you can't even see it."

"I'm not sure what you're talking about."

My arms felt electrically charged, like they might swing at something of their own accord—maybe the lamp. I knew, though, that I could not lose my shit in Todd's office. That I could not scream at him the way I wanted to, or even tell him off calmly. I knew that Todd's story would win out over mine in the end. I could not afford to lose my job, not now that

I had Greta to take care of. I breathed in a sip of air and straightened my shoulders.

"Do you want to just ask me whatever it is you wanted to ask me now?" I said. "Instead of forcing me to miss my child's bedtime to accompany you to cocktails?"

Todd held up a single finger, which kept me there, as if he were the conductor and I was an obedient oboist. I waited as he pulled something out of his desk drawer, which made no sound as it opened. It was a magazine, an arts and literary journal, one that I recognized and often read. It was one of the publications that was considered cool; it was intellectually rigorous with a dash of contemporary pop, designed in a way that made it feel both friendly (warm serif fonts) and casually exclusive (if you knew why it was cool, you knew why it was cool). I had often imagined what it would be like to have a story published in this very publication, but had never let myself actually hope for it. The magazine was discerning, and would likely reject me.

"Have you seen this?" Todd said, nodding at the magazine.

"Sure, I've seen it. They stock it at my local bookstore."

"No, I mean this issue. Have you read it?"

I shook my head, feeling embarrassed. I really, really wished I had already read it. Todd leaned back in his fancy chair, which was much nicer than the chairs the rest of us sat in. I noticed he was wearing striped silk socks.

"Page thirty-eight," he said.

I picked up the magazine and flipped to page thirty-eight, where there was a drawing that I recognized immediately as Megan's; I could spot her wonky, confident lines anywhere. The drawing was the self-portrait I'd seen in her sketchbook, of her reflected image in her phone. Holy shit, I thought. She *published this.*

I looked up at Todd, who gave me a little nod that seemed to mean *keep going.* I turned the page, and there was another drawing, this one of an older woman looking at herself in the mirror. Behind her were many braided strands of garlic. It was so good, especially the garlic. If I could write something that was as poignant as that garlic, I thought, I would know that all my effort had been worth it.

I immediately thought of responding to these drawings, writing something to complement them, as we had done for so long, sending our words and images across the office to each other. I thought about how women looked at each other and themselves, how they saw their own reflections in each others' gazes, found themselves in each others' stories. I thought about the garlic, imagined breaking open the bulb to reveal the flower of the cloves, nestled up against each other like pungent petals.

Todd, growing impatient, turned the page for me and pointed at the final drawing, which was stark compared to the others, mostly blank except for the outline of a pregnancy test, labeled Screen Italia, set diagonally across the page.

"Holy *shit*," I heard myself say out loud, forgetting I was with Todd. The picture transported me back to that bathroom near the train station, holding on to Megan's waist as I squatted over that Italian toilet.

Todd said something, but I no longer cared about Todd, I barely heard him. The more I looked at that sad little Screen Italia stick, the more my feelings morphed, and I began to understand what Megan had done with these drawings. She had done what she'd always aimed to do, pressed the regular up against the sublime, but she'd also done something else, something I wanted to do with writing, which was acknowledge the everyday questions and private hells and particular pleasures and banal maneuverings of womanhood. Peeing on the stick. Looking in the mirror at your constantly transforming face. Releasing the garlic's profound smell as you crushed it with a knife. The guilt, the ecstasy, the billions of moods. Crying in a bathroom near the train station. Your fate altered with that one extra little line. She'd done it. She'd made art out of life. And although a tinge of jealousy arose in me, that she had been published and I had not been, that she had followed through with her art and I had not, I felt something else, too. It was part pride, that my friend had made these pictures, and part power. Megan's work made me feel powerful, even righteous. It made me feel validated, understood, *seen*.

"Emily?" Todd said, leaning forward and trying to meet my eyes. "Did you hear me? I said: *Was Megan pregnant?*"

I realized then that Megan hadn't told Todd about the pregnancy or her abortion, which I hadn't expected for some reason, imagining the heat of their affection for each other meant they would have weathered that storm together. She had gone through all of that alone, without him and without me. It made me incredibly sad to think about it. I knew that if she hadn't told him, it was for a reason, so as satisfying as it would have been to throw her abortion in Todd's face, I held back.

"No, Todd," I said, surprisingly calmly. "*I* was pregnant. Or do you not remember? How I waddled into meetings with my giant stomach? You don't remember that? You didn't notice my ankles? How swollen they got? You don't recall, do you? But you must remember the milk stains, right? The milk, all over my shirt at the swimwear meeting? I tend to overproduce."

"Of course I knew you were pregnant," Todd said, shaking his head. "I'm talking about *Megan*. Why would she have drawn this?"

"For me," I said quietly, more to myself than to Todd. She drew this for me.

I felt myself growing taller. *Just fucking do it*, I heard Megan say, in her husky angel voice.

I looked up. Looked Todd directly in the eyes.

"I know you're not technically my boss," I said. "But I quit."

"Emily," Todd said scoldingly.

"You should quit, too," I said icily. "Before anyone finds out that you fucked my friend and then fired her."

Todd went white, and before he could explain himself, before he

could tell me that he never meant to hurt Megan, that in fact he loved
Megan, that in fact she might have been the great love of his life. He'd
let her go—yes, it had been his recommendation to add her to the list
of layoffs—precisely for that reason, because she'd meant so much to
him, because it was too painful to see her and not be able to have her.
But I didn't catch any of this—I'd already walked out of his office with
his copy of the magazine.

I felt victorious and righteous for exactly one minute, as I stormed
through the halls and heard the door click shut behind me for the
final time. But as I stood in the empty elevator, waiting for it to close
and seal me into its little box, I realized just how unvictorious I was.
Todd would quit or not quit, but either way he'd be fine. He'd become a creative director before he was thirty. He'd shed his grievances,
forgetting the love he'd felt for my friend, and continue to sit in big
offices with his personal lamps, taking credit for other people's work,
basking in other people's glow. Todd would only rise, levitate, be lifted.
It was me—the elevator began its speedy descent—who was going
down.

ELEVATOR TEXTS

Me: *Get home soon, please.*
Wes:
Probably at the airport already, or somewhere without servce. But still:
silence was silence.

URGE

After quitting my job, I returned to the loft in the middle of the day.
Original Greta had taken Baby Greta on a walk, and the place was quiet

and empty. Greta had cleaned up; the dishes were done and Baby Greta's dirty clothes were in the hamper. The blankets had been folded neatly over the back of the couch, which I lay down on and sighed. I knew I was going to regret what I had just done: I would no longer have health insurance for me or my child, I would no longer have an income and would need to rely on my savings. Beyond that, I knew that my job, no matter how much I complained about it, had been a kind of home for me. I thought about the kind and fatherly Chief Marketing Officer giving me high-fives in the hall ever since we bonded over my spilled coffee; the comforting smell of my cubicle; the way Hans made me feel genuinely motivated when he prompted our brainstorm sessions; Reed's razor-sharp humor and Fiona's calming essential oils; the endless well of puns and wordplay I could draw upon to feed my corny, word-loving appetite. Working there, I had been a part of something; a group of people had counted on me to be somewhere every day. To be counted on felt to me like being loved, or perhaps like loving, and I realized I did love that place, those people, that desk, and I would miss them, and I hadn't even said goodbye.

I felt like an old woman, lying down in the middle of the day, which I didn't like. I sat up quickly. I went to the kitchen to get myself some water. My laptop was there on the table, open but dark. It looked inviting and threatening at once: a black hole that could suck me in or spit me out. I thought about Megan's drawings. The drawings themselves, yes, but also how she had published them in that particular magazine, a magazine she knew I read. Had she meant for me to see them? Were they some kind of olive branch? Or were they simply what they were: a marker of Megan's talent and success, a few pages in a perfect bound book?

Regardless of what the drawings meant to Megan, they filled me with that old, familiar urge: I suddenly wanted to write. I sat down at the table. In the afternoon, the sun was on the other side of the building, so the kitchen was shadowed. I liked darkness for writing. It made me feel cloaked and invisible. I could do this. I wanted to. With Wes coming home tomorrow, everything would change: I'd quit my job, so I'd probably be the one who'd have to stay home with Greta now. It felt like a last chance, one last sacred moment of solitude and space. Right now. Now. I opened a document. But just as the blank white square emerged onto my screen, I heard the key in the door. The Gretas were home, and my ideas flew away like doves. I wanted to cry. A switch flipped in my body, and I reached my arms out toward my child desperately, as if she had been gone for days.

DRINKING WINE WITH GRETA

Greta stayed for dinner. We stood in the kitchen after Baby Greta had gone to sleep, ripping lettuce and drinking wine. She showed me how to make a simple red sauce with fresh tomatoes and a few herbs and a chunk of butter. It seemed too easy to be as delicious as it was.

"Paolo and I broke up," she said at one point, without much emotion.

"What!" I said. I feigned surprise even though I had known from the beginning that she and her Italian boyfriend wouldn't stay together forever; long distance never worked for the young.

"I was sad for about an hour," she said. "And then I went out walking around my dorm, and I realized I actually felt so much better. I saw this woman in the park, wearing a silk scarf around her neck. She was looking up at all the cherry blossoms. And I thought: That is what New York is for. For being alone and looking up."

I smiled. I could tell she was already a little bit drunk from her glass of wine; her English had become fluid in the way that second languages do with alcohol.

"You know what I like about it here?" Greta continued. "Is that everybody matters but nobody matters, you know? You could be a big star or a regular person and nobody would look at you. But you also feel like if you were in trouble, people would see you and they would help."

"I couldn't have said it better myself," I said.

"In Italy, I felt like I had to always be happy," she said. "If I wasn't happy, or if I wasn't good enough in school, or if I wasn't helping cook the dinner or clean the house, I was afraid . . . I would make my mom sad." She looked up at me.

"Oh, sweetie," I said, reaching a hand to her face, as I had seen Renata do so often. "You never made her sad. Maybe she was sad for other reasons, but never because of you."

Greta's eyes narrowed. Her eyes seemed to say: *You know that's not true.* I could tell she wanted to say something else, and I knew it was about that moment we'd shared, when she'd overheard her mom, revealing her feelings about her daughters: how angry she was with them for keeping Massimo's baby a secret, how it hadn't been her idea to adopt in the first place. I could feel an accusation in Greta's eyes, or some kind of challenge. She seemed to be begging me to tell the story back to her, to either validate or negate it, to explain to her: Had she cost her mother that much?

I wanted to tell Greta that what she'd overheard was just her mother's anger at Massimo, that she had done nothing wrong. I wanted to tell her about overhearing my own mother outside the confession booth. I wanted to tell her about the conversation I'd had with Renata when I visited last year, about her description of motherhood—how there was no other love that came close, how it had been its own kind of scholarship. I wanted to tell her what I knew for certain now that I had a child of my own: that she and Bene were Renata's best, most precious things. But before I could say anything, my phone vibrated and lit up on the counter between us.

"Sorry," I said, clicking the green button on the screen. "I need to get this."

It was Faith, from work, wanting to know what happened, why I'd stormed out of Todd's office like that, if I was coming back. I got up from the couch and walked to the window with Faith's voice in my ear. I watched the moonlight bounce off in the gutter puddles on Kent Avenue. There were tears in my eyes. I told her that no, I wasn't coming back, that it had become too much for me, that I just couldn't be there anymore.

MIDNIGHT

Greta took the subway back into the city, and I was left alone with the rest of the wine. I drank it and paced the loft. In my mind, Megan's drawings swam around with Greta's words, then caught on Baby Greta's sleepy whimpers. I felt distinctly guilty. It had to do, I knew, with my avoidance, or my silence. Of letting down these women I loved—Greta, Megan, Renata, Ann—in some crucial way. Of knowing what to say but being unable to say it. Of having the stories inside me but being unable to get them out, offer them up for people who might want or need them, all because of my own stupid fear. What was I so afraid of? Of rejection? Of not being good enough? Of hurting someone? But all of that had already happened in other ways; I no longer had anything to lose.

I got up from bed and sat at the kitchen table under the lamp's little circle of light. I opened the literary journal to Megan's drawings again, studied them for a while. Then I got up and went to the junk drawer, where I found that tube of blue paint I'd bought for her so long ago. I also retrieved the blanket I'd brought Greta home from the hospital in, which smelled like Ann's detergent, from when she'd held her for hours while she slept, and Renata's locket, which I squeezed tightly before placing it on the table next to Megan's drawing of the pregnancy test. I breathed in, stretched my arms above my head, and then, very quicky, as if the keyboard were hot, began to write.

DEAR GIRL

It came out as a letter. At first I didn't know who it was to, exactly, but as I wrote I began to see the image of a girl. She was younger than me, unsmiling, wondering what the world was. I could see her there, amorphous but steadily present, in my mind's eye. I didn't know what I was going to say to her, but I knew I wanted to tell this girl what a woman's life was like. Not what it should be, but what it was. Or what it had been for me.

I began with my birth, with the bodily feeling of being left alone in my existence. I cataloged sense memories of my childhood—the ache I'd felt outside of the confession booth, the stifling feeling of Ann's too-clean house, our rigid schedule. I wrote about escaping, about finding my way to San Francisco and then New York, riding elevators in shiny office buildings, meeting Megan, falling in love with her, making our book, flying to Italy together, the electric current of our friendship powering us both toward our secret dreams. I wrote about writing, about how I stole time to do it, how it crackled within me and then blew up my life, acting as a catalyst for the destruction of my truest friendship. I wrote about finding out I was pregnant in Italy, and telling Renata, and telling Wes, how we'd decided to keep it. I wrote about my pregnancy and I wrote about my birth, about seeing my daughter for the first time.

Dear girl, I wrote. *There you are.*

Dear girl, are you part of me, or are we separate? When you hurt, will I hurt? When I hurt, will you? Here, here, drink from my gigantic breast. There you go. It's okay, it's okay, it's okay. There you go. There we go. Shhh. That's it. Shhh. Quiet now. Don't cry, my girl. Don't cry. I'll tell you a story about a horsey with braids in its tail. I'll tell you a story about crab apple trees in springtime. I'll tell you a story about moons with faces and faces in clouds, and cat whiskers, and summer rain in New York City, running down Mott Street with your tongue out, holding hands with your best friend. I'll tell you a story about best friends, about wine poured in ceramic cups and midnight text messages, about holding each other in the back of a cab and crying. I'll tell you about sharing clothes and not washing them so they'll stay smelling like her, so you feel understood every time you put them on. And about the harsh words women can say and not mean, how you'll feel like you can't take them back. This is what I want to tell you, girl: Take them back. Replace them with other words. Words like *seagull* and *spoon* and *soft*.

But I must, too, tell you a story about men. About how exciting they are, their flat bodies and tender forearms, their collarbones and cursed pasts, the way they walk with their shoulders back. How their sturdiness can feel like truth, how it sometimes is. How they can possess a certain kindness, different from a woman's, that is not attached to anything other than itself. How they can move your heart a half inch to the left, and how you feel you might die for them, or are living for them, until you realize, in some anti-climactic moment after their approval of you stops mattering, that you are not. Let me tell you a story about how you are living for *you*, searching for beach glass on a foreign beach, far from any boy you've ever loved, thinking about the book you're reading, a novel about a woman who goes crazy, and how you'll begin worrying, fearing, knowing, that one day you'll go crazy, too, even if only for a little bit, for a hot second, when you see the madness of your existence glimmer like it sometimes does, in the steam from a pot of soup, in the middle of sex, in the aisle seat as the plane rises away from the earth. Let me tell you a story about makeup, about putting it on with anticipation and wonder, about how it both conceals and reveals at once, making you look more and less like yourself. Let me tell you a story about tampons and glitter shoelaces and tiaras and moods. About summer camp and cruelty and cutting off all your hair.

I want to tell you a story, dear girl, about mothers. About how having lost one feels like a hole in your body, just above your belly button. About looking to fill that hole everywhere, in every person you meet, wondering, always: Will this person love me like she would have? Will this person love me even if I am vile, even if I cry, even if I am wrong, even if I embarrass myself, even if I am a disaster? Let me tell you how it will be impossible to find her, how you will search and search and turn up empty-hearted again and again. And how the mother you do have, if you are lucky enough to have one, will disappoint you—how you'll overhear her confessions: how you deterred her dreams, how she cannot handle you, how you're too much, how you've done the wrong thing, how you've let her down. But let me assure you—because I now know this from experience—that she is angry with the world and not with you, and that she is tired. Yes, you make her tired. But you also make her whole. And then suddenly there she is, surprising you. Lifting you up in a piazza and kissing you on the mouth. Standing above you in the hospital room when your child has been ripped from your belly. And in your pain and your horror and your bliss you will look at this person, this mysterious woman to whom you belong, and think: *She's been there all along.*

Dear girl, she will come at the right moment, and she will come in many forms. You will find her in your purse, inside a tube of red lipstick. You will find her when you're far away: she'll appear, like a shape-shifter, in the form of a black-haired professor or a wild-haired eleven-year-old, or a best friend who sits across the table from you, sipping her wine. She's in the eyes of the woman at the pizza shop, in the glint behind the towers. She's there in every character of every story: she is the girl and the beach and the whale, all at once. Your mother is everywhere, inside you and also in every woman who helps build you, who texts to see if you got home okay. Sometimes, she's so omnipresent it feels like she might swallow you up.

Dear girl: I will try not to swallow you up. I will try not to devour the skin around your knees the way I want to, or lick your tears, or breathe your breath. I'll just watch you as you fall asleep. That's it, close your little eyes. Fall into the kind of sleep you'll only ever get now, before the darkness of the world invades your dreams. Dream of milk at body temperature, gauzy blankets, the washes of light that float in and out of your gaze. Do not dream of wars or men or bulldozers. Do not dream of supermarket gleam or overdraft charges. Those things will come later. Right now you

are allowed to be a body, you are allowed to be a sponge, you are allowed
to be taken care of without feeling the guilt of being taken care of. If
you let me be your mother, I will be. I am here, dear girl. I am right
here.

IMPULSE DECISION

I saved the document and closed it. I felt wild—both lighter and heavier
than I ever had, like I was spinning around on a cloud. Wes was going
to be home any minute now; it was already 1 a.m.. It occurred to me,
strangely, that I never could have or would have written any of what I
had just written if Wes had been here, which made me feel a weird dread
at the thought of him walking through the door. I felt time compressing.
The real world closing in again. If I didn't act now, I knew I never would.

My first impulse was to send what I'd just written to the magazine
that had published Megan's drawings. This would be like an extension
of our book project, I thought: publishing things for each other, back and
forth. But for whatever reason, that magazine didn't feel like the right fit:
it was too cerebral, too cool, and I knew in my heart of hearts that what
I'd written didn't belong there. Plus, this piece wasn't for Megan, not exactly. It was mine.

Then I had a thought. Or maybe, a thought that jogged a thought. I
thought of Todd, belowdecks on the ferry, asking me why I'd never gotten
in touch with the editor of my mother's story. I thought of the bomb that
had exploded and then fizzled in my mind; I had never followed up on
his idea, perhaps scared of what I'd find, or wouldn't. But now I opened
a search window without hesitation, as if I were a new woman with new
blood pumping through my veins: brave blood, nothing-to-lose blood. I
found the digitized issue of *The Haight*, quickly scanned the masthead:
Rebecca Simon, editor-in-chief. Another quick Google search to find
that she still worked as an editor, now for an indie journal based out of

Seattle called *Clouds*; they were accepting submissions on a rolling basis. Before I could think about it anymore, before Wes opened the loft door and whatever witchy writing spell I was under evaporated, I submitted the crazy letter I'd just written, along with a breathless note explaining that I was the daughter of Moni Lastra, the writer Rebecca Simon had published so long ago.

A bubble appeared on my screen: This email has no subject line.

The Woman and the Whale, I typed in the subject box.

Click.

Send.

And there were Wes's keys in the door.

JUST STOP

With his duffel over his shoulder and a five-day beard, Wes looked different. I felt my heart leap a little bit, an old nervousness returning to me from a past life, as if these weeks without Wes had negated all the time I'd spent with him; suddenly a series of old questions presented themselves anew: *Who is this person I am standing across from? Does he love me, and will he forever?*

"Hey!" he said now, grinning, tossing his duffel down and embracing me.

"It's you!" I replied, hugging him back.

We kissed and he tasted like traveling. All the questions flew away after the kiss. He was just Wes, wearing a new shirt and his old Levi's. He was familiar and cozy, and I was glad he was home.

"Is she down?" he said, nodding toward the mezzanine, where Greta slept.

I nodded. He put his hand on my lower back. I knew that he would want to have sex—it was what people did after long trips—so though I had no interest—the idea of having another body clinging to my flabby, scarred, tender one made me feel actually sick—I pulled him close to me and tucked my hand into the waistband of his jeans. He didn't stop me, exactly, but he didn't return the advance, so I pulled my hand out. I felt stung but ultimately relieved. He dug in his tote bag for a bottle of retsina he'd brought back, and we sat at the kitchen table to drink it. It burned the inside of my mouth.

"So tell me everything," I said.

"It was wild," he said. "Incredible, and horrifying. How white the houses look against the brown hills, and the ocean is this pure blue-green. And then the contrast of that beauty with what's happening—these people are living in conditions you couldn't even imagine. The camps are either totally flooded, with these giant puddles, or completely overcrowded, to the point where people are literally sleeping on top of each other. I've never seen anything like it. Not even after Katrina, not even close."

I was listening, but I had gotten caught up in the giant puddle, and had been imagining a mother with a baby in her arms trudging through it, like the one in Wes's photo from that Bushwick show. Once I imagined it, I couldn't get it out of my mind. I could see her face, the pleading yet resigned expression, the blank stare of her dark eyes. The look of mothers everywhere.

"Em," Wes said. "You hear me? I have something I need to tell you."

The woman in the giant puddle disappeared.

"Okay," I said to Wes.

"I just want to say first that I love you," he said. My heart and mind started to race. "And that I didn't mean for this to happen." I knew what he was going to say, but I also had no idea.

"Okay," I managed again.

"It's Sarah," he said.

"Oh my god," I said, understanding everything immediately. Sarah Hughes, the writer he'd traveled with. Hotels and hotel bars and hotel beds. The close quarters of collective creativity. The sensuality of captur-

ing a story together. Of course. What an idiot I had been for not imagining it sooner. Or had I imagined it? Had I known all along, from the first
time he'd said her name?

"Nothing happened," Wes said defensively. "I didn't cheat on you. I
wouldn't do that."

"But you like her," I said. I was incredulous, and yet I also felt like I
was seeing something clearly that had been fuzzy for so long. This was
not a new story. The outline of Wes crisped as the truth came into view.
He nodded.

"You want to be with her."

He nodded again.

"Jesus Christ, Wes," I said. I felt dizzy. My whole reality was spinning. I realized I had made the grave mistake of misunderstanding Wes
on a fundamental level. I had, from the beginning, figured him to be, if
nothing else, a loyal person, someone who firmly committed himself to
something once he had chosen it—I assumed he was with people the way
he was with his work. But now I saw that this loyalty pertained only to
himself—he was loyal, to the bone, to his own vision.

"I'm sorry," he said. "It's the worst. This isn't like me—I feel like
absolute shit."

"Then stop," I said, suddenly wanting to plug my ears, or run away,
to forget Wes had ever told me what he'd told me, so that we could go
back to whatever it was we were before this moment. "Stop telling me.
Why are you telling me?"

"I'm not telling you to hurt you, Em. I love you and I love Greta—but
I also feel . . . I also feel like myself for the first time in a really long time.
And I can't just look away from that."

"Wow," I said, shaking my head. "This is really rich. Feeling like yourself. Wow. That must feel really good, Wes. I would have no idea what that
feels like, actually. I can't even imagine. What a beautiful luxury."

"Fuck, Emily," he said. "Can we just have an actual conversation like
actual adults? Like can you look at me as a person who has complicated

feelings, not someone who's out to get you with everything I do? It's not like I feel good about this. This is hard."

"Complicated feelings? How is wanting to fuck someone else complicated? Seems very straightforward to me."

"I don't just want to fuck her, Emily. She inspires me. She actually listens when I talk, cares about the work I'm doing, wants to have a conversation about something other than how big our baby's shit was. When was the last time either of us inspired the other? You and I have been so . . . at odds lately. Even before the baby. We aren't bringing anything to the table for each other, we aren't making each other better. I feel like I disappoint you all the time, like I can't make you happy. All you do is nag me, tell me I'm doing things wrong, push me out of the bed. And you know what the worst part of it is—I was fine alone before you. I didn't need anyone. I don't even know how it happened, but I started needing you, and now . . . now it's all needing and no wanting . . . it doesn't feel like you want me anymore. You only look at Greta. You push me away. And it's fucking lonely."

"You don't think I feel lonely, Wes? Waking up every night, every two hours, sleepwalking through feedings, all alone? Sitting in supply closets pumping milk three times a day? Walking around the neighborhood again and again, trying to get her to sleep in the stroller? Never seeing anyone, never talking to anyone, never having one minute to myself, or for my work? I want to look at you, I do. I want to be good for you, for you to want me. But this is all I have in me right now. This is what I am right now."

"But you *wanted* this, Em," Wes said. "You're the one who wanted this baby."

"You know I've been waiting for you to do this since we decided to have her?" I said. "I've just been waiting for it, knowing it was coming. You blaming it on me. Pushing it all on me."

"I'm not pushing it on you. I'm just saying you must have had some idea it would be like this, that this is what you were getting into. But now

all you do is complain about it. Every little injustice, every little choice
you act like everything is an impossible task, and you're never fucking
happy. Where's the joy, you know? It's honestly exhausting, just being
around you, fielding all this negativity."

"I can't actually believe you're saying this to me right now. I feel so
misunderstood it's actually crazy."

"Well, I'm sorry, but this is what it feels like from the outside. You
don't make it very easy to feel any other way."

"So you're actually going to do this? You're actually going to leave?
Leave your kid? That's actually what you're going to do?"

"I'm not going to *leave her*," Wes said. "I'm going to be here. I'm
going to be Greta's dad. That's the difference here, Emily. I don't think
being Greta's parent is some problem to solve. Something to get out from
under."

"How dare you," I said. "How fucking dare you. Out from under? I
am under. I am all the way under it, Wes. *That's* the difference. You have
one fucking foot in the water. You have no idea what it's like."

"I'm sorry," Wes said. "You're right. I don't know what it feels like to
be you. But I do know what it's like to be in a relationship with you. And
I can't do it anymore. I'm tired of feeling like I'm a bad person all the
time, like I haven't made any sacrifices for you and Greta, because I have,
I make them every fucking day, all day long, endlessly, and you don't seem
to see any of it. In fact, you don't seem to see me at all."

"No!" I practically yelled. "It's you who doesn't see me! It's like you've
always wanted me to be something I'm not. Even the photographs you
took of me, back when you took photographs of me—they never really
looked like me. It was like you saw someone else when you looked at me,
and then when you realized it was just me, that I was *this*, you want to run
away!"

I was crying now, soft, fluid tears running down my hot face.

"Well, maybe neither of us sees the other," Wes said. "Maybe that's
my point."

"Or maybe you're too selfish to actually love someone," I said, knowing it wasn't true as I said it. I knew, even in that moment, that Wes was right, that he and I had passed by each other at some point, that we had changed, that we had traveled too far away from each other. But it didn't keep me from feeling furious at him for being the one to say so. It didn't keep me from not wanting him to go, or feeling the incredible loneliness of the loft without him in it, even when he was still here.

"I'm sorry you feel that way about me," he said. "I do love you and I didn't mean to hurt you. But I understand you're mad. You're right to be. I'll sleep at Kasper's."

"You don't even want to see her?" I said accusingly, knowing I was weaponizing Greta in this moment, trying to make Wes feel bad.

"Of course I want to see her." Wes had a strange, flummoxed look on his face, and I could see him trying to decide whether he should go upstairs to Greta's crib. "I shouldn't wake her up, though, right?"

He looked helpless, like he truly didn't know what he should do.

"Just fucking go," I said. "Go straight to Sarah Hughes's house and fuck her, like I know you want to."

Wes looked at me sadly.

"Stop, Emily. Just stop," he said gloomily, before he left.

FIRST PERIOD

The next day, I woke up alone and puffy-eyed, to silence. I had the brief thought that Greta was dead (this thought occurred almost any time she was quiet), so I rushed to peek in her crib. She was sleeping peacefully on her back, her tiny mouth open just wide enough for a stream of drool to slip out and down her cheek. I breathed in deeply, utterly relieved. A wave of love coursed through my body: warm and real. I wanted to press my mouth onto her mouth in a passionate kiss. Instead, I tiptoed down to the kitchen to make coffee. I cried quietly while the water percolated. I'd gotten good at being quiet so as not to wake Greta, but I felt like bawling loudly, the unhinged kind of crying I'd done as a child. What was I going to do now? Where was I going to live? Why hadn't I seen this coming? What had ever made me think any of this—me and Wes, this baby, this life—would work?

I went to the bathroom while the coffee machine did its thing, where I discovered a cruel dark spot on my underwear—after being missing in action for months, my period had returned. The sight of the blood made me burst into tears again, as if I were experiencing real pain, as if the blood were from a gash I had just gotten. But I *do* have a gash, I wanted to tell someone. But who? Who could I tell that I had a gash? That I was bleeding? That there was *blood coming out of me*? There was no one to tell; I had no one left. I wiped the blood with a wad of toilet paper and inspected the brownish-red mess, the tears still coming. I wanted to smear the blood somewhere, to make some kind of a mark with it, but I knew I wouldn't. I was too scared to do what I wanted, too scared to make any marks. This was why I was all alone, I suddenly realized, because I was fearful of my own desires, my own self: all I ever did was try to seep into other people so that I could barely feel the horror of being individual and alone. But here I was, bleeding out, with no one to witness it. I flushed the bloody wad down the toilet and cried into my hands until I heard Greta crying above me, at which point I leaped up, wiped my face with my sleeve, and ran upstairs as fast as I could to get her.

Look at her, the little wailing mess, rolled up in her silly sleep sack. Look at her wanting someone to scoop her up. *Shhhhhh*, I said as I scooped. But then I corrected myself.

"You know what," I said. "People are going to tell you to be quiet for the rest of your life. Don't be quiet. Go ahead, cry. Cry, my girl. Let it out."

But I was too soothing. Greta quieted in my arms almost immediately, rubbing her cheek into my shoulder. I carried her down the precarious stairs and prepared my coffee with my free arm. I missed Wes's

arms: the way they could do things for me when I needed them to. I
looked over at his desk, where his latest photographs were taped above
his computer. A stranger on the subway wearing a straw hat. A woman
holding a protest sign that read FUCK THE POLICE. A man on his knees,
his face lifted to the sky, as if he was waiting for rain. These were the images that consumed Wes, that inspired him, that moved him. Strangers,
uprisings, communal and individual gestures of pain or glory or plain
old existence. A thought I hadn't had before came to me: When had he
stopped taking photos of me? And why didn't he ever take photos of
Greta? Hadn't he seen me cut open at the belly? Hadn't he seen Greta's
face meet the air for the first time? Hadn't he seen us screaming? Why
hadn't he taken any pictures of us screaming? Perhaps Wes didn't feel
ownership over those gory, tender narratives, thinking they were too personal, too private. Or perhaps they hadn't moved him as they'd moved
me: now these maternal scenes were the only ones I saw when I closed
my eyes.

Greta cried in the specific way that meant she was hungry. I sat down
at the kitchen table and offered her my breast.

I scrolled on my phone while she extracted all the nutrients she
needed from my body. J.Crew was having a sale on ballet flats; Turbo-
Tax wanted me to know their service was easier to use than all the
other services out there; Angela, from HR, wanted to let me know that
today was the last day for me to use my store discount, should I want
to make any final purchases. At first I scoffed at the email, and the
idea of shopping at that stodgy store, until I remembered I needed a
few key items for Baby Greta—a new sleep sack and a few larger PJs.
Their baby things were nice, and I was not one to pass up a discount.
Suddenly convicted, suddenly convinced I could not be in this loft for
a moment longer, suddenly fierce and determined, suddenly a woman
who could and would do everything on her own, I decided I would
put Greta in the baby carrier and haul us both to midtown to get 40
percent off.

VALIDATION

Walking into the department store again felt like entering into another life-warping machine, pulling me into a past existence that now didn't seem plausible. Though I'd been in the store a few weeks ago, I felt like an entirely different person now. How could it have been such a short time ago that I stood in this perfume gallery, listening to the new CEO going on about loyalty? How could I have written the wall text for the sunglasses display just last week? *Bright future, bold shades.* I shielded Baby Greta from the flying particles of Marc Jacobs Daisy and Chanel No. 5 and rushed to the escalator. As we were going up, I saw a familiar silhouette riding down.

It was Essie. Tiny, hunched, wonderful, wearing a classy black tunic, sleeveless with a mock turtleneck collar. I caught her eye for a moment, but it was unclear whether she recognized me. I smiled at her and received no smile in return. She just kept moving slowly down and down, until she reached the main floor. Then—and this nearly broke my soul in half— she shuffled back onto the escalator, going up. I had a sudden revelation: she was the same as me. Here we both were, women caught in the particular loops of our individual existences. We kept being told that the escalators of the world would deliver us out of our present circum- stance and into to the correct department. But the escalators were rigged! They'd been fashioned to keep us on the endless loop of pursuit, holding us hostage in a purgatory of fabricated need, searching for an exit door that was designed to be impossible to find.

Suddenly Greta and I were spit out on the baby floor. I made my way to the sale rack and flipped through the tiny expensive clothes. Sweaters small enough for dolls; brand names waiting to be soiled by sweet potato puree. I found a set of pajamas with elephants on it that looked like it would fit Greta's little body. I felt a pang of missing Essie: her coffee in its little paper cup, her sarcastic *wonderful*, the comfort of being greeted in the same way every day. It was the Essies—the people who were in your orbit

by default, not by any choice of your own—who made up a life. Maybe
the sideburned CEO wasn't so wrong after all. Maybe we had been a kind
of family.

My phone buzzed in my bag. I dug around frantically to find it, my
hand bumping into bottles and diaper creams and pacifiers as I sought
out my hit of cell phone serotonin. A buzz of a phone could mean anything: that you'd won a lottery you hadn't entered; that a plan was being
made and you were an integral part of it; that someone, anyone, loved
you.

Or that someone wanted to publish something you'd written.

What! The buzz was an email from Rebecca Simon. I had not
expected to hear anything back from her, and if I did I thought it might
take weeks. Maybe it was an autoreply, or some kind of spam. But no—
when I opened it, I saw that it was a personal note from Rebecca herself,
telling me that she had read what I sent through.

Emily—

*Normally our interns read submissions first, but your subject line caught my eye. I
remember your mother's story well. I chose it for its brutal simplicity—it said everything
about what it felt like to be a young woman, in such few strokes. In fact, I tried for many
years to get Moni to submit more work. She never did. I never knew what happened to
her, why she stopped writing. But what a gift that story was. And now, this: her daughter writing to me, all these years later. Another gift.*

*I was quite moved by your story. You are a very different writer than your mother
was—she was a minimalist, where you, my dear, are quite verbose—but you share a
recognizable vitality. I do think your piece will benefit from a drastic haircut. (There's
enough for a novel in here, hint hint.) I have some editorial ideas, if you'd be willing to
work with me over the next few weeks to get this in shape for publication. It's a powerful
and brave piece of writing, and I hope to include it, if you're open to working together.
If it is included, we pay $500 per story.*

Sincerely,

Rebecca Simon, Editor

I couldn't quite believe what I was reading. This person—a person who had once accepted the woman who had given birth to me—was now accepting me. Better than acceptance: she wanted to *work* with me, to help me shape my writing to make it better. These days, an offer to help felt like the kindest, most valuable thing, and I coveted it. Someone reaching out toward me, grabbing for my hand. I imagined meeting this editor for a glass of wine, staying for hours. I imagined her nurturing my writing career for decades, staying in touch with weekly progress check-ins. I heard myself laugh out loud. Baby Greta, who had been looking around the bustling store, looked up at me quizzically. What could her mother possibly be preoccupied with that was not her?

I purchased the pajamas and then floated back down the escalators. I felt myself hoping I'd see Essie again, so I could tell her—tell anyone!—about the email I'd just gotten, but I did not. I was delivered to the cosmetics section, offered tests of golden bronzing powder, liquid blush. I smiled and moved forward, out the automatic doors and onto the cold sidewalk. I felt buoyant, incredible, smart, and accepted for who I was.

The street screamed with life. Taxi horns bantered with spring birds. A woman in a pencil skirt stepped out of her high heel accidentally, then laughed at herself when a man kneeled to help her put it back on.

"I'm Cinderella!" she howled, joyfully amused by her own folly.

I grinned. Zara called out to me from across the street. I tried to avoid her gaze and pretend I didn't see her, but she was insistent. *You could find something you love in me!* she called. *I've changed since last time, I promise! This time, no really, I'm serious, this time I'll be just what you need in the ever-evolving moment that is right now!*

I sighed and crossed the street toward her. She opened her air-conditioned mouth for me and I slid in. Oh, Zara. Oh, temporary happiness. Upon entering, I felt the way you feel after the very first sip of a cocktail: the special buzz of possibility. Maybe Zara *had* changed. Maybe their designer rip-offs had gotten so good no one would know the difference. Maybe the fabrics had gotten better. Maybe I'd dip my toes back into fast fashion just this once; no one would have to know. I fingered a billowy jumpsuit. Was that *linen*? If it was, it was linen I could afford, which made it all the more attractive. Also, it was the shape that everyone was wearing these days: it looked like baby coveralls. I wanted to be a baby! I wanted to be a little baby in drop-crotch linen coveralls! I wanted someone to take care of me! Zara, will you take care of me? She whispered in my ear that I deserved to be taken care of. Of course I did; I had finally been accepted by a real editor. I bought the jumpsuit for $69.99 and left the store feeling momentous and in charge. I was a writer with a jumpsuit. I was a writer with a fucking jumpsuit!

I kept grinning as I made my way to the subway, passed through turnstiles as if I were made of water, melted into my plastic seat. Greta fell asleep on me, and I kissed the top of her head while she breathed into my chest. God, I fucking loved her. I opened the email again to look at that word: *novel*. So much possibility there: the word was like a promise. The idea of a novel appealed to me in a way that writing a story did not; it seemed to invite the unruliness that was so much a part of my nature. When I wrote my stories, it was as if they were always butting up against the edges of themselves, fighting against their own constraints, rebelling against their own rules. But a novel, I thought: a novel could hold everything, anything. Birth and Death, Business and Pleasure, Pain and Glory—all of life's bigness, held inside whoever, whatever, I chose to write about. *It said everything about what it felt like to be a young woman*, Rebecca had said about my birth mother's story. What Moni Lastra had done: I wanted to do that, too.

Though it was only four o'clock when I got home, I opened a bottle of wine and toasted myself with half a glass. I turned on a song I liked on my laptop and Greta sat in her bouncy chair and bounced. I smiled until Greta began to cry. I set down my wine and picked her up. I checked her diaper, which was dry. Probably she was hungry. I brought her to the couch and I undid my nursing bra, which I was getting better at. She latched on to my nipple and began to suck. The relief of quieting her was amazing. It lasted for the entire ten minutes of her feeding, which was longer than my excitement about the email did. The excitement had morphed distinctly by the time Greta was finished eating. I felt light-headed and worried. Who would read the story? What would they think of it? What would they think of me? To release something into the world was only to invite potential embarrassment. To try to say something was only to risk others thinking you had nothing to say.

Keys in the door; it was Original Greta, who'd asked if she could come for dinner to escape the drama of her dorm mates, a pair of girls from New Jersey who drank Red Bull vodkas and went clubbing in the Meatpacking District. She plopped down next to me on the couch and stole a sip of my wine.

"You'll never believe it," she said, setting down her bags. "Wait, why do you look sad?"

"Wes left me for a journalist and I might be getting published in a magazine," I blurted.

Greta raised an eyebrow, trying to take in all this information.

"But now I'm freaking out suddenly, and don't know if I should publish it. It might be terrible. Or cruel. Or . . . I don't know. It might be something that I didn't intend it to be."

"Let me read it," Greta said.

"No, you don't have to," I said.

"We're all going to read it at some point," she said.

She was right. I handed her my computer, opened the document. I watched her read.

Like me, Greta furrowed her brow when she was concentrating. Her olive face scrunched into itself, lit by the little screen. She used her two fingers to scroll. At a certain point, her face unscrunched, and silent tears began to roll down her cheeks. She did not wipe them away. She kept reading until the end, and when she was done, she set the computer down

next to her. Then Greta looked up and into my eyes. It sounds strange to
say this, but I don't think I'd looked anyone in the eyes besides my daughter in a while. So when Greta and I looked at each other, I could feel it,
like a cord of trust between us. It brought tears to my own eyes, this look.
I couldn't keep them back.

"Thank you," Greta said.

"I didn't do anything," I said.

"You did," she said, nodding. "This. It feels like . . . like it was for me.
At least a little bit."

I smiled. "It was. I mean, it is."

The wine between us spilled on my couch, tipping the moment. I
rushed to get some baking soda, which never works but the rule was to do
it anyway. I poured the baking soda on the stain and remembered Greta
was going to tell me something.

"Wait, what were you going to tell me, when you first got here?"

"It's Bene," Greta said, as if she were delivering illicit gossip. "She's
engaged."

"What!" I said.

"They're doing it soon, too," Greta said. "End of July. I'm not sure
what all the rush is about."

"She's nineteen!"

"Twenty, now," Greta said. "And apparently it's a good thing? My
mom thinks so, at least."

"I'm assuming she's marrying Fede?"

"Yes," Greta said. "And I like him, so that's good. He's friends with
Paolo."

"So you'll be seeing Paolo at the wedding," I said with a playful smirk,
grateful to be joking around now. Greta grinned and nodded.

"Wow," I said. I was imagining so many things right then, I couldn't
pin anything down. Bene's young body in a white dress. My name in
print. Greta dancing with Paolo at the reception. Wes and Sarah Hughes,
diving into the Aegean Sea at dusk.

"Will you come, Emily?"

"Come?"

"To the wedding," Greta said. "You could be my date."

"I'm afraid you'd have to have two dates," I said, nodding toward the mezzanine.

"You have to be there," Greta said, with a new desperation. I knew she was giving me a blessing, or maybe an offer—she wanted as much as I did for me to be part of their family.

"Of course," I said. It was easy to say, not because of obligation, but because of some other kind of truth I couldn't name but was probably love. "Of course," I said again, just to feel it slide out of my mouth. Then I got up, retrieved Renata's locket from the dish on top of my dresser, and hung it around Greta's smooth neck.

PART NINE

DEATH

RETURN

In July, Baby Greta and I take a sleepless overnight flight to Rome. From there we take a weepy, exhausted train to Bologna Centrale, and here I am again, stepping into the red city with my many bags, shielding my jet-lagged eyes from the bright summer sun. It is early afternoon. Many motorbikes and many teeny Italian cars rush around the traffic circle, picking people up from the station. I manage to hail us a cab, then somehow get all of Greta's gear in the tiny trunk and her car seat in the tiny seat. I dread the brain power it will take to translate what I want to say into Italian, but then it comes out of me almost without trying, as naturally as breath. To the city center, I say. Right past the statue of Neptune.

Over the past few months, everything has changed. Wes moved out of the loft, letting me stay there with Greta so as not to disrupt our routine. He did not move in with Sarah Hughes, but into his own studio apartment in the city, a stone's throw from hers. Probably, I thought, he and Sarah had made a pact. To flourish individually, they'd agreed, it was best to maintain a healthy separateness. It was not a new story.

A few weeks after Wes left, on the first day of June, I returned to the loft to find a letter stapled to the door, alerting me that the landlords were selling the building, and that the developers would be offering to buy the tenants out. Wes's name was still on the lease, but he insisted on giving me half of whatever he made on the place; he considered it both of ours. Though I knew part of this was out of guilt for having left, I also felt moved by Wes's generosity, which I knew was rooted in his deep affection for me, and for Greta. I can't explain this totally, but I somehow knew that

I would always have a place in Wes's heart, both because we had Greta together and because of something else we shared: the dream of ourselves,
the projection of possibility, that we'd cocreated in that early part of our
time together. I knew that this mattered to Wes, like it mattered to me. It
felt comforting, almost, to recall the image of us: two young people, sitting
on opposite ends of a room in an old pantyhose factory, trying to make
something of themselves. Stopping only occasionally to help form the
other's creation—editing a sentence, squinting at an image, punctuating
the story with a stolen kiss. We weren't those people anymore, but each of
us was proof to the other that we once had been.

Within weeks, the loft deal went through and I had more money in
my bank account than I had ever known was possible. I negotiated with
the landlords to stay there through most of July, until we left for Italy
for Bene's wedding. I put our things in a storage unit in Ridgewood, the
same one Megan had stored her things in so long ago; I imagined our
belongings existing together in the dark, like phantoms of who we once
were. I'm not sure when we'll be back to retrieve these boxes of clothes
and books and thrift store silverware. I have not bought a return ticket yet.

We are staying in a small bed and breakfast above one of the fruit
and vegetable markets, because Renata has a full house with her mother
and the girls. The street below us teems with onions and overripe
melons and people shouting. Bulbous hams and thick, powdery salami
hang above giant wheels of cheese, pungent and glowing. Fistfuls of
asparagus lie lazily next to eccentric bushels of frisée; tomatoes as big as
Greta's head, smelling like sun and dirt, nuzzle up to deep purple egg-
plants and fennel bulbs that resemble human hearts chopped off at the
ventricle. The stalls that sell fresh pasta glow yellow, little rooms full of
flour and sunshine, boasting infinite shapes of hand-formed dough: little
ears, little butterflies, curlicues, perfect worms of every length and girth. I
love the sounds of the market: sharp knives hacking through thick stems
and bones, wooden crates banging against other wooden crates, the roller-
coaster cadence of Italian sentences, rising and falling with every impas-

sioned transaction. I love that in Italy people fight about the ripeness of a fig. That there are entire ordeals about which pasta goes with which sauce.

We make it through the hotel's doorway, but Greta's stroller won't fit in the tiny elevator. I have to pull her out, strap her to my body, leave the stroller downstairs, and make multiple trips up with each of our bags. By the time I am finished with this epic task, she is very upset with me. I release her from the carrier and plop her on the bed, give her many kisses on her tight, round tummy.

"Me and you," I whisper in her ear. "Let's get the plane off you."

I undress her, place her in the tiny European bath, scrub her fine hair with the organic shampoo I brought from back home. The warm smell of children's soap fills the bathroom. I think about an artwork Renata showed me in a book from her library, on one of those long nights sitting on her couch. It was a series of photographs by Mierle Laderman Ukeles, in which the artist documented herself dressing and undressing her children in winter clothes, putting on layers just to peel them off again. How many times have I bathed this tiny person, delicately pouring the lukewarm water over her head with my hand? These repetitive, mundane rituals, the new tasks that now fill up my nights and days. I wonder if it would be possible to do with writing what Ukeles did with her artwork—that pure documentation of repeated gestures—or if it would simply become too boring to read, too tedious to even begin to type out.

I rinse Greta's head and towel her off, inhaling the familiar smell of the hotel towel: the ubiquitous Italian detergent, fresh rain and flowers, cut with a strange sourness I can't place. Greta's body is Wes's body: elegant in the shoulders, a bit awkward in the legs, the butt. I love it, it fascinates me. I watch it grow in fits and bursts, as if it is tearing through space to become itself. I am enamored with her little breastless chest. I love her hands, how square her fingernails are, and how tiny. Sometimes I cannot fathom that I had any part in creating this person. Other times, like now, I can see my own eyes in her eyes, feel the warm towel on my own skin as it touches hers, as if we are one being.

"Let's do a *gira*," I say. This is what Italians do: take daily "tours" around town, hoping to bump into each other, yelling salutations from across piazzas that feel as ancient as the earth itself. "*Andiamo*."

Down the old stairs of the hotel and straight into the market. Basil smell already, before we even step outside. Hanging fruits and commotion. Someone ordering a kilo of this. Someone snacking on *un po di* that. I tuck Greta under my left arm, boost her up on my hip, order a basket of blueberries. She rubs the purple juice all over my white shirt and her jumper. I am annoyed until she grins. I puddle when she grins. The world gets brighter. Her grin is the most successful thing I've ever made.

We cross under a portico and emerge into piazza Maggiore, where we sit at an outdoor café and I order a cappuccino. Across from us is the Basilica of San Petronio, with its hulking, unfinished facade—the bottom half is white and pristine, decorated with ornate stonework; the top is plain brown brick, rough and punctuated with holes. When I lived here, I remember feeling oppressed by the building, saddened by the unfinished brick in all its imposing darkness. But now I find myself attracted to the dark half of the building, thankful for it. The brick looks real in a way that the white stone veneer does not; I can see the life in the brick, feel its deep, old warmth: it has seen everything, and the stories of the piazza show through on its weathered face.

As I drink my coffee and watch a pack of pigeons take flight over the church, I am transported into a past version of myself. I am twenty and lonely, searching for belonging in a place I don't belong. I am thirty-one and newly pregnant, utterly confused, sitting across from Megan as she draws the food on our table. I am myself as I am now, holding my tiny child. Suddenly I feel surrounded: all the girls and women I've ever been are at this table, sipping foam, eyeing each other. *I see you have a kid now*, twenty-year-old me says to present-day me, raising her eyebrows skeptically. I remember what it felt like to be her: the judgment I flung around so easily, the flame in my eyes. How I thought I was better than other women because I was younger than them, or freer. How thirty seemed ancient, forty-five impossible. Silly girl, I think, looking back at her now. Marvelous, silly girl.

Greta can always sense when I am somewhere else, and she becomes needy and petulant. She whines pathetically, then wails. I feel unbelievably tired thinking about having to solve her problems, deal with her dirty face and hands. But I dutifully go into the café with her saddled on my hip again, and I ask for a *bicchiere di acqua* to wipe her hands and face with a wet napkin.

"There," I say. "All clean."

She glares at me. Her glassy eyes pierce mine in an accusatory way. I can feel that she wants someone other than me, maybe Wes, who throws her into the air, or Original Greta, who can play peekaboo for hours. Someone who will engage with her fully, without traveling somewhere else in their mind.

"I get it," I tell her.

To want the whole thing of someone but be unable to have it. This is the pain of love.

MOTHER TONGUE

I sometimes think Italian is easier to understand than English, on a language level—the rules of conjugation are easier to follow, and the rhythm feels natural and round in my mouth, rather than clunky or heavy. Strangely, I feel more myself while speaking Italian, even though I am not always getting it right. I wonder if this comes from my birth mother's family, if language, somehow, travels through bloodlines like another kind of DNA. Or maybe I am just good at imitating others; I have heard before that languages come easily to those who are good mimics.

I wonder sometimes if I have mimicked my way through life. If I have simply been able to perform the sounds and acts of friendship, love, and now motherhood, in the same way that I can so easily roll my tongue around a foreign word. Trying so hard, always, to pronounce the word fluently, to not get it wrong, so that I will not be misunderstood, so that I will not go unheard or unloved. But I don't think so, I tell myself now as I show Greta the statue of Neptune. I think it has been more than just words and sounds, this life. Under the language are a thousand hands, reaching out toward each other, offering to touch and be touched.

EVELINA

We run into Evelina, Renata's flamboyant neighbor, on our gira. She blusters up to us from across the piazza, looking like a beautiful, copper-feathered cockatoo. She carries many bags, has a different color of nail polish on each finger.

"*Dio, dio!*" Evelina cries, hoisting her bags to hug me. "And who do we have here? *Madonnnnna che bella ragazza*. But oh, what a sad time to arrive. Did you hear? No? Oh, *dio, dio, Madonna. La povera Renata*. She just broke the news to everyone."

"What news?" I ask, hardly understanding Evelina's Italian, which is delivered with a warm lisp. "Did something happen?"

"It's the grandmother," Evelina says, ducking in close. "Giuseppina. She's sick. They're giving her a few months, maximum, which is why the fast wedding. Bene knew about it before. Greta just found out today. It's the lungs." She pats at her chest with her winglike hand.

"Oh no," I say, gulping. I feel unable to cope with this news for some reason, though I cannot parse out whether it is a selfish feeling of not wanting to navigate someone else's complicated sadness alongside my own, or an empathetic one, feeling genuinely sad for Renata and her family, for Greta, who just learned of this sad news today. Probably both. "Can I do anything?"

"You can bring these over," Evelina says, handing me a woven bag full of tangerines. "I've still got to get the pastries."

The tangerine bag feels like a stone in my arms, as heavy as another Greta. Part of me does not want to go to Renata's, not yet. I don't want to sit by Giuseppina's bed, holed up with their family's grief. I want a day with my daughter, wandering this city that is so familiar and unfamiliar at once, a place where I can feel both held and free, dipping in and out of used bookshops and record stores, creating stories about the author of every handwritten advertisement flapping on the walls of via Zamboni. But another part of me—a new part—knows that I will go to them, the sad women who need other women. *Freedom is overrated*, I can hear Megan saying, and I now know she's right. I let Evelina kiss me on both my cheeks, and I allow myself to feel a little brush of excitement about seeing Renata. I think of her gleaming, knowing eyes, the way they pierce through my outer layer and go somewhere deep.

"Come on," I say to Baby Greta. "Let's go check in on the girls."

THE CLAMS

I had imagined a depressing scene: Giuseppina, pale and frail, tucked under a quilt in the bed under the angels. A grandmotherly smell: bad breath and expired lotion, overcooked food. I had imagined a bedside gathering at which tangerines and truths were passed around in neat slices. I had imagined Renata in tears, kneeling.

But once again, my version of the story is way off. The mood at Renata's does not reflect impending death. No one is in bed; Giuseppina looks healthy and full of life, in Adidas trainers and pearls, with a spray of white hair like a cloud floating just above her head. She's practically running around the apartment, tossing out orders as if she's a commander in chief. *What are these curtains? Change these curtains! Has anyone thought about the guestbook at the wedding? Of course nobody in this house thought about the guestbook. You people are not guestbook people. How did I raise someone who doesn't care about a guestbook? And what about the almonds? Has anyone even thought about the almonds?!*

The tangerines get left on the counter, go unnoticed. When I see Renata emerge from her room I bristle with excitement and nerves. She rushes to me and hugs me tightly, and I feel my body relax into hers—part relief and part reluctance. But it feels so good to see her: her warm skin, crinkling around the eyes; her gaze shifting to Baby Greta's face, leaning onto my shoulder as I hold her.

"She's *you*," she whispers, cupping Baby Greta's chin. I laugh. "No really, she's *you*. Can you see it?"

"Sometimes," I say.

"Do you know you look just like your mamma?" Renata says to Greta. "Which means you're going to have Italian men following you down via Zamboni in long lines! Everybody watch out!"

The room fills with laughter, mine included, and it feels so good: the first authentic laugh I've had in a while.

Giuseppina slowly opens the balcony door and sneaks out with a cigarette.

"Fucking *Mamma*!" Renata screams as soon as she smells the smoke. She launches her body through the door and steals the burning stick from her mother's mouth. "Are you kidding me, Mamma? Do you want to kill yourself?"

"But Rena," Giuseppina says, "didn't you hear the doctor? I'm basically already dead!"

"That's a horrible thing to say to your daughter," Renata says.

"Well, you're a horrible daughter if you don't let me enjoy myself on my last days on earth!" Giuseppina says. "Just horrible!"

For some reason, this makes them both laugh again. I am in awe of this laughter, which comes as easily as their bickering, as if they're riding the same emotional wave. I cannot imagine what Renata is going through, knowing that her mother has a dangerous mass inside her body. Can Renata feel the mass, somehow, in her own chest? Does she worry she might perish when her mother does?

"The clams!" shouts Giuseppina, momentarily forgetting the cigarette.

"The clams!" shouts Renata. They throw open the fridge in a flurry of arms and pull out a giant bowl. They begin a synchronized dance, pulling out clams one by one, inspecting them to see if they've opened, and then dinging them into another big silver bowl. Greta and Bene appear to help, huddling around the kitchen island. Everyone is quiet as they perform this ritual of separating the mollusks. Greta hands me an open clam, explaining that if it doesn't close when I tap it, it may be contaminated. I tap the clam; it stays open. She points to the trash can and I toss the dead clam in.

I watch as Giuseppina pulls a small notepad from her pocket and writes the number 32.

"Thirty-two clams," says Giuseppina, very softly. I suddenly flash on Renata's lecture from so long ago, and Giuseppina's entire life appears like a movie reel: the numbers and photographs and images and beliefs that have made it what it has been. "Oh, how I'll miss these clams," she says, too quietly for the rest of the family to hear.

A REFUSAL

Giuseppina refuses to die. She wants to meet her great-grandbabies, she says, elbowing Bene, and plus, to give herself over to cancer would be an admission she does not want to make, that by smoking her beloved cigarettes she has done this to herself. Giu is not one to admit fault, never has been. It's not her fault her life turned out the way it did, that her husband beat her, that her only daughter had turned into a raging feminist intellectual whose decisions she'd never been able to understand, that her son-in-law had abandoned his family and her poor grandbabies had to grow up practically fatherless—and it won't be her fault when it ends, either. Until it ends, she will stay with her daughter in the newly empty children's room on via de' Poeti. She will sleep in Bene's bed, the one by the window, and she will wake every morning to the sounds of her daughter's life. The sputter of Renata's espresso pot makes her happy, despite everything. Not wanting to be in her daughter's way, not wanting to feel like a nuisance, she'll stay in her bedroom until Renata has gone off to work. Then she'll linger in the scent her daughter has left behind: coffee aroma, rose oil, that godawful perfume.

She'll drive Renata crazy just by being here, she knows. Her daughter considers her stodgy, old-fashioned, out of touch. She'll say all the wrong things. She'll use the wrong slang for *gay*, vote for the wrong party, buy the wrong kind of cleaning products, say something that isn't perfectly politically correct, like her daughter needs everything to be. But she simply can't keep up. It's as if the world has sped up since she was young, and everything changes just as you begin to understand it. Her poor grandbabies, teenagers now, are glued to their telephones, looking at images of themselves, to which they add sparkles and digital makeup and something called hashtags. She worries they will float away. Sometimes it feels like they already have. The speed at which the world is turning means that gravity can hardly hold them down.

But she won't die. Not this week or this month or this year. Giu will be one of the weird miracle cases that doctors talk about on their days off, one of the people whose diagnoses never did them in. Her disease will simply back off, as if it has been shooed away, lingering just outside the door of her existence. Giu's time won't expire until years later, when an unknown virus sweeps around the world and through Italy, rendering her unable to breathe. Her last embodied memory will be sitting at the open window with her daughter, singing, and looking down the street to see that everyone in the neighborhood is singing out their windows, too.

In the final hours, Renata will encourage her to get the respirator, but she'll decline. It's not her fault this time. It's the world's fault. The world has finally killed her, and she will let it. Renata's face above her, and Greta's, and Bene's. The women of her life, floating in her fading view. She'll close her eyes and smile. Renata will kneel over and spread her own body atop her mother's. She'll stop breathing for a whole minute when her mother's breath stops for good. Renata cannot fathom what a life without Giuseppina looks like, or how she will fill the hole her mother has left behind. Who will she fight with at Christmastime? Whose cigarettes will she steal when Giu is making her crazy? Who will make her crazy? Who will remind her that she is alive? That she came from somewhere?

Goodbye, my girls, Giuseppina will whisper to herself as she closes her eyes in that distant future. But for now, as she prepares for her granddaughter's wedding, she will stick with hello. *Hello, my girls. Hello, new bride. Hello, beautiful embossed guestbook. Hello, tiramisu, amaretto, balcony lanterns, lucky almonds, cigarette. Hello, family I did not choose, but who I got anyway. Let's dance.*

CEREMONY

Bene's wedding ceremony is at a tiny church in Bologna, outside the city center. Baby Greta and I have gotten dressed up: I wear the same dress I wore to Grace's wedding, the red one I got in Verona with Megan, and Greta wears a blue sundress, a hand-me-down from a fashionable Brooklyn friend with an equally fashionable child. I've never liked being in churches, myself, mostly because it reminds me of having to go with Ann when I was little, so I have never taken Greta inside one before. I linger too long outside, watching Greta play with the dirt in a planter box, letting the sunlight warm me before we go in. But once we've crossed the threshold from the bright day into the church, it feels cool and kind— vast and familiar all at once. I watch people filter into the pews: a few faces I know and many I don't recognize. All the characters of an old life convening in this holy room, to celebrate Bene's love.

Renata is in the front row with Giuseppina and Original Greta; they wave for us to come join them. Hesitantly, I walk up to the front, where they've saved us a spot in the row just behind them. I don't know what has afforded us these seats, whether it's pity that we don't know anyone else at the wedding, or gratitude for our having come so far, or true inclusion. Across the aisle, Massimo sits with his new wife and their child, who is now a very beautiful preteen. They all look wet with gel and gloss, as if they've just stepped from a cool shower. His wife is wearing a silver dress made of silk, cut on the bias. Renata is wearing a cropped jacket over a navy shift that hits above the knees. She looks beautiful, and I lean over to tell her so. She *tsks* at me, but I know she is thankful for the compliment. I can see her holding her anxiety in her jaw. I can feel it buzzing out of her shiny dark hair.

When Bene finally walks down the aisle to Beyoncé's "Halo," I feel unexpectedly moved, and small tears gather in the corners of my eyes. Renata weeps, sniveling into a hankie her mother hands her. Original Greta beams with pride and jealousy. Baby Greta watches with awe, doesn't dare cry. Bene looks beautiful and confident, her bright eyes scrunched from smiling. She wears her dark hair down and long, and daisies have been threaded into tiny braids running through it like little flower waterfalls. Her dress has a seventies vibe to it, with a high collar and long crocheted sleeves. She looks like a magical forest nymph. As she approaches her new husband, walks toward her new life, she looks young and happy and in love. Beyoncé sings about being addicted to your light, and a shaft of sun from a stained-glass window lands on Bene's groom, who is grinning ear to ear.

When Bene reaches the altar, Renata's hand darts over the pew and grabs mine. She is flanked by her own mother and her own daughter, and yet she reaches backward, for me. Baby Greta looks down at my hand, clasped in this Italian woman's manicured claw. A rush of love and terror wipes through me. Instinctually, I grab Renata's hand and squeeze back. But then I become frightened that my urgency will scare her away, and that she will let go. I loosen my grip, but she keeps her hand there. Bene giggles at the podium, holding the hands of her new groom. No one looks at him; they all look at her. The bride. The woman. The star of this show, dressed in white, virginal and sexy at once, transformed by costume, lifted to societal precipice, adorned with the halo from Beyoncé's song. A concise ceremony, an exchange of vows, and then a kiss. During the kiss, I squeeze Renata's hand again. She squeezes back. A Morse code of palms and fingers, saying things we'd never been able to say.

What does Renata see in me? What could I possibly give her that she doesn't already have? While she offers me the hand of a mother, a teacher, a friend, what do I offer in return? What does my squeeze do for her? I have wondered this about all my relationships: how I figure into them, what I bring. I keep waiting for her to realize that my hand is clammy, that I am scared, that I know nothing, that I can offer nothing. I wait for her to retract. But she doesn't. Through the whole ceremony, and through Bene's walk back up the aisle, and for the standing and the cheering, Renata grips my hand as if she cannot let go.

THE PAINTED MOTHERS

The Gretas cannot see their mothers. Not really, not all the way. When their mothers reach for each other, they cannot understand it, the need for another woman's hand, for the acknowledgment that comes through touch. They cannot see that their mothers' hands have not touched any bodies but their daughters' in months, maybe years. They cannot see that they—the Gretas—changed the shape of their mothers' lives entirely with their entrance into the world. That before them, these women were the kind of women who might stay out walking well into the evening without ever thinking of having to go home. Who read entire books. Who tried to write them.

When they look at their mothers, the Gretas see only watercolor shapes, blurred and leaking at the edges. They see blobs of comfortable skin, no longer taut. They see a lot of bending: the way their mothers' bodies move when they are trying to carry many grocery bags at once, or reach to pick up a fluttering napkin while carrying coffee, or lean over vacuums or brooms. They see tools and milk and loneliness and chests that have gotten leathery from too many years of sun. They see the backs of wrists against eye sockets, wrists in sinks full of water, bunions, the scandalous dark triangle between a pair of fair legs.

The Gretas cannot know their mothers completely; it's impossible. Though Original Greta knows her mother is a professor, she cannot know how serious her scholarship is, and how vibrant her mind is. She has not read the articles her mother has published about the Italian feminist artists of the 1970s, not because she isn't interested but because she cannot let her original conception of her mother go. She needs her mother to be as she once understood her: consumed only with keeping her, Greta, alive. Though she understands that there is an aspect of denial in her unwillingness to see her mother as a cosmos of experiences and thoughts that do not concern Greta whatsoever, she cannot change this mode of thinking—and does not necessarily want to. She is impervious to her mother's truths; she is a sieve through which they cannot pass. Later, when she goes to therapy in her late forties after a divorce from Paolo, with whom she will have a baby boy, she will admit that she was jealous of those artists that her mother studied with such vigor. Her mother's interest in her was so much different: responsible rather than inspired.

Baby Greta is too young to understand what her mother does, of course. But later, when she is in her twenties like Original Greta is now, and her mother has written many more stories and one book, she will experience her mother's work much like Original Greta does, her intrigue overwhelmed by reticence. When she sees her mother's book on a bookstore shelf, she often will touch its spine and pull it from its hiding spot, placing it in a more visible location in the store. But she will never read the book, and for this she will have no good explanation or excuse.

Always, the Gretas each want more from their mother, but cannot seem to get it, no matter how hard they cry or beg. They want the whole thing of her, every inch and aspect, her skin and her smell and her thoughts and her time. Their mother's private life threatens this, and they do their best to try to abolish those inner worlds with their own needs, their incessant requests, their love. But it doesn't work all the way, and they see her, stealing away at night after she puts them to bed, furiously writing in her notebook, sipping from a glass of wine. Who is she? They wonder as they watch her eyes drift away from them, toward something they cannot know. Who is this woman who has formed me? Why am I not enough for her? Why am I too much? Why can't she see me standing here, and why can I not see her? Her outline is wobbly, viscous, permeable. Her shape merges with mine, but then separates. Why is she clutching hands with this other woman now? Another amorphous shape, extending as the pigment of their color merges. Weak beige colors, made stronger when blurred.

MEANWHILE ON IOS

In a farther-south section of the Mediterranean, on a hilltop on the island of Ios in the country of Greece, Megan is also sitting in a church. She is also wearing the dress she bought in Verona, the blue one that looks like water. She is also watching people walk down the church aisle, and those people are also crying, though their tears are sad rather than celebratory. They are mourning the death of a man named Art, who is the father of Rhea, the woman who worked at the hotel Megan and I stayed at in Verona so long ago. I will learn of Art's existence and his death simultaneously, in the context of Megan's story, which she'll tell me days later over wine and olives at a restaurant overlooking the Aegean Sea.

At the ceremony, Megan is very tired. She slept not at all the previous night, anxiously anticipating this day. When she roused herself, the whole village was already moving in the direction of the church, forming a long line up the hillside toward the tiny white building with the cross on its hat. Megan had joined the group and followed them into the church, where they'd arranged themselves on the dark wooden benches. The church is plastered white inside, and has three paneless windows on each side, letting in the sun and heat.

It is boiling hot. Megan has sweat stains on her dress, and her scalp is wet. Her stomach lurches at the thought of seeing Rhea, who she has reason to believe is interested in her in a romantic way. Why else would Megan be the first person Rhea told about her father's death, in a 2 a.m. text message sent to Megan's burner phone, the one she purchased to replace her iPhone when she decided, after Italy, to move to Greece and stay here? *Papa is dead*, Rhea had written. *He died just now.* And then, after Megan had texted a cursory apologetic response, a long-winded message that had brought tears to Megan's eyes.

I know we don't know each other so well, Rhea had written. *So this will seem weird, sure. But I feel close to you for some reason, and I felt close to you even before you lived with my family. Just seeing you and your friend come into the hotel. It felt like I knew you very well, like I had known you my whole life. I could see something in your face, like you would understand me. When you left Verona, I liked to imagine you with my family. I know my father was hard to get to know, but I knew my mother would love you. She does love you. She writes me emails from the internet café. She says you are a good soul, and that you are very helpful. She said that you bring life into the house. And then when we spent those nights together at Christmas I could see it, the way you lit my family up.*

Megan has been living on the same land as Rhea's parents for over a year now, in the little barnlike cottage behind their house. This came to be in a strange way that Megan still doesn't totally understand, when Rhea had appeared at her hotel room door in Verona like some kind of olive-skinned angel, right when Megan was about to fall into the darkest spiral of depression she'd ever experienced. She was prone to these depressions; she'd had three or four of them since she was a teenager, patches of darkness that drifted in and out of her life like ominous clouds. The first and most powerful one had come when her parents divorced, when she was fourteen; she'd believed it to be her fault somehow, and the guilt of it solidified like a stone in her belly and sank her. Another came after a high school kegger, where she'd had sex with a guy named Teague in the girly bedroom of the little sister of whoever was throwing the party. She hadn't wanted to go all the way with Teague, and she'd asked him to stop, but he didn't, and she didn't say anything more, and so he just kept on going. The rock in her stomach grew lava hot and heavier. The third depression arrived out of nowhere, was spurred by nothing, as if the sense memories of her previous depressions could be called forth at any time. This was perhaps the scariest of all: the darkness that came for no reason.

When Megan read my notebook, read the story I'd written about her and Todd, seen the questions I'd posed about her character, she could feel the old darkness coming for her again. Strangely, it was the ways I'd portrayed her goodness that hurt her most, that made her question everything. In much of what she'd read, I had portrayed Todd as the bad guy, pursuing her doggedly while she did whatever he said. But she knew that it had been just as much her fault as his, that she was just as bad as he was. She was also the bad guy, the monster, as I had put it. The badness bloomed within her: it had always been there, no matter how hard she tried to exorcise it. No matter how hard she exercised. No matter how much she tried to shape herself into the shape of least resistance, the shape everyone wanted her to be, there she was: a lumpy, shitty person without a moral compass. She blamed her eyes. She knew they had power, and she knew how to wield it. One look across a conference table could cut straight to a heart, ruin a life.

As she read my story, she saw the real version of herself alongside the fictional version, and felt that she knew the truth, that she was worse than anybody had even thought. The story made her long to be a different kind of woman, a better woman, a woman who didn't destroy everything—marriages, fetuses—but instead nurtured and gave life, like women were supposed to. But she was not that woman, and no matter how hard she tried she couldn't make herself be, and she became paralyzed; two days after I had left for Bologna, Megan still hadn't left the Verona hotel room. She knew that our flight was sometime that evening, but she'd already decided she wasn't going to be on it. She didn't know what she was going to do, but she couldn't go home. At some point, after not having fed herself once during these two days, inevitable hunger arrived, and she made her way downstairs with considerable effort. She asked the receptionist where she could get some takeout.

"There's an osteria on the street," the receptionist said in clunky English, referencing the place Megan had gone with me before our fight.

"I don't want to sit down to eat," Megan said, knowing she sounded exasperated, probably rude. "I want to bring the food back here."

"Oh, I see," said the receptionist, whose slicked black hair seemed to be tugging on her eyes. "There's not much of that here. But I could order you a pizza from a place where I know the waiter? I'd be happy to bring it up to you."

Megan nodded. "Thank you," she said. The receptionist smiled warmly, and Megan noticed a gap between her small teeth.

An hour later, after Megan had showered and put on a clean shirt, the receptionist knocked on the door and passed Megan her pizza. Megan handed her a fistful of euros and thanked her again, started to close the door. But the woman lingered there, as if she wanted something more.

"Oh shoot, did I not tip enough?" Megan said, grabbing for her purse.

"No, no," the receptionist said. "I just . . . I just wondered if you were okay? You were supposed to check out yesterday. But I see nothing is packed. And this room is reserved for the day after tomorrow."

Megan looked around the room; her shit was everywhere. "Yeah," she said. "I'm sorry. I'm going to go, yeah. Do you know of anywhere around here to stay? Maybe somewhere that rents by the week?"

The woman thought for a second. Megan noticed that her jawbone was very pronounced, and that her neck extended from her head in a graceful way. "I don't know of anything here, because I am so new to this place. I just came from Greece a few months ago."

"Greece sounds nice," Megan said.

"It is nice," the receptionist said. "I miss it. My family is all still there. They have a small farm on Ios."

"I don't miss anything about home," Megan said, surprising herself with how forward she was being with this person she didn't know. "I don't really have any reason to go back."

The receptionist made a sad expression, the corners of her mouth curling up. "No family?" she said.

Megan looked up quickly, taken off guard. The receptionist was clearly getting too personal too fast, and yet, strangely, Megan didn't mind. In fact, she found herself willing to explain herself to this stranger, perhaps *because* she knew she'd never see her again.

"No, I do have a family, yeah, but they live across the country from me," Megan said. "I moved to New York alone when I was eighteen—not because they weren't great parents, they helped me a lot, but after they got divorced it was like I had to divide myself in half, I never felt like one person, if that makes sense. I had this idea that I was going to make my own life, be my own person, find my own place. I guess you could say my friends are my family now, but I don't know, I feel far away from them, too, at the moment. It's all a big mess. Or maybe I'm the big mess."

The receptionist didn't say anything, but her brow furrowed in a way that showed she was interested and listening, perhaps even sympathetic, which prompted Megan to keep talking.

"I feel like I just need to start over, totally, from scratch. Go somewhere where no one knows me for a while, just to see who I am without . . . without them, or without anything. Without social media or text messages or friends or men who aren't worth the energy I put into caring about them. I know it sounds trite, but I feel like I need to be peaceful for a second. To find some kind of peace."

The receptionist nodded sincerely, with her head tilted.

"I know exactly what you mean," she said. "That's why I came here. It's very lonely, this starting over. But sometimes you need to be lonely to see things clearly."

Megan smiled at the receptionist.

"I'll ask around for you," the receptionist said, turning to go. "About places to stay here in Verona. In the meantime I'll extend your reservation for this room through tomorrow?"

Megan nodded, smiled. The receptionist's presence had changed the air in the room while she was in it, but now it was back to being stale, stifling. She no longer wanted the pizza, and so she moved it from the bed to the floor, where it sat until morning, untouched.

The next morning, the receptionist returned with breakfast—a pale croissant and a cappuccino—and a proposition. Megan had just woken up; her eyes were bleary and her head still clouded with dreams.

"I was thinking about you last night," the woman said, letting herself partway into the room to set down the precarious little plates. Megan felt her body tense in a way that was both nervous and pleasant. The receptionist had been *thinking about her last night*?

"About what you told me," she went on. "About wanting to get away. I thought, if you are looking for somewhere to go, I know that my parents would love some help on the farm. There's no internet there, unless you go down to the café in town. It's very quiet. My mother is trying to learn English, maybe you could help her with that, too."

"In Greece?" Megan said.

The receptionist nodded. Megan had felt it then: the heat of her gaze, when they'd locked eyes for a quick second, when she had looked up to see if this woman could possibly be serious. She was, that was clear. And she was looking at her like that, it was too obvious to mistake; there was kindness but also something fiery in her eyes, which Megan knew was the particular heat and reflection of desire. It was all very confusing but also convincing: the gaze, the offer. Megan imagined milking a sheep, learning how to turn its milk into feta cheese.

"Think about it," the woman said with a half smile. "Oh, and I'm Rhea, by the way."

"Nice to meet you, Rhea," Megan said. She liked the sound of that name in her mouth; she involuntarily ran her tongue over her teeth after she said it.

A few days later she was on a train to Bari and then a ferry to Athens and then another ferry to Ios, heading to Rhea's parents' farm. She'd planned on staying two weeks. She ended up staying all year.

Sometimes she couldn't believe that she was still here; it seemed impossible. This place was so far removed from the life she'd known in New York—a little piece of land with a few olive trees and some roaming sheep; she had not yet learned how to make feta, it seemed somehow to make itself, appearing in front of her on worn ceramic plates, doused in olive oil and herbs. Bartering at the market and cooking dinner with all the women in the village on Sundays. Long walks through the arid hills and down to the water, where she'd dive in and sometimes swim until the sun set. Waking in her bright room, making coffee, drawing for hours without interruption. Back in the city, Megan had been known as a fun and productive person, a competent worker with a vast knowledge of New York's best restaurants and stylish brands. In Greece, no one cared about any of those things. They saw Megan as a human with as many humanlike qualities as any other human, who was helpful with the olives and who laughed easily for no good reason. For the first time in a long time, she felt distinctly happy.

Over Christmas, Rhea had come home from Italy to visit with her family. As there were many other family members visiting, there was no room for her in the house, so she shared the back cottage with Megan, set-

ting up a cot on the floor, insisting that Megan keep the only bed. Megan
had initially thought this would be an awkward setup, being that Rhea
was basically a stranger, but it had ended up feeling easy, even natural.
After a lively, boozy dinner with the family, they'd gone down to the beach
and dived into the cold ocean, then stayed up late drinking more wine.
Drunkenly, she'd shown Rhea her sketchbooks, of which she'd filled six
since she'd arrived on the island.

Rhea furrowed her brow as she inspected the drawings thoughtfully,
then, with a burst of inspiration, asked Megan if she could tear out some
of the pages. Megan nodded, intrigued and oddly trusting. Rhea spent
a long while arranging her favorite images into clusters, pairings or trip-
tychs that told some kind of story or played off each other visually, and
then taping them on the wall.

"You've got to do something with these," Rhea said. "They can't just sit
here, wasting their beauty on my parents' sheep. People need to see them."

Megan laughed.

"If you say so," she said.

"I do say so," Rhea said seriously, pouring them both more wine.

Rhea's conviction rubbed off on Megan, and a few days later, after
Rhea left to go back to Italy, perhaps because she wanted to linger in
the emboldened state Rhea had conjured or perhaps because she knew,
somewhere deep, that the art she'd been making was actually good, Megan went to the internet café in town, where she used their scanner to
make JPEGs of the drawings. Then she uploaded them slowly into the
body of an email, rapping her fingers impatiently on the desk as her lines
emerged on the screen. She had only one idea about where to send them,
which was a literary journal that I always had lying around my apartment, one of those too-cool publications that all the hipsters pretended
to read on the train; she'd seen that they'd published artwork alongside
the written pieces, figured it was worth a try. She received a generic email
saying the drawings had been received. She went back up the hill and
made herself and Rhea's mother some coffee.

A few weeks later, by some miracle, she got word that the drawings had been accepted. She imagined me seeing them, and the thought filled her with a certain anticipation, the kind she'd always felt when she sent me a drawing for our book. The issue of the magazine was due to come out in April. She planned to take a trip to Athens to pick up a copy from an art bookstore there that stocked American publications.

It was in Athens, in April, that Megan saw Wes. It was almost violent, the shock it gave her, to see someone from her old life in this foreign city. What the hell was he doing here, at a café on Lisiou, his camera draped around his neck and a cigarette smoking in his hand? And who the hell was he with? A woman she'd never seen before, in wide-legged sailor pants and an expensive-looking spring jacket in the fleshy blush color that was so popular right now, her hair knotted atop her head like a scoop of ice cream. The woman was very elegant, and she seemed to be very interested in Wes.

Megan knew all these moves from her days with Todd: The excessive laughter, even when things weren't funny. Little touches on the arm or shoulder. Overly expressive conversation and lots of leaning in. A glass of wine in the middle of the day. And then—there it was—the reach of the woman's hand, effortlessly moving through the space between them to land on top of Wes's. A tender touch that told Megan everything: that Wes was sleeping with this woman, or if he wasn't, then he was going to.

Megan's breath stopped. She felt a prickly anger tingling under her skin, though she realized that it could very well be for no reason; she didn't even know whether Wes and I were still together. Could it be that we had broken up, that I had actually heeded her advice and left him, and that this was his new girlfriend, in which case, who cared? But her intuition told her this was not the case—there was something illicit that she recognized in the way the two of them were behaving—and she knew she had to find out for sure if this was what she suspected it was: a blatant betrayal of her friend.

Yes, she still considered me her friend, despite everything. Despite the things we'd said to each other, despite the fact that we hadn't talked in over a year. She hadn't meant to leave our friendship hanging like that, it had just happened that way. Her stubbornness had kept her from reaching out, hoping that I would be the one who'd eventually come back to her. In the dynamic of our friendship, she, Megan, was supposed to be the stubborn one. I was supposed to claw my way back. She'd wondered about my abortion, of course, and she knew it was shitty of her not to get in touch back then, but she also knew I would be fine, that I'd get through it like she had, and that I had Wes. But now she wondered if that was even true. She stepped into the street and crossed through the traffic, her gaze trained on Wes's mirrored sunglasses.

He looked up at her, but kept the glasses on.

"Megan?"

She nodded.

"Whoa!" Wes said, rising to hug her. "What are you doing here? This is crazy!"

Megan felt stunned by Wes's joy. She couldn't bring herself to ask what she'd come over here to ask. Instead she tossed her hair and said, "I live here."

"You do? For how long? Where? How?"

Wes seemed genuinely curious, possibly even impressed, so Megan went on to tell him about the farm, and Rhea's parents, and her decision not to return to New York.

"I wonder if there's something on the farm?" the woman with the ice cream hair said, almost like a secret, to Wes. "An agrarian moment, maybe?" And then, to Megan: "Can I ask you if the farm employs any refugees?"

The woman's tone, the way her sentences were all questions, reminded Megan of all the women she'd ever known in New York: ambitious, serious women who still questioned every single thing that came out of their own mouths.

"It's not that kind of farm," Megan said icily.

"No worries," the woman said, holding up her hands.

"Wes," Megan said. She could feel her blood racing through her heart and veins. "Can I talk to you for a second? Inside?"

"Sure," Wes said, standing, suddenly looking nervous. "Just a sec, Sar." He followed Megan inside the café, which was a junky old art lounge with green-painted walls. They stood at the bar.

"Are you still with Em?" Megan said.

Wes nodded awkwardly. "Yeah, why?"

"I need you to tell her," Megan said.

Wes swallowed, straightened his back.

"Tell her what?" he said, in a stabbing attempt at denial. "What are you talking about?"

"I saw how she touched your hand," she said.

"Touched my hand? Are you kidding me, Meg?"

Megan shook her head. "No," she said. "I'm not kidding. I need you to tell Emily about this woman and whatever is going on between you two. And if there's nothing going on, I need you to tell her that, too. Or else I will."

Wes looked at the floor, coughed, and then looked back up at Megan.

"Fuck," he said. He pressed his palms into his eyes. "Nothing has even happened. I swear"

"Congratulations," Megan said.

"Okay," he said with a sigh. "I'll tell her. Just don't call her, okay? I'll tell her myself." He walked back out of the café and put his sunglasses back on. But in the threshold of the doorway, he turned back toward her.

"When was the last time you talked to her?" Wes said.

"I got rid of my phone," Megan said. "So, since Italy."

Wes paused, hesitating. Then he said: "She had the baby. Or, we had the baby. A little girl. Greta."

Megan's hand flew to her chest, her fingertips hovering over her heart.

"Oh, Em" was all she could say, after Wes had disappeared through the door.

—

Silently and without warning, the family of the dead man enters through the front door of the church. They all carry bundles of lavender and rosemary, and their heads are bowed. They are wearing simple outfits, black dresses and shoes. They are all women. Megan sees Rhea at the back of the line, trailing her mother. She thinks of Rhea's mother's soft garlicky smell, the way she bats at flies. She thinks about how Rhea's mother barely spoke to Rhea's father, but how they communicated through gestures, making zigzagging pathways around the house and the farm. Rhea's mother would milk the goat, then leave the bucket of milk at the doorway. Rhea's father would turn up just as her mother left, to carry the bucket to the barn and bottle the milk, then stock it in the icebox. One of them would take over the cooking from the other seamlessly, as if they could read each other's minds. It had been that kind of love.

Tears stream down Rhea's face in the church. Later, after the ceremony and after many small glasses of retsina, on the twin horsehair mattress in the cottage next to her parents' house, these tears reappear. They cascade down Rhea's cheeks, onto her neck, over her collarbone, down her breasts. Megan licks these tears. They are salty and bitter. Rhea smells like lavender and goat milk and synthetic perfume and fish. The mattress smells like hay. Her father would have killed her, Rhea says as the tears stream. If he had known she was like this.

Like what? Megan asks stupidly, though she knows what Rhea is talking about. Her father would have killed her for liking women. For shoving her fingers inside Megan and knowing just where and how to move them. For rubbing her sweat into Megan's sweat. For gyrating her leg against Megan until she cried out with pleasure. Her father would have disowned her for this pleasure, Rhea explains. But it doesn't matter now, does it? Now he is dead.

Salt oceans from Rhea's eyes. Sea salt on her skin. A vigorousness

Megan had forgotten she possessed. A desire for herself she no longer knew was possible. Megan's breasts sag. She rubs them against Rhea's. They kiss and sigh into each other's necks all night, and as Megan comes for the third and fourth and fifth times, she cries, too. She cries for Rhea for losing her father, and for herself for losing her way for so long. She cries for me, too, she'll tell me, though she doesn't know exactly why. Because I had been wronged by Wes? I'll ask. Because I was born into aloneness? Because I was a mother now, and she hadn't been there to witness it?

Because I missed you, Megan will tell me, her hazel eyes reflecting the red and setting sun.

Rhea's tongue is on her thigh now. She can feel a chasm inside her closing up, a distance shortening, her self returning to her, as if she is her own old friend.

YES, PLEASE

A few days after Bene's wedding, Renata and Original Greta and Baby Greta and I take a train to Bari, where we board a ferry headed to Greece. The boat is full of women. There is a conference in Athens, something to do with skin care, and so the women are all glowing from the neck up. They move about like radiant suns, from bow to bow, and then below-decks to refresh their drinks and layer serums onto their faces, and then up into the sea air again.

We stay at the front of the boat, letting the wind hit our faces. We don't talk because the boat and the breeze are loud, filling in the silence. But there is an ease between us that feels comfortable enough. I feel proud for some reason, standing here with Renata and her daughter, though I'm not sure why. I feel like I have done right by them in some way, by inviting them to come to Greece, where we'll stay for four nights in an Airbnb I rented with the loft buyout money. I know it is self-centered to think that I am giving Renata something she could not have attained on her own—companionship, adventure, a vacation from dealing with the pain of her sick mother, from cleaning her kitchen yet again, from real life. Renata is just fine without me, and always has been. It is I who need her. And perhaps this is why I am proud: I have articulated a need for someone, and acted upon that need. Without clawing, without changing myself to erase the distance between us, without hedging against inevitable abandonment. I just got on a boat, asked another person to join me, and then let them. In fact, I am acting upon my own needs twice at once. This ferry is docking on Ios, where I am going to find Megan.

Ironically, it was Wes who told me she was here. In June, just after the loft sold, he called me and asked if I could meet him for coffee. Something in his voice felt urgent, so I told him I could come now if he was ready. Original Greta was already over at the loft studying, so I asked if she could stay with Greta while I ducked out for a coffee. She was one of the only people I believed when they said something wasn't a problem at all.

We met at a tiny place on Wythe, a place we'd often gone in our first year together. It was romantic, with French blue walls and tiny tables, and a nook in the very back that no one really knew about so it was almost always empty. We tucked into it and sat across from each other on the little floral cushions they put on the metal seats; they were purely aesthetic, always sliding off. We ordered coffee that came in bowls, and granola that also came in bowls. I felt weirdly happy to be with Wes, especially without Greta. There was sun on our table and the coffee was good. I felt like some old version of myself that I now missed.

I asked Wes what he wanted to talk to me about; I assumed it had something to do with him and Sarah, maybe that they were moving in together, or that he wanted to have more days with Greta, or fewer days—some logistical matter that would probably put me out in some way. Despite knowing I might be put out, I felt open to these things. I had decided I didn't hate Wes, that it felt better not to hate him. I knew he was only shitty because of what he'd done, not who he was, and that those were not the same thing. I also knew that I no longer loved him. The love I'd once felt for him had found a new home in Greta, as if it were a flock of birds who had migrated, found new trees in which to land and rest.

"Okay, so precursor," Wes said, sounding slightly nervous. "This was my therapist's idea."

"You have a *therapist*?" I said.

Wes nodded. "I started getting these really bad anxiety attacks," he said. "Ever since we broke up."

This admission made me feel validated in some way, that our breakup had affected him. As petty as it was, it was nice to be affecting.

"But that's not the point of why I'm here. The point is that I saw Megan. When I was in Athens."

"What? My Megan?"

"Yes, your Megan."

"What's she doing in Greece?"

"She's been living there. On Ios, actually. On a farm. She was in Athens for the day when I ran into her."

"*What?*" I said again. I was incredulous. "My Megan? On a *farm*?"

"She went there after you guys were in Italy. Got off the grid, doesn't have Wi-Fi or anything. Anyway, I ran into her at this café near the hotel I was at."

Wes looked down at his hands, which were fidgeting in his lap. Wes had nice hands, soft and strong. Sometimes I did miss his hands. And his collarbone. I missed his collarbone.

"Megan saw us together," Wes said, pulling off the Band-Aid. "She saw Sarah touch my *hand*. And she had some kind of spidey sense, I guess; she said she knew something was going on, even though nothing had happened yet."

An electric charge ran through me as I imagined this scene. Wes sitting outside of some Grecian café with pretty, accomplished Sarah, and Megan looking on. More than anything, I felt excluded. A whole story had unraveled on some far-off island that I hadn't been told. How many stories were out there that I'd never know? How many private islands did every person carry within them? Why the fuck had Megan gone to Greece?

"Megan was the one who told me I needed to tell you about Sarah," Wes said. "Which isn't to say that I wouldn't have told you—I would have, eventually. But I just thought—or, well, my therapist thought—that I should tell you she had your back like that, even though I know it makes me look like more of an asshole."

I was quiet, stunned.

"She told me to tell you that she missed you," he said. "Megan, I mean. Not my therapist."

Wes's eyes flicked in the way they did when he wasn't telling the whole truth, but for some reason I didn't care. Just thinking of her saying that, even if Wes had made it up for my benefit—it made my heart lurch. Here I was getting this strange news about Wes and his therapist and Sarah touching his hand, and all I could think about was Megan. Megan with her hair in a messy bun, in the sandals she liked to wear to cover the bunion that was emerging on her left foot, her hand over her eyes, shielding them from the sun. She might have said she missed me; she might not have. Either way, as Wes had said, she'd had my back, tried to protect me from the pain of Wes's mistake, and that was enough. It turned out that was all I had needed to be prompted to rush, as quickly as I could, toward her.

I sent her an email. It didn't include a story, or an explanation, only a simple question. *Can I come see you?* Her answer, which I received a few days later, was just as simple. *Yes, please.*

Now, as I look out over the choppy gray-green water, with Greta's breath against my neck and the ferry churning like a workhorse beneath us, I feel an overwhelming sense of calm, the feeling of heading home after a long time of being gone.

NEW WOMAN

Renata offers to take Baby Greta for a while, to go explore the ferry, and I go belowdecks to get out of the sun and use the bathroom. I feel the relief of being alone, even for a moment, and relish the silence of the bathroom stall—no baby crying, nobody asking me for anything, at least for now. When I am washing my hands, one of the skincare women catches my eye in the mirror. She has brown hair and tanned, glossy skin, and is wearing a white linen dress that flows over her body like cloud wisps, without catching on any bulk or curve. She smiles and the whole room brightens. I smile back.

"You have beautiful skin," she says in Italian. No one has ever told me this before, so I know it's probably a line she uses on everyone, to start a skin-care conversation. And yet I accept the compliment gladly, decide to hold on to it. I thank her and turn to leave, but she stops me with a light touch of her fingers on my arm.

"Can I try something on you?" she asks, pulling a glass vial from her purse.

"Okay," I say, caught in the glow of her sun face, pulled in by her kindness, feeling stunned. In a charming moment of violence she cracks the glass, allowing the sparkling serum to flow out onto her hand.

"Close your eyes," she says, so I do. I feel her soft fingers graze my left cheek, and then my right one. Then they slide over my forehead and the bridge of my nose. It feels incredible, calming and electric. I think of the "spice-amnesia" of makeup, as Barbara Ras referred to it in a poem that once changed my life, and Renata's creamy pot of blush, and Ann's one tube of mascara that I stole when I was eleven, and Megan's skin regimen. And then, as can happen in moments of closed-eyed calm, I have an idea. I will rewrite the story I've already written once, the one about Megan and Todd. But this time, I will tell it differently. I will not tell it to surprise myself, or to play out my own questions on the page, or to enact revenge against the man who hurt my friend. I will tell it like it happened, I will tell it clear as glass, how two people looked at the same piece of art at the same time and their human souls touched for a second. And how they made mistakes, and how they regretted them, and how they lost respect for themselves, and how they suffered. How we suffer. How we close our eyes in suffering and wait for someone to touch us. *Never stop touching me*, I think as the skin-care woman's fingers press gently into the space beneath my eyes.

"It's just vitamin C," the woman says, "but you already look brighter."

"I feel brighter," I say with a laugh. I am not lying; I really do. When I look in the mirror, I see that I am new, as if some part of me has died and come back different. I am radiant.

More of the skin-care women enter the bathroom, and they smell like sandalwood and suntan oil. I have a sense that we are getting closer to where we are headed, and I imagine us all getting off the boat together, traipsing over the decks and up onto the island. Its mountains will be dotted with the barnacles of whitewashed houses. The sky will be fierce and blue. We will be an island of women, I think, reachable only by boat, surrounded by salt water. We will take care of each other's children, make meals for each other, pass each other the wine. Our limbs will entangle when we fall asleep in the middle of the day, unencumbered by jobs and roles and societal contortions that do not serve us. We will serve each other. We will make a new life together, tending to our collective fire in the middle of this vast, dark sea.

I ask the woman if the vitamin C is for sale. She places a new vial in my palm and closes my fingers around it for me: a gift. I squeeze tightly. I will crack open the glass and put some on Megan's face, when I see her. And Renata's, too. And Greta's, when she's bigger.

ACKNOWLEDGMENTS

Thank you to my agent, Claudia Ballard, for your rock-solid support, helpful decisiveness, great ideas, and generous friendship.

Thank you to my editor, Alison Callahan, for being patient while I found my way, pushing me to write what burned, and for your patent editorial prowess.

Thank you to the Scout Press/Simon & Schuster team: Jen Bergstrom, Aimée Bell, Taylor Rondestvedt, Lisa Litwak, Alexis Leira, Erika Genova, Caroline Pallotta, Emily Arzeno, Jessica Roth, Mackenzie Hickey, and John Paul Jones. And to the team at WME: Camille Morgan, Oma Naraine, Laura Bonner, and Fiona Baird. You have all been instrumental in giving this book a life.

Thank you to my wise and trusted readers of this project and others that have preceded or informed it: Sarah Fontaine, Elena Schilder, Melissa Seley Scordelis, Laura Pancucci, Lily James Olds, Paul Felten, Marisa Paiva, Megan Walsh, and Megan Linehan. And to Medaya Ocher and to Melissa Seley Scordelis for publishing "Eravamo Noi"—the short story that gave birth to this novel—in the *Los Angeles Review of Books*.

Thank you to my parents, Nikki Silva and Charles Prentiss, for modeling a life driven by limitless creativity and curiosity, and for your unconditional love and support. Dad, thank you for your colors and your witty wisdom and your steadfastness. Mom, thank you for taking notes and telling stories and counting bell chimes, and for being my everything, all the time, for always.

Thank you to my sisters, Grace Carlson, Kate Prentiss, Maddy Baer, and Annie Baer, for inspiring me with your superwoman strength and life intelligence, for unknowingly offering up feminine fodder for these pages, and for laughing with me the way only sisters can. And to Carlos Prentiss, Colette DeDonato, Pete Carlson, Scott Shelton, Danny Judy, Sam Scott, Matt Clarke, Maxx Lewinger, Stefan Lewinger, and Lizzy Lewinger, for your siblingship and love. And to the small humans you've all helped create: thank you for bringing us so much bright happiness.

Thank you to all the women who have helped to raise, nurture, and guide me throughout my life, especially Mary Bennett, Davia Nelson, Dorothy Silva, Marian Watt, Patti Pruitt, Sue Struck, Joanne Bauer, Sara Paul, Laura Folger, Sara Prentiss-Shaw, Carolyn Prentiss, and Flavia Santonico. You, too: Chris Baer, Bobby "A" Andrus, Craig Shaw, Alan Lewinger, David Bill, and Greg Becker. And a special thanks to Jo Aribas for the tender support and creative friendship.

Thank you to Carey Denniston and Carmen Winant for the never-ending conversation about our daily lives as women and mothers, for inspiring me with your work as artists and humans, and for your best-friendship. And to Ainslee McAndrew, Jessica Chrastil, and Kate Bonacorsi, whose banter and companionship I covet.

Thank you to my book club full of geniuses who make reading even more fun. To the work friends who became real friends and real friends who became work friends—with special shout-outs to the writers: Melissa (again!), Desi Gallegos, Steven Jessop, Aimee Walleston, Bora Chang, Penny Saranteas, and the dearest Abbye Churchill. .

Thank you to the people who cared for my daughter so that I could write and work, especially Ali Bill and Tricia Langley McCormick, who brought such warmth to those early days.

Thank you to my daughter, Valentine, for expanding the world as you entered it. I don't think we knew what joy was before you. I just don't think we knew.

Thank you, most of all, to my husband, Forrest Lewinger, without whom I would not have been able to write this (or any) book. You are brilliant and beautiful—my forever flame.

—

The two poems I've mentioned and excerpted in this text are listed here, should you want to read them in full. Thank you to these poets and all of the poets.

"You Can't Have It All" by Barbara Ras
(from *Bite Every Sorrow*, Louisiana State University Press, 1998)

"Paula Becker to Clara Westhoff" by Adrienne Rich
(from *The Dream of a Common Language, Poems, Selected and New, 1950–1974*)

The novels I refer to in this text are:

Little Labors by Rivka Galchen
The Folded Clock by Heidi Julavits
I Love Dick by Chris Kraus

ABOUT THE AUTHOR

Molly Prentiss is the author of the novel *Tuesday Nights in 1980*, which was longlisted for the Center for Fiction First Novel Prize and the PEN/ Robert W. Bingham Prize for Debut Fiction, and shortlisted for the Grand Prix de Littérature Américaine in France. Her writing has been translated into multiple languages. She lives in Red Hook, New York, with her husband and two daughters.